PENGUIN BOOKS

ONE LAST KILL

Acclaim for *Choke Point*

'If Tarantino ever got a crack at Bond, chances are the results would resemble one of Eisler's novels' *Entertainment Weekly*

'With each book Eisler climbs ever further up the ladder of excellence with well-crafted plots and adrenalin-filled action scenes that keep the suspense razor sharp' *Daily Record*

Acclaim for *Rain Fall*

'Eisler is exactly my kind of writer and his deadly main character John Rain is exactly my kind of guy – highly recommended' Lee Child

'Stunning. John Rain is one of the most compelling characters in recent crime fiction . . . a taut, brilliantly paced debut thriller' Amazon

'A tense, cleverly plotted thriller' *Sunday Telegraph*

'A hypnotic thriller. Dazzling plot, deft characterization and imagination, it's got it all' *James Ellroy*

'A superior thriller with much forensic detail on how to tail crooked government officials, break into their flats and fake their deaths by heart attacks' *FHM*

For my love, Laura

The way of the samurai is found in death.
YAMAMOTO TSUNETOMO, *Hagakure*

Part One

I

Killing isn't the hard part. Gangbangers and other fear biters do it every day. Anger pumps you up, panic cancels consideration, you grab the gun, close your eyes, pull the trigger, Christ, an ape could do it, you don't even need to be a man.

No, the truth is, killing is the easy part. Getting close to the target, though, that takes some talent. And making it look 'natural,' which is my specialty, well, I've known of only one other operator who could consistently get that right, and I'm not sure he should count because I'm the one who killed him. And leaving no trail back to yourself, that's no cakewalk, either.

But the hardest part? The part that you can't plan for, that you can really understand only when it's already too late? Living with it after. Bearing up under the weight of what you've done. That's the hardest. Even with limitations like mine – no women, no children, no acts against non-principals – you're not the same person after. You never draw the same breath again, or dream the same dreams. Trust me, I know.

As much as you can, you try to dehumanize the target. Accepting the target as human, a man just like you, creates empathy. Empathy makes killing more difficult and produces caustic regret.

So you employ euphemisms: in Vietnam we never killed people; we only 'wasted gooks' or 'engaged the enemy,' the same as in all wars. When possible, you prefer distance:

air strikes are nice, bayonet range is horrible. You diffuse responsibility: crew-served weapons, long chains of command, systematic replacement of the soldier's sense of self with an identification with the platoon or regiment or other group. You obscure features: the hood is used not to comfort the condemned, but to enable each member of the firing squad to pull the trigger without an anguished face to remember afterward.

But it's been a long time since any of these emotional stratagems has been available to me. I typically operate alone, so there's no group with whom to share responsibility. I don't discuss my work, so euphemisms would be pointless. And what I do, I need to do from a very personal distance. By the time I'm that close, it's too late to try to cover the target's face or otherwise conceal his humanity.

All bad enough, even under the usual circumstances. But this time I was watching the target enjoy a Sunday outing in Manila with his obviously adoring Filipino family just before I killed him, and it was making things worse.

The target. See? Everyone does it. If I'm different than most, it's only in that I try to be more honest. 'More' honest. A matter of degree.

Manheim Lavi was his name, 'Manny' to his business associates. Manny was an Israeli national, resident of South Africa, and citizen of the world, which he traveled much of the year sharing bomb-making expertise with a network of people who put the knowledge to increasingly grisly use. Vocations like Manny's once offered a reasonable risk-to-reward ratio, but post-9/11, if you sold your expertise to the wrong people, you could lose your rewards pretty fast. That was Manny's story, as I was given to understand it, a tragic fall from a certain government's grace.

Manny had arrived in Manila from Johannesburg that

4

evening. A black Mercedes from the small Peninsula fleet had picked him up at Ninoy Aquino Airport and whisked him straight to the hotel. Dox and I were already staying there, outfitted with first-rate ersatz identities and the latest communication and other gear, all courtesy of Israeli intelligence, my client of the moment. Dox, an ex-Marine sniper and former comrade in arms of mine, had recently walked away from a five-million-dollar payday to save my life in Hong Kong. Bringing him in on this job was in part my way of trying to repay him for that.

Dox was waiting in the lobby when Manny arrived. I was in my room on the sixth floor, a tiny, flesh-colored, Danish-designed wireless earpiece nestled in my ear canal, a wireless mike secured to the underside of the left lapel of the navy blazer I was wearing. Dox was similarly equipped.

'Okay, partner,' I heard him say softly in his southern twang, 'our friend just got here, him and the world's biggest, butt-ugliest bodyguard. They're checking in right now.'

I nodded. It had been a while since I'd worked with a partner, and not so long ago Dox had proven himself a damn good one.

'Good. Let's see if you can get the name he's using and a room number.'

'Roger that.'

Having to get this information on our own wasn't ideal, but the Philippines wasn't exactly the Israelis' backyard, and they hadn't been able to offer all that much. Manny traveled to Manila frequently from his nominal home in Johannesburg, taking as many as ten trips in a year. He never stayed for less than a week; the longest of these visits had lasted two months. He'd been doing this for a decade: presumably because customs control in Manila isn't as tight as it is in, say, Singapore, making the Philippines a good place for meetings with the MNLF, Abu Sayef, Jemaah Islamiah, and other violent groups in the region; possibly because he liked the price and variety of Manila's well-known nightlife, as well. He always stayed at the Peninsula. There were a few surveillance photos. That was all.

With less than the usual dossier to go on, I knew we would have to improvise. Where to hit Manny, for one thing. The hotel was our only current nexus and so presented a logical choice. But if Manny died in the hotel, it would absolutely have to look natural; otherwise, there would be too much investigative attention on the other guests, including Dox and me. Staying elsewhere wouldn't have helped; it would have kept us too far from the action.

The level of 'naturalness' a hotel hit itself would require isn't easy, but there were other problems, as well. Most of the ruses I typically use to get into someone's room depend on the target's anonymity, yet Manny was well known to the hotel. And even if I did get into the room while Manny was out and then waited for him to return, what if the bodyguard swept the room immediately before his arrival? What if Manny came back with a bar girl? In the current terrain, I couldn't control for these variables, and I didn't like that.

Still, I wanted the room number. Partly in case a better opportunity didn't present itself and we had to use the Hotel Room Expiration as Plan B; more important, so we would know on which floor to place the video camera that we would use to track his movements. We could have tried placing a camera in the lobby, which would have been easier because it would have saved us the trouble of finding out what floor he was on. But there were downsides to the lobby, too. With all the people coming and going through the hotel entrance, we'd have to scrutinize the grainy feed

and an accompanying room number. We'd tested the system earlier, and it had worked perfectly. Now that we had the right name, it was time to see whether it would work when it counted.

Five minutes later there was a knock on my door. I padded quietly over and flipped up the small piece of cardboard I had taped over the peephole – no sense blocking the light from behind with my approach and alerting a visitor to my presence – and looked through. It was Dox. I opened the door. He came inside wearing his indefatigable grin.

'You're smiling like that, you better have good news,' I said, closing the door behind him.

The grin broadened and he nodded. 'That, and I'm just happy to see you, partner, it doesn't have to be one or the other.'

I gave him a nod in return, knowing that anything more would encourage him. I couldn't pretend to fully understand Dox. In many ways he was a contradiction, a conundrum. He was a talker, for one thing – not a breed I've ever been particularly comfortable around – and a loud one at that. And yet every other sniper I've known, and I've known more than a few, has been reserved, even taciturn. Every environment has a certain flow to it, a rhythm, a connectivity, and snipers instinctively and habitually enter into that flow without disturbing it. But Dox liked to stir things up – in fact, his nom de guerre was short for 'unorthodox,' an accolade awarded by consensus in Afghanistan, where the Reagan-era CIA had sent men like us to arm and train the Mujahedeen against the invading Soviets. His constant boisterous clowning there had put me off at first, and I'd initially figured him for nothing but a braggart. But when I'd seen his effectiveness and coolness under fire, I knew I'd been wrong. When he settled behind the scope of his rifle, there was an eerie transformation, and the good ol' boy persona would fade away, leaving in its shadow one of the most focused, deadly men I've ever met. I didn't understand the opposing forces that combined to create his character, and I knew I would never have trusted him but for what he'd done at Kwai Chung. Of course, that single act couldn't eradicate my lifelong tendency to doubt, but it seemed in a way to have eclipsed it, or at least to have created an uncomfortable exception.

We walked into the room. I sat down at the small desk and flipped open the Mac PowerBook I'd brought along for the festivities. It came out of sleep mode and I typed in the password. Dox handed me the camera.

'You sure you got a shot of the page with Manny's name on it?' I asked.

He gave me a theatrical sigh. 'There you go, hurting my feelings again.'

'Does that mean you got it?'

He sighed again. 'Didn't I tell you I'd get it?'

I attached the camera to the laptop. I hit the 'sync' key, then glanced at him and said, 'Let's see if I have to apologize for my outrageous lack of faith in your infallibility.'

'Don't worry, partner, I'll be gracious about it. I hate to see a grown man grovel.'

It took just a few seconds for the images to download. The first of them was an alphabetical listing of hotel guests, A through F. I closed the image and opened the next one. G through M. Including one Randolph Hartman, Room 914. Bingo.

'How'd you get the clerk to give you a shot of G through M?' I asked. 'You're checked in under Smith, right?'

'Yeah, Mr Smith first told the clerk that he couldn't

remember his room number, but that she could charge the Snickers bar he was buying to Mr Herat.'

Cute. Herat is one of the northern cities of Afghanistan.

'And then?'

'Well, the nice young lady – pretty little thing, by the way, and I think she liked me – she flipped to the page with the H names on it and told me there was no Mr Herat registered at the hotel. I told her, 'That's odd . . . Oh, wait a minute, that's right, the room is under my name, not my partner's.' Should be under Smith, I told her, and okay, now I'm remembering, it's room 1107, Ayala Tower. Which is indeed where Mr Smith is staying.'

I looked at him. 'Did she seem suspicious?'

He rolled his eyes. 'Shoot, partner, I was trying to buy a damn candy bar, not cash a check. She couldn't have cared less. Besides, it was pretty obvious she was distracted by her blossoming feelings for me. I think I might stop by again later, see what time she leaves work.'

'Hey,' I said, looking at him, 'if you need to get off, Burgos Street is a two-minute cab ride from here. I don't want you trying to make it with the hotel staff. That kind of shit gets noticed.' Even as I said it, though, I realized it would be pointless. Dox was genetically wired to be conspicuous. In some ways, I supposed, the tendency could be an asset. In an environment like this one, Dox came across more like an ugly American tourist than an undercover operator. He was hiding in plain sight.

He shrugged. 'All right, don't get your panties in a wad. It's just that I hate to disappoint the pretty ones, is all.'

'"The pretty ones"?' I said, still annoyed. 'Dox, you'd fuck an alligator if it would hold still for you.'

'That is not true, partner, Marines do not engage in

congress with reptiles. We prefer whenever possible that our partners be mammalian.'

I gave up. 'Oh, okay. I don't know how these rumors get started.'

'Lot of nasty people in the world, man, that's all,' he said, giving me the grin. 'I mean a sheep is one thing, but an alligator? I'm surprised you'd think so little of me.'

I didn't know how Dox was able to maintain his constant good cheer even as he prepared to go operational. When I'm gearing up, I get serious, even dour. Harry, my martyred hacker friend, had always been nervous helping me with ops, and had often provoked an unfamiliar clownishness in me. But Dox and I seemed to polarize the opposite way.

But he'd done well so far. I wasn't yet confident in his social engineering skills. He was too consistently brash, too direct, and, I had to admit to myself, his style was just too different from mine. Getting Manny's room number had been a test. I'd resisted the urge to tell him how to go about it, and he had come up with something close to what I'd thought of myself. More important, something that worked. It wouldn't come easily to me, but I'd have to try to give him more slack as we went along, as he continued to prove himself.

'Let's see,' I said, closing my eyes. 'He's in nine-fourteen. That's around the corner from the elevators. Unless the bodyguard is positioned at the elevators while Manny is in his room, I ought to be able to get some video in place.'

'Yeah, nice having a way to know when he's leaving. I hate hanging around in the open, waiting for someone to go out.'

In the dark, though, I knew Dox could wait for days. He had the kills to prove it.

I opened my laptop bag and took out a camera, a wireless

unit about twenty millimeters square and weighing less than an ounce. I clicked it on, then worked the laptop's keyboard for a minute, watching as the screen filled with input from the unit. 'It's transmitting all right from here,' I said, 'but at nine hundred megahertz it's only rated to about a thousand feet. I might have to install a couple of repeaters along the way. You wait here and monitor the screen. Tell me if you're getting reception and the right view of the elevators once I've got it in place.'

'Roger that.'

We took earpieces from the laptop bag and slipped them in place. I walked over to the door and checked through the peephole. The hallway was empty.

I walked out, hearing a loud clack as the door closed behind me. 'You there?' I asked quietly.

'Roger that,' I heard back. Okay, the commo gear was still working.

I took the elevator down to the lobby level, not wanting to go to Manny's floor directly from mine. To satisfy anyone who might be watching through the dome security camera peeking down from the elevator ceiling, I got out and bought a pack of gum at the gift shop, then came back and headed up to the ninth floor. There were no stops along the way, and a minute later the doors opened on nine. I walked out and looked around. The hallway was empty.

There was a wooden credenza against the wall opposite the elevators with a mirror behind it. I walked over, supported myself against the credenza with my left hand, and ran the fingers of my right through my hair. There was another dome camera mounted on the ceiling in front of the elevators, and if anyone was watching right then, all they would see was a man concerned with his appearance. In fact, I had slipped the adhesive-backed unit underneath the left edge of the credenza, where it would have a wide-angle view of the approach to the elevators.

'How's the image?' I asked quietly.

'No go. Too grainy. Signal's falling off before it reaches the receiver. I think we need the repeater to boost it.'

'Okay. Hang on.'

I walked down the hallway for a few paces, then returned to the elevator, just another hotel guest who'd absent-mindedly gotten off on the wrong floor. This time, I stopped on six. As I got off, I checked my room key and looked around in slightly theatrical confusion, thinking, *Gosh, these floors all look the same, where was I staying again?* just in case someone was watching. Then I placed a repeater in front of the elevators the same way I had put the camera in on Manny's floor.

The moment I clicked it on, I heard Dox's voice: 'Okay, there we go. Now that's a beautiful view.'

I moved out of the way. 'The approach to the elevators?'

'Yeah, and it beats the wide-angle shot of your crotch I was getting a minute ago. Someone should call *America's Funniest Home Videos.*'

I thought about a retort, but then this was exactly what he wanted. I let it go and walked back to the room.

2

The two men who'd offered me the Manny job a week before had never explicitly acknowledged their affiliations. They might have been Mossad; they might have been attached to one of the elite Israeli military units, like the Sayeret Matkal. All I knew was that they were compatriots of Delilah, who had vouched for them. Her involvement had been enough to convince me to meet them.

Delilah and I had first crossed paths in Macau, where we discovered we were both focused on Achille Belghazi, an arms merchant I had been hired to kill but whom Delilah's people needed alive for the extraction of critical intelligence. We'd managed to create an uneasy truce, though, and things had worked out well in the end. Very well, if you included the month Delilah and I had spent together in Rio afterward, before she had to return to her world and I to mine.

But despite our personal chemistry, I didn't trust Delilah completely: she was an operator, after all, with her own professional agenda. So I had insisted that her people travel to Nagoya, a large Japanese city two hundred miles west of Tokyo. For me, Nagoya would be native terrain, but for a couple of visiting Israelis, and any uninvited guests they might decide to bring, it would be unfamiliar and uncomfortable, and they would be reassuringly conspicuous there. Tokyo might have served my purposes instead, but I preferred to travel there infrequently. It had been two years since I'd faced off with Yamaoto, the puppet-master behind much of Japan's endemic corruption, but I knew the

15

man had a long and bitter memory and would be looking for me in Tokyo. Nagoya was better.

My prospective clients followed my instructions, and on the appointed day and time we met at Torisei, a small *yakitoriya* in Naka-ku. Yakitori is down-home Japanese fare, primarily chicken, other meats, and vegetables grilled over an open charcoal barbecue and served on wood skewers. It's usually supplemented by *chazuke,* a soupy mixture of tea and rice, and always washed down with copious portions of beer or hot sake. *Yakitoriya* tend to be small, cozy, and unpretentious, and are often located near subway stations to make it easier for their *sarariman* and student patrons to duck in for a quick meal at a corner table or the easy camaraderie of the counter.

I was sitting in a tea shop across the street, wearing an unobtrusive *sarariman*-style navy suit and reading the *Asahi Shimbun,* a Japanese-language daily paper, when they arrived. I saw them approach from the north, pause to glance at Torisei's sign, and go inside. Although they were out of their element in Nagoya, they didn't refer to directions or other written instructions to confirm that they'd found the place, and I sensed from this that they were accustomed to operating sterile, something that in professionals becomes a habit.

I waited and watched the street. After ten minutes, I got up and followed them in. As I parted the establishment's blue *noren* curtains, I was thinking in Japanese and maintaining a Japanese persona. In my peripheral vision, I saw that they had taken one of the small tables. They both looked up when I arrived, but I ignored them. I expected Delilah would have given them a description, but I doubted that would be enough for them to pick me out if I wanted to stay anonymous. I took a seat at the counter, facing them and

with the entrance door to my right. I ordered *yaki-onigiri* –
grilled rice balls – and an Asahi Super Dry, opened my
paper, and started to read. After a few minutes, when I felt
they would have concluded I wasn't of interest, I glanced
around.

I liked what I saw. They were dressed neatly, blazers
but no ties, and seemed relaxed and comfortable in the
doubtless unfamiliar environment. But for a slightly heightened sense of alertness that only someone like me would
have recognized, they could have been a couple of visiting
European tourists, or businessmen pleased to have discovered an authentically Japanese place to eat after a day of
interminable meetings in some generic office conference
room.

I looked around and didn't see anyone or anything that
set off my radar. After another moment, I explained to the
counterman that my acquaintances were already here and I
had somehow overlooked them. I was going to go join them
at their table, and, when it was ready, the waitress could just
bring my order there.

I got up and strolled over. I left my newspaper at the
counter, wanting to reassure them in the face of this small
surprise by keeping my hands empty. They watched me
coming.

When I reached their table, I said, 'Boaz? Gil?' These
were the names I had been given.

They both stood up. The one with his back to the door
said in lightly accented English, 'I'm Boaz.'

The other said, 'Gil.'

'Sorry,' I said, 'I didn't see you here at first.'

Boaz laughed at that. They knew damn well I had seen
them.

We shook hands and I sat down next to Gil. Boaz looked

at the all-Japanese menu and asked with a smile, 'Do you want to order, or shall I?'

His smile was reassuring and I returned it. I said, 'Maybe you should let me.'

As we ate and talked, I found myself impressed. They were in their early forties, senior enough to have advanced within their organization, presumably on merit, but not so senior that they would have lost touch with the field. They were comfortable in their cover: although I sensed by a dozen small tells that they were ex-military, nothing in their outward appearance would have revealed their backgrounds to a casual observer. They eschewed G-Shock wristwatches, aviator shades, too-short hair, and the other indicators of an ongoing attachment to a military past. Instead they wore their hair at a civilian length; dressed tastefully, even stylishly; and either were comfortable unarmed or were carrying weapons I wasn't able to detect. They were confident, but not arrogant; businesslike, but not cold; obviously serious, and even grave, about the business at hand, but not without a sense of humor.

Of the two, Gil was quieter. His eyes were a contradiction – partially hidden by heavy lids that made him appear relaxed, almost ready to doze, and yet lit by a strange glow from within. In those eyes and in his unaffected tone I recognized a fellow killer, a man who had taken lives at close range, and who was prepared to do so again. Boaz, short, balding, and slightly chubby, had a warmer persona, and I judged him the less lethal of the two. In fact, he had an infectious laugh and insisted on telling me several American jokes, which I didn't find unfunny. If they were a team, Boaz was the front man and Gil the trigger puller, a division of labor that, I imagined, would be fine with Gil.

They had initially insisted that Manny's expiration would

have to appear natural. I pressed them for a more precise definition. Certainly a heart attack is natural, about as natural as it gets, and I've been known to cause one when conditions are right. But I wasn't sure I could get that close to someone like Manny, wasn't sure I could establish the necessary control over the environment. I asked them about an accident, or a suicide. These were possible, they said, if things could be made to look convincing. I told them there were no guarantees, not with the little they were giving me to go on. I told them that in the end it might have to look like a crime – a robbery or a kidnapping gone awry, foul play, yes, but not foul play that had been directed specifically at Manny. And therefore not attributable to anyone who would be happier in the absence of such attribution.

In the end, we had agreed on a sliding scale of compensation, with the richness of each potential payment tied to the degree of 'naturalness' of Manny's demise. Sure, there were some gray areas that a good lawyer might have been able to better define. But I was confident that any disputes would be resolved in my favor. Trying to take advantage of someone like me is usually unwise, and smart people tend to know better.

I noted the way they made decisions. There was no 'We'll get back to you on that' or 'We'll just have to check with headquarters first.' They examined the facts and made up their minds on the spot. Obviously their organization gave them a healthy amount of operational autonomy. I sensed a deference on Gil's part toward Boaz, and took Boaz's likely rank as further evidence that he was more the brains, Gil more the brawn of the operation.

I asked them why they had come to me rather than doing the job in-house. Boaz laughed his infectious laugh. He looked at Gil, then at me, and said, 'You think the two of us would blend in in a place like Manila?'

'I know this might come as a shock to you,' I told them, 'but not all Asians look alike. I don't look particularly Filipino.'

Boaz said, 'We don't mean to imply that all Asians look alike. We're familiar with the differences. I only mean that an Asian would blend there better than a Caucasian. I don't think that's an inaccurate statement, is it?'

In fact I wasn't worried. Although it's true I don't look like the average Filipino, there are plenty of ethnic Chinese in the country and all sorts of other mixes, too, along with a significant expat population. With the tan I had acquired in Rio, where I had been living since leaving Japan, I knew I could blend in just fine. But I didn't want them to think this would be easy. They might try to price it accordingly.

We were quiet for a moment. Boaz said, 'Also, you were highly recommended.'

'Delilah?'

Gil said, 'And other sources.'

I wondered whether there really were any other sources, or whether they were just trying to seem more connected than they really were. Cops, intelligence agents, interrogators . . . puffery about how much you know is a venerable technique for establishing control.

'Recommended on what grounds?'

Boaz shrugged as though the answer were obvious. 'Reliability. Discretion.'

Gil, his eyes flat, added, 'Lethality.'

I glanced around and confirmed that no one was within earshot. The Japanese education system's ubiquitous efforts to teach English as a second language are sometimes endearingly useless, but there are plenty of success stories wandering around, too, and you have to be careful. I said, 'I'm glad my references checked out.'

Gil shrugged. 'Delilah seems to think highly of you.'

The comment was redundant after Boaz's assurance that Delilah had recommended me. That, and something in Gil's tone, suggested to me that he wasn't entirely pleased by Delilah's enthusiasm. If he was jealous, it was sloppy of him to show it. On the other hand, it was clear to me that Gil was employed for talents other than his knack with people.

'To be more specific,' Boaz said, 'lethality without weapons.'

His smooth catch of the conversational ball made me feel I had been on to something in thinking that Gil might have some issues with Delilah. I raised my eyebrows, and Boaz went on.

'Firearms present a problem in Manila. All the public venues – hotels, shopping centers, theaters – have guards and metal detectors. Lots of bombings in the region, and these are countermeasures. So if you're carrying a gun, you'll limit your mobility.'

Gil said, 'But we understand you don't carry.'

'Depends on the terrain,' I said, deliberately non-committal.

'But you don't need one,' Gil pressed, as though intrigued.

I shrugged. 'A gun is a tool. Sometimes it's the right tool to carry, sometimes not. Like I said, it depends.'

They nodded: Boaz, seemingly satisfied; Gil, as though mentally confirming that, in a pinch, he could drop me. Christ, he was in his forties, he really should have been past that sort of shit. Well, I guess you never get past it.

After a moment, Boaz said, 'Regardless, we would prefer if he died of something other than lead poisoning.' He raised his eyebrows, and I nodded to indicate I understood the joke. He smiled.

Gil added, 'As we've explained, the less this looks like an assassination, the better.'

'The ultimate point being deniability,' I said.

To that, they both nodded.

I wanted to ask about that, but I sensed it might be a sensitive subject, so I decided to hold off for a moment. 'Tell me,' I said, 'what has our friend Manny done that's made you want to wish him other than a long, prosperous life?'

The truth was, I didn't particularly care why they wanted him dead. What I needed was who, and where, and when. But I've learned from experience in the business that their ostensible reasons, and what I might glean from between the lines of their response, could help me protect myself from unpleasant surprises.

Gil took a briefcase from the floor and placed it on the table, then reached inside. Although we were in a public place and all seemed comfortable enough, I noted that he moved reassuringly slowly. The implication was: *If you have a problem with me reaching into a bag, just say so, and I'll stop.* The move was courteous and showed experience.

Gil took out a sheaf of about a dozen color photographs and handed them to me. Holding them so that no one in the restaurant could get a casual look, I started leafing through them.

Boaz said, 'The top one is Bali, October twelfth, 2002.'

The photo was of a demolished building. Charred bodies were everywhere, lying among burning palm trees and smoking rubble. A dismembered hand was front center, a man's wedding band prominent on the fourth finger, bloody tendons protruding from the stump of the wrist like wiring ripped from the back of an electronic appliance.

'You're saying Manny did this?' I asked, my tone dubious. 'I thought Bali was Jemaah Islamiah.'

'Yes, JI carried out the op,' Boaz said. 'The Malaysian Azahari Husin was the bombmaker. But where did Azahari acquire his expertise? From our friend.'

'Lavi is a chemist by training,' Gil said. 'He has special expertise in the explosive properties of various materials. That expertise is now for sale.'

'Take Bali,' Boaz said. 'The Bali bomb used lots of low explosives – potassium chlorate, sulfur, aluminum powder, alum, and chlorine – and only a small amount of TNT. The mixture created a shock wave and blistering heat. Most of the victims were roasted alive.'

'He's Israeli, and he's doing this?' I asked.

Boaz nodded. 'It's . . . how do you say, "infamy"? But yes, just like everyone else, we have some people who will do anything for money. There are Israeli soldiers who've been prosecuted for selling weapons to Palestinians in the West Bank and Gaza – the same weapons that are then used to kill their own brothers in the army.'

Gil shook his head disgustedly and said, 'I don't understand why we bother prosecuting them.'

Boaz reached over and showed me another photo. 'This is the Jakarta Marriott, August 2003. For this bomb, the terrorists used sulfur, potassium chlorate, gasoline, and TNT. The resulting bomb was both smaller and more powerful than the Bali device. This mixture created a shock wave and again a horrible burning effect.'

He pointed to the next photo. 'The Australian embassy in Kuningan, Jakarta, September 2004. This time we have sulfur, potassium chlorate, and TNT. The mixture created a tremendous shock wave followed by fire. Again, more powerful than the Bali bomb.'

Gil said, 'This is Lavi, learning by experimentation.'

Boaz said, 'Lavi isn't just disseminating his knowledge. He's refining it. He's briefed on the composition of these bombs, he analyzes the results, and he proposes "improvements." Lavi is one of the linchpins of a worldwide terrorist knowledge base. He helps these monsters improve their tools and tactics all over the world. What is learned in Southeast Asia is passed on in Europe, in the United States, in the Middle East.'

'How long have you known about what he's up to?'

'Not long enough,' Boaz said. 'A chance observation of a meeting with an Azahari cutout, more focused attention after that. We want him removed as soon as possible. As you understand, though, and personally I consider it unfortunate, we need deniability.'

'Otherwise,' Gil said, 'the list of volunteers for this job would be long.'

It was clear to me that Gil would be first in line.

'Knowledge,' I said, musing. 'How can you stop it? Isn't the genie out of the bottle?'

'We do what we can,' Boaz said, without any trace of his characteristic good humor, and for a moment I wondered whether I had misjudged in thinking that between them Gil was the only killer. 'We do our part.'

I went through the rest of the photos. Boaz gave each a place and date in a monotone: first World Trade Center attack, 1993; Buenos Aires Jewish Community Center, 1994; US embassies in Kenya and Tanzania, 1998; USS *Cole*, 2000; others. Gil explained Manny's behind-the-scenes involvement, and how his participation was increasing the lethality of the bombs and furthering knowledge of how to create them.

'So you see,' Boaz said when I was finished and had

handed the sheaf back to Gil, 'to us, eradicating Lavi is like curing a fatal disease. We can't bring back the people he has already murdered, but we can save the lives that will be lost if his life were to continue.'

'We think you can help us,' Gil said.

Boaz added, 'And we think you can do it the right way.'

I got the point. The main thing was, they weren't looking for something foolproof, only something deniable. If they had insisted on a heart attack, I would have taken it to mean that their fundamental concern was that no questions even be asked. I would then have assumed that Manny was an unusually connected target, and would have reevaluated accordingly. Instead, they seemed willing to have questions asked, as long as the answers didn't lead back to them.

I found it interesting that they had approached me directly. They might have used someone else, and insulated themselves with cutouts. My guess was that, in their judgment, the extra insulation afforded by the cutouts would have been outweighed by the greater chance of discovery. If Manny were to die of a headshot from a high-powered rifle, somebody might feel compelled to look very hard for whoever was behind it. Sure, there would be some insulation then, but the method of the hit would make the insulation necessary. My methods, and my track record, were such that they must have been more confident of my ultimate success. Less insulation, less need for it. A trade-off. And regardless, Delilah had brought me in. She'd pitched the work to me, she'd brokered the meeting. It would have been pointless to try to run things under a false flag after that.

The flexibility we'd agreed on was helpful, but overall I was still operating in a relatively constrained universe of possibilities. The whole thing would have been simpler if I could have just learned Manny's routine and then positioned Dox to blow his head off from a thousand yards away. But I didn't mind the constraints, really, and I suppose I never have. After all, they're part of what justifies my prices. And 'natural' means no investigation, perhaps not even any questions. I can slip away afterward without pursuit. And make fewer enemies in the process.

'One thing concerns me,' I said. 'I don't understand the need for deniability. With the kind of stuff he's been up to, I would think that you or anyone else could kill Manny any way you wanted.'

They glanced at each other. Obviously I'd been right in sensing that this would be a sensitive topic.

After a moment, Boaz said, 'We have reason to believe that Lavi is a CIA asset.'

In my mind, the price of the job instantly doubled.

'You have reason?' I said.

He shrugged. 'We're not positive. But obviously, if there is a relationship, we don't want to have to apologize.'

'Why would the Agency want this guy as an asset? Why not just put him six feet under?'

'The CIA has exaggerated ideas of its own capabilities,' Gil said. 'They think they can do more good running people like Lavi than they can by just killing them. They think the intelligence they get from Lavi and his type serves the "big picture" and the "greater good."'

Boaz asked, 'You know A. Q. Khan?'

'The father of the Pakistani bomb,' I said. 'And a whole lot of illegitimate children, too, if the news is getting it right. The Paks arrested him for running an international Nukes R Us, then pardoned him pretty much the next day.'

Boaz nodded. 'Makes you wonder what you have to do to get thrown in jail over there.'

Gil said, 'Khan sold his nuclear starter kit to Iran, Libya, North Korea, and others, possibly including some nonstate actors. It turns out the CIA was watching Khan for thirty years. Everything he did, he did right under their noses. Twice the CIA persuaded Dutch intelligence agents not to arrest Khan because the CIA wanted to follow his trail.'

'What about your people?' I asked. 'Sounds like Khan was ripe for an accident.'

'We very stupidly deferred to the CIA on how to handle him,' Gil said. 'With Khan, everyone was too clever by half. We're not making those mistakes anymore.'

'So you think the Agency might be taking the same approach with Manny that it took with Khan.'

'Similar,' Boaz said. 'Not the same. Khan was never a US asset. We think Lavi might be. But either way, we're no longer interested in trying to get these characters to lead us to other characters. That's all just a . . . what do you say, "circle jerk"?'

'I think you could call it that, yeah.'

He smiled, pleased at his use of the idiom. 'Well, we've learned from our mistakes. Now, when we find people like Lavi, we just make them dead. In this case, for the reasons we've shared with you, dead with discretion is preferable.'

We were all quiet for a long time. Then I said, 'If this might offend the CIA, there's more risk. The prices we discussed a few minutes ago won't do it.'

Boaz looked at me and said, 'Tell us what will.'

3

Over the next few days in Manila, Dox and I learned two important things. First, Manny wasn't actually staying at the hotel. He would show up there once or twice a day, typically in the early afternoon, and sometimes again in the evening. He would stick around for about an hour, then depart again for parts unknown. Second, a hotel car, one of a small fleet of four identical black Mercedes S-classes, was taking him around. We never saw the car, license plate MPH 777, except when it pulled in to deliver Manny, and then the driver would wait in the carport until Manny had reemerged. It didn't even come back at night. Manny must have reserved it on a twenty-four-hour basis, possibly for the duration of his stay.

I was tempted to call the front desk – 'Hello, this is Mr Hartman, can you remind me, how long did I reserve the hotel car?' – which might have given us an indication of how long Manny planned to be in town. But I decided the call would be unnecessarily risky. Given Manny's long association with the Peninsula, the staff might know his habits, perhaps even his voice.

But maybe there was a better way. Among the goodies we had brought along for the job was a miniature GPS tracking device. It was a slick unit, with an internal antenna and motion activation to preserve the battery when the car wasn't running. If we could place it in the vehicle, we could track Manny's movements remotely.

That day, I hired one of the cars for a trip out to Lake

Taal. In a thick Japanese accent, I told the driver that I wanted to see the lake and the active volcano that had conceived it. On the fourth finger of my left hand I wore a gold wedding band, purchased for cash from a Manila street vendor. I gave the driver plenty of opportunities to see it.

The journey, my first beyond Metro Manila since arriving in the city, was strangely beautiful. We drove first past the area's slums, shanty cities clinging precariously to the undersides of highways and train tracks, their rusted corrugated walls provisional, yet also, somehow, timeless; their inhabitants sitting, sometimes squatting, before their wretched domiciles and among chickens and foraging dogs, watching uncomplaining as the Mercedes crawled past them in the thickening morning traffic. Beyond EDSA, the highway that encircles Manila like a traffic-choked noose, the city gave way to rice fields and green hills in the distance, and I had the odd and not unpleasant sense that I was being driven back into Vietnam. We picked up speed. Goats and gaunt cows observed our passage without evident interest. We passed a thin boy riding a water buffalo alongside the highway. He ignored our passage, but I noticed that he was smiling dreamily to himself as he swayed atop the animal, and I wondered for a moment what random thoughts might have provoked such gentle rapture. The lake itself, utterly placid, surrounded the cone of an active volcano that seemed to be merely sleeping, perhaps soon to stir. Because of the earliness of the hour no tourists had yet alighted, and I was gratified to have a moment to contemplate the water, the sky, the buzz of insects, and the calls of tropical birds before heading back to the density of Manila and the weight of the operation.

Back at the hotel, Dox and I took turns monitoring the feed from in front of the elevators for a sign of Manny's return. It was boring work, as surveillance inevitably is. This time we were lucky: he showed up at a little after two in the afternoon, having kept us waiting only a few hours. As soon as we saw him and the bodyguard moving past the camera, I walked out to the carport.

In a heavy Japanese accent and broken English, I explained to the bell captain what had happened. One of the cars had taken me out to Lake Taal, I said, and somehow I had misplaced my wedding ring during the trip. The man seemed genuinely sympathetic: he must have understood how it would look to my wife when I tried to explain that I had lost my wedding ring in Manila, a city notorious for its pleasure quarters. He examined some paperwork, then gestured to one of the cars. 'There, Mr Yamada, the one on the far left, that's the one you were in. Please, have a look.'

I thanked him and made a show of feeling around in the gaps in the seats and looking under the floor mats. Strangely enough, my ring was nowhere to be found.

'Not there,' I said, shaking my head in apparent agitation. 'You are certain . . . that is correct car? All look same.'

'Quite certain, sir.'

I rubbed a hand across my mouth. 'Okay if I check others? Please?'

He nodded and offered the sympathetic smile again. 'Certainly, sir,' he said.

I made sure to search license plate MPH 777 next, going through the back in the same thorough fashion I had used a moment earlier. But this time, I left behind the GPS unit, adhered to the underside of the driver-side seat. The driver was chatting with another of the hotel staff by the front door and seemed neither to notice nor to care about my brief intrusion.

My search of the third and fourth cars was similarly

fruitless. I thanked the bell captain sheepishly and asked him to please call me right away if anyone found a gold wedding band. He assured me that of course he would.

If an opportunity presented itself when we were done with the op, I would retrieve the unit. If I didn't, eventually someone would find it. But so what? The driver would be reluctant to report it lest he somehow cause trouble for himself. If he did report it, his supervisor would suffer from the same inhibitions. Even if the incident reached management, the hotel could be counted on to take the high road of not advertising that someone had been surreptitiously tracking a guest through the hotel's own fleet. And thus do greed and shame become progenitors of complicity.

Over the next few days, we used the GPS to track Manny's movements. He seemed to travel widely within Metro Manila, but there was one commonality: a suburb called Greenhills. He would typically arrive there in the early evening, and, although he would sometimes go out again an hour or two later, he would always return for the night.

'Why do you suppose he's going out to the suburbs every day and not even staying in the hotel?' Dox asked as we charted his movements.

I paused and thought about that for a moment. 'I'm not sure. It could have to do with security, with the multiple locations creating a shell game dynamic. But two shells isn't much. And his timing is more regular than I would be comfortable with.'

'I reckon he's got a woman out there.'

'He could get a woman a lot easier in Makati, near the hotel.'

'Maybe this one is love.'

I shrugged. 'Only one way to find out.'

Upon arriving in Manila three weeks earlier, I had rented

an unobtrusive gray Honda Civic, which I had garaged at the Peninsula. In my mind, I was an advance man for a Japanese boss, scouting locations for his arrival in the city. The cover was simple, provided for a wide range of behavior, and would be difficult to disprove. The *yakuza* maintains a sizable presence in the Philippines, a country that supplies many of Japan's female 'entertainers,' and my story, including a reticence about details, would be adequate to survive any foreseeable inquiries.

I drove out to Greenhills late in the afternoon, before Manny's usual arrival time. With the GPS information, we knew to within a meter where the car was stopping. It was always in front of 11 Eisenhower Boulevard, which turned out to be a brick-and-glass high-rise condominium that looked like new money. I sat and waited in the window of a Jollibee, the local McDonald's equivalent, in a shopping mall across the street. I had noted that, with the sun overhead and continuing to move westward, the store glass was mirroring a lot of light, making it difficult to see inside from the street.

I'd spent time in Manila while with the army in Vietnam, but of course that had been long ago, and the city had changed. Enclaves like what was now called Greenhills had once been rice paddies. The city was denser now: more people, more cars, more frenzy. There was a new air of commercialism, too, with mega-malls visible from auto-choked highways and billboards advertising teeth-whitening toothpastes and modern high-rises emphasizing by contrast the eternal shantytowns and slums around them. For the three weeks before Manny arrived, I had taken in these changes while indulging myself with a Manila-and-environs refresher course. The itinerary varied, but there was certainly a theme.

I might have been researching a unique guidebook, some-thing like *Trouble in Paradise: Ambush, Escape, and Evasion for the Independent Operator in Metro Manila.* The more you sweat in training, the less you bleed in combat, an army instructor once told me, and I've never forgotten the lesson. If I ever die during an op, it won't be because I was too lazy to prepare properly.

Manny showed up at dinnertime. I saw the black S-class round the corner on Eisenhower and pull up in front of the condo. The bodyguard got out first. He spent a moment scanning the street for trouble, but failed to spot it eating a cheeseburger behind the reflective plate glass of the Jollibee. When he was satisfied, he opened Manny's door, his eyes still periodically roaming the street. Manny got out and the two of them walked inside. Two uniformed guards in front of the building nodded to Manny as he went past, and I realized he was well known to them. Getting to him inside, while offering certain advantages, would obviously pose a challenge. We would have to keep watching for a better opportunity.

I left the Jollibee and entered the shopping mall. I called Dox from a prepaid cell phone I had bought with cash. Dox was also using a prepaid. He had his own GSM unit, but I'd told him to keep it switched off while we were operational. There are ways of tracking a cell phone, and I didn't know who might have had Dox's number.

'He's here,' I told him. 'The condominium in Greenhills.'

'I know. I'm watching the little arrow moving around the computer. I saw the car pull up ten minutes ago. Anything interesting?'

'There's a lot of security at the building. We're going to need to watch him some more.'

'Roger that.'

'What's the earliest he's left the building so far?'

'Hang on a minute.' I heard the sound of the keyboard. 'Oh-seven-hundred. Seems like he's typically on his way by oh-eight-hundred.'

'All right. I'm leaving. I'll come back in the morning. I've seen him arrive. Maybe I'll learn something watching him go out.'

I returned at just before seven the next morning. It was Sunday. I ate at the Jollibee again. The morning crew was new. Even if they'd been the same as the previous afternoon, I doubted that they would have noticed me. When I want to, I have a way of just being part of the scenery.

Manny came out forty-five minutes later. He was with a pretty Filipina and a boy of about seven or eight who looked to be of mixed heritage. Manny was wearing dark trousers and a cream-colored silk shirt; the woman, dark-skinned, petite, showed a nice figure in a yellow floral dress. The little boy was wearing a blue blazer and khaki pants. He was holding Manny's hand, and in the instant my mind put all the pieces together in some sort of preconscious shorthand, I realized, *He's just happy to be with his daddy,* and was surprised at the acuteness of the pang that accompanied the thought.

They got into the back of the Benz and I watched as it pulled away from the curb. My cell phone rang. It was Dox.

'He's moving,' he said.

'I know. I'm watching.'

'What do you see?'

I paused, then said, 'He's not staying at the hotel because he's got a family here in Greenhills. A woman and a son.'

'How do you know?'

'I just saw them all together. From the way they're dressed on a Sunday morning, I'd say they're on their way to church. And it makes sense. The file says Manny has a family back in Johannesburg. My guess is that somewhere along the line, say seven, eight years ago from the apparent age of the boy, Manny knocked up a Filipina. That's why he's been coming out here so regularly and for so long. It's not business, or at least it's not just business. He keeps a room at the hotel so his Johannesburg wife doesn't get wise, and he goes back there once or twice a day. Think about the times he shows up at the hotel – morning and afternoon in South Africa. Probably calls home from the room so she can see the caller ID readout.'

'I thought old Manny was of the Israeli persuasion. When I was growing up, I didn't go to church too often, but I don't remember seeing a whole lot of Jews there at the time.'

I thought for a moment, then said, 'If I'm right about where they're going, he's probably doing it as an accommodation to the woman. Filipinas can be pretty serious about their Catholicism.'

'All right, I'll buy that. Any angle on how we reach out and touch him?'

'We've got a pretty good idea of where he's actually staying. That's a start. Keep me posted on where the car is heading, and I'll follow them from a distance until they stop. Maybe I'll learn more.'

'Roger that.'

As it turned out, they weren't going far: a nearby gated community called East Greenhills. I had to show a guard my ID, which was fake in any event, but he let me in when I told him, following my hunch, that I was there to attend morning Mass. He could have tested me on the liturgy if he'd wanted. My American mother, who was Catholic, had taken me to church regularly enough for the experience to have made an impression.

The approach to the church was clogged with cars, and I had to park some distance away and walk. That was fine. I preferred to keep the car out of view, so as not to give the bodyguard too many opportunities for multiple sightings.

Inside it was crowded, nearly full. I recognized the subject of the sermon, which was being delivered in English – spoken almost universally, along with indigenous Tagalog, throughout Manila. The priest was discussing the prayer of St Francis of Assisi, who opined, among other things, that it is in dying that we are born to eternal life.

My own experience has led me to contrary conclusions, but I didn't see the point of arguing.

The priest's voice echoed from the front of the long room, competing with a series of wall-mounted ceiling fans that swayed forward and back as though alternately entranced by and then distracted from the cadences of his speech. The room was open on three sides to the outside, and the air was heavy with tropical moisture.

I sat in back on one of the varnished wooden pews, feeling the weight of the edifice settle in around me. It had been a long time, a lifetime, since I'd been in a church, and that was fine with me.

I could see Manny and his family, to the left and six rows forward. The boy sat between Manny and the woman. I sensed I'd been right in suggesting to Dox that periodic church attendance was an accommodation Manny made to the desires of the woman. Probably he didn't really give a shit on a religious level. Or maybe the whole thing was uncomfortable for him. Either way, that he was willing to participate was further evidence that he cared a lot about the woman, and, I assumed, about the boy, too.

I watched from where I sat, wondering what the boy made of the ritual to which he was being subjected. I didn't know if his father's participation would make things better for him, or worse. My own visits to church had always been exclusively with my mother, over the silent protests of my Japanese father, who objected to such silliness, and, I realized later, to the Western infection it would impart.

Yes, I thought. *Four-hundred-plus years ago, the Spanish infect the natives. And now the infection perpetuates, persists. The woman passes it on to the boy.*

My own father was killed when I was eight, in a Tokyo street riot. Since then there have been a number of what I suppose might be called 'defining moments,' but that first death was the original. I can still feel the terrible fear and shock as my mother broke the news to me, trying and then failing to hold back her own tears. If I choose to, and I usually don't, I can vividly recall the years of strange dreams after, in which he would be back with us and alive but always insubstantial or mute or dying or in some other way less than whole. It had taken me a long time to recover from all that.

I realized that seeing Manny with his family was stirring up this shit. And being in a church, that wasn't exactly a plus, either.

I thought of the photos Boaz and Gil had shown me. If Manny were to die in an accident today, there was no question that many innocent lives would be saved. How could it be a sin, then, to facilitate his demise? On the contrary, wouldn't the sin lie in forbearance? Wouldn't such forbearance, in fact, be a form of complicity in those later deaths?

But I also knew that Manny's death would leave this boy bereft, crucify him in grief and loneliness. I knew that very well.

All at once I hated being faced with this dilemma. I

resented all the forces, past and present, that had conspired to impose it on me. I wanted to be one of the ignorant, the undeserving recipients of the fruits of awful choices like this one, who could sleep secure in their beds and dream innocent dreams and enjoy the profits of the sacrifice I was about to impose on this child, and the sacrifice I would make in the process, without bloodying their own hands in the process. They didn't deserve the benefits any more than this boy deserved the burden, and goddamn if I was going be the one to present them with such a bloody gift.

And then I thought, *Maybe this is the sacrifice that's required of you. This is the sacrifice that you owe. All those lives you've taken . . . do lives saved count against them?*

I shook my head, confused. I've been at this for more years than I care to acknowledge, and I'd never been troubled this way before. At least not in the middle of the proceedings. Sometimes you learn something afterward, or see something when it's too late to turn back . . . it bothers you later. But not like this.

It's the boy, I told myself. *You never want to see that the target has a family. And the boy is reminding you of yourself. Perfectly normal reaction. It'll pass, like it always does. Focus on the job, on doing the job. That's all you can trust, that's the thing that gets you through.*

I took a deep breath and let it out. Right. The job.

Mass lasted another forty minutes. When it was over, I drifted behind Manny and his family, staying well back in the crowd. As we exited the church, the boy clambered onto Manny for a piggyback ride. I could hear his delighted laughter carrying across the tropical air. I watched the three of them load into the Mercedes, then walked back to my car.

I called Dox. 'They were at church. My guess is that

they're on their way to a meal now. Let me know where they're heading and I'll stay with them. This might be our chance, too, so be ready to move.'

'Already am.'

With Dox apprising me of the direction they were taking, I was able to follow them without maintaining a visual. It turned out I was right about the meal. They stopped in the Ayala Center, a sparkling mega-mall almost across the street from the Peninsula. I got to the mall only a minute behind them, and took my best guess, based on where they had parked, on where they had gone inside. From there, it was mostly a matter of checking restaurants. It took me only a few minutes to find them, in the main food court on the third floor. They were sitting in front of a place called World Chicken, already working on a meal. The bodyguard was standing off to the side. I picked him up in my peripheral vision, but gave no sign that I was aware of him. I felt confident he hadn't noticed me. The area was crowded with shoppers and diners and I had plenty of cover.

I called Dox. 'I'm on him again. They're at the Ayala Center, right across the street from you. Walk over and you'll be here in less than ten minutes.'

'I'm on my way.'

'Switch to the commo gear when you get here.'

'Roger that.'

I bought a coffee from one of the vendors and sat down on the other side of the food court. After a few minutes, I heard Dox.

'I'm here,' he said. 'First-floor atrium. Where are you?'

'A place called Glorietta Food Choices, third-floor Glorietta. One floor under one of the cineplexes, right next to a video game arcade. I'm sitting near the windows, farthest from the escalators. Our friend is getting lunch ten feet in front of the escalator. Guard is staying with them. Come up and move to your left right away and he won't see you. Then stay at the periphery until you ID the players. I don't want him to recognize you from the hotel.'

'Roger that.'

A minute later, I saw Dox enter. He circled wide as I had suggested, keeping the crowd between himself and the principals. I saw his eyes move past me without stopping.

I realized that Manny hadn't taken a restroom break since church. I was thinking that at some point, maybe after lunch, he was going to heed a call of nature. The bodyguard would be watching for anyone moving in after him. But it wouldn't occur to him that some antisocial someone might be in there already.

I felt a small wave of adrenaline coming ashore.

'Hey,' I said.

'Yeah.'

'There's a men's room on this floor. I'm going to wait inside it. I have a feeling our friend is going to go after he finishes his lunch. With luck, he'll come alone.'

'I'll watch your back, partner.'

'Good.'

Restrooms are nice because they're one of the last urban places where you can't find a security camera. I would wait inside, come up behind him, break his neck, and be out the door before he hit the floor. There were no cameras in the vicinity of the restroom, so my entrance and exit would go unrecorded. No one would check on Manny for at least two minutes, and probably more like five, giving Dox and me plenty of time to slip away unnoticed. Not quite the level of naturalness that the Israelis were hoping for, or that I would have liked to be paid for, but I thought it would do. The police can be as lazy as anyone else, and for anyone disinclined to fill out a lot of paperwork, a broken neck would be easier to file under 'slip and fall' or 'accident' than would a bullet hole in the forehead. The main thing was that no one would be able to attribute it to my client.

I imagined Manny's family, waiting for him to return. Two minutes becomes three, three becomes four. Someone makes a joke about how Daddy must have fallen in. The woman goes to the door and calls for him. There's no answer. She feels confused, possibly a little concerned. She pokes her head inside and sees Manny on the floor, his head at an impossible angle. She screams. The boy comes running. He stops at his mother's leg and looks through the door she's holding open. The image carves itself into his brain and never, ever leaves him.

I heard Dox's voice in the earpiece: 'You all right, partner?'

I looked around the food court. 'Yeah, fine. Why?'

'You looked a little spooked there, for a while. Thought maybe you saw something I didn't.'

'I'm all right.'

'Well, you've got company, coming up from behind you. I was afraid you hadn't noticed.'

'What kind of company?'

'The kind that's wearing a big bulge under the back of a suit jacket.'

'Bodyguard?'

'That's right.'

I wondered how he had managed to get a gun inside. He must have been licensed. Manny had been coming to Manila for a long time and was probably well connected.

'Tell me if I need to turn, let him know I see him coming.'

'I think you're okay. His hands are empty. But he's definitely coming to check you out.'

I knew what had likely drawn the man's attention. It wasn't something I did. It was something I am.

No one can completely obscure the signs of a profound acquaintance with violence. The obvious ones are the hard cases. These are men who've lived through the shit and have no ability, and certainly no inclination, to hide the predacious air such survival conveys. This type, which includes gangbangers, ex-cons, and a certain breed of former soldier, gives off the strongest, most distinctive vibe, and is the easiest to detect.

There's another type, too, as intimate, if not more so, with violence as the first, but better aware of the scent they now carry and more inclined and better able to conceal it. This type, which includes your average undercover operator, is harder to detect, but is often noticeable anyway not so much by the presence of a particular vibe as by the absence of any vibe at all. These people have become aware of the danger signals they put out and have reacted, or in a sense overreacted, by retracting everything. Within the energy of a given social environment, these men show up as an absence, a missing something, like gray in a color canvas, or a black hole against a tableau of stars.

The third type is the hardest to pick up, and is probably unrecognizable to the first two and certainly to civilians. It, too, includes men who have been forged in violence, but who also are natural camouflage artists, chameleons. These men hide their predator's mark not so much by trying to retract the vibe, but by concealing it behind a new persona that they recognize in civilians and then imitate and project like a hologram. I know this type because I call it my own.

But even the third type is detectable sometimes, at certain moments, if you know what to look for. I find it impossible to articulate just what gives the chameleons away.

Sometimes it's something in the eyes, something that doesn't fit with the clothes, the gait, the speech patterns. Sometimes it's something that feels like a ripple at the edge of the persona, a not-quite-perfect fit in the façade. Whatever it is, it's something the intuitive mind can flag, but that remains too subtle for the conscious mind to label. And as I sat in the food court, troubled by my thoughts, something must have surfaced in my expression, and it was this the man coming toward me must have keyed on and felt worth examining more closely.

Operators don't let people move in from their blind side, so if I didn't turn or otherwise let him know I was aware of his approach, it might help persuade him to ignore whatever had caught his attention, to conclude that I was a civilian after all. He might then simply move on after taking a sniff. Or, if he got too close and forced me to act, he would be less likely to be properly prepared for what he encountered.

'How close?' I asked, without moving my lips. I picked up a packet of sugar, tore it open, and started pouring it into the coffee cup. If you're trying not to be spotted, it helps to do mundane things, and, if possible, to think mundane thoughts. Don't ask me why, but it does.

'Eight yards. Seven. Six . . .'

'Hands?'

'Still empty. Four yards.'

At four yards, I should have heard his footfalls. Either he was naturally stealthy, or he was deliberately approaching quietly. Either way, I knew I was dealing with something more than typical rent-a-cop security.

'Three yards. He's stopped, next to a big old potted plant for partial concealment. Hands are still empty. I don't think he knows what to make of you, but I don't think he wants to be friends, either.'

43

I busied myself swirling sugar into the coffee with a wooden stirrer, thinking, *Hmmm, I hope this tastes good, I prefer my coffee black, well, this coffee was fairly bitter anyway, maybe it's an arabica, yeah, dark-roasted, I wonder what country it's from . . .*

I heard Dox's voice again: 'All right, he's heading off. Must have decided you weren't interesting after all.'

I took a sip of the coffee. Actually, with the sugar it was pretty good. 'I'm not,' I said.

I heard him laugh.

When the bodyguard had moved off, I got up and walked away, shuffling like a typical Japanese *sarariman*. I sensed him watching me go, knowing that he would take my exit as further confirmation that I didn't present a threat.

But at the far end of the food court, with the arcade between us, I ducked into the restroom. The room was rectangular, about five meters by six, with the entrance on one of the short ends. Three urinals along one long side; two stalls on the other, sinks against the connecting wall. Two Filipino teenagers were zipping up when I came in and left a moment later.

I went into the corner stall and closed the door.

'I'm in,' I said. 'Tell me when he's moving.'

'Roger that.'

I waited ten minutes. Then: 'They're getting up. Looks like he's saying good-bye to the woman and the boy. Yeah, they're heading down the escalator.'

They were splitting up. Good.

'Bodyguard's staying, though. No surprise there.'

'No, no surprise.'

A moment passed. Then: 'He's coming toward your position. I think your hunch was good.'

I felt another adrenaline wave roll in, bigger than the first. 'With the bodyguard?'

'No, he's hanging back. Okay, our man is walking down the corridor to the restroom right now. Ten more seconds and he's inside.'

'Good.'

I heard the bathroom door open. I took a deep breath, then slowly exhaled all of it through my mouth, its passage smooth and silent in counterpart to the thudding of my heart.

I looked through the gap alongside the stall door and saw Manny. He walked over to a urinal. His back was to me.

I opened the stall door. I took two silent steps forward.

Dox, in my ear: 'Shit, partner, the woman and the boy are back. The boy's heading toward you. Must have told his mom he needs to take a leak.'

Shit. Shit.

I started back into the stall. I heard no sound, but adrenaline was closing down my hearing and there must have been some noise of which I was unaware, because Manny turned his head and looked at me.

In the moment before the kill, I never look at the target's face. My gaze tends to focus on the torso, the movement of shoulders, hips, and hands. Doing so offers the advantage of spotting defensive movement, and of avoiding having to see the target's eyes, his expression, his fucking humanity.

But this time I looked. Maybe it was morbid curiosity. Maybe it was misplaced instinct, something that would have been noble in other circumstances, a desire to face the consequences of my deeds. Regardless, I looked.

Our eyes met. In his I saw earnestness, perhaps some surprise. No recognition. Not yet any fear.

The door opened. It was the boy.

And then I froze.

There's no other way to put it. My thoughts were clear.

45

Likewise, my perception. But I couldn't move my body. I seemed rooted to the spot. I thought, absurdly, *Move! Move!*

Nothing happened.

I felt beads of sweat popping out on my forehead. Still I couldn't move.

Manny looked at me, his surprise fading into concern, then to fear, then to resolution. He pulled himself back into his pants, and his right hand dipped into his front pants pocket. The word *knife!* flashed in my mind, but still my limbs were locked.

But it must have been some sort of panic button, not a knife. Because a second later, I heard Dox in my ear: 'Shit, partner, something's up. The bodyguard's heading in fast.'

I couldn't answer. I heard him say, 'Are you there, man? Say something!' Then, 'Fuck, I don't know if you can hear me, but I guess you can't answer. All right, I'm coming in.'

Manny started backing toward the door. He turned and swept the boy up in his arms. A moment later, the door flew open and the bodyguard burst inside, nearly running into the two of them. He saw my face and pulled up short, recognizing me, realizing he'd been wrong to dismiss me earlier, knowing now that he should have listened to his gut.

He shoved Manny and the boy to his right and reached behind and under his own jacket. Sweat was running down my face but I still couldn't move a muscle.

The door burst inward again and Dox barreled into the room. The bodyguard turned, his gun coming out.

And then, finally, when I saw that he was going to get the drop on Dox, my paralysis broke. Roaring something unintelligible, I took two steps forward and grabbed the gun with both hands as it came out and around. My decades of gripping and twisting the judo and jujitsu *gi* have given me abnormal hand strength, and once I had gotten ahold of the guard's gun I knew it was mine. I twisted hard, keeping the muzzle pointed away from me and Dox. The guard cried out and his hand gave. The gun went off as I took it away from him, the small room suddenly reverberating with the report.

Dox slung an arm around the guard's neck from behind and yanked him off his feet. The man's hands flew to Dox's massive forearm and his feet kicked wildly. Manny and the boy slipped past them. I looked for a shot at Manny, but Dox and the guard were in the way. Manny yanked the door open and he and the boy spilled out of the room.

Dox transitioned to *hadaka jime,* a sleeper hold, and the guard's struggles intensified, his body twisting and his legs churning the air.

The door crashed inward again. Two men, both Caucasian, burst into the room. Both had guns drawn.

'Down!' I shouted at Dox. But he was still struggling with the bodyguard. Still, he did the next best thing: he spun, pulling the guard in front of him like a shield.

Both men dropped to one knee, reducing the size of the target they offered, the smoothness of the move demonstrating training and experience. Dox and the bodyguard were between us – in what was about to become the crossfire.

A crazy thought zigged through my brain: *How the fuck are they getting these guns in here?*

His considerable muscles no doubt supercharged with adrenaline, Dox dropped one hand to the back of the guard's belt and heaved him into the two men. He used the force of the throw to hurl himself to the floor in the other direction.

Both men tried to get clear of the oncoming mass of the bodyguard. Only one succeeded – the one nearest the door, who jerked away just in time. His partner took the impact. But in avoiding the bodyguard, the first man had been forced to momentarily give up his focus. And in that moment, I put two rounds into his chest.

The other man was on his back now, he and the bodyguard hairballed up against the wall. He was trying to reacquire me, but too late. I swiveled and squeezed off two more shots. The first hit the bodyguard in the back of the neck. The second caught the downed man in the shoulder, jerking him partway around. He recovered, started bringing the gun toward me again.

No way, shitbird, it is not your turn now. You don't get a turn.

I moved in, keeping the gunsight on him, and pressed the trigger back twice more. The first shot caught him in the sternum, the second in the face. I tracked to the bodyguard – *Pause. Breathe. Aim* – and put one in the back of his head, then a final one in the head of the man I'd shot in the chest.

The room was suddenly, eerily quiet. My ears were ringing. The air was acrid with gunsmoke.

Dox was looking up at me from the floor. His eyes were wide. 'Damn, man, where did you learn to shoot like that?'

I stepped over to the bodyguard and felt along his belt. There, a spare magazine. I pulled it free, ejected the current magazine, and popped in the new one. I stuck the gun in the back of my pants where it would be concealed by my shirttail. The used magazine went into my pocket. There was no time to wipe these items down and otherwise ensure that none of my DNA or anything else incriminating had adhered to them. Besides, from where we were to where we needed to get, the gun and the rounds left in the first magazine might prove handy.

'Come on,' I said, myself again. I would think about what

had happened to me later. 'We've only got a few seconds. Follow my lead now.'

'Your lead?' he asked, coming to his feet.

I struggled not to get impatient. It seemed so obvious to me. 'Look, some nutcase was in here shooting up the place. Security guards are going to be converging any second. We're running from it, same as anyone would.'

'Okay, you're persuading me now.'

We each pulled a hat from a pocket. Mine was a baseball cap; Dox's was for fishing. Witnesses tend to remember gross details only, such as shirt color or the presence of a hat, and elementary precautions like ours can save a lot of grief later.

We moved to the door. 'Ready?' I asked.

'Right behind you, partner.'

I looked at him. He was grinning.

'Goddamnit,' I said, 'we were the victims, remember? You need to look scared.'

'Man, I am scared!'

'Try to show it better,' I growled.

'Fuck, man, I'm telling you this is how I look when I'm scared!'

Our eyes locked for a moment. His grin didn't budge.

I shook my head and said, 'Here we go.'

I opened the door. The corridor was clear. No sign of Manny or the boy. Just outside the corridor, though, the mood among the dining crowd had clearly been disrupted. The people with good sense and experience with the sound of indoor gunfire were wisely heading down the escalators. The curious, the deniers, and the simply stupid were lined up and gawking. For their benefit, I turned my head back toward the bathroom and shouted, 'They're shooting in there! Somebody call a guard!'

I heard Dox add, 'I'm scared! I'm scared!'

An unhelpful thought flashed through my mind – *My partner is insane* – but I kept moving. My quick scan of the crowd hadn't revealed my biggest concern – that individual or handful of individuals you will always encounter in a crisis who, sometimes by instinct but more often by experience, are not fleeing and not in denial, but instead calmly watching and evaluating, and perhaps looking for an opportunity to intervene. Ordinarily, these people simply make better than average witnesses later on, although sometimes they can access some deep-seated protective impulse and actually attack. I kept my head down and avoided anyone's eyes, and we joined the crowds hurrying down the escalator. In my peripheral vision, I saw two white-shirted security guards heading up opposite us. Neither had drawn his gun; they weren't sure what the trouble was and weren't yet taking it fully seriously.

On the second floor, the crowd was less agitated but still distracted. People were looking around, trying to figure out what had happened, what was the disturbance, whether they needed to do anything or if they could just get back to their shopping.

We moved laterally, heading in the direction of the next set of down escalators. As we walked, we each automatically removed the hats, then, one at a time, pulled off and balled up our outer shirts, which were navy blue. Underneath we both wore a second shirt, in cream – typical Filipino attire.

'We need to split up,' I said. 'Big white guy, Asian guy, that's about as much as people are going to remember, but it's enough to ID us right now.'

'Yeah, I know.'

'Go straight to the airport. I'll get the gear from the hotel. We'll meet at the backup in Bangkok.'

'You saved my life back there, partner. You really did.'

'Bullshit.'

'That bodyguard would have drilled me clean if you hadn't gotten to him first. I saw his eyes, and he meant business.'

I shook my head. There was no time to explain. And I still didn't understand what had happened to me in there.

'Think those guys were Agency?' he asked. 'They sure got there fast and they moved like pros.'

The agitation was behind us now; the next set of escalators, and the exits below, just a few meters away.

'That's one of the things we need to find out,' I said. 'But first we have to get out of Manila. I doubt Manny is going to report this to the authorities – it would mean too much attention for him. But I don't want to stick around waiting to find out.'

We reached the escalators and paused for a moment.

'You go down here,' I said. 'I want to lose the gun and the mag. I'll drop them in a toilet tank in one of the bathrooms. With a little luck I can find some bleach or other cleaning supplies in a janitor's cart and douse them first.'

He grinned like a schoolboy about to brag of a prank or some other exploit. 'I guess I need to break my date with the girl at the concession stand,' he said.

In the craziness of the moment, half of me wanted to laugh. The other half wanted to strangle him. I looked at him for a moment, shaking my head, and in the instant before I walked away his grin actually broadened.

4

The arrivals area of Tel Aviv's Ben Gurion Airport was crowded, bustling, and noisy. Tourists in tee-shirts and shorts jostled with *haredi,* the tremblers before God, in their black suits and hats. Announcements in English and Hebrew reverberated off the long concrete walls. The sun was setting beyond the western windows, and for a moment the terminal's interior burned headache bright with its sideways orange glow.

Delilah no longer felt comfortable here. Although her employer arranged for her to return at least annually to visit her parents and other relatives, the years of living a foreign cover had pulled her inexorably from the shores of the Levant, farther and farther until finally she had lost sight of land. This was her country, but she was no longer supposed to be here. The extraordinary security measures that accompanied these visits – false papers, disguise, countersurveillance – were testament to that. She was more comfortable now ordering *pain au chocolat* in French in Paris than she was giving instructions to a taxi driver in Hebrew in Tel Aviv. She told herself that this was the natural and perhaps not undesirable consequence of her commitment to her work, but still it was odd, to feel that you were forgetting who you are, or anyway who you used to be. The point of it all could wind up seeming so remote, so abstract. She wondered at times whether other operators were similarly afflicted, but knew she would be wise to discuss her concerns with no one. Regardless, she understood that this growing sense of estrangement from things that had once seemed inalienably hers would be known, in other endeavors, simply as the cost of doing business.

Her business was what the domestic media called *sikul memukad,* or 'focused prevention,' a construction she preferred to the more straightforward 'assassination.' The former was, to her thinking, more descriptive, and more associated with its purpose of saving lives than with its means of snuffing them out. She wasn't one of the trigger pullers, but at times she wished she were. After all, the men with the guns had the easy side of the division of labor. They never had to know the target. They didn't have to spend time with him. They certainly didn't have to sleep with him. They got close only once, only for an instant, and then they were done and gone. Emotionally, it was the difference between parting after a one-night stand, on the one hand, and dissolving a marriage, on the other.

Still, she was quietly proud of her sacrifices, proud that she made them for her own reasons and not for the recognition of her peers. Recognition, that was funny. Notoriety would be more like it. Her superiors acknow-ledged her unique talents and employed them with ruthless calculation, but deep down, she knew, they looked at her as somehow stained by what they called upon her to do. The best among management was merely uncomfortable with a woman who wormed her way into the lives of her victims, who slept with the monsters night after night, who knew even as she took them into her body that she was guiding them to their deaths. Management's worst, she suspected, thought *whore.*

Sometimes she felt coldly angry at the men who harbored such thoughts; other times, she almost pitied them. Their problem was that they couldn't get beyond the limits of their own inherently male experience. Men were simple: they were propelled by lust. And so they assumed that women should be the same. That a woman might sleep with a man for her own, more calculating reasons, even reasons of state security, put them off balance. It made them wonder if they were as vulnerable as the woman's victims, and this made them fidgety. If the woman was attractive, and they secretly desired her, the fidgeting became a squirm. *Whore* was their way of reassuring themselves that they were the ones in control.

She wondered why they had called her in this time. Things were going well with her current op, a straight-forward 'honey trap' of a certain Paris-based Saudi diplomat who had become distracted from his Wahabi religious convictions by her long, naturally blonde hair, and the way it cascaded around her shoulders when she chose to wear it down; by her blue eyes, endlessly enthralled, of course, by the man's awkward palaver; by her tantalizing Western décolletage and the porcelain skin beneath it. The man was smitten with her story of an absentee husband and her longing for true love, and was therefore nearly ready to hear the tearful tale that someone had learned of their illicit passion and was now blackmailing her with exposure – exposure that would of course encompass the Saudi himself – unless he could take certain actions, trivial in themselves, but which over time would compromise him further and further until her people would own him completely. Why recall her when she was so close? They had used the ordinary communications channels, with no abort signals, so she knew she wasn't in any danger, that the current op wasn't compromised. But that only made the reasons behind the recall even more mysterious.

Her papers were in perfect order, and her Hebrew,

though no longer her primary language, was still native, so she and her carry-on bag passed quickly through customs. She caught a cab outside the terminal and headed directly downtown. She needed to get to the Crowne Plaza on Hayarkon, a nice, anonymous business hotel and the site of the meeting to which she had been directed. The participants would arrive and depart separately to keep her affiliation sterile, and they wouldn't use the same hotel for months. After the meeting, she would call her parents and go see them, then spend the night at their house in Jaffa. She never announced these visits; they understood that her work, whatever it was, precluded notice. But business first.

She changed cabs several times and used a variety of other techniques to ensure that she wasn't being followed. When she was satisfied, she made her way to the hotel. She took the elevator directly to the fourth floor and headed toward room 416. She didn't have to look hard – there were two crew-cut men outside it, each with an earpiece and an Uzi. The obvious security was unusual. Something was definitely up.

One of the men examined her ID. Apparently satisfied, he opened the door and then immediately closed it behind her. Inside, three men were sitting around a table. Two she recognized – Boaz and Gil. The third was older by perhaps two decades, and it took her a moment to place him. She had met him only once.

Good God. The director. What was going on here?

'Delilah, *shalom,*' the older man said, getting up from his chair. He walked over and shook her hand, then continued in Hebrew, 'Or should I say, *bonjour*? Would you prefer to use French?'

She liked that he asked. Moving in and out of cover, out of two separate identities, was stressful. She shook her head and answered him in Hebrew. 'No. She's not supposed to be here. Let's let her sleep. She'll wake up when she's back in Paris.'

He nodded and smiled. 'And then this will all seem like a dream.' He gestured to the other men. 'You know Boaz? Gil?'

'We've worked together, yes,' she said. They stood, and the three of them shook hands.

Boaz was one of their best IED – improvised explosive devices – experts. She liked him a lot, as everybody did. He was serious when the situation called for it, but his default persona was boyish, at times mischievous, and he had an easy laugh that could almost be a giggle. He never came on to her, and in fact treated her as much like a sister as a colleague, which made him rare in the organization and, had the director not been present, deserving of a hug.

Gil was different – gaunt, moody, and intense. People admired Gil, but he also made them uncomfortable, and both for the same reason: he was extremely good at what he did. On two of Delilah's assignments, Gil had been the shooter. In both instances, he had emerged from the dark to put a .22 round through the target's eye and then disappeared without a ripple. He worked with others when he had to, but at heart, Delilah knew, he was a loner, and never more in his element than when he was silently stalking his prey.

Once, in a safe room in Vienna, he had made a pass at her. His move had been crudely direct, and Delilah hadn't liked the underlying assumption of entitlement and expectation of fulfillment. She knew the sex would have given him a kind of power over her – that in fact this was part of the reason he wanted it – and she wasn't about to surrender one of her few mysteries, her few levers of influence, with a colleague. Her rebuff had been as un-ambiguous as his proposition. It shouldn't have been a big deal – he was hardly the first – but on the few occasions on which she'd seen him since then, he always looked as though he was remembering, and not without resentment. There was a breed of man that was inclined to feel humiliated by a woman's demurral, and she suspected that Gil was such a specimen.

The table was set up for four, which told her they weren't expecting anyone else. They all sat down. The director gestured to the sandwiches. 'A little something to eat?' he asked.

She shook her head, not yet comfortable. 'They served dinner on the plane.'

Gil took a sandwich and bit into it. Boaz picked up the teapot and smiled at her. 'Tea, then?' he asked.

She smiled back and extended him her cup. 'Thank you.'

Boaz poured for everyone. They all sat silently for a few moments, sipping. Then the director said, 'Delilah, let me explain why you've been called in. You may have been wondering, eh?'

She nodded. 'A bit, yes.'

'We've had a problem in Manila. We think you can help solve it.'

We've had a problem, she thought. Wasn't that what those *Apollo 13* astronauts had said as their spaceship was breaking apart? And his use of the inclusive pronoun, that was interesting, and vaguely worrisome, too.

'All right,' she said, wondering what was coming.

'Recently we used a contractor for a job in Manila. A part-Japanese fellow named John Rain.'

She didn't hesitate. 'Yes, I brokered that introduction.'

She wondered for a moment why the director was playing

dumb with her. If the problem were serious enough to warrant his presence at this meeting, he would have been fully briefed on all the details, including Delilah's early involvement. He must have been testing her, looking for opportunities to gauge her reactions.

'Yes, of course,' he went on. 'You met Rain in Macau. The Belghazi op.'

'Yes.'

'Everything we were able to learn about this man, including your own evaluation, indicated that he was extremely reliable.'

Including your own evaluation. Something had gone wrong, and she was going to take some heat for it.

'Yes,' she said again, sensing that it would be better to say less.

He paused to take a sip of tea, and she recognized that he was attempting to draw her out with his silence. She resisted the urge to speak and instead took a sip of tea herself. After a moment, he went on.

'The man Rain was hired to remove is named Manheim Lavi. He goes by "Manny." An Israeli national, currently residing in South Africa. He has contacts in the Philippines, and, it now seems, a second family there. Recently we learned that he had turned traitor. He has been sharing bomb-making expertise – extensive expertise – with our enemies.'

The director wouldn't be telling her any of this if she didn't need to know. Nothing formal was being said, but she was being brought in on the op. He had mentioned her 'evaluation' to let her know she was partly to blame for whatever the problem was; the information he was now sharing was to inform her she would be responsible for the problem's resolution.

She looked at Gil. 'Why did you use a contractor? Why outsource the operation?'

'Manny is connected,' Gil replied. 'We believe he's a CIA asset. The CIA doesn't take kindly to "friendly" intelligence services erasing its people.'

'So instead you brought in a contractor who screwed something up?'

Gil's eyes narrowed slightly, and she smiled at him to let him know he had definitely just received a 'Fuck you' for talking down to her. And her response served another purpose: it indicated to the director that, although she knew Rain, she had no interest in downplaying whatever his screwup had been or in otherwise protecting him.

'You told us he would be reliable,' Gil said, and she was gratified by the touch of petulance in his voice.

The director waved a hand like a father dismissing a squabble among children at the dinner table. 'It doesn't matter how we got here. What matters is what we do next.'

Everyone was quiet for a moment, and the director continued. 'Rain tried to hit Manny in a restroom in a Manila shopping mall. Manny got away, but Rain killed three other people. A bodyguard.' He paused and looked at her. 'And two CIA officers.'

He paused to let it sink in. Delilah said nothing, but thought, *Oh my God.* She asked, 'Can the CIA connect the mess to us?'

'That,' the director said, 'is the question.'

'Here's what we know,' Boaz said. 'Rain called in yesterday to brief us. He told us he had followed Manny and his family into a Manila shopping mall. Manny was with a woman and a boy. When the woman and the boy seemed to leave the scene, Rain anticipated that Manny would use the restroom, and moved there ahead of him to wait. Manny came in, but then the boy showed up. When Rain saw the boy, he hesitated.'

'Apparently, Rain won't harm women or children,' Gil added.

Delilah looked at him. 'Do you have a problem with that?'

'It depends on how badly he's screwed things up.'

Delilah turned back to Boaz. 'And then?'

'Then the bodyguard burst in. Rain thinks Manny hit a panic button. Rain disarmed the guard just as the two CIA men arrived. Rain didn't know who they were, and still doesn't, so far as we know. But they were armed, too.'

Gil said, 'Rain managed to kill everyone but Manny.'

Delilah looked at him. 'The boy?'

Gil shrugged as though this was irrelevant. 'Not the boy, either.'

She looked at Boaz again. 'How good a look did Manny and the boy get at Rain?'

'Rain says he's not sure.'

Gil added, 'That's bullshit. How could this have gone down without someone seeing his face? Someone got a good look, and Rain knows it. Otherwise he would have just told us he got away clean. Anyway, it's in his interest to downplay his exposure here. We have to assume if he acknowledges Manny got any kind of a look, it means Manny got a damn good look.'

She couldn't argue with any of that. She nodded.

'So here's what's happening right now,' Gil went on. 'Manny is freaked out. He's sitting down with his CIA handlers. They're showing him photos of known Asiatic operators. That should be a stack about what, three or four photos high? If they have pictures of Rain, and Manny can ID him, the CIA is going to be hunting for him. Hunting hard.'

She saw where this was going. A refrain started buzzing through her mind: *Shit, shit, shit*. She said nothing.

'Manny has lots of enemies,' Gil continued, 'but I think we can safely assume that, when the CIA draws up a list, we'll be at the top. So if they get to Rain, our status will change from "prime suspect" to "proven culprit."'

The room was silent for a moment. The director looked at Delilah and sighed. 'You understand what's at stake here?' he asked.

She nodded.

'Not just your career,' he went on. 'Not just theirs.' He glanced at Boaz, then Gil, letting the comment sink in, then back to her. 'Not just mine. We would only be the first casualties. The government would quickly and rightly sacrifice us to try to contain the damage. But if the damage couldn't be contained . . . there's no telling. It could affect billions of dollars in aid from the United States. Not to mention arms deliveries. Access to satellite imagery and other intelligence cooperation. Do you understand? This is not an organization problem. It's a geopolitical problem. We have to get it under control.'

'I understand,' she said.

He nodded as though satisfied, then said, 'Tell me, how well do you know this man?'

She should have seen this coming. Now she understood.

She shrugged. 'Our paths crossed in Macau. Some people' – she looked at Gil – 'wanted to take him out there because he was after Belghazi and might have killed him before we acquired what we were after. I argued there were better ways to manage him.'

'You were wrong,' Gil said. 'It's true things turned out well, but that was all luck. Rain might have killed Belghazi before we had what we needed.'

'I was managing him,' Delilah said, and immediately realized her mistake in letting Gil goad her.

'You spent time with him, then?' the director asked.

She shrugged again. 'I told you, yes. I persuaded him to stand down for a while, for long enough. Then we tracked him to Rio. I traveled there and made the pitch. Boaz and Gil took it from there. This is all in the file.'

'How did you contact him at the time, again?' Gil asked.

Fuck Gil and his games. 'Did you not review the file?' she asked, with an innocent smile.

He clenched his jaw and tried to recover. 'It was an electronic bulletin board, wasn't it?'

'Are you asking because you don't remember? It's not like you to forget details, Gil. Usually you remember everything.'

His jaw clenched again. She knew he would be hating her for one-upping him in front of the director, especially in this insinuating way, and at the moment the knowledge was deeply satisfying.

'Can you contact him now?' Gil asked, abandoning his losing game.

'I don't know. I suppose so, if he's kept the bulletin board and still checks it.'

Gil started to say something, but the director held up a hand. 'Delilah. Do you know this man in any way not reflected in the file?'

'I don't know what you mean,' she said. Although of course she did, but damned if she would answer the question without at least having him endure the discomfort of asking it.

'Did you ever have a . . . personal relationship?'

She paused, then said, 'I'm not going to answer that.'

In her peripheral vision, she saw both admiration and sympathy in Boaz's eyes. In Gil's she saw surprise that she would doom herself this way, something he would never have had the integrity to do himself. Poor Gil. He didn't understand that her advantage in this game was that, for her, the stakes were so much lower. Gil was moving up in management. He wanted a career here. She knew that was impossible for her. In just a few years, she would be too old to do what she did, and then they would give her a desk job or a training position and she would be bypassed, ignored, and forgotten. Under the circumstances, what did she have to lose?

The director drummed his fingers on the table, then said, 'I'm not asking you for personal reasons. I'm asking you professionally. Because the information will affect the way we proceed in a very serious matter.'

Delilah looked him in the eyes. 'I'm still not going to answer. I'm not going to let you cross that line today. If I do, you'll cross it again tomorrow.'

He looked at her for a long moment, then smiled at her chutzpah and pressed no further. She gave him credit for that. But why would he press? In her refusal, she had already answered his question.

Gil looked confused, then nonplussed. Had she actually just *scored* points with the director?

'Delilah,' Boaz said. 'Do you think . . . Can you get close to Rain?'

'You mean, can I set him up?'

Boaz nodded.

'I'm not sure. I can try.'

The three of them settled slightly in their seats as though a bit of tension had been suddenly drained from their bodies, and in that instant she understood completely the nature of the conversation that had preceded her arrival: *Do you think she slept with him? Will she do this? Can we trust her?*

'But why do you need me?' she asked. 'You've met him, presumably you have a means of contact?'

'If we ask for a meeting now,' Boaz said, 'he'll be suspicious. We need something to lower his guard.'

'He might be suspicious with me, too,' she said. 'Under the circumstances.'

'We're counting on you to dissolve his suspicions,' Gil said. 'You're the best at that.' His tone indicated that her abilities, although useful, also were somehow suspect.

She looked at him, but ignored the comment. 'How are you going to do it?'

Gil waved as though it would be nothing. 'You contact him. Go somewhere with him, a romantic getaway. When the moment is right, you contact me.'

'Who's the shooter?'

'I am.'

'He knows your face. How are you going to get close?'

'He'll never see me.'

She almost laughed. 'You don't understand who you're dealing with.'

'He's a fuckup. He's going down.'

She thought of the way Rain had dealt with that guy in the elevator on Macau. He had gone from calmly talking to her to breaking the man's neck without anything in between.

'If he sees you,' she said, 'he'll know I set him up.'

'Do it yourself, then.'

She didn't answer.

'He won't see me,' Gil said. 'Anyway, you know how to handle yourself.'

There was a long silence. She was used to making hard decisions quickly and under pressure, and by the time the director spoke, she had already made up her mind.

'You'll do this?' he asked, looking at her, his expression open, his tone affable.

'When have I ever refused?' she replied.

'Never,' Gil said, and in those two syllables she heard an echo of *whore*.

She looked at him. When she spoke, her voice was frozen silk.

'Well, there was one time, Gil.'

He flushed, and she smiled at him, twisting the knife.

The director, pretending to ignore what he fully understood, said, 'It's settled, then.'

5

The day after the Manny debacle, I made my way to the Bangkok Baan Khanitha restaurant on Sukhumvit 23, the backup Dox and I had agreed upon in case things went sideways – as indeed they had.

I chose an indirect route to get to the restaurant, as much to indulge an incipient sense of nostalgia as for my usual security reasons. Sukhumvit, I saw, had changed enormously in the decades since the concentrated time I had spent here during the war, yet in its essential aspects it was still the same. There had been no high-rises back then, true, and certainly no glitzy shopping malls, and the traffic, although chaotic, had not yet reached today's level of biblical-style calamity. But the smell of the place, the vibe, then and now, was all low-level commerce, much of it sexual. In my mind, Sukhumvit has always been about lasts: the last party of the last evening that everyone wants to prolong because tomorrow it's back to the war; the last chance for nocturnal behavior that will surely be the source of regret in the light of the oncoming day; the last desperate stop for those women whose charms, and therefore their prices, have fallen short even of the standards of nearby Patpong.

I walked along Sukhumvit Road, letting the crowds carry me and flow past me, then carry me along again. My God, the area had grown. I'd been back several times since the war, of course, and had even done a job here once, a Japanese expat, but somehow my frame of reference, which was over three decades out of date, seemed unwilling to oblige the area's changing topography. There were vendors back then, yes, but not this many. Now they had overgrown the sidewalk and were selling every manner of bric-a-brac: ersatz luggage, knockoff watches, pirated DVDs, tee-shirts proclaiming 'Same-Same' and 'No Money, No Honey.' Hawkers wheedled and cajoled, competing with the hum of the crowd, the roar of passing bus engines, the distinctive, sine-wave growl of motor scooters and tuk-tuks weaving back and forth through the constipated traffic. I smelled diesel fumes and curry, and thought, *Yes, same-same, it all really is,* and was surprised at an overwhelming sense of sadness and loss I couldn't name. Nothing looked the same here, but to me it smelled the same, and the dissonance was confusing.

I walked on. And then, with a burst of mixed pleasure and horror, I came upon an artifact: the Miami Hotel, which was still here at the top of Soi 13. Squalid and moldering from the moment it went up in the late sixties to house US troops on R&R, the hotel now felt like an architectural middle finger extended to the rich, upscale Bangkok that was growing up around it. As I moved past, I caught a glimpse of a grizzled expat looking out from one of its windows onto the street below, his expression that of a man serving a life sentence for a crime he doesn't understand, and I thought it possible that I had just seen one of the original inhabitants, as stubborn and anachronistic as the hotel itself. I walked. Arabs and Sikhs in turbans smoked cigarettes and sipped coffee under the corrugated eaves of collapsing storefronts. Prostitutes lurked in the vestibules of massage parlors, passersby ignoring their sad eyes and desperate smiles. An amputee, filthy and in rags, rattled a cup at me from the sidewalk where he lay. I gave him some baht and moved on. Half a block later, the vendors' tables parted momentarily and I saw a sign for the Thermae Bar & Coffee House, the lowest of the low, which had once housed the women who serviced the Miami's soldiers. I wondered if its patrons still called it, appropriately and inevitably, the Termite. The original building, it seemed, had been torn down, but the Termite had been reborn, demonstrating in its reincarnation that although the body might fade and die, the spirit, for better or worse, is eternal.

I passed a vendor selling knives, and took the opportunity to arm myself with a knockoff Emerson folder with a wooden handle and a four-inch, partially serrated blade. For a long time I had gotten by without carrying a weapon, and I had liked it this way. For one thing, you tend to comport yourself differently when you're armed, and there are people who can spot the signs. Also, my lawsey, lawsey civilian cover would have been compromised somewhat if I'd been picked up carrying, say, a folding karambit or other concealed cutlery. And then there's the matter of blood, which can get all over you and severely compromise your attempts to blend with the crowd after a close encounter. But I sensed that the balance of costs and benefits was changing now. I wasn't as fast as I once was, for one thing. Or as durable, for another. I wondered whether what had happened to me in that restroom with Manny, also, was in part the consequence of age. I had needed Dox to bail me out there, as he had at Kwai Chung a year earlier. On top of all this, being back in Sukhumvit was itself a reminder that I had aged in the intervening years, and that things I had once ably done with my hands might now be accomplished more effectively with tools.

I caught a tuk-tuk for the final leg over to Sukhumvit 23. Dox and I were supposed to meet at the restaurant at noon, but I arrived early to scope the area out, as I always do on those rare occasions when I agree to a face-to-face meeting. A sneak preview tends to prevent surprises. In this case, though, the surprise was already waiting for me, in the form of Dox. Resplendent in a cream-colored silk shirt, he was sitting in one of the cushioned teak chairs at the back corner of the main room sipping some tropical concoction from a tall glass through a long straw, and looking, I had to admit, utterly at ease and at home in his surroundings.

'I knew you'd get here early,' he said, grinning. He put down the drink and got up from the table. 'Didn't want to be rude, keeping you waiting.'

I walked over, looking around the restaurant as I moved. The clientele was about half local, half foreign, and all seemingly more interested in the Baan Khanitha's excellent traditional Thai food than in whatever might be going on around them. I realized, though, that I was doing my security check out of habit, not because I thought Dox would have brought trouble. And then I was surprised, almost stunned, to realize that I trusted someone this way. I looked at him, and my discomfort must have showed, because he raised his eyebrows and said, 'You all right, man?'

I gave him a nod that was half exasperation, half pleasure at seeing him after our scrape in Manila. 'Fine. I'm fine.'

I reached for his hand, but he ignored it, instead clapping his arms around me and pulling me in for a hug. *Jesus,* I thought. I patted his back awkwardly.

He stepped back from me, looked at my face, and laughed. 'Hey, man, you're blushing! You don't have a crush on me or something, do you?'

I ignored him. 'Any problems on the way over?'

He laughed again. 'No problems. Hey, it's good to see you, man, even if you're starting to have unnatural feelings for me. You want to eat here, or should we go somewhere else? I recommend we stay. The *poo nim pad gra pow* is the best in the city.'

I looked around again. Dox might have known his *poo nim,* whatever that was, but his tradecraft wasn't always up to my standards. Although in fairness, I don't know whose would be.

'You're leaving your cell phone off, right?' I asked.

'Yeah, Mom, I'm leaving it off. Disappointing all the ladies who want to reach me.'

'You sure you weren't followed?'

He rolled his eyes. 'C'mon now, you've got to get over this lone-wolf, international-man-of-mystery shit. You can't live like that twenty-four-seven. It'll bum you out, man, I've seen it happen.'

'Does that mean you weren't followed?'

He frowned. 'Yeah, that's what it means. You know, I might not be quite the urban ghost you can be, but I do know how to be careful. I've made my way doing this fucked-up thing of ours for a long time on my lonesome, and I'm still breathing even though there are plenty of people who'd rather I wasn't.'

'Weren't.'

He clasped his hands to his head and said, 'Somebody save me, my partner's a schoolmarm!'

I raised my hands in surrender. 'All right, all right.'

'"John Rain, killer and grammarian." You ought to put it on a business card.'

'All right,' I said.

'Use the subjunctive correctly or he'll take your life.'

Jesus, I thought, looking around. 'Look, let's just eat here,' I said.

'Well, thank God. I'm starving.'

70

We sat down at his table. The waiter came over and Dox ordered the food. He knew what he was doing – even his Thai seemed passable. We also asked for a couple of iced coffees. It had been a long few days.

'Okay, what's the status?' Dox asked, when the waiter had departed. 'I hope the Israelites aren't pissed.'

I had told him who the client was. They, of course, didn't know about Dox. They didn't need to.

'I'm not entirely sure,' I said.

'Meaning?'

'Meaning as soon as I was out of Manila, I contacted my friends Boaz and Gil. I told them what had happened. They seemed to take it in stride. They were disappointed that Manny got away, and concerned that he would harden his defenses now. But they were reassured that I had made it out of there without further incident.'

'You mean without being caught and implicating them.'

'Yes.'

'They're probably a little despondent that you weren't just killed in the fracas.'

'It's just business.'

'Wishing it is just business. Trying to bring it about is different.'

'I don't think we need to worry about that. It wouldn't be worth it to them. It looks like I'm clear of it, so they are, too.'

'Yeah? Whatever happened to the professional paranoid we all know and love?'

'I'm being careful. I told you what I think is likely, but I don't assume anything.'

'What did you tell them happened?'

'That two unknown players that I hadn't managed to spot popped onto the scene and turned it into a shooting gallery.

That said players were good and might have been CIA.'

'What did they say to that?'

'Like I said, they were concerned. But they'll verify the body count easily enough. It's in all the English-language Philippine newspapers today.'

'You checked?'

I nodded. 'Spent the morning online.'

'Well, what do the papers say?'

'One dead Filipino, two dead foreigners whose identities are being checked. Witnesses seem to think there were two shooters. Both Asian.'

He smiled. 'Both Asian, huh?'

I nodded. 'Even in the best of circumstances, people don't see straight. Add adrenal stress, they don't remember what the hell they saw. They could be searching for Martians right now. Boaz and Gil are looking into the dead men's identities, too. When they learn more, they'll tell us. In the meantime, we just have to monitor the situation and wait.'

The waiter brought over our food and departed. *Poo nim* turned out to be sautéed soft-shelled crab. Dox hadn't been exaggerating. It was excellent, soft and fresh and redolent of basil.

'I think they were Agency,' Dox said.

'They could have been, I don't know. You didn't see them before heading into the bathroom?'

'Sure, I saw them. They were sitting in the food court, just the two of them. But they didn't look like hitters to me. Although I admit I might have been distracted by what was going on with Manny and the bodyguard, and not paying attention to the little signs like I might have other-wise. What about you?'

'The same. Damn, they were low-key, I'll give them that.' I dug into the crab. 'My guess is they were hooked up with

Manny in some way. They weren't there to harm him, otherwise they would have looked to drop him as he exited the bathroom, like I did. They were trying to protect him.'

'Yeah, I kind of picked up on that. More bodyguards?'

'Maybe. But we hadn't seen them earlier. I think they were there for a meeting.'

'With Manny?'

'Yeah. They didn't look like locals, so figure they were staying at a hotel – maybe the Peninsula, the Mandarin Oriental, the Shangri-La. They're all a stone's throw from the Ayala Center, and that's where Manny took his family for lunch, even though Greenhills shopping center would have been closer.'

'So he has lunch with the family, says good-bye, the woman and the boy leave, and he gets down to business with the people who are waiting for him.'

'Yes. And when they see a huge, goateed, dangerous-looking guy busting into the bathroom along with Manny's bodyguard, they realize something's going down. They go in, too.'

He nodded. 'Well, I'll buy that. They were cool and their tactics were good. And like you said, they wore their cover well. I didn't make them until it was too late. That's my fault, man, and I'm sorry. I told you, you saved my life there, you really did.'

I wanted to tell him the truth – that by bursting in as he had, Dox had saved my life, not the reverse.

Instead I said, 'The thing is, we still don't know for sure who they were. Who they were with. Why they were meeting Manny. If we knew those things, we might get a second chance.'

'You think we could still get that close?'

'Depends. I hate to leave things unfinished, though.'

He laughed. 'You mean like an uncashed paycheck?'

I nodded. 'That's part of it. And letting Boaz and Gil know that I'm still after Manny gives me an excuse to be in touch with them, and an opportunity to continue to evaluate them.'

'To make sure they haven't changed their minds about just letting the whole thing go.'

'Of course. And they're also a potential channel of information.'

'About who those shooters were.'

'Etcetera.'

We ate quietly for a few minutes. Then Dox said, 'There's one thing I want to ask you.'

I raised my eyebrows and looked at him.

'When I got in there, I was surprised Manny was still vertical. I know what you can do up close with your hands. You were alone with him for long enough.'

I didn't say anything.

'You going to tell me what happened?' he asked.

I looked away. 'I don't know, exactly.'

'Are you leveling with me, partner?' I heard him say.

I paused, then said, 'I don't know. He came in, his back was to me, I moved out of the stall. Then you told me the boy was coming. I went to move back into the stall before the boy came in, but I must have made a sound, because Manny turned. I looked in his eyes . . .'

'Whoa, why'd you look in his eyes, man?'

I shook my head. 'I don't know.'

'Shoot, man, when I look through the scope, I never look in the eyes. Or if I do, I just look at one of them, and then all I see is a bull's-eye, you know what I mean? I never see a man. Only a target.' He looked at me, then added, 'If you see a man, you might . . . hesitate.'

I thought of several things to say, but none of them came out.

He took a sip of iced coffee and looked upward as though contemplating something. Then he said, 'Well, each of us has only so much courage in the well. You draw from it too many times, eventually you come up dry. I've seen it before. I guess one day it'll happen to me, too.' He paused, then smiled and added, 'Although probably not.'

'That's not what happened,' I said.

'Then what?'

I looked at the wall, images flickering against it as though it were a screen. 'It was something about the boy. Seeing him with his family . . . I don't know.'

There was a pause. He said, 'Sounds like you spent a little too much time watching them this week, man.'

'Yeah, maybe.'

'Well, that happens. It can make it hard, it's true.'

I felt like an idiot. What was wrong with me? Why had I frozen? Why couldn't I explain to a man I'd fought along-side, a man I trusted?

Trust, I thought. The word felt slippery in my mind, dangerous.

'That's not it,' I said. 'Or, it's not the only thing.'

'What else?'

I shook my head and exhaled hard. 'I haven't had a partner in a long time.'

'Hang on now, this is my fault?'

I shook my head again. 'That's not what I meant. It's just . . . I didn't trust you before, when you first came for me in Rio.'

'Yeah, I got that feeling.'

'But then, after what you did at Kwai Chung . . . I saw that I'd been wrong. That's hard for me.'

'Guess I should've just shot you and taken the money for myself. At least that way you'd have been right not to trust me.'

'Did you think about it?'

He laughed. 'Jesus, man, you almost sound hopeful.'

'Did you?'

He shook his head. 'Not even for a minute.'

'Goddamnit. I knew it.'

'You want an apology?'

I shook my head. 'No.'

'You don't owe me anything. Like I said at the time, I know you'd have done the same for me. Wait, don't respond to that, it'll spoil my reverie.'

The waiter came by and cleared away our plates. We ordered mango and sticky rice for dessert. I watched the man leave.

There was something I wanted to ask Dox, something I'd been thinking about, on various levels, for a long time, and particularly after Manila. It wasn't something I'd ever said out loud before, and I found myself reluctant to bring it up. Partly because doing so might make it feel more real; partly because it would probably all seem so silly to Dox. But I'd told him a lot already. I wanted to finish it.

'I've got a question for you, too,' I said, looking at him.

He pushed his chair away, leaned back, and laced his fingers together across his belly. 'Sure.'

'You ever . . . you ever bothered by what we do?'

He smiled. 'Only when I'm not paid promptly.'

'I'm serious.'

He shrugged. 'Not usually, no.'

'You don't ever feel like . . .' I chuckled. 'You know, like God is watching?'

'Oh, sure he's watching. He just doesn't care.'

'You think?'

He shrugged again. 'I figure he's the one who made the rules. I'm just playing by 'em. If he doesn't like the way things have turned out down here on planet Earth, he ought to speak his mind. I would if I were him.'

'Maybe he is speaking his mind, and no one's listening.'

'He ought to speak a little more clearly, then.' He looked up and added, 'If you don't mind my saying so.'

I studied my hands for a moment. 'It bothered me, thinking about that boy losing his father.'

''Course it did. If it didn't, you wouldn't be the good man you are. That's why it's best not to get too close to the target. "If it inhabits your mind, it can inhibit your trigger finger," as one of my instructors once told me.'

'Yeah, that's the truth.'

'The thing is, you can't make the decisions and also carry them out, you know what I mean? The judge and the executioner, they're different roles. The judge does what he does, and then the executioner carries things out. That's the way it is. We're just doing what we're supposed to.'

'That's an interesting way to look at it,' I said, feeling uneasy.

'It's the only way. I didn't know you were such a philosopher, partner. In fact, I think this is the most I've ever heard you talk.'

'Sorry.'

'No need to apologize. But I do think that pondering too deeply might not be highly recommended for men such as ourselves. We might start thinking we're the judges or something, and where would we be then?'

The waiter brought the mango and sticky rice. It was good, but my mind was elsewhere.

Dox asked, 'Well, what's the next step? With Manny, I mean.'

I considered. 'We can't get close to him again the way we did. He got too good a look at me, for one thing, and I think we can expect him to be taking extra precautions, for another.'

'Yeah, I'm thinking the same thing.'

'We need a new variable, something to shake things up. And the only one I see coming our way is information from Boaz and Gil. If they can find out the affiliations of the two guys we took out in that restroom, we might have something to go on. Otherwise I think the op is dead.'

'So nothing to do but wait and see what the Israelites can offer.'

'That's right.'

He leaned back in his chair and grinned. 'Well, in my not inconsiderable experience, there's nowhere in the world better to wait around than here in Bangkok.'

I sighed, feeling like a parent about to remonstrate with a teenager. 'We still have work to do. You're not going to be useful drained of all bodily fluids and nursing a binge hangover.'

He laughed. 'Yes, Mom.'

'Look, just be available in case I get a call and we need to move quickly.'

He nodded, then said, 'Tell you what. Best way for me to be available is for us to stick together. Why don't you come out with me tonight?'

'No, I think . . .'

'C'mon, man, when was the last time you got yourself properly laid? Or even laid at all.'

I shook my head. 'A night out with the prostitutes isn't really my thing.'

'Who said anything about prostitutes? The local girls will be throwing themselves at you when they see you with a handsome stranger like me. And by the way, I think you're avoiding my question.'

I thought of Delilah, but said nothing.

'C'mon, man, we can get you some of that black market Viagra.'

'I don't think so.'

'Hey, with a double dose, you'll do fine. Plus, you've still got a quart of my blood sloshing around in you. That ought to be a help.'

He was reminding me of the transfusion he'd given me after I'd nearly bled out at Kwai Chung.

'I mean I don't think I'm in the mood for One Night in Bangkok,' I said.

'What, are you worried you might have fun? Tell you what, if I see you laugh and have a good time, I promise not to tell anyone. I know you've got your reputation to protect.'

I thought about it. Maybe I would take a long walk through some of the city's less-traveled boulevards. I could pass by some of the places where I had once caroused with other teenagers hardened by war, who were yet, in retrospect, still astonishingly innocent, and observe these relics to see how my memories animated or distorted them as they might exist in Bangkok today. But as I considered these possibilities, I was surprised to find I didn't really want to be alone.

'All right!' Dox said, taking my hesitation as a yes. 'We can get dinner, hit a few bars, talk to the ladies, who knows. Hey, you like jazz, right? I know a new place on Silom that'll be right up your alley. I tend to favor the discos myself, but I know you're a man of sophisticated tastes and I'm willing to indulge you.'

79

I nodded in capitulation. 'All right.'

The grin got wider. 'You made the right decision, Mr Rain, and I promise you won't regret it. You checked into the hotel yet?'

We were staying at the Sukhothai, which offered the right combination of high class and low visibility. Something like the Oriental had plenty of the first but none of the second; innumerable Bangkok hotels would have offered the opposite combination. But the Sukhothai had been built for both beauty and discretion. The property, with its acres of flower gardens and lotus ponds; its long, symmetrical lines and soft lighting; and its traditional accents of Thai architecture and art was certainly a triumph of form. But from my perspective, the hotel was also highly functional: its small, intimate lobby was utterly unlike the grand, bustling thoroughfares that greeted visitors at, say, the local Four Seasons, which was well designed for people who wanted to see and be seen, but uncomfortable for those who favored invisibility instead.

'I got an early check-in this morning,' I told him. 'You?'

'The same. Nice place, too. I like those big bathtubs. You can get three people in one of them, did you know that? With all those mirrors, you can have a lot of fun. This one time . . .'

'Why don't we meet in the lobby, then?' I said.

He grinned at the interruption. 'All right. Twenty-hundred?'

'You need to rest up first?'

'No, son, I need to go out and buy you that double dose of Viagra.'

Trying to get the better of Dox was a losing proposition. I signaled the waiter for the check and said, 'Eight o'clock, then.'

6

Jim Hilger never got upset. It wasn't that he didn't show agitation; he simply didn't experience it. The crazier things became around him, the calmer he felt at his center. The quality had made him one of the best combat shooters in the Third Special Forces during the first Gulf War. When someone was firing at him, it felt almost as though his personality had floated out of his body, leaving a machine to handle things in its place. He knew that, had he lived in the age of dueling, he would have been fucked with by nobody.

He knew, too, that his imperturbability was a useful leadership skill. In combat, when his men saw how calm and deadly he was, they became calm and deadly, too. And now, in his new role, he had found that his flatlined demeanor gave him power over the people he managed. The more upset they became in a crisis, the more his temperature dropped, cooling the people around him in the process. It was as though people assumed he must know something they didn't; otherwise, he would be coming unglued, too. In fact, he doubted that he really knew more than others. It was just that he had come to rely on his own coolness, to believe that his coolness was the one thing he could count on to get him through, as it always had before. He didn't believe in anything more than that.

When Manny had called him the day before, nearly hysterical with rage, Hilger's calmness had been put to the test. 'Just tell me what happened,' Hilger had repeated while Manny had fulminated and threatened. It took a little while, but eventually he had brought Manny around. And Jesus, a little hysteria almost seemed to be in order. Someone had tried to hit Manny in Manila, and Calver and Gibbons, two of Hilger's best men, men from his Gulf War unit, had been killed in the process. A critical first meeting with an asset, which Hilger had been trying to set up with Manny's help for over two years, and which Calver and Gibbons had gone to Manila to take care of, had been aborted. The whole thing was a mess.

As Manny had hyperventilated the news to him, Hilger automatically shifted into problem-solving mode.

'Where is VBM?' he asked, using the cryptonym they had established for the new asset.

'I don't know,' Manny told him. 'I don't have an immediate way of contacting him. He probably went to the meeting site, and when we didn't show up, he left.'

Shit. Not quite the first impression Hilger had been hoping for.

'Can you reestablish contact?' he asked. 'Set up another meeting?'

That produced a minor explosion. 'Another meeting? Someone just tried to kill me! In front of my family!'

Hilger realized he wasn't demonstrating the proper priorities. All right, one thing at a time.

'Look, there's not much we can do over the phone,' he told Manny. 'We need to meet. You'll give me every detail. And then we'll figure out what to do.'

'But how do I know I can trust you?' Manny had whined. 'How do I know you weren't behind this?'

'Those were my people who were killed,' Hilger told him. 'I can't give you better proof than that.'

Manny wasn't being rational. He said, 'Maybe it was a trick, maybe it was a trick.'

Hilger sighed. He said, 'Let's work together and we can solve this problem the way it needs to be solved.'

There was a long pause. Hilger's heart rate was slow and steady.

Manny said, 'All right, all right.'

'Good. Where do you want to meet?' Giving Manny the choice would help ease his ridiculous suspicions.

'Not in Manila. I can come to . . .' He paused, and Hilger knew he had been about to say Hong Kong and then had thought better of it. Hong Kong was Hilger's home base, where he lived his financial-adviser cover. Manny didn't want to offer him any advantages just now, and, probably because he felt spiteful, was glad to deny him any convenience, as well.

'Jakarta,' Manny said. 'I can come to Jakarta.'

Hilger didn't want to fly to Jakarta. Manny was being a pain in the ass.

'Sure. But I've got a few things here I need to wrap up first – it'll probably take a few days. Are you sure you can't make it to Hong Kong?'

There was a long silence. Hilger said, 'Look, we can meet anywhere you want, but Hong Kong will be faster, and I'd like to get started on this right away. Anywhere in Hong Kong, fair enough?'

That closed it. The next day, they were sitting in a coffee shop off Nathan Road in Kowloon, just a fifteen-minute cab ride from Hilger's office through the Cross-Harbor Tunnel. There weren't quite as many white faces in Kowloon as there were in Central, where Hilger worked, but there were enough so that neither of them would stick out, and there was a lower chance that Hilger might run into someone he knew. Not that anyone would recognize Manny – it wasn't as though the man's face appeared on post office walls, although probably it should – but it was better to be safe. Hilger had taken the usual precautions to ensure that he hadn't been followed, and hoped that Manny had been equally thorough. He had indulged Manny his mandatory hysteria. When he felt he had been nodding sympathetically for long enough, he began his debriefing.

'Tell me exactly what happened,' Hilger commanded, and he knew that his calm would now be reassuring. 'Not just that day, but every day, from the moment you arrived in Manila.'

Manny complied. When he was finished, Hilger began to drill into the details.

'You say there were two of them.'

'I think so, yes. Someone came in after the bodyguard.'

'But you didn't see his face.'

'Not well. He was big. I think Caucasian. I'm not sure.'

Hilger considered. 'It doesn't matter. Even if you hadn't seen him, I could have told you he was there. The first guy, the Asian, you say he was already in the bathroom, is that right?'

'Yes.'

'He'd been following you for a while before he decided to anticipate you in the bathroom. But he wouldn't have done that if he didn't have backup continuing to watch you. Otherwise, if he'd been wrong about you coming to the bathroom, he would have lost you.'

Manny nodded and said, 'Yes, that makes sense.'

'You think you could recognize the Asian?'

Manny nodded. 'If I saw him again, yes. I got a good look at his face. Can you find him? And the other one?'

Hilger thought for a moment. He said, 'I have some photos I'll show you before you leave. We'll see if the men I have in mind are the ones you saw.'

84

'Then you can find them.'

Hilger knew that if he was right about the men in question, identifying them would be a trivial exercise compared with actually finding them. Still, he said, 'I think so.'

Manny leaned forward. 'You better. And when you find them, you make them suffer first. They were following me with my family, they might have harmed my son!'

Hilger nodded to show that Manny could count on him. He said, 'And VBM? You can contact him, set up another meeting?' Letting Manny know that there was something of a quid pro quo here.

Manny shrugged. 'I've already left him a message. But he's not an easy man to reach. And he might be spooked when he hears about what happened in Manila.'

Hilger doubted VBM would spook that easily. Men like him tended to be tougher than that. But no sense contradicting Manny's assessment.

'If he's spooked, he's spooked,' he said. 'But if you told him about what my people can do for him, I think he'll still want the meeting.'

'I told him.'

'Good. Keep trying to contact him. When you do, tell him that the people behind the problem in Manila have been taken care of. Tell him . . .'

'I'll tell him that when it's true.'

'By the time you contact him, it will be true,' Hilger said, his voice as even as his gaze.

Manny nodded, and Hilger went on.

'Tell him I'll come to the meeting myself. That we can do it anywhere he likes. And give him my cell phone number. He should feel free to contact me directly.'

Manny nodded again and said, 'All right.'

Hilger detected a slight churlishness in the set of Manny's

mouth, no doubt precipitated by Hilger's willingness to discuss matters not directly related to Manny's recent difficulties. Partly to continue the debriefing, partly to assuage the man, Hilger asked, 'Who do you think might have been behind this?'

Manny leaned back and shrugged. 'How should I know? It could have been anyone.'

'"Anyone" doesn't help me narrow it down.'

'Who do you think?'

'Manny, I have my own ideas, but I doubt anyone is in a better position to say than you are. Are you holding something back from me? That's going to make my job harder.'

Manny shook his head. 'I'm not holding anything back. I just don't know. It could have been the Mossad, I suppose. They might not like my choice of friends, the fucking hypocrites.'

Hilger had already thought of the Israelis. They were at the top of his short list. 'Who else?' he asked.

Manny looked at him. 'The CIA, of course.'

Hilger nodded. 'My contacts there are already looking into that. Any others? Maybe BIN?'

'BIN?'

'The Badan. Indonesian intelligence. They've had a lot of problems – Bali, the Jakarta Marriott, the Australian embassy . . .'

'BIN, yes. Maybe. Maybe.'

Hilger realized that Manny wasn't going to be helpful here. He was the kind of man who was uncomfortable acknowledging that he had real enemies – which, given his activities, was almost funny. It seemed that this was the first time Manny had come face-to-face with the reality that someone really, truly, wanted him dead and was actively trying to make it so. It would take Manny a while to adjust to the reality of that. In the meantime, Hilger would just have to investigate on his own. Well, he was used to doing things alone. Sometimes it was the only way to get the job done.

Hilger decided to return to the previous line of questioning, on which Manny was more useful. 'You say the Asian saw you and seemed to freeze,' he said. 'Could it have been your son that he saw?'

Manny scowled. 'I think it was me.'

Hilger wondered about Manny's recollection. He didn't expect it to be particularly accurate in any event; he knew that memories of traumatic incidents rarely are. Also, Manny probably wanted to believe that the men who had come after him were vicious, subhuman killers. This would make Manny feel virtuous by comparison. That one of these men might have hesitated at the sight of a child wouldn't fit with this view, would detract from the accompanying sense of comparative righteousness, and would likely be rejected. The mind of a man like Manny had so many ways of unconsciously pleasuring itself. You had to be careful.

'Still,' Hilger said, 'I find it odd that the man seemed to hesitate at all, regardless of the reasons. Hesitation tends to be an affliction of the inexperienced.'

Manny scowled. 'Maybe these men were inexperienced.'

'Inexperienced men wouldn't have been able to drop your bodyguard and my people with him. They were all dispatched with tight shots, headshots. Take my word for it, the shooters were not inexperienced.'

'Then why? Why did he hesitate?'

Hilger shook his head. 'I don't know yet.'

'My son is traumatized,' Manny said. 'He and his mother have gone to stay with her relatives in the provinces.'

'I can arrange for extra protection.'

'They're okay where they are. But I need a new body-guard.'

This was the closest thing Hilger had heard to an expression of sorrow about one of the men who had given his life in the course of saving Manny's. *Me, me, me,* Hilger thought. It wasn't just Manny. It was the state of the fucking world.

'Otherwise,' Manny went on, 'I can't continue to help you.'

Hilger sighed. Manny was always making poorly timed, even unnecessary, threats.

'I've already taken care of it,' Hilger said.

'And the men who tried to kill me?'

'My people will find them.'

Manny clenched his jaw and said, 'Find them soon. You're not my only friend, you know.'

Another silly threat. Hilger had seen it coming. He said, 'Manny, I know you have many friends. Has any of them been as reliable as I have?'

Manny was silent for a moment, then burst out, 'You told me that your friendship would protect me! That something like this would never happen!'

Hilger looked at him. For the first time in the conversation, he let some emotion creep into his voice. Part of it was for effect. But not all of it.

'Two of my best men just died protecting you,' he said. 'And a bodyguard who I set you up with.'

Manny didn't answer. Hilger found his silence characteristically petulant. Three men had just died for him, and he couldn't even say, *All right, that's a fair point.*

'If you go to other people,' Hilger went on, 'it complicates my job. Give me some time to solve the problem before you do something to complicate it, all right?'

'I have other friends,' Manny said again.

Hilger sighed. Time for a reality injection.

'Manny, the people you're talking about aren't your friends. They're people you know, who have interests. If those people decide that their interests are out of alignment with yours, you'll find that they become decidedly unfriendly. How will I protect you then?'

Manny looked at him, resenting him for not being more fearful of the threat, and for making a veiled one of his own.

'Make them suffer,' he said again, demanding something to save face.

Hilger nodded. More because he was thinking of his men than out of any particular desire to appease Manny, he said, 'I will.'

7

There were a few hours to kill before I met Dox for our evening out, so I took a cab to nearby Silom to look for an Internet café.

I rarely take down an electronic bulletin board once I've established it. Clients need a way to reach me, and maintaining the bulletin boards provides it. But when business necessity doesn't justify the continued maintenance, pleasure, in the form of nagging hope, provides the necessary motivation instead. If I'd ever established a board with Midori, who had loved me, then shunned me after learning that I had killed her father, I would probably check it all the time. In lieu of a board, I commune with my hopes for Midori by listening to her CDs, four of them now, each deeper, more soulful, more daring than the last; by imagining enthusiasts applauding her piano in the dark jazz joints of lower Manhattan, for which she had left Tokyo; by whispering her name every night like a sad incantation that always summons, along with certain qualities of her spirit, the continued pain of her absence.

Checking the bulletin board I had established with Delilah, I told myself, was a mix: business and pleasure. The introduction she had provided was what led to the Manny assignment, and, if I could straighten out the aftermath of that one, there might be more where it came from. But business wasn't really why I kept the bulletin board, or why I continued to check it almost every day. The real reason, I knew, was the stolen time we had spent together in

Rio after our initial run-in in Macau and my subsequent near-death experience there.

It wasn't just the sex, good as it had been; nor was it only her stunning looks. Instead it was something deep inside her, something I couldn't reach. What that thing might be I couldn't really say: regret over her role in so many killings; bitterness at her ill treatment at the hands of her organization; sorrow over the normal life, the family, that she had chosen to forgo and that probably now would be denied to her forever. She hadn't been the perfect companion with me. She could be demanding, sometimes moody, and she wasn't without a temper. But sweetness and perfection were the charade I assumed she played with the targets of her work. The uncertainty and the barriers that spiced her relationship with me made her feel real, and led me in the direction of trusting her. And trust, as I was discovering with Dox, is a dangerous narcotic. I thought I had weaned myself from its rapture, gotten the monkey off my back. But then I had a little taste, and that thing I'd lived without for so many years was suddenly indispensable.

I had the cab let me off at Silom Road under the Sala Daeng sky train station. The sky train had opened a few years earlier, and this was the first time I was back in Bangkok to witness its effect. I wasn't sure I liked it. No doubt its presence made the city easier to traverse, bringing together points once rendered impractically distant by automotive gridlock. But there was a price. The overhead passage of steel tracks and concrete platforms smothered the streets below in shadow, and seemed somehow to compress and amplify the noise, the pollution, the pent-up weight of the whole metropolis. I smiled, without any mirth, because I had seen the same thing done to Tokyo with the elevated expressways, to the long-term regret of everyone bar the construction companies and their corrupt government cronies, who profited from the implementation of such schemes and who would no doubt profit again when the city planners determined that now it was time to banish those dark monstrosities they had once seen fit to invoke. By building a subway across the sky, the custodians of Bangkok had made the streets below effectively subterranean. I could imagine a time, not too distant, when the sky train would be so dramatically expanded and agglomerated with food courts and wireless shops and video outlets that life on the streets below, the pedestrians and the cars and the stores, would without conscious planning or the apportionment of blame become by default the city's true subway, its final stop for those denizens who had fallen through the cracks and who would now lie unseen in a darkness from which they could fall no further.

I walked, zigzagging along the sois and sub-sois – the main streets and their arteries – between Silom and Sura-wong, passing several storefront places advertising Internet access and overseas phone calls. Most of these were tiny spaces in larger buildings that had probably gone unused until the Internet arrived and created the possibility of profit for places with a half-dozen tables and chairs and terminals. Soon enough, I found one whose looks I liked. It occupied a ground-floor niche in a gleaming Bank of Bangkok building, and seemed almost to be hiding there. Inside there were ten terminals, several of which were occupied by women who looked to me like bar girls, who were perhaps now sending e-mails to those *farang* customers foolish enough to provide addresses, telling interchangeable stories of sick mothers and dying water buffaloes and the other reasons for this one-time-only, embarrassed request for the *farang*'s dollars or pounds or yen. I chose a table that put my back to the wall.

The girls, intent on their correspondence, gave me barely a glance.

Before getting started, I downloaded some commercial software from a storage site I keep and checked the terminal for keystroke monitors and other spyware. When I was sure it was clean, I went to the bulletin board I had established with Delilah, not with any more than the usual inchoate hope.

But there was a message waiting. My heart did a little giddyup.

I entered my password and went to the next screen. The message said, *I've got some time off. Do you?* Followed by a phone number starting with 331 – the country code for France and city code for Paris.

Damn. I looked around for a second, a reflex in response to having my sense of aloneness unexpectedly disturbed. The girls typed determinedly away, their eyes filled with calculation and hope.

I looked at the screen again. The message had been left the day before. I wrote down the number, using my usual code, exited the bulletin board, and purged the browser to erase all records of where I'd just been.

I got up and walked back out onto Silom. My heart was racing, but my brain hadn't shut itself off. It was hard to believe that the timing of her call was a coincidence. More likely it had something to do with the Manny op. Although I couldn't be sure.

I stopped and thought, *You can't be sure? What the hell is wrong with you?*

I've never believed in coincidences, not for things like this. Sure, maybe they exist, but you act as though they don't. Most times, the thing that might have been a coincidence wasn't, and your doubt helps you survive it. And if you're wrong, and the thing was a coincidence? Well, what's the downside? There is none.

But now there was a downside, apparently, and it was as though my mind was trying to warp my worldview accordingly. What I wanted to believe wasn't the point. What I needed to believe was everything.

Then ignore the message. Don't call her. At least not until Manny is straightened out.

The thought was depressing. Even painful.

Dox hadn't known, and I would never tell him, but his comment about the last time I 'got laid' had hit home. Yeah, I pay for recreation from time to time. You have to take care of your physical needs. Something real, though, something worthwhile? Not since Delilah, and there hadn't been many before her, either.

How could I know what this was about, what she had in mind, unless I saw her? She might have the information I would need to get close to Manny again. She might be able to give me insight into her people's thinking about what had happened in Manila, about their related plans. Yes, there would be risks. But there always are. And I could control the risks. I always do.

My gut told me it was worth taking a chance. For a moment I was afraid that I couldn't trust my gut, that maybe the instinct that has always served me well had somehow been distorted, the internal navigation instruments compromised. But then I thought, *If your gut's no good anymore, you're done anyway.*

Which might itself have been a distortion. But the hell with it.

I found an international pay phone and called the number. As the call went through, I felt my heart beating harder and felt foolish for it. Dox would have ribbed me if he'd known, told me I was acting like a kid or something.

She answered after one ring.

'*Allo,*' I heard her say.

'Hey,' I said, staring out at the street, afraid of my hopes.

'Hey,' she said back. When I didn't answer, she asked, 'How have you been?'

Whatever I'd been expecting, I hadn't expected it to be awkward. 'Good. You?'

'The same. I've been working on a . . . project, but I can get away for a few days, if you can.'

No mention of business. Either this was a personal call, as I wanted to hope, or it was business disguised as personal, which among the current range of possibilities would probably mean the worst.

'Yeah, I can get away. I'm in the middle of something that's quiet for the moment, but it might heat up suddenly.'

I wondered if she would react to that. She didn't. She said, 'I can come to you, if that's better.'

I considered for a moment. I needed to stay in the area, in case Boaz and Gil turned up something that could put Dox and me back in the game with Manny. And I wanted to meet Delilah someplace that would pose difficulties for her if she was thinking of bringing company. Just in case.

'Can you make it to Bangkok?' I asked.

'Sure. I can probably get a nonstop from de Gaulle.'

'Put your itinerary on the bulletin board and I'll meet you just outside customs.'

'All right. Are you sure you want to do Bangkok, though? They say taking a date there is like bringing a lunch box to a restaurant.'

I smiled. 'I know the kind of food I like.'

She laughed, and the tension eased a little. 'All right, then. I'll make the flight arrangements, and leave the rest to you.'

I recognized the concession to what Dox might call my paranoia. She knew that letting me choose the final destination, without telling her in advance, would be more comfortable for me.

'I'll need to know the name you're traveling under,' I said. 'To make reservations.'

'I'll put it all on the bulletin board.'

'Okay, then.'

There was a pause. She said, 'It'll be good to see you.'

'Yeah. I'm glad you got in touch.'

'*Jaa,*' she said, displaying a little knowledge of Japanese. Well then.

I smiled. '*À bientôt.*' And hung up.

I walked for a few minutes, then went into another Internet café. I did the usual spyware inspection, then checked on flights to Bangkok from Paris. The only non-stops were on Thai Air and Air France. The Thai flight left daily at 1:30 P.M. Let's see, it was already 1:15 P.M. in Paris, so she'd missed that. The Air France flight left daily at 11:25 P.M. and arrived at Bangkok International at 4:35 the following afternoon.

I thought for a minute. Either she had some sudden free time, as she'd said, in which case she would want to make the most of it, or, more likely, she was coming on business, which would entail its own form of urgency. Either way, I could expect her to move promptly, which would probably mean that evening's Air France flight. All right, I'd bet on that.

I thought about where to take her, and how to go about it. It had to be someplace special. Partly, I had to admit, because I wanted to impress her. More important, because I wanted her to feel far away from whoever might have sent her. A sense of distance, of disconnection, would increase the likelihood that she would talk openly, or at least that she would slip. The place also had to be secure. And we'd have to get there in a way that would give me the opportunity to satisfy myself that she was traveling alone.

I checked the bulletin board again and saw that she had already left me the name she would be traveling under. Good. I spent the next half hour making the appropriate reservations online. I thought it all through again when I was done, and was satisfied in all respects. The only problem was a sudden feeling of impatience. Everything was set, and I had nothing to do but wait. The next day would feel like nothing more than killing time.

Ordinarily, killing time in Bangkok would mean taking in a Thai boxing match at Lumpini or Ratchadamnoen, or jazz at Brown Sugar or in the Bamboo bar at the Oriental, maybe an evening with one of the girls from Spasso in the Grand Hyatt. But tonight, it seemed, I would simply go out with a friend.

The thought felt strange. Not unpleasant, by any means. But strange. It was like hearing a song I had enjoyed a long time ago, and had then somehow forgotten, a simple tune that at the time had been rich and fresh and full of promise and that now, by its unnoticed loss and unexpected reappearance, had been alchemized into something haunting, a reminder not only of what was but also of what had been lost in the accumulated years, the melody now tinged with hope that what was gone might be recovered and fear that its loss instead was irretrievable.

Dox and I met in the lobby as planned and, after the appropriate precautions, caught a taxi to Silom. I asked him where we were going on the way, but he refused to tell me. It was a measure of the degree to which I had come to trust him that I didn't just stop the cab and leave. But the childishness of his demurral was irritating.

We got out in front of the State Tower Bangkok building and took the elevator to the sixty-third floor, the building's highest. Emerging from the elevator, we walked through a pair of floor-to-ceiling glass doors and were greeted with what I had to admit was an impressive sight.

Stretching out along the open-air roof below us was a tableau of symmetrically arranged tables covered in white linen and, at one end of the arrangement, a circular bar on a promontory glowing in red, then blue, then yellow. To our left was a higher terrace, upon which a jazz quartet was making music for the diners below. The restaurant's floor, stone and dark teak, stretched all the way to the edges of the building, beyond which in all directions twinkled the endless lights of the city, the Chao Phraya River, expressing itself only as a sinewy absence of light, winding its way silently through it. A glass sign at the bottom of the stairs announced discreetly that the place was called Sirocco.

'Well, what do you think?' Dox asked. 'Do you like it?'

'I do,' I admitted, failing to keep the surprise out of my voice.

'What did you think, I was going to take you to a go-go bar or something?'

'Is that a rhetorical question?'

He frowned. 'Sometimes you don't give me enough credit, man.'

I was surprised by that. Dox played the buffoon so often and so well, it seemed odd to me that he would want to be acknowledged for occasionally possessing some good taste.

'How did you hear about it?' I asked.

He shrugged. 'I spend a fair amount of time out here, so I keep my ear to the ground. Just opened a few months ago, and it sounded like your kind of place. So I figured we could give it a try.'

I looked at him and said, 'Thank you. I didn't mean . . .'

He grinned. 'Ah, forget it.'

'I was just going to say, I'll order the wine.'

The grin started to fade, then came back at double voltage. 'Whatever makes you happy, man,' he said.

The hostess brought us to our table. The menu, consisting of what Sirocco called 'Inspired Mediterranean Dining,' was as good as the view. We ordered garlic-rosemary marinated grilled double lamb chops, grilled Phuket lobster with lemon and aromatic olive oil, confit of duck and pan-seared foie gras appetizers. I took care of the wine: a '96 Emilio's Terrace Cabernet Sauvignon Reserve. It would be a little young, but some air would bring it around.

'Damn, this is good,' Dox said, after the waitress had opened and decanted the bottle and we had taken our first sips. 'I don't know who Emilio is, but I'd sure like to shake his hand. How do you know so much about wine, man?'

I shrugged. 'I don't know that much.'

'Cut the modesty routine. I can tell you do.'

I shrugged again. 'For what I do, I need to be able to blend in a lot of different strata of society. To do that, you need to know the little things, the tells. Could be wine, could be the right fork to use. Could be the right clothes to wear. Or the right words. I don't know. I just watch and try to learn. I'm a good imitator.' I took a sip of the Emilio's Terrace. 'But also, I just like wine.'

'So you can just . . . put these things on, then take them off, like they're a disguise?'

'I guess so. You do it, too, although a little differently.

You've got a way of disappearing when you want to, I've seen that.'

'Yeah, that's from sniper school. You just . . . draw in all your energy, like. It's a Zen thing. Kind of hard to explain. A buddy of mine once told me it's like what that creature did in *Predator,* or a Klingon warship with a cloaking device. I think that's about right. I wouldn't mind being able to move comfortably in all those different societies like you do, though. Still, it must be strange, to be able to move in them but not really belong in any of them, you know what I mean?'

I nodded. 'Yeah. I know.'

The meal turned out to be an unexpected pleasure. The food and wine were first-rate, and the feeling of being in the heart of, and yet above and isolated from, the dense metropolis around us was invigorating, almost heady. The weather was Bangkok's finest: cool and relatively dry, and a few stars were even visible through the polluted pall above. We talked a lot about Afghanistan, which was the conflict we had in common: the men we had known there; the crazy things we had done; the unintended consequences of an armed and well-trained cadre of Islamic fanatics that had followed in the wake of the departing Soviet army we had helped to drive out.

We talked, too, of Asia. I was surprised at his knowledge of and affection for the region, and his inquiries about Japanese culture, in particular, were intelligent and insightful. He told me about his love for Thailand, where he had been 'sojourning,' as he liked to put it, for years, staying longer and longer with each visit, and how he hoped to retire here. How he no longer felt at ease in the States.

I understood his feelings. There's something accepting about Thai culture, and there are species of *farang,* foreigners, who find themselves drawn to it. On the dark side of the phenomenon are pedophiles and other deviants who come to indulge their secret sicknesses. And there are the aging middle-management types, who anesthetize regrets about failed ambitions and the implacable, day-by-day approach of death by renting women with whom they are in any event too old and too far gone to function, and by reassuring themselves of their worth by living in a neo-colonial style that the locals can't afford. But there are many who stay for more benign reasons. Some, in a sense, are Easterners trapped in Western bodies, who find their truer natures liberated in Thailand's 'foreign' climes. Some are simply adventurers, addicts to the exotic. Some are refugees from a misguided affair, or divorce, or bankruptcy, or other such personal trauma. And some, like Dox and me, are soldiers who found themselves too altered by the things they did in war to return to the lands of their youth. For some, the distance between who you were and who you have become is unbridgeable, and the dissonance attempted repatriation creates is a constant reminder of the very changes that you want so badly to forget.

When we were finished with the meal, and lingering over enormous mugs of cappuccino, I told him, 'I need your help with something.'

He looked at me. 'Sure, man, anything, you know that. Just name it.'

'My Israeli contact. The one who brokered the meeting with Boaz and Gil. She just contacted me. She wants a meeting.'

'Maybe this is the break we've been waiting for, then. Some new info on Manny.'

I shook my head. 'She didn't say anything about Manny. She says she just wants to see me.'

He cocked his head and looked at me. 'I don't get it. Why would she want to see you, if it's not about Manny?'

'Before she set things up with Boaz and Gil, I spent some time with her.' I gave him the *Reader's Digest* version of how Delilah and I had met in Macau, of what had happened between us there and then in Rio after.

He listened quietly, his expression uncharacteristically grave. When I was done, he said, 'You're thinking about seeing her.'

I nodded.

'Are you going to do this because you think she might have some operational intel, or because you just want to?'

For a guy who liked to play the hick, Dox had a way of going straight to the heart of the matter. I could have equivocated, but I decided to play it straight with him. He deserved that.

'I just want to see her.'

He nodded for a moment, then said, 'I'm glad you said so. I could tell it was that from how you just talked about her, and I would have been awfully concerned if you'd tried to bullshit me. I would have wondered if you were bullshitting yourself, too.'

'I don't know if I'm bullshitting myself or not.'

'Partner, that in itself is a profound species of honesty.'

I sipped my cappuccino. 'She might still have something operational for us. I doubt that the timing of the meeting is just a coincidence.'

'If it's not a coincidence, and she told you she was calling just because she missed your charming personality, she wasn't playing straight with you. There might be something nefarious at work.'

'"Nefarious"?'

'Yeah, you know, it means "immoral" or "wicked."'

I frowned. 'I know what it means.'

He smiled. 'Well, if you know what it means, what do you think?'

'You might be right.'

'But you want to meet her anyway.'

'Yeah.'

He pursed his lips and exhaled forcefully. 'Sounds like unsafe sex to me, partner. And I'm not sure I want to be the condom.'

I nodded. 'When you put it that way, I'm not so sure, either.'

He gave me a medium-wattage grin. 'Well, tell me what you want, anyway.'

'She's coming to Bangkok. I told her I would meet her outside of customs. If she puts people there to anticipate me, you can spot them.'

'Okay . . .'

'We'll take a taxi from the international terminal to the domestic. You'll be tailing us, so you should have some opportunities to tell if we're followed. If I'm clean, we'll go through security on the domestic side. I'll have two tickets for Phuket, which is where Delilah and I are going, and you'll have a ticket for somewhere else. That way you'll be able to get through security, too, and you'll have another chance in the boarding area to confirm that we're alone.'

'Phuket, huh? Hope you talked to your travel agent. There are still a few places that aren't back on line after the tsunami.'

'I know.'

'Or you could go to Ko Chang, it's in the Gulf of Thailand and they didn't get hit at all. Plus it's less built up and only about a four-hour drive from Bangkok.'

'I know. I want to fly. We'll be harder to follow that way.'

'Ah, that's a good point. Well, Phuket sure is nice, anyway. Where are you planning on staying?'

I balked for a second out of habit, then said, 'Amanpuri.'

'Hoo-ah! Paradise on earth! Stayed there once and saw Mick Jagger. My kind of place, although I believe I do slightly prefer the beach at the Chedi next door. I won't need one of the villas or anything like that. Just a pavilion ought to be fine. With an ocean view, of course. No sense being in paradise if you can't see the water.'

'No, I don't think . . .'

'Hey, how am I going to watch your back if I'm not there? She could call her people once you arrive, and you'd be all on your own.'

'I can take care of myself.'

'Then why are you asking me for my help?'

'Look, I don't know if I can get another room there. I was lucky to get the one on such short notice.'

'Come on, man, you know their bookings are off because tourists think the tsunami damage is worse than it really is. All on account of them CNN camera crews going in and asking the locals, "Can you take us to a scene of appropriately picturesque destruction that'll increase our ratings back home?" And then their viewers think, "Shit, that's the whole island, I better just go to Hawaii instead." But you and me, we know better, don't we?'

I didn't see any room for negotiation in his expression. I sighed. 'All right. But this woman is sharp, understand? She notices what goes on around her and she remembers faces. If you stay in sniper mode, you'll be fine. But if you slip, she'll make you in a heartbeat. And that could multiply our problems.'

He grinned. 'I promise to behave.'

I looked at him. A part of me was shaking its head, thinking, *Nothing good can come of this.*

But I only said, 'All right.'

'Well, I'm glad to be getting an all-expenses-paid trip to Amanpuri, but I still don't like it, partner. Mixing business and pleasure like this ain't smart. It's apt to leave you confused. And you getting killed would be a piss-poor way to clarify the confusion.'

I took another sip of my cappuccino. 'There's some risk, but there's a reward, too. If I don't meet her, I'll blow a chance to learn what the Israelis know, what they might be planning.'

'Yeah, son, but that ain't the only reward that's on your mind here.'

'No, it's not.'

'All right, you're a grownup, I'm not going to tell you what time to go to bed or who to take there. I hope she's worth it, though.'

I nodded. A breeze picked up, and for a moment, the terrace was actually chilly. I wondered about the wisdom of what I was doing, and about the fairness of involving Dox.

The stars, which had been briefly visible, were gone now, reclaimed by the polluted sky. I looked out at the lights of the city. The meal over, I no longer had the pleasant sense of being above it all, removed from it. Rather, I felt that I was right in the middle of something, probably more than I knew.

8

Hilger sat at his desk in his eighty-eighth-floor office at the International Finance Center. Two IFC was one of the newest buildings on Hong Kong and, at 1,362 feet, the tallest. He had to admit, he really liked the place. It wasn't just the views, the amenities, the feeling of being on top of the world, detached, all-powerful, untouchable. The building was also the perfect cover. The lease itself was so breathtakingly expensive that it was inconceivable that a government or any other nonprofit could be footing the bill for it. And, indeed, Uncle Sam wasn't paying for Hilger's lease, or for any other aspect of his operation. These days, Uncle Sam pretty much left Hilger alone, enjoying the quality of his intelligence but preferring not to know too much about how he came by it. All of which suited Hilger just fine.

The room was done in natural oak and off-white wool Berber carpet. The desktop supported only a few items: a brushed nickel Leonardo Marelli halogen reading light; a Bang & Olufsen Beocom 2500 telephone, with CIA-issue Secure Telephone Unit circuitry installed; and an anodized aluminum Macintosh thirty-inch flat panel display with a wireless keyboard and mouse. The overall look, which he had put to good effect with numerous clients, was solidity, focus, money, connections. The view, of the skyscrapers of Central and Victoria Harbor, was part of the impression, and Hilger liked it a lot. Tonight, to minimize reflection and reveal the glowing cityscape without, he had the room illuminated only by the desk light. Gazing out at the view soothed Hilger's mind, helped him figure things out. Which was good, because at the moment there was a lot of figuring to be done.

The situation wasn't entirely positive, certainly, but things were still fixable. Yes, he'd lost two men, but he'd lost men before and understood that losing men, perhaps losing his own life, was part of any mission. It was the mission that mattered, the operation. The operation had to succeed and he would ensure that it did.

He took things backward. The goal: protect the operation. Which meant: ending the threat to Manny, who was a critical part of the operation. How to do that? Easy enough. Find out who had been behind the hit and who had tried to carry it out, and then, insofar as possible, eliminate both.

The problem was doing it all under pressure. After meeting Manny in Kowloon that morning, he had returned to his office. There was a message waiting for him from someone in his network who was currently stationed at Langley. Hilger had called him. The man had offered a heads-up: the news that Calver and Gibbons had been gunned down in Manila had reached the top immediately. Manila Station had liaised with the Metro Manila police, who had checked the dead bodyguard's records and learned that his only client was one Manheim Lavi, Known Major Scumbag. Lavi was currently unreachable, but the inference was that the bodyguard had died protecting, and that the two dead ex-spooks had been mixed up with, said Known Major Scumbag. The burning question, his man had said, was: What were Calver and Gibbons doing with the Scumbag, and who else was involved? Hilger knew he had to tie up all the loose ends before someone grabbed hold of them and unraveled the whole fucking thing.

Well, on the first front, finding out who had tried to carry out the hit, he had managed to move quickly. From the description Manny provided, Hilger had immediately suspected John Rain, who he knew had done the Belghazi job at Kwai Chung in Hong Kong last year. Hilger had been against that op, and had even tried to have Rain killed to stop it. Rain had proven a hard man to deter, though, and he'd gotten to Belghazi anyway. Which, strangely enough, turned out to have been all right: that bastard Belghazi had been trying to move radiological missiles right under Hilger's nose. If Rain hadn't wound up doing the job, Hilger would have had to do it himself.

What a mess that had been, though. Some of the assets he'd been so carefully cultivating had suspected he'd been involved. If it hadn't been for Manny, he doubted he would have been able to regain their trust. And then there was the heat from the CIA, which wanted to know exactly what the hell his involvement had been and why none of the proper paperwork had been filled out. There, too, outside intervention had made the difference. His National Security Council contact had effectively bought off the Director of Central Intelligence by telling the DCI the Agency could take carte blanche public credit for stopping a terrorist operation at Kwai Chung. It had all been in the news the next day, with the heroes of the CIA, the DCI foremost among them, standing squarely in the adulatory spotlight. And there had been some side benefit, too: because the National Security Council spoke in the name of the President, the fact that the NSC had intervened aggressively on Hilger's behalf told the DCI that Hilger was protected, all the way to the top. The DCI, the DDO, and pretty much everyone else who mattered in the Directorate of Operations left him alone after that.

But there was a new DCI now, this guy Goss, and with all

the firings and resignations, all the people who had been intimidated were now gone. The good news was that Goss didn't have a clue, at least not yet. He had so many things he was trying to get under control that Hilger could probably fly under his radar for a while. If there were another slip, though, or if Goss took it into his head to assert himself by getting in Hilger's face, things could get messy again. Yeah, maybe he'd be able to call in another round of favors and get the mess cleaned up, but he preferred not to have a showdown with the new management so soon. Even if Hilger won, there would be grudges after. Hunters don't like to be interrupted in the act of pouncing on their prey.

Rain's involvement suggested that the CIA had ordered the hit, as it had with Belghazi. The thought was almost sickening. If those idiots had any idea what Hilger was up to, of what in three short years he had managed to accomplish, they would know to get out of his way and leave him alone. Leave him alone, hell, if they had any sense of proportion they would fucking genuflect.

He drummed his fingers along the edge of the blond wooden desktop and watched the lighted barges inching like water bugs along the dark surface of the harbor a quarter mile below. He didn't know why his men believed in him, exactly, but they did. They always had. He sensed that, at just south of forty years old, he had become a sort of father figure to them. It would be too much to say that they worshipped him, but his opinion of them mattered hugely, as did his understanding, his forgiveness, for the things their work required them to do. He'd never had anyone like himself in his own life, but he understood the power, and the responsibility, of the position. He could pat a man on the back, sometimes literally, and tell him that it was all right, that he had done the right thing, that the images and the smells, the fears and the doubts, the corrosive effects of conscience, all these were in fact part of the man's nobility for not having taken the easy, the common path of shying away from what needed to be done. And because no one could ever know of their quiet heroics, of the anonymous sacrifices they made, because there would never be medals or ticker-tape parades or the thanks of a grateful nation, his understanding and, when necessary, his forgiveness were all his men had to comfort them. It wasn't enough to remove the weight, true, but it was enough to lighten it. Sometimes he wished he had someone he could turn to in a like manner, but he didn't, and he supposed this was part of the burden of leadership, to bear the doubts, and the hard memories, alone.

Manny had said there had been another man, a big white guy. That wasn't much to go on by itself, but Hilger had more. There had been a sniper at Kwai Chung. Maybe it had been Rain, but Hilger knew that Rain had no sniping background, and the gunman at Kwai Chung had been a pro. He'd taken the heads off those two Transdniester bagmen from far enough away so that no one had even heard the shots. That didn't feel like Rain, who worked from close up. Hilger couldn't be sure, but he suspected the shooter had been a CIA contractor called Dox. Hilger, through an intermediary, had tried to hire Dox to eliminate Rain and save Belghazi. Afterward, he wondered if the damn ex-Marine had decided to work with Rain instead of against him. He knew they had 'served' together in Afghanistan, helping the Muj chase out the Red Army. He'd expected Dox's mercenary instincts to be more powerful than any sense of comradeship the man might still feel from that shared conflict, but it seemed in that respect Hilger had misjudged.

He had his own files on both these men, complete with photographs. The photo of Rain was out of date, but Hilger had used some Agency software to update it. He'd shown the photos to Manny before Manny returned to Manila, and Manny had given him a positive ID on both.

So far, so good. But who had been behind the hit was proving more difficult to divine. The CIA had been his first guess, but he hadn't been able to find out anything there. Of course, his inquiries had to be somewhat oblique, lest someone connect him through Manny to the men who had died in Manila, but he had his sources, and all of them had come up blank. The CIA might have wanted Manny dead, but it seemed they hadn't tried to bring it about.

Who, then? Manny hadn't wanted to face it, but, as they'd discussed the day before, the list was anything but short. The problem was that Rain had no known connections with any of the primary suspects. He had a history with the Japanese Liberal Democratic Party and of course with the Agency, the latter dating all the way back to Vietnam, but he wasn't known to work with anyone else. That didn't mean there weren't any other clients, of course; Rain was a free-lancer, a mercenary. But expanding a client base in Rain's line of work isn't easy. You can't just hang out a shingle, or take out a few ads. New clients come slowly, if at all.

Well, there was a fairly straightforward way to get to the bottom of this. All he had to do was ask Rain or Dox. They might not want to tell him, true, but they'd be inclined to believe him when he said that he understood they were just contractors, that he had no personal beef with them nor any professional reason to want them removed. Hell, after he'd cleared this whole thing up, he'd be happy to have them on his team.

What would make it sound appealing was that it was very

nearly true. It would be true, in fact, except they'd killed Calver and Gibbons, which did indeed make things personal. And they had scared Manny's boy, ruining any chance that Manny might want to just let bygones be bygones, as well.

All he needed to do was get to them. A clean snatch, the back of an unmarked, unobtrusive van. A reasonable, man-to-man conversation, if possible. Electrified alligator clips attached to their scrota, if not. Either way, he would get the information he wanted.

He took a deep breath. Yes, he needed someone who could snatch them, then interrogate them. And who knew the region well enough to be able to make it all happen quickly.

There were several men he could have chosen, but one name stood out: Mitchell William Winters. The man was an expert. He had trained with the famed FBI Hostage Rescue Team and rendered more than his share of bad guys. And he had worked in Asia, doing security consulting for companies that needed such assistance in the region. Winters was into martial arts – Hilger remembered hearing about *kali* or something like that in the Philippines and Thai boxing in Bangkok. He didn't particularly care about the karate stuff – Hilger's choice of martial art was a SIG P229, concealed in a belly band carry, and he had yet to meet the Long Dong Do master who could block a bullet from it – but the experience in Asia would be critical.

And Winters had another plus: Hilger knew he was a graduate of an off-the-books CIA hostile interrogation program. The program was ostensibly designed to teach operators to resist torture, but it was well known in the community that, in doing so, the program taught torture itself, and that this was its true purpose. Some people took to the course material more readily than others. Winters, Hilger knew, had a knack.

The sky was beginning to grow light behind Central off to his right. He consulted his directory, then picked up the phone.

9

After dinner, Dox insisted on heading over to the go-go bars in Patpong. I wasn't happy about it, but I supposed I would just have to accept that the man was large enough to contain multitudes: lethal and loud; cultured and crude; profound and party-going. And what he had said earlier, about having been doing fine on his own, was of course true. Maybe I was being unfair to him. I decided I would try to trust him more. The thought was strange and uncomfortable, but it felt like the right thing to do.

I stopped by an Internet café to check on Delilah's plans. There was a message waiting from her: she was coming in on the Air France flight, and would be arriving in Bangkok the following afternoon at 4:35. All right. I made the necessary reservations for Dox, went back to the Sukhothai, took a hot bath in the excellent tub, got in bed, and slept.

But my sleep was restless. I dreamed that I was a little boy again, in the apartment where I had grown up, and that something was chasing me there from room to room. I called for my parents, but no one came, and I was terrified at being alone. My father had kept a *katana*, the Japanese long sword, which had belonged, he said, to his great-grandfather, on a ceremonial stand in my parents' bedroom, and I ran in there and slammed the door behind me. Then I went to grab the *katana*, but instead of one, there were two, and I couldn't choose which to pick up. I froze. My mind was shouting, *Just pick one! Either one!* but I couldn't move. And then the door started to open . . .

I woke and sprang off the bed into a crouch. I remained like that for a long time, catching my breath, feeling the sweat dry on my body, trying to shake off the dream and come back to myself. Finally I straightened, used the toilet, then took another bath.

But this one didn't help me sleep at all. I lay in bed for a long time afterward, thinking. It bothered me that I'd frozen again, even in a dream. Two swords within easy reach – an embarrassment of riches if you're in danger, you would think. And yet I couldn't choose either one. If I hadn't awoken, whatever had been pursuing me in the dream would have killed me.

Dox and I went to the airport early the next afternoon to give ourselves time to establish a countersurveillance route and walk it through. We were using the commo gear from Manila. If Dox had to warn me of anything, he could do it at a distance and right in my ear. This would give us a better range of options than if he had been trying to protect me from afar without contact.

The area outside customs was crowded with people waiting for arrivals: families, Thai and expat; hotel car drivers in white livery; greasy-haired backpackers in sandals with adventure-seeking friends coming in from Europe and Australia. No one set off my radar, but the area was too crowded to be sure. If there were trouble, I expected it would look Israeli. After all, part of the reason Delilah's people had brought me in to begin with was their lack of Asian resources. The 'lack' was relative, of course: through both the gemstone trade and the underground arms market to groups like the Tamil Tigers in Sri Lanka, Israel does have contacts in Thailand. Still, if they wanted to move quickly enough to take advantage of any intel Delilah might have supplied them, I didn't think they'd be able to outsource. None of which is to say I ignored people who didn't fit the profile, but it does help to keep certain guidelines in mind as you go.

I set up far to the right of the exit, where I would be able to see her as she emerged from customs but where she would have to look hard for me. Dox was positioned a few meters behind me and to my left, and when I casually checked in his direction, it took me a second to spot him, even though I knew him and I knew where to look. He really did have that sniper's knack for disappearing into the background.

There were two possibilities: first, they would have someone pre-positioned outside of customs, where I had told Delilah I would meet her, along with when. Second, they would have someone on the plane with her, who would have to follow her if his presence were going to serve any purpose. Of the two, I thought the second the more likely, as well as the easier to deal with. More likely, because their probable lack of Asian resources would prevent them from getting someone in place that quickly; easier, because whoever it was would have to be close to Delilah coming off the plane and would have a hard time staying submerged once I started moving her. Either way, I wasn't unduly worried about someone making a move inside the airport. The levels of surveillance, security, and control over ingress and egress involved would make an airport job almost impossible to pull off cleanly.

The plane arrived ten minutes ahead of schedule, with nothing noticeably out of place in the crowd beforehand. I saw Delilah immediately as she came through. She was wearing a navy pantsuit and brown pumps, her long blonde hair pulled back into a loose ponytail. A crocodile carry-on was slung across her left shoulder, the bag resting comfortably against her opposite hip. The surface brand was looks, money, confidence, style. There was a lot more to her than just that, I knew, but she wore that outward persona well.

I reached into my pocket and turned off the commo gear, then turned on the mini bug detector Harry had made for me in Tokyo and that I've relied on since. The former would have set off the latter, and I wanted to make sure Delilah wasn't wearing a transmitter.

She looked around, saw me, and smiled. I felt something going on down south, like a slumbering dog stirring in response to an enticing aroma, and I thought, *Down, boy. Don't embarrass me.*

She walked over and put the bag down, then leaned in and kissed me lightly on the mouth. I put my arms around her and pulled her close. She smelled the way she did the first time I'd kissed her, clean and fresh and with a tantalizing trace of some perfume I couldn't name. The warmth of her, the feel of her against me, her scent, it all seemed to ease in under my clothes, and in the crowded airport the embrace was suddenly private, focused, almost naked in its intimacy.

She pulled her head back and looked at me, one hand resting against the back of my neck, the other dropping gently to my chest. The dog was coming fully awake now. Another minute and the damned thing would sit up and beg. I eased away and looked at her.

She smiled, her cobalt eyes alight with good humor. 'I guess this is when I'm supposed to ask, "Is that a gun in your pocket . . ."'

I felt myself blush. 'No, I'm definitely just glad to see you.'

She laughed. 'Where are we going?'

The bug detector slumbered peacefully in my pocket.

She wasn't wired. I struck a casual pose, my hands in my pockets. I switched the bug detector off and powered the commo gear on. I heard a slight hiss in my ear canal where the flesh-colored unit was inserted.

'A little place I know in Phuket,' I said.

'Wonderful! I've heard it's beautiful, but have never been. How are things there, after the tsunami?'

'The place we're going is elevated from the beach and did fine. Actually, most of the island is recovering nicely. How much time do you have?'

'Three days. Maybe longer. You?'

'I don't know. I'm waiting for something. I hope it'll take at least a few days to materialize.'

'Well, let's not waste any time. Where do we go?'

'The other terminal. Our flight leaves in an hour.'

I eschewed the shuttle bus, instead choosing a route that required a walk through the terminal and a descent to the level below us. She knew what I was doing but didn't comment on it. On the level below, I flagged down a cab and had it take us to the domestic terminal. A minute after we had pulled away from the curb, I heard Dox in my ear: 'All right, so far, so good. It doesn't look like anyone's trying to stay with you. If they are, they're sure not being obvious. I'll head over and see if we see any familiar faces.'

The cab pulled up in front of the domestic terminal. I paid the driver, got out, and held the door for Delilah, checking behind and around us while I did. She saw what I was doing – I wasn't trying to be subtle, and she would have spotted it anyway – and again, she didn't comment. I logged her failure to protest as a possible source of concern. In Rio, we had moved past the point where I was treating her as a potential threat, and I knew that my willingness to relax my guard had been important to her. That my mistrust had apparently resumed should have been the source of insult, and, I knew from experience with her occasional temper, of anger. Unless, of course, she was aware of the reasons behind the resurgence and was misguidedly trying to lull me.

We went inside the terminal and headed down to gate eight. A few minutes later, Dox moved in, keeping to the periphery. I heard him again in my ear: 'Okay, partner, there is no way you were followed over here. Also I don't see anyone here who was waiting outside international arrivals. So unless someone knew where you were headed and got here before us, you are in the clear. I think the next point of concern will be our destination. She might make a call or something, tell her people where you are after you've arrived. That way they wouldn't have to give themselves away trying to follow you. If I was her, sorry, if I *were* her, I know you're sensitive about that, and I had bad intentions, that's the way I'd do it.'

Enough, I thought. It's not as though I hadn't already worked this all through myself. In fact, Dox and I had already discussed it all. He was feeling awfully talkative.

Delilah and I made some small talk about the flight. She had flown first class and had slept the whole way, and was refreshed and ready for an evening in a tropical paradise. But Dox kept jabbering, and with Delilah right there next to me, I had no way of telling him to knock it off.

'And damn, man, I have got to tell you, that is one fine-looking woman! Why didn't you say so? I would have understood right away why you wanted to see her. Hell, I'd have tried to see her myself. I would have done your countersurveillance for free, partner, if I'd known she was going to be the subject, you wouldn't even have had to pay for my vacation. Well, too late now, a deal's a deal.'

He stopped, and I thought, *Thank God.* But a moment

later it started up again: 'And here I thought you'd been leading a lonely life with nothing but your tired right hand for comfort! I judged you wrong, man, and I'm big enough to admit it, too. From now on, you're my hero, I'm taking all my romance cues from you.'

Once we were on the plane I knew I was safe, at least temporarily, and I took the earpiece out, satisfied to think that Dox would now be talking only to himself.

Delilah and I caught up some more. The conversation was largely small talk, but I was probing, as well. So far I had two pieces of data, and both pointed to a problem: the timing of her call, and her failure to react to my obvious security moves. The jury wasn't in yet, but the evidence was piling up. It bothered me, at some level, that it had come to this. In Rio it had been good, it really had. I should have just been able to deal with it – she was a professional, and business is business – but yeah, it was bothering me.

God, she was beautiful, though. You could see why she was so effective in her work. There was something about her, an aura, a magnetism, that I'd never encountered in anyone else.

And despite my suspicions, it felt good to be with her. Maybe I was wrong. Maybe the data would start to accumulate in a more favorable direction.

The approach and landing were smooth, and a hotel car was waiting outside arrivals to take us to Amanpuri. The sun was getting low in the sky as we drove along Phuket's two-lane, narrow roads toward the resort. I knew what she must be thinking: *This is it? It's actually not that much.* But we were still somewhat inland. The island's beauty doesn't really unfold until you hit the coast. At which time, I knew, her diminishing expectations would make Amanpuri that much more breathtaking.

We pulled in off the resort's winding, gated drive just as the sun was setting behind the steep, Thai-style rooflines of the bungalows and pavilions and the Andaman Sea beyond them. Palm trees swayed in silhouette to a gentle ocean breeze. A teak terrace flowed from the edge of the driveway to a long, black-bottomed pool, its surface like polished onyx against the darkening sky. In the tenuous golden light, we might have been looking at a movie set.

A porter opened the car door and we got out. 'Welcome to Amanpuri,' he said, pressing his palms together under his chin and bowing his head in a formal *wai,* the Thai attitude of greeting and gratitude.

Delilah looked around, then at me. Her mouth was slightly agape.

'What's that wonderful smell?' she asked.

'*Sedap malam,*' the porter said. 'Brought here from Indonesia. It means "heavenly night" because it offers its scent only in the evening. I think in English you call it the tuberose.'

I smiled and looked at her. 'Well? Do you like it?'

She paused for a moment, then said, 'Oh, my God.'

'Does that mean yes?'

She nodded and looked around again, then back at me. Her face lit up in an enormous smile. 'Yes,' she said. 'Yes, it does.'

We checked in under the rafters of the open-air entrance pavilion. A woman named Aom gave us a quick tour of the facilities – the fitness center, the library, the spa. Everything was teak and stone and seemed to rise up out of the hilly terrain as indigenous as the surrounding palm trees. I noted the presence of multiple guards, all extremely discreet. Amanpuri is a celebrity magnet, and the resort takes security seriously. Which, to me, was part of the attraction. Even if

Delilah informed her people of our whereabouts, they would have a hell of a time getting in here unannounced and unobtrusive. As for Delilah herself, from what I had seen of her organization's MO, her role was to set up the bowling pins, not to knock them down. Also, without checked bags, her ability to carry weapons would be limited. Knowing all this, and also, inevitably, influenced by the blissfully beautiful surroundings, I began to relax. I felt as though we'd been granted some sort of time-out, during which I might learn what I needed to know. Maybe I could turn the situation around, if that's what was called for. Yeah, we'd faced a conflict of interests before and found a way to work things out. Maybe we could do it again.

Aom took us to our pavilion – number 105, with a full ocean view. The room was low-key and luxurious. The walls, floor, and simple furniture were all teak, with the porcelain of a long tub, a cotton duvet, and oversized thick towels all gleaming white by contrast. Everything seemed to glow with the golden light of the sun, which was still visible through the pavilion's western doors.

Delilah was starving, so we decided to eat at one of the property's two open-air restaurants. We sat along the railing overlooking the ocean. The sun was now completely below the horizon, and but for a thin line of glowing red between them the water was now as dark as the sky. The restaurant, like all Amanpuri's facilities, wisely eschewed any piped-in music, instead allowing the breeze swaying the palm trees and the waves lapping at the beach to supply the necessary ambience.

We ordered roast duck sautéed with morning glories, soft-shelled black crab sautéed with chile paste, stir-fried mixed vegetables, and stir-fried bean sprouts with tofu and chili. I started us with a '93 Veuve Clicquot.

'I have to tell you,' Delilah said as we ate. 'I've been to some of the most beautiful places on earth. Post Ranch in Big Sur. The Palace in Saint-Moritz. The Serengeti Plain. But this is right up there.'

I smiled. 'There aren't many places that can make you forget everything. Everywhere you've been, everything you've done.'

She raised her eyebrows. 'Where are the others? For you.'

I thought for a moment. 'A few places in Tokyo, believe it or not. But they're more like . . . enclaves. Oases. They can protect you from what's outside, but you still know it's there. This . . . it's another universe.'

She took a sip of the champagne. 'I know what you mean. There's a beach in Haifa, where I grew up. Sometimes, when I'm back there, I can find a quiet spot at night. The smell of the sea, the sound of the waves . . . it makes me feel like I'm a girl again, innocent and unblemished. Like I'm alone, but in a good way, if you know what I mean.'

'To be unaccompanied by constant memories,' I said, quoting something a friend had once said to me, 'is to find a state of grace.'

'Grace?' she asked, taking the reference literally. 'Do you believe in God?'

I paused, thinking of my conversation with Dox, then said, 'I try not to.'

'Does that help?'

I shrugged. 'Not really. But what difference does it make, what you believe? Things are what they are.'

'What you believe makes all the difference in the world.'

I looked at her. We'd been down this road before, and I didn't like the implicit criticism, maybe even condescension, in her comment. Then or now.

'Then you better be careful about what you believe in,' I said. 'And about what it might cost you.'

She looked away for a moment. I wasn't sure if it was a flinch.

We finished the champagne and I ordered a '99 Lafon Volnay Santenots. Delilah had a disciplined mind, I knew, but no one does as well in the presence of wine and jet lag as in their absence. And if she were here for something 'nefarious,' as Dox had put it, the discord between her feelings for me from before and her intentions for me now would be producing a strain. I wanted to do everything I could to turn that strain into a fault line, the fault line into a widening crack.

We talked more about this and that. She never let on that she knew anything about Manny, or that the botched hit in Manila had anything to do with her presence here now. And as the evening wore on, I realized I couldn't accept that the timing of her contact had been a coincidence. So the absence of any acknowledgment had to be an omission. A deliberate omission.

If she had been anyone else, and if this had all happened just a year or two earlier, I would have accepted the truth of what I knew. I would have acted on it. Doing so would have protected my body, albeit at some cost to my soul. But sitting across the table from her, no doubt affected by the wine, as well as by the surroundings and the feelings I still had for her, I found myself looking for a different way. Something less direct, less irredeemable, something that might have as its basis hope instead of only fear.

And there was something strangely attractive about the feeling that I was taking a chance. It wasn't anything as base as the thrill of 'unsafe sex,' as Dox had suggested. It was more a sense of the possibilities, the potential upside. Not just the possibility that, if I confronted her and she cracked, she might give me information that would help me understand where I stood regarding Manny. I was aware, too, of a deeper kind of hope at work, for something more than information alone, something intangible but infinitely more valuable.

After a dessert of fruit and Thai sweets followed by steaming tureens of cappuccino, we strolled back to the pavilion. We left the lights dim and sat on a low teak couch facing the sea, present by the sound of the surf but unseeable in the darkness without. The silence in the room felt heavy to me, portentous. My previous, oblique conversational gambits had afforded me only hints and clues. I decided it was time to be more direct. My mouth felt a little dry at the prospect, part of me perhaps afraid of what I might discover.

'Did your people tell you about what they've involved me in?' I asked.

She looked at me, and something in her expression told me she wasn't happy with the question. This wasn't why we had come back to the room. It wasn't part of the script.

'No,' she said. 'Everything is "need to know." If I don't need to know, it's better that I don't.'

'They sent me after a guy in Manila.'

She shook her head. 'Why are you telling me this?'

'I don't want what's between us to be nothing more than "need to know." If it is, we're just gaming each other.'

'Protecting each other.'

'Would you protect me?'

'From what?'

'What if something went wrong?'

'Don't put me in that position.'

'What if you had to choose?'

Her eyes narrowed a fraction. 'I don't know. What would you do?'

I looked at her. 'It's easy for me. I don't believe in anything, remember? I can make up my own mind.'

'That's not an answer.'

'It's more of an answer than what you just told me.'

'I told you I don't know. I'm sorry if that wasn't the answer you were looking for.'

'I'm looking for the truth.'

'You know who I am.'

'That's what I'm asking you.'

She laughed. 'Look, I'm like a married woman, okay? With a family I always have to return to.'

I didn't respond. After a moment she said, 'So stop pretending you don't know all this.'

That sounded dangerously close to a rationalization, one with which I'm all too familiar: *He knew what he was getting into. If he hadn't been in the game, they wouldn't have wanted him dead.*

Of all the potential angles, the possible gambits, it seemed to me that the truth would be what she was least prepared for. The closer I got to it, the more it was putting her off her game.

'You're here only for personal reasons?' I asked her.

She shifted a fraction on the couch. 'Yes.'

'Look in my eyes when you say that.'

She did. A long beat went by.

'I'm here only for personal reasons,' she said again.

No. I knew her, from the time we'd spent together in Rio. If what she just said were true, my suspicions would have provoked her instantly. But now she was trying to manage her behavior in the presence of fatigue, conflicting emotions, and alcohol, and under pressure from my questions, and the unaccustomed effort was showing.

I looked at her silently. She returned my gaze. A long time went by – ten seconds, maybe fifteen. I could see some color coming into her cheeks, her nostrils flaring slightly with each exhalation.

All at once she looked away. I saw her shoulders rising and falling with her breathing. 'Goddamn you,' she said, her voice just above a whisper. 'Goddamn you.'

She glanced around the room, her head moving in quick, efficient jerks, here and there and back again.

She got up and started pacing, slowly at first, then more rapidly, her head nodding as though internally confirming something, trying to accept it. She looked everywhere but at me.

'I have to get out of here,' she said, more to herself than to me. She walked over to one of the dressers, pulled open a drawer, and started shoving things into her bag.

'Delilah,' I said.

She didn't answer, or even pause. She pulled open a second drawer and stuffed its contents into the bag, too.

I stood up. 'Delilah,' I said again.

She threw the bag over her shoulder and headed toward the door.

'Wait,' I said, and moved in front of her.

She tried to go left around me. I stayed with her. She went right. That didn't work either. She moved left again, more quickly. No go.

She had become almost oblivious to my presence. Something had gotten in her way, she had been blindly trying to go around it. But her lack of progress forced her to change her focus, and all at once she saw that the obstacle was me. Her eyes narrowed and her ears seemed to settle back against her head. In my peripheral vision I took in a shift in her weight, a slight rotation of her hips. Then her right elbow was blurring in toward my temple.

I retracted my head and shrugged my left shoulder, bringing my left hand up alongside my face as I did so. Her elbow glanced off the top of my head. Her left was already coming in from the other side. I covered up, dropped through my knees, and deflected it the same way.

She shifted back and shot a left palm heel straight for my nose. I weaved off-line and parried with my right. Other side – same drill.

She took two more quick shots, hooks to the head. I avoided the worst of both. She grabbed my arm and tried to drag me to the side, frustration and anger eroding her tactics.

If there's one thing my body learned in twenty-five years of judo at the Kodokan in Tokyo, it's grounding. She might as well have been trying to move one of the room's thick teak posts.

She made a sound, half rage, half desperation. She stepped back and whipped the bag around at my head. I dissipated some of the blow's force by flowing with it, and absorbed the rest by covering up with my shoulder, bicep, and forearm. She reloaded and swung again. Again I flowed and absorbed.

She started swearing something in Hebrew and hammering at me with the bag, with no obvious goal now other than to vent her fury. I let her pound on me, taking most of the impact along my arms and shoulders. She was in shape, and it took longer than I would have liked for her to tire. But eventually the power of the blows lessened, the interval between them lengthened. She stood, the bag hanging at her side, her breath heaving in and out. I lowered my arms and looked at her.

She glanced around the room. I realized she was looking for a better weapon of convenience than the bag. I tensed to grab her before she could pick up something heavy and blunt, or something sharp.

She must have sensed that I was on to her. Or she didn't see anything that looked likely to do the job. Regardless, she stopped scoping the room and looked in my eyes. Her pupils were huge and black – dilated by adrenaline.

Her panting punctuated her words. 'Get. The fuck. Out. Of my way.'

'Not until you tell me what's going on.'

She sucked wind for a moment, then said, 'Fuck you.'

I looked at her. 'This is going to be a long night.'

'What do you want?' she asked.

'I want . . .' I started to say.

But it had only been a feint. She dropped her right shoulder and charged into me, trying to knock me off balance. The move surprised me and might have worked, but I caught her shoulders with both hands and used her body as a momentary brace. She reared up under me, looking for a head butt, and connected with my chin. My teeth slammed together, narrowly missing my tongue.

Enough. I grabbed her by the biceps and shoved her against the wall.

'Tell me what's going on,' I said.

She dropped the bag and tried for an uppercut to my gut. I took hold of her wrists and slammed her arms up against the wall on either side of her head. Our faces were inches apart.

I felt her knee coming up and pressed my body against hers to stop it. She twisted right, then left. My cheek was pressed against hers and her smell, that perfume I liked, now mixed with sweat and fear and rage, got inside me and wrought some weird alchemy. I dropped my face to her neck, feeling first as though I was just going to brace it there, but then I was kissing her instead. I heard her say, 'No, no,' but she wasn't fighting me anymore, or at least not the same way.

Keeping her arms and body pinned to the wall, I brought my face around to kiss her on the mouth. She twisted her head away. I let go of her wrists and took her face in my hands. She tried to push me away for a second, but then she was kissing me back, almost attacking me with her mouth. I ran my hands down around her breasts and squeezed her waist, her ass. I realized I was kissing her as hard as she was me.

I reached up and tried to undo one of the buttons on her blouse but my hands were shaking and I couldn't do it. *Fuck it.* I slipped the fingers of both hands into the gap between the buttons and pulled hard to the sides. The buttons all popped free. The bra beneath was lace, with a front snap. I could feel her nipples, hard, through the fabric. I struggled to get the snap undone. Fabric tore. The bra opened up and her breasts were in my hands. Her skin was smooth and hot and damp from exertion.

Kissing me so hard I was forced to step back from the wall, she reached up and tore my shirt open the same way I had done hers. Then she reached down for my belt buckle. *No,* I thought. *You first.* I yanked her blouse and bra down to her wrists and spun her around so that she was facing the wall. We started to struggle again. I took her left arm in a wristlock and bent it behind her back. I held it high, almost to her shoulder blades, with my left hand, and shoved her up against the wall. I reached under her skirt with my right. She was wet through her panties. I pushed her skirt up, pinned the fabric against her ass with my hip, and tore her panties away. She snapped her head back and caught me on the cheek with a rear head butt. I saw stars. I pushed against her harder and pressed the side of my face against hers so that she was pinned entirely to the wall. I reached down and began to touch her. She closed her eyes and groaned. I moved my fingers inside her and her body shook.

I looked around wildly. To our left – the dresser. I shoved her over to it. There was a stack of travel magazines on top. I swept them to the floor with my free hand. Then I bent her over the dresser, bearing down on her arm and pinning her upper torso. She struggled but the wrist hold was too tight. I stepped to her side, opened my belt, and undid my button and zipper.

I stepped on the cuff of my left pants leg with my right foot and dropped my pants, stepping clear of them with my left leg as soon as they hit the floor. No way was I going to deal with her with a pair of trousers pooled around my ankles. I repeated the procedure with my right leg, then slipped off my boxers. My erection was straining upward like spring-loaded cement.

I stepped between her legs and pushed up the skirt. Her breathing was more like gasping now, and so, I realized, was mine.

Still pressing her down with the wristlock, I started touching her again. I don't know what I was waiting for. Maybe I wanted to torture her a little, to torture both of us.

'Do it,' I heard her gasp. 'Do it, or I'll kill you.'

My heart was hammering so hard I heard it thudding in my skull. My fingers and toes were tingling. I kicked her feet farther apart, wiped some of her wetness onto myself, and entered her in one smooth motion.

She gasped so loudly I felt the sound of it run back up into me, like a feedback screech through a microphone. I started driving into her, my hips sliding up and forward, my gut and ass clenching and releasing with each profound stroke.

I looked down at her. The side of her face was pressed against the dresser, her eyes squeezed shut, her mouth open and panting, in pain or ecstasy or both I didn't know. Her cheek was streaked with tears. I kept going. I didn't slow down at all.

A minute went by, maybe two. I forgot who she was, who I was, why we were there. There was only the room, the heat, a singularity generating a rhythm as old as oceans.

I heard a deep groan and realized it came from me. Or maybe it was hers. She opened her eyes and looked back at me, pleading for something. I let go of her wrist and took hold of her hips. She gripped the edges of the dresser and moved up onto her toes, raising her ass higher. Her lips were moving but if there were words I couldn't hear them. Her legs were trembling. I felt her start to come and it took me over the edge. I dug my fingers more deeply into her hips. The pounding in my chest and in my head seemed to fuse together with everything else, my legs, my balls, my gut, her body beneath and before me, everything. Through it all I could hear her swearing in Hebrew again, could feel her coming in waves under me and all around me and myself coming with her.

Finally it subsided. I eased down on top of her, supporting some of my weight with my arms. We stayed that way, our breathing abating, our sweat drying, coming back to ourselves.

After a while, I eased myself up and stepped to the side. I touched her shoulder.

She pushed herself up off the dresser and looked at me. Neither of us said anything.

'You okay?' I asked, after a moment.

'Yeah,' she said. 'I'm okay.'

'You want to talk?'

'No, I want to get out of here.'

'Is that going to help?'

'No.'

'Then maybe we should talk.'

There was a pause. She looked down at what was left of her blouse and bra, then let them slide off her arms to the floor. She stepped out of her skirt.

'Tell me one thing, okay?' she asked.

'Yeah.'

'Tell me that you haven't done that before. Without a condom, I mean.'

I thought of Naomi, and, even more, of Midori. 'Not in a few years.'

She nodded. 'Good. Although at this point AIDS or whatever ought to be the least of my worries.'

'Tell me what's going on.'

She walked over to the shower and took a robe off the peg next to it. She pulled it on. I walked over and did the same. We moved over to the bed and sat on it.

'Those men you killed in Manila,' she said, looking at her hands. Her voice was slightly husky. 'Two of them were CIA officers.'

I looked at her. I saw that she was being straight with me. 'Shit,' I said.

She didn't respond. After a moment I said, 'How bad is it?'

'My people are afraid the Agency will find you and you'll talk. They don't want to take that chance.'

'So they sent you.'

She shrugged. 'What would you have done?'

'You came here to set me up?'

'I thought I did. Now I'm not sure.'

'That's not quite what I was hoping to hear.'

'It's the truth.'

'Couldn't pull the trigger yourself?'

'What I do is hard enough.'

We were silent for a minute while I digested the news. I said, 'What's next?'

She brushed away a few strands of hair that were clinging to her face. 'I'm supposed to call my contact, let him know when and where you'll be vulnerable.'

'What are you going to tell him?'

She looked up at the ceiling and said, 'I have absolutely no idea.'

'What changed your mind?' I asked, and thought, *Maybe you haven't, though. Maybe this is just the best set-up you've ever pulled off.*

I'd have to keep testing for that. I didn't think the way her body had responded could possibly have been acting. But maybe there were a bunch of dead men out there who had all convinced themselves of the same thing. And maybe I would be a fool to assume that the body would always follow the mind. Or vice versa.

There was a long silence. Then she said, 'You've been lucky so far. I don't know anyone who's been luckier for longer. But nobody's bulletproof. I can't keep bailing you out.'

'Bailing me out?'

'I warned you about that guy in your room in Macau.'

'I didn't need your warning.'

'No? You took it.'

I let it go. 'And this time?'

She looked at me. 'Enough, all right? You know why. I

134

don't want to be responsible for your death. You fucked up in Manila and I don't know if you're going to survive it. I just don't want to be the one who kills you. Or helps make it happen.'

'I wouldn't want to put you out.'

She glared at me. 'Stop being a child. You caused this situation, and now I'm caught in it, too.'

I paused and took a breath. I needed to think. There had to be a way out of this.

'What did they tell you happened in Manila?' I asked.

'Only what you told them. That you tried to hit Lavi in a restroom but his son came in and got in the way. Then the bodyguard and the other two guys burst in and Lavi and the boy got away.'

'Yeah, that's about right.'

'Why don't you give me your perspective, with details?'

I told her, leaving Dox out of it.

When I was finished, she said, 'That tracks with everything my people told me. At least they were being straight.'

'Do they know what Manny was doing with Agency operators?'

'If they do, they didn't tell me. Other than to say that Lavi is a known CIA asset.'

Something was nagging me, jostling for my attention. I parsed the facts, tried to identify the assumptions. Then I realized.

'How do your people know those men were CIA?' I asked.

She shrugged. 'I don't know. I didn't ask.'

I thought for a moment, then said, 'From what your people told me, Manny is a world-class bad guy. Not the kind of person the Agency can acknowledge is on the payroll. In fact, even post–nine-eleven, employing a character like

Manny is highly illegal. If it got out, there would be a lot of embarrassment. The people involved would probably have to take a fall.'

'I don't understand.'

I nodded. 'No, you don't, and your people might be having the same problem. You all work for a small, tightly knit organization that operates with little oversight and few constraints. But the CIA isn't like that. I've worked with them on and off for years and I know. They've been ripped apart again and again – the Church Commission, the purges under Stansfield Turner, now again with this guy Goss – and they've developed a Pavlovian aversion to risk. Should they be recruiting terrorists? Absolutely. But if you're the guy who does it, if you recruit, run, and God forbid pay someone who has American blood on his hands, and if the paperwork has your name on it, the first time some Congressional committee starts trying to assert its prerogatives, or the first time someone needs a sacrificial lamb, or the first time you make a bureaucratic enemy, you will absolutely be crucified.'

'You're assuming they were running Lavi. They might have been there to kill him, like you were.'

I shook my head. 'That wasn't it. The way they rushed into that bathroom after Manny hit the panic button, they'd spotted trouble and were on their way to protect him. Trust me, I know the difference.'

'All right, so they weren't there to harm him.'

'That's right. You see what I'm getting at? Something's not right here. Manny's not like some Second Secretary in the Chinese Consulate that everyone wants to take the credit for. He's an explosives guy, a terrorist with American blood on his hands. If someone's running Manny at the CIA, they're going to treat him like he's radioactive. They wouldn't send two officers to meet with him face-to-face. It doesn't make sense.'

She looked at me. 'If they weren't CIA . . .'

'Then I don't have a problem with the CIA. Or at least no more of a problem than usual. Maybe the situation is more fluid than it seems right now. Maybe I can take another crack at Manny.'

'I see your point.'

'Can you find out how your people know what they think they know?'

She glanced to her right, a neurolinguistic sign of construction. She was imagining how she was going to go about this. 'I'll see what I can do,' she said.

'What are you going to tell Gil?' I asked, trying to plug into exactly what she was envisioning.

'That . . .'

She looked at me, realizing what I'd done and how she had slipped. But the damage was done and she went on. 'I'll call him in the morning. I'll tell him I'd suggested we go snorkeling at a certain beach at a certain time, and that the suggestion had made you suspicious. That when I woke up you were gone.'

I figured it would be Gil. A killer knows a killer.

'Will he believe that?' I asked.

'He'll suspect. But it'll buy us time.'

'Do you trust him?'

She frowned. 'He's very . . . committed.'

'Yeah, I got that feeling.'

'But he's a professional. He does what he does for a reason. Take away the reason, and he'll move on to the next thing that keeps him awake at night.'

I nodded. Her assessment tracked with my own.

She rubbed her eyes. 'I need to sleep.'

I leaned over and touched her cheek. I looked in her eyes, wanting to know what I would see there.

Whatever it was, it was good enough. There was nothing more to say. We turned off the light and got under the covers. For a long time I listened to her breathing in the dark. After that I don't remember.

Delilah slept deeply for two hours, then woke from jet lag. She lay on her side and watched Rain sleep. God, what a mess.

She had come here convinced that he had screwed up and that there was no other way to solve the problem he had caused except for him to die. That he knew the risks and so in some ways deserved the outcome. But she realized now that all of this had been rationalization, psychic defense against an involvement she dreaded. Seeing him hadn't clouded her judgment, it had cleared it.

They'd hired him for a job, and he'd done the best he could without a lot to go on. What did they want him to do, slaughter a child? Had it come to that? With Gil, she knew, it had. If she confronted him, Gil would talk about 'greater evil and lesser evil' and 'collateral damage' and 'theirs and ours.' She didn't buy any of that. She didn't want to. That Rain was still able to make the moral distinction after so much time in the business – more time than Gil – impressed her. It gave her hope for herself. She wasn't going to help set him up for acting in a way even Gil, if pressed, would publicly profess was right. Yes, there was a problem, but the director, Boaz, Gil . . . they had simply proposed the wrong solution. She saw that now. All she had to do was find a better way. She felt confident that she could. If she couldn't . . . No, she didn't want to go there. Not unless she had to.

She was aware, on some level, that she was rationalizing, that her people would view her determination to find a third way as a betrayal. She didn't care. They weren't always as smart as they liked to think. And their investment was different than hers. To them, Rain was not much more than a piece on a chessboard. To her, he had become much more than that.

She liked him a lot, more than she had liked someone in a long time. The sex was good – God, better than good – but that was only part of it. She was also . . . comfortable with him. Until she had spent time with him in Rio, she hadn't noticed the absence of that kind of comfort in her life. It had disappeared so long ago, and she had been so overwhelmed with so many other things at the time, that it had never occurred to her to mourn its loss.

There had been many affairs, more than she could count. But none of those men, not one, knew what she did. No matter how intense the infatuation, no matter how satisfying the sex, she was always aware that they didn't, couldn't, really know her. They couldn't understand her convictions, sympathize with her doubts, soothe her frustrations, ameliorate the periodic ache in her soul. No wonder she tended to tire of them quickly.

Rain was different. From early on she realized he knew exactly what she did, although she had never spelled it out for him. He seemed to understand her without her ever needing to explain herself. He was patient with her moods. He knew, yes, but he didn't judge her. More than that, she sensed that he even admired her beliefs, the personal sacrifices she made for the cause that defined her. She had identified the absence of, and the longing for, a cause of his own as one of the key attributes of his persona, and remembered, with a slight pang of conscience, how she had reported on this to her people as something potentially exploitable.

There was comfort, too, in context: there was no

uncertainty about their status, no foolish hopes about where this might be leading. There could be no hurt or recriminations about why someone hadn't called or had to break an engagement. Even their different affiliations, and the potential conflicts of interest those affiliations might present, as indeed they had, were understood. In French they would call it *sympa,* simpatico. In English, the banal but perhaps more descriptive 'same sheet of music.' In its quiet way, it was really quite wonderful.

All of this mattered to her, but there was something more important, more improbable, still: she knew he trusted her. Of course he never abandoned his tactics, she wouldn't expect that. His moves were as subtle as she'd ever seen, and usually disguised as ordinary behavior, but she knew what he was doing. Meeting her at the gate in Bangkok and taking her to the domestic terminal by taxi had been a particularly nice, albeit undisguised, way to play it. If Gil or anyone else had been with her, the game would have been over right there. She suspected that there were other layers, possibly involving electronics, in his countermeasures, layers she hadn't detected. And she was aware from time to time that his 'innocent' questions involved hidden meanings and traps. But all of this was reflex for him, habit. She sensed the tactics were his way of reassuring himself that he hadn't gone soft, that he was still protected, that he wouldn't be so foolish as to trust someone like her.

She never would have told Gil or anyone else, but she knew from the moment they asked that Rain would take the meeting. She wondered what series of rationalizations he must have employed in agreeing to see her in Bangkok. Probably he told himself that it would be worth the risk because she might be able to tell him more about Lavi. And maybe he had been hoping for something like that, but she knew the real reason. The real reason was trust.

Watching him sleep, she felt a surge of gratitude so strong it brought tears to her eyes. She wanted to wake him with a kiss, hold his face in her hands and look in his eyes and thank him, really thank him, so that he could understand how much that trust, which not even the men she worked with extended to her, was worth. She smiled faintly at the ridiculous urge and waited for it to pass.

He was a strange man in many ways, and she found his strangeness appealing. Sometimes what she saw in his eyes reminded her of what had settled into her parents' after her brother had been killed in Lebanon. She found herself moved by that look, and by the way he would force it away if he saw her watching too closely. Once she had asked him if there had ever been a child. He told her no. She hadn't pressed, sensing that whatever equivalent events could produce that expression had to be approached gradually and obliquely, if at all.

She knew the odds were against them, but she didn't want to think about that now. She thought instead about how, when things were fixed, they would make up for how they had almost been set against each other. They'd been together in Macau, Hong Kong, now Thailand. All his territory. And, of course, Rio, which was somewhat of a neutral corner. She found herself wanting to take him to Europe, which felt like home now even more than Israel. Maybe Barcelona, or the Amalfi Coast. Somewhere he had never been, somewhere their time together would be fresh and unburdened by memory.

She watched him. She had never known a man who slept so silently. It was almost unnerving, that someone could be stealthy even in his sleep.

After a long time, she joined him.

10

I woke up early the next morning. Delilah was still sleeping. I got out of bed and padded silently over to the living area, sliding shut the teak doors that divided it from the sleeping area behind me. I picked up my cell phone and inserted one of the spare SIM cards I had purchased in Bangkok, effectively giving the phone a new identity. Then I went into the toilet stall, closed the door behind me, and turned the unit on. I needed to make two calls, and for the moment I wanted to keep them private. Ordinarily I prefer not to use a cell phone from a fixed location, but with the new SIM card the unit would be sterile. And the conversations would be brief.

First Tatsu, my old friend and nemesis at the Keisatsu-cho, the Japanese FBI. Tatsu owed me a lifetime of favors for having taken out Murakami, a *yakuza* assassin he'd wanted dealt with extrajudicially, and it was time for me to call one of those favors in.

His cell rang only once. Then I heard his voice. Never one to waste words or even syllables, he said only, *'Hai.'*

'Hello, old friend,' I said in Japanese.

There was a pause, and I imagined a rare smile. 'Hello,' he said. 'It's been a while.'

'Too long.'

'Are you in town?'

'No.'

'Then you are calling for information.'

'Yes.'

'What do you need?'

'Four days ago there was a shootout in a Manila shopping mall. I want to know everything you can tell me about the men who died there.'

Tatsu would be wondering whether I'd been involved, but he knew there would be no point in asking. 'All right,' he said.

'Thank you.'

'Everything is good?' he asked.

'The usual.'

'I'm sorry to hear that.'

I chuckled. 'Thank you, my friend.'

'Call me if you're ever in town. We can make small talk.'

I smiled. Tatsu was congenitally incapable of small talk, something I used to rib him over.

'We'll do that,' I said.

'*Jaa.*' Well then.

'*Jaa.*' I hung up.

The next call, I knew, would be more problematic. Higher risk, but also higher reward.

I punched in the number and waited while the call went through. I told myself that, if the men in Manila really had been CIA, I was in a world of shit anyway and the call couldn't do much to worsen my position. If they weren't, though, a call to the CIA itself would be my best chance of finding out.

This time, too, the phone was answered promptly with a curt '*Hai.*' I smiled, wondering briefly whether Tatsu was mentoring this young man. I suspected he was.

Tomohisa Kanezaki was a third-generation Japanese American and rising star at CIA Tokyo Station. We had found ourselves involved in several of the same off-the-books projects over the last couple years, and, as was the case with Tatsu, we had managed to work out what seemed to be a mutually beneficial modus vivendi. It was time to test the limits of that ambiguous relationship.

'Hey,' I said to him in English, knowing he would recognize the greeting and my voice.

There was a pause, then he said in English, 'I've been wondering when you would get in touch.'

'Here I am.'

'Looking for work?'

'Have you got any?'

'Not like we did. The post–nine-eleven urgency is beginning to fade. For a while there, we were really in a take-no-prisoners mindset, but that's going now. Shit, if we were the Department of Wildlife and Fisheries, we'd call what we've got now a "catch and release" program.'

'Sorry to hear that.'

'I'm sorry to say it.'

'I'm not looking for work anyway.'

'No?'

'No. I'm staying out of that business. It's too dangerous.'

He laughed.

'I need a favor,' I said.

'Sure.'

'I heard there was a shooting recently. In a Manila shopping mall.'

There was a pause, then he said, 'I heard the same thing.'

Shit. I couldn't imagine he would have heard about the shooting if the CIA weren't in some way involved. Maybe I shouldn't have called him. Well, too late now.

'You know anything about the deceased?' I asked. 'I heard they were company men.'

There was another pause. Then: 'They were ex-company.'

Ex-company. Interesting.

'You know what they were doing there?' I asked.

'I don't.'

'I think I might know something. If I tell you, can you see what you can find out?'

'I'll do what I can.'

Not exactly a binding promise, but I'd take what I could get.

'They were there for a meeting with a guy named Manheim Lavi. Israeli national, resident of South Africa. Check your files, you'll find out who he is.'

There was a pause. 'How do you know this?' he asked.

It was only reflex. He knew I wouldn't answer.

'Check your files,' I said again.

'I know who Manny is.'

I should have realized. When we were last in touch, Kanezaki had been responsible for a number of antiterrorism initiatives in Southeast Asia. If he knew his brief, and of course he did, Manny would be very much on his radar screen.

'All right. Any ideas about why some ex-company guys would be meeting with him in Manila?'

'All I know is that they were named Calver and Gibbons. They retired from the Agency two years ago. They were with NE Division – the Middle East. I didn't know them while they were here, but enough people did to make their deaths pretty big news. Everybody's talking about it.'

'If you can find out more, I'd like to know. Who they reported to when they were with the government, what they were up to lately. That kind of thing.'

There was a pause. 'Tell me you weren't involved in this,' he said.

'I told you, I'm not doing this stuff anymore.'

'Yeah? What are you doing instead?'

'I'm thinking about the greeting card industry.'

'That's funny. You going to wear a shoe phone?'

I smiled. 'Anything you can tell me, I'd be grateful.'

'You know where to look,' he said. Meaning the bulletin board.

'Thanks.'

'And don't forget. This isn't a one-way street. I'm taking a lot of chances here. I expect good information in return.'

'Of course.' I clicked off and shut the unit down.

I pulled on a pair of shorts and did my daily two hundred and fifty Hindu push-ups, five hundred Hindu squats, several minutes of neck bridges, front and back, and a variety of other bodyweight calisthenics and stretches. What you can get done with nothing more than a floor, your body-weight, and gravity in thirty minutes of nonstop activity would put the fitness equipment industry out of business if people caught on.

When I was done, I got in the shower. I lathered up to shave and winced when I touched my cheek. I checked in the mirrored surface of the shower door and saw that my cheek was bruised. Then I noticed that my forearms were black and blue, too. Damn, I was lucky that bag hadn't been filled with something heavier. And that I'd turned my face away from her head butt in time.

Delilah joined me just as I finished shaving. She looked at my cheek and said, 'Ouch.'

I looked at her. 'Don't worry, I accept your apology.'

She gave me an odd look – half smile, half glare. 'You deserved it,' she said. 'And then some.'

I decided to respond to the smile, not the glare. I put my arms around her and pulled her close.

Some time passed before I got to finish showering. This

time was slower, and a lot more tender. Thank God.

Afterward, Delilah stayed in the shower. I changed into jeans and an olive polo shirt and packed my bags.

I sat on the couch and waited for her. When she was done, she walked out into the suite naked. No makeup, wet hair. She looked great. I wished I could have had more time with her. Well, maybe there would be another chance. If we were lucky.

She pulled on a pair of navy silk shorts and a cream linen blouse. She sat next to me and brushed some wet hair back from her face.

'I've got some preliminary information,' I told her.

She raised her eyebrows, and I went on. 'I have a contact at the Agency. According to him, those men weren't active duty. They were retired.'

She frowned. 'What did you expect? You called the CIA, and your questions confirmed your guilt. Your contact reacted by lulling you, telling you there's less to worry about than you first thought. That's exactly what you would expect him to say.'

She had a devious mind. Probably she thought I was telling her this so she would feed it to Gil and company, maybe get them to rethink. She was discounting the information accordingly.

I shook my head. 'I've known this guy for a while. I don't think he would play it that way.'

'Let's hope not.'

'Check on your end. We'll see if we can resolve the apparent discrepancy. If we can find proof, or something like proof, maybe your people will get them to change their assessment before things turn really ugly.'

She nodded slowly as though considering, then said, 'I meant to tell you – I saw a big man, sandy-colored hair, outside the arrivals area in Bangkok and then again after dinner here. Did you notice him?'

'No,' I said, shaking my head automatically as though it was no big deal and probably just a coincidence. Damn, she'd caught me by surprise there.

She nodded. 'I thought it was odd that he was at the airport in Bangkok at the same time we were, and then here afterward, but that he wasn't on our flight.'

'Maybe he was waiting for someone and they caught a later flight.'

She looked at me. 'I'm surprised I spotted an incongruity and you didn't. I know you're attuned to the environment.'

Fuck. I knew she had me. Still, I struggled for a moment longer. I said, 'I guess I'm not as sharp as I used to be.' Given the less than adroit way I had just handled her probe, my words rang worryingly true.

'If you didn't know him and you hadn't noticed, I would have expected you to be more alarmed to learn of his presence,' she said, relentless.

I didn't say anything. Dox was blown. There was nothing I could do.

'Who is he?' she asked.

I sighed. 'My partner.'

She nodded as though she had already known, as indeed she had. 'He was with you in Manila?'

I shrugged. There was nothing to say.

'You might as well call him, then. We should talk.'

I realized I had never been with Dox in front of civilized company. The prospect made me uncomfortable.

'I don't think that's a good idea,' I said.

But she misunderstood my reticence. 'It would be more efficient for us to put our heads together.'

For the second time in as many days, I thought, *Nothing good can come of this*.

And for the second time I found myself saying, 'All right.'

I took out my cell phone and called him. He answered immediately. 'Everything okay?' he asked.

'Peachy,' I said, the code word to tell him that everything was indeed okay, that I wasn't under duress. 'But my friend noticed you at the airport, and again here. She'd like to meet you.'

'Oh man, how did she notice me? You must have told her.'

'I didn't. She just noticed you.'

'How? Damn, this is embarrassing.'

I looked at Delilah. She was smiling slightly, enjoying what she must have been making of the other side of the conversation.

'I told you, she's good,' I said.

'Yeah, apparently so. You going to give me a hard time about this?'

'God, yes.'

There was a pause. 'All right. I reckon I've got that coming. But not in front of her, okay? This is embarrassing enough.'

'All right.'

'Promise me.'

Christ. 'I promise.'

'Okay, where do you want to do this?' The tone was of a little boy resigned to a spanking.

'I think my room would be best. No sense the three of us being seen together.'

He sighed. 'I'll be there in a minute.'

I clicked off. Delilah asked, 'Was he upset?'

I shrugged. 'Embarrassed.'

She smiled. 'I would be, too.'

'I promised him I wouldn't be hard on him in front of you.'

Her smile broadened. 'That's what you were promising?'

I nodded and added innocently, 'But that was only me. You didn't promise anything.'

She chuckled and said, 'There's a streak of cruelty in you, I see.'

I looked at her.'How did you make him? Really.'

'I told you, the incongruities. But also . . . he's a big man, but when you look at him, it's almost like he's not there.'

I nodded. I saw no sense in telling her about his sniping background. I said, 'He's like Dr Jekyll and Mr Hyde. Most of the time he's as loud and obnoxious as an ambulance siren. But when he goes dark, he can damn near disappear.'

'That's what tipped me. I didn't notice him, but then I noticed that I didn't notice, you know what I mean? I took a second look, and realized how big he is. That's what told me he was a pro. It's not easy for a big man to make himself fade away like that. Even for a small one, it's rare.'

There was a knock at the door. I walked over, stood to the side, and leaned over to glance through the peephole. It was Dox.

I opened the door. He nearly blotted out the sun behind him. I turned and waved him inside.

Delilah stood. Dox looked at her a little sheepishly. Then he turned to me. His eyes widened slightly at the sight of my bruised cheek. His glance dropped to the wear and tear on my arms. His face lit up in his trademark grin.

'Well, I don't know what ya'll were doing last night, but I hope it was consensual,' he said.

Shit, I thought. Well, Dox had to be Dox. There was nothing anyone could do about it.

Delilah looked at him. Her expression was somewhere between mild amusement and gentle reproach. 'Really, is that any way to introduce yourself?' she asked softly, holding Dox's eyes.

Dox returned her look, and something strange came over him. The grin faded away and color crept into his cheeks. He dropped his hands in front of his pants as though he was holding a hat there, and said, 'Um, no. No, ma'am, it's not.'

I thought, *What the hell?*

She gave him an encouraging *that's better* smile and held out her hand. Her head was high, her posture erect and formal. 'I'm Delilah,' she said.

He reached for her hand and shook it once, his head bowing slightly as he did so. 'People call me Dox.'

She raised her eyebrows. '"Dox"?'

He nodded, and I noticed him unconsciously straighten, mirroring her posture. 'It's short for "unorthodox," ma'am. Which some people seem to think I am.'

Good God, it was like watching a ferocious-looking dog charge into a room, then roll over to have its belly scratched.

Her eyes twinkled with understanding and shared good humor. 'You don't seem unorthodox to me,' she said.

Dox's expression was almost grave. 'Well, I'm not,' he said. 'I'm the normal one. It's all those other folks who are unorthodox.' He paused, then added, 'Although I do kind of like the nickname. I've had it for a long time. You can use it, if you like.'

She smiled. 'I will. And please call me Delilah.'

He nodded and said, 'Yes, ma'am.' He reddened, and I could imagine him thinking, *Dumbass.* 'Delilah, I mean.'

'Why don't we sit down?' I said.

Dox turned to me as though suddenly remembering that I was in the room. He nodded. Then he turned to Delilah and gestured to the couch like the perfect southern gentleman. She smiled and walked over. I sat next to her. Dox took the chair and pulled it around so he was facing us.

Delilah and I briefed him on what we had discussed the night before and on what I had learned that morning.

When we were done, he said, 'I knew those boys were hitters from the way they moved. And I was afraid they might be of the CIA persuasion. Too bad, really. Ordinarily, I try to make it a habit not to offend spy organizations and their ilk.'

'That's the question,' I said. 'What organization we've really offended.'

'What about your people?' Dox asked, turning to Delilah. 'John tells me you're with the Mossad, or one of their affiliates.'

She raised her eyebrows and glanced at me. 'Is that what he says?'

Dox shrugged. 'Professional outfit, if you don't mind my saying so. I worked with some Israeli snipers some years back.'

Snipers. Shit, he might as well have handed her his CV.

'What did you think?' she asked.

'I liked them a lot. Arrogant badasses – uh, guys, I mean – with every reason to be. They taught me as many tricks as I did them.' He broke out in the grin. Talking about sniping was more familiar territory for him. He glanced at me and said, 'It takes a special kind of karma to offend the CIA and the Mossad, and both at the same time. If it had happened to someone else, I'd be laughing about it.' Then he looked at Delilah and his expression sobered again. 'I sure hope you can do something to help us out of this situation we're in before it gets any nastier.'

Delilah nodded. 'I'll try.'

Dox bowed his head. 'Well, I'm grateful to you. So's my partner.'

Delilah looked at me. 'How do I contact you?'

I gave her one of the cell phone SIM card numbers. I would leave the phone off most of the time so that no one could track it. But I could check the voice mail from time to time securely enough, and more frequently and easily than I could the bulletin board.

'All right,' I said. 'Time to beat a hasty retreat. I'll take care of the checkout.'

Dox and I stood up. I leaned over Delilah and kissed her.

'Thank you,' I said.

She shook her head. 'Don't thank me yet.'

Hilger had gotten back to his apartment on Lugard Road in the Mid-Levels at well past sunrise that morning. He was sleeping with the aid of a black eyeshade when his cell phone rang on the bed stand next to him. He sat up instantly, pulled off the eyeshade, and blinked at the light coming through his bedroom window. He breathed in and out hard and cleared his throat. He had a feeling he knew who might be calling, even though there was no rational reason for his confidence.

He picked up the phone and said, 'Hilger.'

'Hello, Mr Hilger. Our mutual friend gave me your number.'

The voice was soft and assured, lightly Arabic-accented. Hilger smiled. He had been right. It was VBM.

'Good,' Hilger said. 'Thank you for calling.'

'This line is secure?' the voice asked.

'Absolutely,' Hilger responded.

The voice stayed oblique anyway. 'It seems there was a problem in Manila.'

'Yes, there was,' he responded, staying oblique himself to keep the man comfortable. 'Our mutual friend has enemies, as you know.'

'And?'

'The problem has been resolved.' It didn't feel like a lie because he expected it to be true soon. Hell, maybe it was true already.

'All right.'

'If you're still in the area, I hope we can still meet. I'd like to come to the meeting personally.'

'You weren't able to make it personally last time?'

The man was pressing. Maybe he was the petty type. Maybe he was just testing Hilger's mettle. It didn't matter. Hilger said, 'I wasn't. But perhaps that's for the best.'

He heard the man chuckle. All right, that was good.

'Where do you propose we meet?' the voice asked.

'Why don't you come here, to Hong Kong? You'll be my guest. I'll put you up in the best hotel. We can charter a boat, go to the horse races, whatever you like.'

'I'm afraid I'll be pressed for time.'

Yes, the man was the petty type. He wanted to show that he was setting limits, that he was in charge. But the main thing was that he had implicitly agreed to the substance of what Hilger had proposed. The trick now was to close on that substance and at the same time let the man feel he was in control.

'I understand,' Hilger said. 'Still, if your schedule permits, I think you'll find a first-class, all-expenses-paid visit to Hong Kong to be very enjoyable.'

There was a pause, and he could feel the man considering. In Hilger's experience, the wealthy were typically the cheapest, greediest people on the planet. With the people he had behind him, this guy could probably buy half of Hong Kong, yet he was salivating at the prospect of someone buying a tiny part of it for him.

'We'll see,' the voice said.

Hilger knew that meant yes. He smiled and said, 'Why don't I make a few arrangements and post them on the bulletin board. Would tomorrow for dinner be possible? We can discuss business then, and after, if you have time, you can stay for a few days as my guest.'

'Dinner tomorrow will work,' the man said, committing to the only part Hilger gave a shit about.

'Excellent,' Hilger said. 'I'll make the arrangements and post them right away.'

'Very good.' The man hung up.

Hilger got up and walked over to his desk. He fired up his laptop, then spent a few minutes thinking. With Calver and Gibbons gone, it made sense to bring Winters to the VBM meeting. Winters was coming to Hong Kong anyway, to brief Hilger on what he got from Rain and Dox. VBM might not like the slight surprise, but at that point he wouldn't back out. It would be worth temporarily ruffling the man's feathers to have backup at the meeting, and to have someone to whom he could delegate after. And he'd still need Manny there to offer his imprimatur. That would make a nice party of four. Hilger knew just the place.

He spent the next hour on the phone and the Internet, making the arrangements, alerting the players. When he was done, he checked one of the secure bulletin boards.

Son of a bitch, he thought, feeling a flush of pride at the quality of the men he worked with. There had been a break, a bit of luck that had enabled Hilger's people to track Dox to Bangkok. The man had made a mistake, and it was going to cost him. If Rain was with him, as Hilger was betting he was, it would cost them both.

His phone rang again.

'Hilger,' he said.

'It's me,' the caller said.

Hilger recognized the slightly nasal voice on the other end. His contact on the National Security Council.

'Go ahead.'

'We've got a new problem.'

Hilger waited.

The contact said, 'I got a call this morning. A reporter from the *Washington* fucking *Post.*'

Hilger's concern expressed itself in a feeling of almost deliciously cool calm.

'What did he want?'

'He wanted to know about a rumor that the men in Manila were CIA officers and had died while meeting with a known terrorist.'

'Did he have anything else?'

'Not that he said.'

'Maybe he was fishing.'

'I doubt it. His information was pretty accurate in certain respects. I think it's more likely that he has a source.'

Shit, someone was putting together the pieces pretty quickly.

'He's going to run a story?'

'I don't think so. Not yet. I think he's looking for more information, corroboration.'

'Then we still have time.'

'Listen, I used up a lot of capital to straighten things out after Kwai Chung. I don't know if I can do that again.'

Hilger breathed once, in and out. He said, 'You won't have to.'

'You need to put this thing to sleep quickly,' the voice answered. 'We can't afford the scrutiny. Not again.'

Yeah, no shit.

'It's being handled today,' Hilger told him. 'I'll call you when it's done.'

'Okay. Good.'

Hilger clicked off. He looked at his phone, wondering how it was going in Bangkok. For a moment, he thought that maybe he should have been there himself, to oversee things. But no. Winters was the best. Hilger had seen him in action and it wasn't a pretty sight. But the man got results.

Hilger glanced at his desk clock. Maybe he was getting those results right now.

Part Two

12

Delilah waited an hour to make sure that Rain and Dox had sufficient time to depart, then called Gil on his cell phone.

He answered on the first ring, and she imagined him as she always did at this stage in an operation, sitting alone in a dim hotel room, needing neither food nor other sustenance, the cell phone placed on a table or desk in front of him, silently and patiently waiting for the unit to ring so that he could venture wraith-like into the world and do what he was best at.

'*Ken,*' she heard him say in Hebrew. Yes.

'It's me,' she answered. There was no response. Ignoring what she interpreted as one of his little power games, she went on. 'Our friend left this morning. Packed his bags and took off.'

There was a pause, then he said, 'Shit. Where are you?'

'Phuket.'

'Why didn't you call sooner?'

'I never had a chance. I was with him the whole time.'

'Doesn't he sleep?'

'Do you?'

There was a pause, no doubt while he tried to think of a good response. When he couldn't, he said, 'So he took you to Phuket.'

She caught the innuendo and felt a surge of anger. 'You know how it is, Gil,' she said. 'Some men just have the right touch with women. They know how to get what they want.'

As soon as it was out, she regretted it. Mostly, her deep-seated need not to take shit served her well, but this time it was going to hinder her. She wanted information from Gil. To get it, she had to manage him, manipulate him, not react by reflex to his constant, petty provocations. Yes, she was counterpunching, but he was still making her fight his kind of fight. The way to win was to change the game entirely.

Gil was silent on the other end of the phone, and she considered the possibility that her comment had actually wounded him. The thought softened her anger, made her feel more generous. She sensed that this feeling might be useful.

She considered. Maybe what Gil needed was just a victory in their constant verbal sparring. Maybe it would restore his sense of manhood, allow him to behave in some way other than trying to hurt her. She'd often thought that this was what the government needed to do with the Palestinians. After all, it was only after the Yom Kippur War, after giving Israel a bloody nose, that Egypt had been willing to make peace. Maybe Gil was the same. And maybe, if he found himself enjoying an unfamiliar position of success and power, he might be generous, or anyway careless, with information. Yes, that was the way to play it. Let him win.

After a moment he asked, 'Well, what happened?'

'I think he got suspicious.'

'Any idea about where he's gone?'

'No.'

'Shit,' he said again.

Shit, sure. For Gil, not being able to kill someone he had fixed in his sights must have felt like coitus interruptus.

'Where are you?' she asked.

'Bangkok.'

She had expected that. She had told them she was

traveling to Bangkok to meet Rain. Gil would have wanted to be as close as possible so he could move quickly.

'I have to pass through Bangkok to get wherever I'm going next,' she said. 'Why don't we meet there and I'll brief you?' And then, as though she had only just thought of it and hadn't actually been planning this, she added, 'Or you could come here. It's beautiful and I don't know when either of us will have another chance.'

There was a long pause. Then he said, 'It's better if you come here.'

The pause told her he had been tempted by her suggestion of Phuket as the venue, perhaps by the way she had subtly conjoined the two of them with her use of the plural pronoun. The reply itself told her he was suspicious; otherwise, the temptation would have prevailed.

'Okay,' she said. 'I'll catch the next flight and call you when I arrive. It should be just a few hours, if that.'

'Okay,' he said, and hung up.

She nodded. An unfamiliar place, just the two of them, far from the people they knew . . . all an ideal environment for getting someone to relax and open up. She had seen it many times before. Hell, John had just used it on her.

She had the hotel car take her to the airport and was able to get a Thai Air flight that left less than an hour later. She called Gil when she arrived at Bangkok airport. He asked her if she could get to the Oriental Hotel and meet him on the restaurant veranda, overlooking the river. She told him she would be there within an hour.

The midday traffic wasn't too awful, and the ride took less than forty minutes. The moment she saw the hotel, she understood why Gil had chosen it. A classic colonial structure, it sprawled across a city block and would have entrances and exits all over. Guests could leave via cab, tuk-tuk, or some sort of river taxi adjacent to the hotel entrance. And the security, though subtle, was everywhere, in the form of surveillance cameras and guards with earpieces. All of which would make it hard to establish a choke point for an ambush, hard to carry out the ambush without being captured on videotape, and hard to follow someone out of the hotel without staying unacceptably close. Gil wasn't just suspicious; he was downright worried that she had gone over to the other side.

For a moment, she felt the familiar indignant anger rising. Then she realized: *He's not entirely off the mark.*

She walked through the lobby and out onto the veranda. Gil was leaning on the balcony as though in appreciation of the tourist-perfect river scene beyond. But he checked his back within a moment of her arrival and saw her. He straightened and nodded. As she approached, she saw him look behind her, then to his flanks. He was wearing an untucked, short-sleeved, button-down shirt, like most of the other tourists here. The difference being that, in Gil's case, the casual local attire would make it easier for him to conceal the pistol Delilah knew he carried. Gil was right-handed, and, with the shirt out, he probably had the gun on his right hip, which she judged to be the appropriate compromise here between concealment and access. Not that her take on all this was particularly relevant at the moment – this was Gil, after all, and, even if he was an asshole, they were on the same side – but such assessments had become second nature to her, and went on in the background regardless of whom she was meeting.

'Nice place,' she said, ignoring his obvious suspicions.

He nodded and said nothing. He was coiled tight, she could feel it. She would have to find a way to calm him down.

'What do you want to do?' she asked. 'Stay here? Go somewhere else?'

He looked at her for a long moment, then shrugged. 'We can stay here.'

'Good. I'm hungry.'

They ate at the Verandah Restaurant overlooking the river. It was a beautiful scene, and she was able to take in all of it because Gil took the seat that put his back to the water. Having her back to the door wasn't her favorite way to sit, but many of her targets had some security consciousness and she was used to the disadvantage. Call it an occupational hazard.

They ordered *khao phad goong* – they were in Bangkok, after all, and might as well take advantage of the local cuisine – and talked. She explained how things had gone with Rain since she had first met him at the airport in Bangkok. She let Gil ask the questions. At first, he indulged himself with some periodic innuendo. She had anticipated this, and planned to ignore it, but after a few annoying jabs she found herself saying, 'Look, can we just be professional about this?' That seemed to sober him, and she realized that her reaction, more genuine than the gambit she had originally planned, had been the better choice. From then on, he kept the bullshit in check, and she answered his questions as forthrightly as he would expect. She wanted this to feel more like a debriefing than a briefing. That would be more comfortable for him. It would make him feel in charge.

He glanced around frequently. To an outsider, it would have looked like he was enjoying his exotic surroundings, trying to take it all in. Or perhaps that he was waiting for someone, looking up from time to time to see if the other party had arrived. But she knew where it was coming from.

And she didn't like that it wasn't going away. She decided to call him on it.

'Am I making you nervous?' she asked, during one of his perimeter checks, with a friendly, slightly amused smile.

He looked at her. 'No.'

Her smile broadened, but its gentleness remained. 'I thought for a moment that you didn't trust me.'

'I don't trust anyone.'

That, she suspected, was the sad truth.

'But me, in particular,' she said, as though this was something she regretted.

'It's not personal.'

'Are you sure?' Her tone had just the right mixture of sadness and uncertainty.

He shook his head, afraid or unwilling to go there. 'What would have tipped him off?' he asked.

She recognized that the gambit hadn't succeeded. It was all right, she would keep playing it by ear. She shrugged. 'He's naturally paranoid. Up until my suggestion of a private beach, he'd been in charge of the arrangements. Someone else proposing the time and place . . .'

'You shouldn't have been in such a hurry. That's what spooked him.'

Ordinarily, that kind of comment would cause her to go for the jugular. That's what Gil was expecting, and prepared to deal with. But she'd sparred with him enough today. If he wanted to push hard, she would just step out of the way. Let's see him keep his balance then.

'I know,' she said, looking down as though this was a difficult admission, as though he had worn her out. 'I'm sorry. I should have been more subtle with him. It's my fault.'

There was a pause while Gil digested this. Then he

said, 'It's not like you, that's all. Your instincts are usually good.'

Ostensibly a compliment, but really a way of demonstrating that it was his purview and prerogative to judge. And therefore, again, a comment that would ordinarily set her off.

She smiled wanly, as though both appreciative of his expression of confidence and embarrassed by what had precipitated it, then looked away.

After a moment, he said, 'Don't worry about it. We'll find another way.'

Her earlier realization that she had hurt him had softened her, and now her apparent surrender was having the same effect on him. Good.

She looked at him and said, 'Thanks.'

He shook his head and looked away as though embarrassed by her gratitude. She saw her opening and said, 'Gil. Why are you always so . . . hostile to me?'

His expression was of someone trying to look perplexed and not quite pulling it off. 'Hostile to you? I'm not hostile.'

'Come on, you know you are. I can feel it all the time.'

He shook his head again. 'Look, I've got a job to do and I'm serious about it. I don't always have time to be diplomatic. Some people don't understand that.'

Sure, that's part of it, she thought, respecting his instinct for offering up something that wasn't untrue, but simply half true.

She offered a self-conscious laugh. 'Okay, maybe I'm being too sensitive.'

'You've got a hard job, too,' he offered. 'I know that.'

She looked down, as though his kindness had touched some deep part of her psyche, as though she wanted to tell him something more, but didn't know how to find the words. She noted that he hadn't done one of his visual scans in almost a minute.

They were halfway to a connection. She knew he would be finding the prospect attractive, and wouldn't want her to pull back from it now.

'I'll put up another message on the bulletin board,' she said. 'Tell him I'm offended that he would leave me like that. Maybe I can get him to meet me again.'

Gil nodded. She sensed that he would have preferred to stay on a less operational track. That he might unconsciously be willing to jump through a few hoops to get back to it.

'Or maybe we could get a lead from the CIA,' she went on. 'They're looking for him, too. Have they made any inquiries with us?'

'No.'

'No? I would have thought they might check with friendly intelligence services.'

'Not yet.'

She nodded, then said, 'You know, I was thinking about something. It'll sound strange, but ... Are we sure those men were CIA?'

He nodded, probably enjoying the feeling of having information that she lacked, enjoying being in a position where she would have to ask him. 'We're sure,' he said.

'Because, you know how the Americans are. It would be hard for them to run a guy like Lavi. If Congress found out, someone could get in trouble.'

Gil laughed. Making fun of CIA fecklessness was like fishing in a barrel. And the joke had reminded him subtly that, c'mon, Gil, we're not like that. We're on the same team.

'Look,' he said. 'About a year ago, when we first got

suspicious about what Lavi might be up to, I led the team that monitored him with spot surveillance and electronically. We saw him meet more than once with an American who I knew in the first Gulf War as Jim Huxton, but who now seems to go by Jim Hilger. At the time, Hilger was with America's Third Special Forces. The two Americans who Rain killed in Manila were part of Hilger's unit. After the war they all left the military to work for the CIA.'

She was surprised that his ties went back so far. 'You . . . worked with them?'

He nodded. 'Targeting Hussein's mobile SCUD missile launchers. I don't know what else they were up to. They certainly didn't tell us about it.'

She considered. 'They told you they were going into the CIA?'

He shrugged. 'You know. Nudge, nudge, wink, wink. But Hilger's behavior with Lavi confirms it, not that any confirmation was necessary. We've got electronic intercepts. Hilger has a CIA cryptonym: "Top Dog." You want to know the crypt they gave Lavi?'

She nodded.

'Jew-boy,' he said.

'Wow.'

He shrugged again. 'That's how we know.'

'Do we know what those men were doing with Lavi in Manila?'

'We don't. We didn't know they were going to be there, obviously, or we would have warned Rain off.'

'What do you think the Agency was getting from Lavi?'

'I don't know. Whatever it was, they weren't sharing it with us. If they were, we might have decided Lavi was more useful alive than dead, at least for a while. As it is, the government just wants people like Lavi . . .' He waved a hand as though throwing something away, disposing of it.

'So someone else can take his place,' she said, with a genuinely sad smile.

'You know how it is. Disrupt and deprive is the name of the game. Taking out Lavi will disrupt networks that rely on him. And deprive them of his expertise.'

She nodded. Now was the moment to return the conversation to its more personal flavor. She would oblige him, but not in the way he was hoping.

'Remember that time in Vienna?' she asked, looking at him.

He returned her look but didn't answer. She knew he wanted to say 'yes' to get her to continue, but that he was afraid that uttering the word would be to confess to something he didn't want to acknowledge.

'It's not that I didn't want to. But I can't. With colleagues, I have to have distance. Otherwise I would lose my mind. Can you understand?'

He nodded uncomfortably. What else could he do?

'I admire you for what you do,' she went on. 'I know it must be difficult. I just . . . just wanted to tell you that.'

The subtext was, there are so many other things I would like to say. Feeling admired, even desired, couldn't help but soften him. Or fail to distract him from the more substantive inquiries she had just made.

'It's okay,' he said, and gave her a fleeting and hesitant smile.

She had gotten him to agree that nothing was going to happen this time. And to hope, by implication, that there might be a time in the future.

She gave him a smile of her own. Men were so easy.

13

Back in Bangkok, Dox and I checked into the Grand Hyatt Erawan on Ratchadamri. It wasn't as discreet a hotel as the Sukhothai, but I'm not usually comfortable using the same place twice in a row. What it lacked in low-key charm, though, the Erawan made up for operationally: it offered multiple entrances and exits on two floors and a significant security infrastructure in the form of guards and cameras. Ordinarily, surveillance and security are a hindrance to me and I try to avoid them. But this time, I wanted to be some-place that would offer obstacles to anyone who might think to visit me unexpectedly. Not that anyone knew where I was, but I always sleep better with multiple layers in place. And if one of those layers takes the form of 300-thread count cotton sheets . . . well, there aren't so many perks to this profession. I take them when I can.

There was nothing to do now but wait, and I let Dox talk me into another evening on the town. I had enjoyed our meal together a few nights before, enjoyed it much more than the usual solitary night in a hotel room, and he didn't have too hard a time persuading me. This time, though, I got to choose the venue.

I headed down to the lobby to meet him at eight o'clock as we had agreed. He was early again, and again looked very much the local expat in an untucked, short-sleeved, cream-colored linen shirt and jeans. He seemed to be absorbed in a book. As I got closer I noticed the title: *Beyond Good and Evil.*

'You're reading Nietzsche?' I asked, incredulous.

He looked at me. 'Well, sure, why not?'

I struggled for a moment, concerned that whatever I said next would be insulting. 'Well, it's just . . .'

He smiled. 'I know, I know, everybody thinks a southern boy can't be intellectual. Well, my father worked for a big pharmaceutical company, and I grew up in Germany, where he was posted. I studied old Friedrich in school, and I liked him. All that stuff about the will to power and all. When I read it now, it comforts me.'

'Who'da thunk it,' I said, imitating his twang.

He laughed. 'Hey, how did you even recognize what I was reading, cowboy? That's more than I would have expected.'

I shrugged. 'When I was a kid, I always seemed to be on the wrong side of one gang or another. I found the best place to hide was the library. They never thought to look for me there. Eventually I got bored and started reading the books. I never stopped.'

'Never stopped getting on the wrong side of gangs?'

I laughed. 'It seems that way, doesn't it. Never stopped reading, is what I meant.'

'So that's where you get some of those big words you like to use. I found myself wondering from time to time. Plus you never seem put off by my own extensive vocabulary. Even a word like "perineum," it seems like second nature to you.'

'It's good of you to say.'

He closed the book and stood up. 'Well, where are we off to tonight? Discotheque? Massage parlor?'

'I was thinking more along the lines of taking in a fight at Lumpini, then maybe a bar. An adult bar.'

'Sure, I love to see a little Thai boxing. Not sure about the adult bar, though . . . Is it like an adult video? I like those a lot.'

'You might be disappointed, then. But you should still give it a try.'

He grinned. ''Course I'll give it a try. Hell, I'm a trisexual, partner, I'll try anything once.'

We took the stairs to the basement, then exited through the Amarin Plaza shopping mall. Out on the street, Dox started to flag down a cab.

'Wait,' I said. 'Let's move around a little first.'

'Move around . . . Look, man, is that really necessary? We did a route on the way to the hotel earlier. We know we're clean.'

'Just because you were clean before doesn't mean you're clean now. You took a shower yesterday, right? Does that mean you don't need one today?'

'Yeah, but . . .'

'There are ways to track someone other than physically following them. Think about what Delilah said. We've got some motivated people looking for us. Let's not make it easy for them.'

He sighed. 'All right, all right. I just don't want to miss the fights, is all.'

We walked to Chit Lom station and took the sky train one stop to Phloen Chit. We waited on the platform until all the passengers had cleared, then got back on and rode back to Siam. We took the elevator down to the street level, then ducked across one of the sois to Henri Dunant, where we caught a cab.

Dox looked at his watch. 'Satisfied now? We're going to miss half the fights.'

'The good fights start at nine.'

He looked at me. 'You know Thailand better than you've been letting on, partner?'

I shrugged. 'I've spent some time here. Not lately, though, and not like you.'

'You're a mysterious man, Mr Rain.'

I winced slightly at the mention of my name. All right, I know I'm paranoid, as Harry used to tell me: the name wouldn't mean a thing to the cabdriver, who had picked us up utterly at random and who doubtless spoke no English regardless. But what was the upside of using a name? If your paranoia doesn't cost you anything, I figure, why not indulge it? It's worked for me so far.

But I let it go. I was learning that with Dox, as perhaps in all things, I had to pick my battles.

The cab ride to Lumpini stadium took ten minutes. We bought ringside seats for fifteen hundred baht apiece and went inside.

Muay Thai, or Thai boxing, is Thailand's indigenous form of pugilism. The contestants wear gloves, and in this and a few other respects the art is superficially similar to Western boxing. But Thai boxers also legally and enthusiastically fight with their feet, knees, elbows, and heads, even from grappling tie-ups that Western referees would immediately separate. The feel of a match is different, too, with none of the trash-talking that has come to dominate so many American sports. Instead, Thai boxers warm up together in the ring, largely ignoring each other as they perform the *wai khru* dances by which they pay homage to their teachers, and they fight to music, a blood-maddening mix of clarinet, drums, and cymbals. During my years in Japan I worked with an ex-fighter who had come to the Kodokan to study judo. We taught each other many things, and I came away

174

with a lot of respect for the ferocity and effectiveness of this fighting system.

The stadium was purely functional: three tiers of seats, pitted concrete floors, stark incandescent lights shining murderously into the ring. The air reeked of accumulated years of sweat and liniment. The second tier of seats was the most crowded, and the most uniformly Thai, as this was where the hard-core betting went on, and each solid shin kick or roundhouse was greeted from that section with a chorus of cries that had as much to do with commerce as with bloodlust.

We caught the last three fights of the evening. As always I was impressed with the skill and heart these men brought to the ring, and this time I found myself a little envious, too. When I was their age I had been at least that quick, and my speed had pulled me through any number of unpleasant close encounters. But my reflexes, though still good, and despite a careful diet, supplement, and exercise regimen, weren't the same anymore. I touched the knife in my pocket, and thought, *Well, that's what toys are for. Along with evolving tactics.*

Dox was characteristically boisterous, hollering enthusiastically during the fights and even getting up to offer some congratulations in Thai to the winners as they left the ring. I would have preferred it if he had been able to keep a lower profile, but I recognized that this would be impossible for him. I reminded myself that, if I wanted this fledgling partnership to go anywhere, I would have to try to accept Dox more or less as he was.

When the last match had ended, we headed outside. Dox said, 'Well, the night is young. Are we going to hit that "adult bar"?'

I nodded. 'Yeah, if you're not too tired.'

He grinned. 'I'm good if you are. Let's get a cab.'

He saw my expression and said, 'Oh, man, not again . . .'

'Just down the street. We'll walk along Lumpini Park. We can get a cab from there. It'll be easier, there are fewer people.'

'Along Lumpini Park? There won't be any people.'

'Well, that's even better. No competition at all.'

He sighed and nodded, and I realized with an odd sense of gratitude that he was doing the same sort of 'if I want this thing to work' calculus that I was.

We walked, then found a cab. It took only a few minutes to get to the place I had in mind: Brown Sugar, Bangkok's best jazz club.

The club was on Soi Sarasin, opposite the northwest corner of giant Lumpini Park. It announced its presence quietly and with confidence: a simple green awning with white lettering that proclaimed 'Brown Sugar – The Finest Jazz Restaurant.' A redbrick façade and a lacquered wooden doorway, the door propped open, inviting. A window with rows of glass shelving displaying odds and ends – a ceramic bourbon decanter sporting a map of Kentucky, an antique martini mixer, a collection of tiny glass bottles, twin coffee canisters, a demitasse, ceramic soldiers in Napoleonic garb. A few wooden tables and chairs along the sidewalk in front, illuminated only by whatever light escaped from the club inside.

I was gratified to find the place still thriving. It was bracketed to the right by an alley and to the left by a cluster of neon-lit bars with names like Bar D and The Room and Café Noir. Unlike Brown Sugar, which had a classic – some might say run-down – feel to it, the others all looked new. I had a feeling that none of the upstarts would be here a year from now. Brown Sugar might be older, but it had what it takes to go the distance.

We got out of the cab, crossed the street, and went inside. A sign by the door said the band playing was called Anodard. Anodard turned out to be two guitars, sax, keyboards, drums, and a pretty female vocalist. They were doing a nice cover of Brenda Russell's 'Baby Eyes,' and the main room, a cramped, low-ceilinged space that could hold probably thirty people on a good night, was about three-quarters full. The décor was exactly as it should be: dim lighting, a bare ceiling, worn tables and floor, fading jazz memorabilia on the walls. I hoped no one would ever think to give the place a face-lift. We took a table on the right side of the bar, with a view of the band. Brown Sugar's only real failing is its unimaginative selection of single malts, but I made do with a Glenlivet eighteen-year-old. Dox ordered a Stoli rocks. We settled back, sipped our drinks, and listened to the music. It turned out to be more pop than jazz, but Anodard was good and that was the main thing.

It was a little odd to take in live music with a companion. Usually I go to a club alone, coming and going quietly and unobtrusively and without having to worry about whether anyone was enjoying the experience as much as I. About a half hour in, when the band took a break, I said to Dox, 'Well? What do you think?'

He frowned as though in concentration. 'Well, it's taking me a little getting used to. Most of the Bangkok establishments with which I'm acquainted have girls dancing on tabletops and wearing numbers on their bikini bottoms. But I can see the appeal.'

I nodded. 'All right, there's hope for you.'

'And that singer is sexy, too.'

'Faint hope.'

He laughed. 'You know, partner, that Delilah's a classy lady. I don't know what she's doing with a reprobate like you.'

'I don't know, either.'

He gave me a smile that was half leer. 'Looks like she smacked you up pretty good there. Didn't know you liked that kind of thing.'

I glanced around for the waitress.

'I like it when a lady isn't afraid to get passionate,' he went on in a thoughtful tone, apparently unperturbed by my lack of response. 'Damn, just thinking about it is turning me on.'

'Feel free not to share,' I said.

'Oh come on, we're partners and friends and we're here in the great state of Bangkok, land of smiles! We can let our hair down a little.'

'Dox, your hair's never been up.'

'I'll take that as a compliment. Anyway, I think your lady is going to help us. I've got a good feeling about her.'

'Yeah?'

'Yeah.'

'You can't always go on a feeling.'

'Well, partner, lacking your well-developed sense of universal paranoia, I'm often left with nothing more than my gut to fall back on. And it's served me well so far, seeing as I'm even here to talk about it.'

I was surprised to find that his words stung a little. Ever since we'd left Phuket, I'd been half-consciously playing scenarios through my head, testing my hope that Delilah was being straight with us. I thought she was. I just wished I could have Dox's simple confidence.

'We'll see,' was all I said.

The waitress came by, and we ordered another round. Periodically a new couple or group would drift in from outside. I was pleased to see Dox checking the door each time this happened. In professionals this should be a quick, unobtrusive reflex, performed as unconsciously as breathing.

You always want to know who's joining you, to maintain your sense of the crowd.

At one point, I looked up to see a striking Thai girl enter the club. She was wearing a pewter silk jacquard blouse, sleeveless and with a mandarin collar, a clingy black silk skirt, cut just above the knee, and strappy, open-toe stilettos. Her makeup was perfect, and her hair was done in a neat chignon that accentuated her perfect posture and confident gait. Drop earrings that looked like jade gleamed under each ear.

She sat down at the bar like royalty on a throne and looked around the club. Dox nudged me and said, 'You see that girl who just came in?'

I nodded, wondering whether I'd been giving Dox too much credit for what I thought were perimeter checks. It looked like the more likely explanation might be excessive horniness.

The woman saw Dox and smiled. He smiled back.

Great, I thought. *Here we go.*

'You see that, man?' he asked. 'She smiled at me.'

I looked back at him. 'She's probably a prostitute, Dox. She smiles at everyone. Especially Westerners who she assumes have money to buy her jade earrings.'

'Partner, I don't care how she makes her living. She might freelance a little, who could blame her? That ain't the point. The point is, she likes me. I can tell.'

'She likes your money.'

'She might like that, too, and I might even tip her, as a show of my appreciation and just to help her out generally. But I wouldn't be attracted to her if she didn't want me for me. Watch, you'll see.'

He looked over again and gave her a long smile. She smiled back, then said something to the bartender and got up. She started heading in our direction.

Dox looked at me. 'What did I tell you?'

The confidence she displayed in brazenly approaching Dox told me I'd been right in suspecting she was a prostitute. But it occurred to me that her presence here was a little odd. The high-end hookers tended to troll dance clubs and bars like Spasso at the Grand Hyatt, not authentic, out-of-the-way dives like Brown Sugar. Well, she might not have been having any luck in one of the places next door, and might have drifted in here for the music, or for the hell of it. Still, as it always does in response to something out of place, my alertness bumped up a notch. Although I had already been keeping a routine, low-level awareness of what was going on in the room, I glanced around just to confirm that nothing else was wrong. Everything seemed okay.

The girl came over to our table. I checked her hands. Right hand empty, left holding a tiny black evening bag, probably weighed down by no more than a cell phone, lipstick, and a mirror. I didn't pick up any danger signals. But my sense that something was out of place wasn't entirely placated, and I remained watchful.

She glanced at me, then at Dox. 'Hi,' she said, in a voice that was both sweet and slightly husky. 'My name is Tiara.' She had a heavy Thai accent.

'Well, hello, Tiara,' Dox said, offering her an enormous grin. 'I'm Bob, and this here is Richard. But most people call him Dick.' He glanced at me and his grin broadened.

The girl held out her hand to Dox, who shook it. She offered it to me. I caught her fingers and gave them a gentle squeeze. Her fingertips were smooth, with no calluses. As she withdrew from my grasp I glanced at her hand. Her fingers were long and perfectly manicured, and the light caught her polished nails as though they were little jewels.

'Would you like to join Dick and me for a drink?' Dox asked.

The girl offered a radiant smile and made some microscopic adjustment to her hair. 'Yes, very much,' she said. I expected this kind of conversation would be all that was comfortable for her in English. This, and maybe, 'Oh, you so big dick! Oh, you make me come so much!' and the other such Shakespearean phrases of the trade.

I got up and offered her my chair, adjacent to Dox's, facing the bandstand. 'Here,' I said. 'I just need to use the men's room. You and Bob get acquainted and I'll be right back.'

The girl nodded and took my seat. Dox grinned and said, 'Well, thank you, Dick.'

In fact, I wasn't particularly in need of the restroom. I just wanted a chance to scan the room from other vantage points. To observe our table the way someone else might be observing it. It would make me feel better.

Brown Sugar has two back rooms, and I checked each of these. Both were occupied by groups of middle-aged Thais talking, eating, and laughing lustily. The other tables were filled by unremarkable twenty- and thirty-somethings, foreign and Thai. No one set off my radar. But something was still bothering me. Not a lot, but it was there.

Maybe you're just jumpy. You're not used to being out in the open with company, with someone approaching you uninvited.

Maybe. I used the men's room and returned to the table. Dox and the girl each had a fresh drink. They were holding hands and murmuring to each other. Well, it looked as though I was going to finish up the evening on my own, after all.

I walked over to her left and said, 'You know, I'm actually feeling a little tired.'

The girl glanced up and back at me. From this angle, the high collar of her dress pulled away slightly from her neck. Beneath her smooth skin I saw the slight bulge of the cricothyroid cartilage – the Adam's apple.

I'll be damned, I thought. All at once I understood what had been making me twitchy. I had to stifle a laugh.

'Oh come on, Dick, it ain't past your bedtime. Stick around, you might even have some fun.'

Oh, I'm going to have some fun, I thought. *I'm sure of that.*

I smiled at him, trying to stop short of the shit-eating grin my mood was suddenly demanding. 'Well, okay. Maybe just for another song or two.'

'There you go,' Dox said. He gestured to the chair across from him. 'Have a seat. Tiara and I are drinking Stolis. You want another one of those whiskeys?'

'Why not?' I said. Dox signaled the waitress and magnanimously ordered everyone another round. He and Tiara leaned close again and went back to murmuring.

Oh, this was going to be good. I didn't know what I'd done to deserve something so beautiful, but here it was. And it could only get better.

The drinks came. I enjoyed mine in silence, my focus alternating between the bar, the room, and my distracted drinking companions. The girl's arm had disappeared beneath the table. From the angle of their bodies, I recognized that her hand was, at a minimum, on Dox's thigh. Possibly it had come to rest somewhere farther north.

The girl whispered something to him. Dox nodded. The girl smiled at me, got up, excused herself, and headed toward the restroom.

Dox took a last gulp from his drink and leaned across the table. His face was flushed. 'Well, partner, you know I'm going to miss you, but duty calls.'

I smiled. 'I understand completely. You're going to make her very happy, I can see that.'

'Well, I reckon she's going to make me happy, too. Did you see her, man? When was the last time you saw something so fine? A little flat-chested, it's true, but that doesn't bother me a bit. I'm sure her other charms will make up for it.'

'Oh, definitely. I'm sure she's otherwise . . . very well equipped.' Keeping my voice even wasn't easy. One hitch, one chuckle, and I knew I'd be lost in a hurricane-force laughing fit.

'Thanks for your understanding, man. It's time for this young lady to have the experience of a lifetime. It'll be nothing but disappointment for her after tonight, but that's the price of a love-filled evening with Dox.'

I nodded. I knew if I tried to speak I'd be done.

He must have misinterpreted my silence. 'Shit, man, there's no need for you to spend the night alone. You're not a bad-looking guy, and the ladies won't know about your deficiencies until it's too late, anyway. You could meet someone if you wanted to.'

Part of me, a bigger part than I cared to admit, wanted to let him go through with it. And I would have paid almost anything to be there at the moment of truth. But he was a good friend. Hell, he'd saved my life. I couldn't do it to him, even if he did deserve it.

I closed my eyes and took a deep breath. 'Dox. She's a *katoey.*'

Katoey, or 'lady-boy,' has a range of meanings, from a guy who likes to dress in drag from time to time all the way to a man who has had transgender surgery and is now effectively a woman. They can be found all over Thailand and are generally accepted, if sometimes difficult to spot, within the society. Regardless of the differences, what they all have in common is that presumably Dox wouldn't want to sleep with one.

He scowled slightly and cocked his head. 'Now that's not like you, man. Don't go trying to spoil my night just because you haven't gotten one of your own.'

'You didn't notice her hands? They're just a little big for her frame, don't you think? And did you get a look at her Adam's apple? Women don't have Adam's apples, and she's wearing that high collar to conceal it.'

Some of the color drained from his face. 'Don't fuck with me,' he said.

I shook my head and stifled a laugh. 'I'm not.'

The girl walked back from the restroom as though on cue. Dox stood and turned to her. 'Honey,' he said, 'Dick over here thinks . . . he thinks . . .'

I smiled gently and said to her, 'I just didn't want there to be a misunderstanding. Bob didn't know you're a *katoey*.'

She smiled back, then looked at Dox, her eyes wide. 'You no like *katoey*?'

Dox lost a little more color. 'I . . . I . . .' he stammered.

'Me, I think you know,' she said. 'So I no say.'

'No, I didn't know!' he said, his voice anguished.

'Most men, no problem. When it dark . . .'

'I ain't like that.'

She smiled. 'Please, honey? I like you.'

Dox's expression was about halfway to physical illness. 'Look,' he said, 'I don't mean to be rude, but could you just go?'

She hesitated, then nodded. 'Okay. Thank you for drinks with me.'

'You're welcome,' Dox said, his tone the quintessence of forlornness.

184

She got up and left the club, no doubt disappointed that her investment of time had yielded so little. Dox looked gut-shot.

He slumped into his chair and looked at me. 'When did you spot that stuff about her hands and her neck? You let that go on for an awfully long time there, partner.'

'Dox, I thought you knew. It was so obvious.'

'It was not obvious. No, sir.'

'You sure you don't want to take her back to the hotel? If you hurry . . .'

'Hell, yes, I'm sure.'

'Because, c'mon, you had to know. At some level.'

'No, I didn't know at any level, not until you told me.'

'Really? I mean, you pointed out that she was a little flat-chested. And I don't know how you could have missed the hands and the Adam's apple. Dox, she might as well have been wearing a sign.'

'No, she was definitely not wearing a sign, man. Although I think she ought to.'

I smiled. 'Maybe you would have enjoyed it.'

'Stop it.'

'I mean, if she'd only given you a blow job, you would never even have known. You'd just think it was the best head you'd ever gotten. It would have become one of your most cherished memories.' I started to laugh. I couldn't help it. 'You never would have stopped telling me about it.'

'Do you want another drink?' he asked. 'I think I need one.'

'How many, Dox? That's the question. How many times before.'

He signaled the waitress for two more, then shuddered. 'Damn, that was a near thing. I'd thank you, if you'd stepped in a little sooner and were enjoying yourself a little less.'

'Enjoying?'

'Yeah, yeah. Very funny.' He drained his Stoli and shuddered again.

I thought about going on, something about how, with all his local expertise, he had still almost unintentionally gone off with a lady-boy. Or presumably unintentionally. But he looked so glum that I decided to give it a rest.

The band started up again. A few minutes later, Dox leaned over to me and said, 'If you don't mind, I'm ready to try something different. You're welcome to join me, but I don't know that where I'm going is apt to be your kind of place.'

'Topless girls with numbers attached to their bikini bottoms?'

'I'd say that's likely, yes.'

'Good. If they're undressed, you'll have a better chance of making sure . . . you know.'

He scowled. 'Are you coming?'

'No, I'd better let you go alone. I wouldn't want to interfere with a man's quest to recover his masculinity. On the other hand, who's going to warn you if you run into another . . .'

'I'll be fine alone, you Yankee degenerate.'

I smiled and held out my hand. 'All right then. We'll talk in the morning?'

'In the morning,' he said, and we shook. He got up, tossed a few hundred baht on the table, and headed for the door.

I chuckled to myself. It was going to be good to have something in my arsenal that I could bring up anytime Dox gave me grief.

I chuckled again, a little more softly. It was odd that she'd been in here, though. She seemed to have been on the make, and Brown Sugar was the wrong place for that. Sure, she could have come here to enjoy the music, to take a break, whatever, but the way she'd been looking around right away, the way she'd immediately zeroed in on Dox . . .

Maybe that was opportunistic.

Didn't feel opportunistic. It felt focused.

I chewed on that. Then, in a sort of semiconscious short-hand that was more suddenly present in its entirety than deduced piece by piece, I realized:

If someone wanted to get to you and Dox, the first thing he'd look to do would be to separate you. To do that, if he were smart, he would employ some means that could distract, at least temporarily, your sensitivity to disparities in the local environment. Give you something you could focus on. A katoey, for example. Make you say, that's what was bothering me — she's not really a woman! *Or, if you didn't spot it, and one of you went off with her . . . boom, there you go, you've found your way to divide us.*

Maybe it would have been easier, more straightforward, to use a real woman as the bait. But a katoey *would have certain advantages. A lady-boy could take better care of himself in a scrape. And he'd be used to acting, to passing himself off as something he wasn't, to fooling people, lulling them.*

I felt the blood draining from my face, my heart begin to pound as an adrenaline dump kicked in. If Dox had still been at the table, he would have laughed at me. I didn't care. There were certain things I would try to change about myself to accommodate our partnership. The way I go with my gut would never be one of them.

I stood up and walked briskly to the door, as fast as I could move without being obvious. I was hoping I was wrong, but I knew I was right.

14

For an instant after exiting the bar, I didn't focus on any one particular thing. I let it all in: the placement of the sidewalk tables and patrons, the parked cars, the pedestrians.

Movement straight in front of me: a muscular Thai man in a black tee-shirt, mid-twenties, leaning against a cab at the curb, coming to his feet. 'You need taxi?' he asked, in a thick Thai accent. He started moving toward me. 'I give you ride. Use meter. Very good.'

His hands were empty and he was still more than three meters away. I did a quick scan for Dox. He had walked out less than half a minute before me; he might still be in the area. I didn't see him. But I didn't have time to look further, or to worry about what might have happened to him.

I checked my flanks.

Left flank: Caucasian male, late forties, alone at one of the sidewalk tables.

Right flank: two Thai men, mid-twenties and in shape like the first guy, watching me with a certain intensity, and getting up smoothly from their table.

Would any of this ever stand up in court? *Your Honor, my partner left after an encounter with a lady-boy. I stepped outside. Someone asked me if I needed a cab, and the men to my right were watching me with 'that look,' if you know what I mean. That's why I killed them all.*

Of course it wouldn't stand up. But one of the things that separates people like me from live civilians and dead operators is an absolute ability and an absolute willingness to act decisively on evidence that in polite society would get you laughed at and that in court would get you thrown in jail. When you know, you know. You don't wait for more evidence. You act. If you act wrong, you live with the consequences. You act wrong the other way, you don't live at all.

The man in front of me was now two meters away. 'You need taxi?' he asked again. His right hand was out, motioning in a 'Come this way' gesture.

'Sure,' I said. I stepped toward him as though I intended to move past him on his right. He smiled, a smile that was supposed to look friendly but that to me was at least half-predatory.

I smiled myself, an 'Aren't you kind to help me, I'm so clueless' kind of smile. He nodded, reassured that this was going to be easy.

But it wasn't going to be easy. It wasn't going to be easy at all.

Just before I pulled alongside him, I snatched his right wrist in my left hand and fed his arm over to my right. I hooked his tricep and dragged him past me. My weight on his arm pulled him forward, and as I circled clockwise behind him, I saw his mouth dropping open in surprise. Apparently my reaction wasn't part of the rehearsal.

I reached around his waist with my left hand and caught his right wrist. I cinched him in close and he grunted as some of the breath was driven from his lungs. We were both facing the bar now. The two men who had gotten up were two meters away to our left. I saw their faces hardening. Their hands were empty and I realized this was supposed to be a snatch, not a kill. Otherwise they would have had weapons and would already have used them.

I sucked in a breath and bellowed, 'Dox!' in the loudest

voice I could muster, half to warn him if he was there, half to call for his help.

The two men to the left started to charge forward.

The guy I was holding took a wider stance and dropped his weight to create a more stable base, and I realized from the reaction he was trained. He tried to snap a head butt back at me, but my face was too far to the right and pressed up close against his shoulder. I reached down to my right front pocket where the knife was clipped in place. In one motion I cleared it, opened it, and thrust it forward from behind his spread legs into his perineum and balls.

There's a certain pitch of human scream that's impossible to ignore, that drills directly into the most primitive parts of the brain. The kind that makes your hair stand up, your scrotum retract, your feet freeze dead in their tracks. That's the scream that tore loose from this guy when my knife hit home, and it was exactly the scream I wanted. His partners moving in from the left were involuntarily stopped by it. Their conscious minds were thinking, *What the fuck was that?* Their unconscious minds were shouting, *Who cares what it was! Run!* They both pulled up short about a meter away from me.

I didn't wait for them to get the circuits clear. I shoved the man I'd been holding into them and turned to my right, ready to bug out. But another Thai man was coming from that direction, fast enough to have already closed the distance. He must have moved out from the alley to the right of the bar. The scream that had frozen his comrades hadn't had the same effect on him. Either he was very brave, very stupid, or very hard of hearing. Regardless of the explanation, he was now in my way.

I had already flipped the knife around in my hand to a reverse grip so that the blade was concealed along my wrist and lower forearm. Even so, Mr Hearing Impaired must not have been paying proper attention, or he would have put two and two together: I was holding something in my hand, something that had just caused his partner to shriek like the eunuch he now was, and that something was probably sharp and pointy. Or the explanation for his failure to hesitate as his comrades had was indeed stupidity, because there is nothing quite so stupid as showing up for a knife fight unarmed.

He paused a meter in front of me and raised his fists as though we were about to box. I noted, half-consciously, scars around his eyebrows and the bump of a previously broken nose, and realized, *Muay Thai, these guys are Thai boxers.*

I detected a slight shift in his weight, a grounding of the left leg, and then his right shin was whipping in toward my left thigh. Thai boxing shin kicks can hit like baseball bats, and if I hadn't seen it coming and so hadn't had a fraction of a second to prepare, he would have blasted my leg out from under me and then I would have been fighting three men, or maybe more, from the ground.

But I had that fraction of a second. I used it to move closer, just inside the sweet spot of the kick, and to drop my weight so my hip would take the main impact. I caught his leg as it hit, wrapping my left arm around his calf. He reacted instantly: he grabbed my head, braced himself on the captured leg, and leaped upward and toward me, his left knee coming around for my face, just as he had doubtless done countless times in the ring.

But they don't let knives in the ring. The sport wouldn't be the same if they did.

I raised my right arm and turtled my head in. The knee hit my forearm. It hurt, especially with the bruises Delilah had given me, but it beat a broken jaw. He started to return to the ground. I moved the knife out from along my forearm so that I was gripping it ice pick style, edge in, and plunged it into his right inner thigh where it connected to the pelvis. In the heat of the moment and pumped full of adrenaline, he seemed not to notice what had happened. But then I ripped down and back, tearing open his femoral artery and a lot of other real estate, too, and that seemed to get his attention. He howled and jerked convulsively away from me. I swept his good leg out from under him in modified *ouchi-gari,* a judo throw, and let him go as he fell, not wanting to take a chance on getting tangled up with him on the ground.

I turned back to the other two guys, and was gratified to see them backing away. There was no doubt now that a knife was in play, and no doubt that it was being used by someone for more than just show. Apparently this was all more trouble than they wanted or had been led to expect. They turned and ran.

I looked the other way. The white guy who had been sitting outside the bar had stood up. 'Are you all right?' he asked, in American-accented English.

I glanced all around. The people who had been sitting at the other tables outside were frozen in place, in shock. The men on the ground were moaning and writhing. From the wounds I had given them and the amount of blood spreading out on the pavement, I expected they would be dead in just a few more seconds.

'I saw everything,' the white guy was saying. He started moving toward me. 'They attacked you. It was self-defense. I'm a lawyer, I can help.'

I thought, crazily, *Great, just what I need, a lawyer.*

And then something came into focus. Maybe it was intuition. Maybe it was my unconscious sifting data that was invisible to my conscious mind, items like the way he'd been sitting at that table, with his feet firmly on the ground as though ready for quick action; or his position, in what had been one of my blind spots as I exited the bar; or his calm and forthcoming expression of concern just now, when all the other onlookers were frozen or fleeing.

He never gave off the vibe, none at all. I'd even overlooked him to start with. Maybe that was part of the plan: I was looking for more Thais, not a white guy. Maybe it was just that, whoever Perry Mason here was, he was definitely very good.

He continued to move toward me. His hands were empty . . . or was that something in his left? I wasn't sure. I shouted, 'Stop right there!'

He shook his head and said, 'What are you talking about? I just want to help.' And kept moving in.

When you tell someone who's moving toward you to come no closer, with the appropriate air of gravity and command in your voice, and particularly when that air is augmented by the presence of a knife with which you've just killed two people, and the guy keeps coming anyway, you are not dealing with someone who needs a light for a cigarette, or directions, or the time of day, or whatever else was his ostensible excuse for invading your space. You are dealing with someone intent on taking something that you would prefer not to part with, up to and including your life, and his failure to heed your command is more than adequate proof of this, and of how you must now handle it.

I did a quick perimeter check. Other than the shocked onlookers, some of whom were now coming to their senses and scurrying away, it looked like it was just the two of us. I started to move toward him.

Suddenly, Perry Mason changed his tune. He started

backing up. But it wasn't a retreat, just a tactical pause. Because, as he moved smoothly backward, his free hand dropped equally smoothly to his right front pocket and pulled free a folding knife. It was opening even as it cleared his pants, and I could tell from the liquid ease with which he withdrew it that this man was no knife dilettante, but rather someone who had trained long, hard, and seriously to develop the proficiency and confidence I had just witnessed.

I paused. I wasn't sure if the display was to warn me off, or if he intended to close. Maybe killing me was the backup plan if snatching me didn't work out. No way to know. Regardless, I didn't want to fight him. I just wanted to get away. I would have been happy to kill him to make that happen, but obviously if he was armed, killing him might no longer be the easiest means of exit here.

He started circling, moving closer. His footwork was smooth and balanced. He was just inside the distance that I would have judged safe for turning and running. I moved with him, conscious of my flanks in case the two who had run off reconsidered. I held my knife in my right hand with a saber grip, close to my waist, with my left hand open and partially extended to block and trap if we closed. If we did, I didn't know if I would make it. What I did know is that he surely would not.

I heard a voice booming from behind me. 'Partner, get down!'

It was Dox. I dropped into a squat, keeping the knife close to my body, and glanced over to see the giant sniper moving in with a wooden chair raised over his head. I ducked down lower. He lunged forward and let the chair go like it was an F-14 being catapulted off the deck of an aircraft carrier.

When a man of Dox's size and strength throws a chair, there are many places you might want to be. In front of the chair is not one of them. In this sense, Perry Mason was unlucky. The chair caught him full in the chest and blasted him to the ground.

Dox and I were on him in an instant. Dox grabbed his knife and something else, whatever it was that I thought I had seen in his left hand, both of which had clattered onto the sidewalk next to him. I knelt across his chest and almost cut his throat to finish him, but then I saw that he was already helpless. He was grunting and starting to cough blood.

I did another perimeter check. Still okay. Returning my eyes to Perry Mason, I said to Dox, 'Quick, give me a hand.'

Dox knelt next to me. I saw that he was scanning the street and sidewalk, and I was gratified to know that, this time, the behavior had nothing to do with sex and everything to do with survival.

'What do you want to do with him?' he asked.

I inclined my head in the direction of the alley, about twenty feet away. 'Pull him over there. The dark.'

We grabbed him under the arms and hauled him up and over. He tried to resist, but the chair had broken him up inside and he didn't have much fight in him.

There were no streetlights over this stretch of sidewalk, as is the case throughout most of Bangkok's lesser thorough-fares, and once we had moved off to the side of Brown Sugar we were enveloped by darkness. In the alley, just in from the sidewalk, someone had parked a white Toyota van. The sliding door on the van's passenger side was open, facing the clubs to the left. I saw this and instantly understood that their plan had been to drag me into the vehicle, then drive away and interrogate me at their leisure.

We shoved Perry Mason up against the front passenger-side door and patted him down. He had a Fred Perrin La

Griffe with a two-inch spear point blade hanging from a neck sheath – obviously backup for the folder. I cut the neck cord and Dox pocketed the knife and rig. In his front pants pocket, we found a Toyota car key and a magnetic key card for the Holiday Inn Silom Bangkok. I pressed the 'open' button on the car key and the van chirped in response. Yeah, the vehicle was definitely his. Beyond all this, and a Casio G-Shock wristwatch, he was traveling sterile.

I pocketed the keys and looked in his eyes. Blood was flowing steadily from the sides of his mouth. He was still conscious, though, still with us. Good.

'How did you find us?' I asked.

He shook his head and looked away.

Dox grabbed his face and forced him to look at me. 'How did you find us?' I said again.

He gritted his teeth and remained silent.

I reached down and started probing his abdomen. He winced when I got to his ribs. Either they were broken, or there was some damage underneath, or both. I pressed hard and he grunted.

'We can do this easy or we can do it hard,' I said. 'Answer a few questions and we'll be gone. That's all there is to it.'

He looked away again. He was trying to focus on something else, to let his imagination carry him away from here.

I knew the technique. There are ways of resisting interrogation. I've been schooled in them, and so, I had a feeling, had this guy. What they teach you is that you have to accept that you are in a position you can't survive. Your life is over. There will be some hours of pain first, yes. Your body is going to be broken and ruined. But then death will deliver you. Concentrate on that coming deliverance, let your imagination go forth to meet it, and use the anticipation of that impending rendezvous to hold out for as long as you can. If you can do this, you can detach yourself from what's happening to your body and make your mind much harder to reach.

I had to interrupt his reverie. Shake his confidence that his acceptance of death had put him in paradoxical control of the situation. Shock him out of his assumption that we were playing a binary game of live or die, life or death, with no other possibilities in between.

I pulled out my folder with my right hand and flipped it open. I grabbed his face with my left and forced him to look at me.

'No matter what happens here,' I said to him, 'you are not going to die. We're not going to kill you. You are going to live.'

I pressed the knife against his cheek, so that the point was resting just below the bottom edge of his left eye. 'But if you don't answer my questions,' I said, 'I'm going to blind you. One eye, then the other. Now. How did you find us?'

The guy didn't answer, but I could tell from his increased respiration that I had his attention, that I had hauled him back some distance from the relatively safe place to which he had tried to flee.

'Your choice,' I said, and started slowly driving the knife upward.

He squeezed his eyes tightly shut and tried to jerk away. Dox shoved his head against the side of the van and I kept the knife slowly going north.

The guy's breathing worsened, approaching the cadences of panic. His eyeball was moving upward ahead of the knife. Another millimeter and it would reach the limits of its give and be skewered.

'Cell phone,' he said suddenly, panting. 'We tracked a cell phone.'

I paused the knife but didn't lower it. 'Whose cell phone?'

'His. Dox's.'

Goddamnit, I thought, I told him to keep that fucking thing off. Then: *Not now. Deal with that later.*

Dox said, 'Hey, asshole, how do you know my name?'

I shot him a murderous *shut the fuck up this is my show* glance, then looked back at Perry Mason. 'How did you get the number?'

'I don't know. It was just given to me.'

Bullshit it was just given to you. 'If I have to ask you again, you lose this eye.'

There was a pause, then he said, 'I don't know for sure. I was told it came from some Russian outfit.'

I knew Dox had done some work with the Russians not so long ago. I glanced at him, my eyebrows raised. He gave me a *yeah, I guess that's possible* shrug in return.

All right. I had deliberately started with a question about tools and tactics, something this guy could give up without feeling he was compromising his integrity. This would warm him up, help him rationalize his responses to the tougher inquiries that would follow. We'd started with *how,* and that had gone well. What I really wanted to talk about was *who.* But I sensed he still wasn't ready for that, not even at the cost of his eyes. As a bridge between what we had accomplished and what still remained to be done, I decided to use *why.*

'Why are you coming after us?' I asked.

He paused, then said, 'You tried to take out an asset in Manila.'

'What asset?' His neck was stretched taut with his efforts to stay ahead of the pressure of the knife. 'Lavi,' he said. 'Manheim Lavi.'

'Why? Retaliation?'

I already knew the answer to that one: information, not retaliation. If it had been simple retaliation they were after, they would have just tried to kill Dox and me. They wouldn't have bothered hiring a bunch of locals to grab us and stuff us into the back of a van. But I wanted to keep him talking just a little more before we got down to brass tacks.

'Information,' he said. 'We needed to know who was behind the hit so we could straighten things out.'

'What do you mean, "straighten things out"?'

'We have to protect our people. If there's a threat, we deal with the threat.'

We were running out of time. The patrons in front of the club might discover some misplaced courage and decide to interfere. And certainly the police would be here soon.

Okay, here we go. 'Who is "we"?' I asked.

He shook his head. I pushed the knife up a fraction and he cried out.

'Last time, and then you lose this eye. Who is we?'

He started to hyperventilate. He'd been standing on the very tips of his toes and his legs were trembling. But he wasn't answering my question.

I didn't want to do it – not out of any misplaced squeamishness, but because once you start hurting the subject, you start to lose your leverage. Fear is the ultimate motivator, but what you're afraid of is by definition the thing that hasn't happened yet. Once the thing has happened, you're not afraid of it anymore. Once I'd taken out an eye, the loss of that eye would no longer be a threat. It would be one less thing the fear of which would motivate him.

But if you threaten and then fail to act, your subsequent threats lack credibility. It's not pretty, but that's the way a high-pressure interrogation works.

It occurred to me that there was one more problem.

Whoever was behind this guy, if he were found *sans* an eye or two, they would know he had died after being interrogated. They could then be expected to change their plans, their security, to protect whatever their man might have compromised under duress. And, although in fact he had compromised very little, we had his hotel room key now. That presented some interesting possibilities I would have preferred not to foreclose.

Damn, it was a dilemma. But before I had a chance to resolve it, Perry Mason started to scream. Not so much in pain, or even to call for aid, but in outrage and desperation.

Dox slammed his hand over the man's mouth, but the screaming decided it for me. We were exposed here, and too much time had gone by since the start of the incident. It was past time for us to bug out.

I looked at Dox. He nodded and I thought he understood. I took a half step back and kneed the guy in the groin. The screaming was displaced by a grunt and his body tried to double forward, but Dox was holding him too tightly. I changed my grip on the knife so that I was holding it ice pick style, blade in, and plunged it into his upper left pectoral, just below the clavicle. I ripped down and across, lacerating the subclavian artery.

I pulled Dox aside. The man spilled to his knees. He let out a long, agonized groan and pitched forward, but managed to get his arms out and caught himself before his head hit the pavement. There wasn't much blood – the artery was transected, and the bleeding would be mostly into his chest and lungs – but there was no question that he would be unconscious in seconds, and dead shortly after that. I stepped in and slashed him twice across the forearms and he collapsed onto his face. He lay there, moaning and writhing.

I saw that I'd gotten blood on my hands – from his mouth or his chest, I didn't know. I pulled a handkerchief from my back pocket and cleaned up the best I could. I handed the handkerchief to Dox and gestured for him to do the same. His eyes were wide and he seemed a little stunned, but he used the handkerchief. We'd be more thorough later.

One more thing. I glanced inside the open sliding door and saw what I was looking for: cell phone tracking equipment, strapped with duct tape to one of the back seats. Other than the equipment, the interior was clean. I used the handkerchief to open the van's passenger door, then to pop the glove compartment, hoping to find registration or some other clue to Perry Mason's identity. There was a first-aid kit inside. I opened it, and saw vials of atropine and naloxone, and syringes. Interesting. But no registration, nothing to identify the people who had rented the van.

'Come on,' I said to Dox, who had been uncharacteristically quiet for the last minute or so. 'We need to get out of here.'

We walked briskly across the street to the Lumpini Park side, where it was comfortingly dark. I glanced back at the sidewalk in front of the bars as we moved. The patrons had all gone inside. The two men on the sidewalk weren't moving. We cut over to a sub-soi paralleling Ratchadamri, then started walking south and looking for a cab. Under the reflected glow of a collapsing storefront sign, I paused and looked at Dox, who still hadn't said a word in a record-breakingly long time. 'Hey,' I said quietly. 'Look at me. Am I okay? Do I have any blood on me? Anything?'

He looked me up and down, then shook his head. 'No. You're okay.'

I gave him a once-over, as well, and nodded. 'You are, too.'

He didn't say anything in response. I never thought I'd be concerned that Dox was being too quiet, but it wasn't like him.

'You all right?' I asked.

He closed his eyes, took two deep breaths, leaned forward, and vomited.

I looked around us. There weren't any pedestrians on this section of road. Even if there had been a few, I doubted they'd be overly interested. It wouldn't be the first time anyone had seen a *farang* who'd had a bit too much to drink.

When he was done, he wiped his mouth and straightened. 'Damn, that's embarrassing,' he said.

We started moving again. 'Don't worry about it,' I told him.

'That's never happened to me, man, never.'

'It can happen to anyone.'

'Did it ever happen to you?'

I paused, then admitted, 'No. But I don't know that's something to be proud of.'

'I just didn't know you were going to do that, stab him like that. If I'd known, I could have gotten ready.'

'Sorry. Couldn't warn you without warning him.'

'Why'd you slash his arms, man? I saw where you cut him, he was already dead for sure.'

'I wanted it to look like he went down fighting, not being interrogated. If his people think he was interrogated, they'll assume he gave up information. I want to keep them in the dark.'

'So if he was fighting . . .'

'Then he would have defensive wounds on his forearms.'

'Oh. All right. Glad you weren't just being sadistic. Is that why you didn't take out his eye?'

'That's why.'

'Would you have?'

I paused, then said, 'Yeah.'

'Damn. I was afraid you were going to.'

I could tell Dox didn't have much experience with hostile interrogations. I thought he ought to count himself lucky for that.

A cab came by and we flagged it down. I told the driver to take us to Chong Nonsi sky train station.

As we drove away and it began to seem as though we'd made it, the enormity of what had just happened started to settle in. Yeah, Dox had helped me out, but his stupidity had caused the problem in the first place. I had told him about the damn phone. Told him specifically. Why couldn't he listen? What was so hard about turning off a cell phone? I tried not to say anything, thinking it pointless at the moment, but then it started coming out anyway.

'What did I tell you about that fucking phone?' I whispered. 'What did I tell you?'

He looked at me, his expression darkening. 'Look, man, I am absolutely not in the mood.'

'There's equipment that can triangulate on a cell phone. They had it in that van. It's accurate to about twenty-five feet. Tiara, the lady-boy who liked you for yourself? Her job was probably to go to the adjacent bars to help narrow it down.'

'How was I supposed to know that? You didn't know either, not until after.'

'Is it on now? Is it still on?'

He blanched and squirmed forward in his seat to reach into his pocket. He pulled out his phone, flipped it open, and pressed a button. It issued its cheery farewell melody and powered off.

'Why?' I asked. 'Why would you leave that thing on?'

'Look, man, I've got clients, okay? There are people who need to reach me.'

'Not when we're operational!' I paused, then said, 'Clients, my ass. It was a girl, wasn't it? Or girls.'

His nostrils flared. 'What if it was?'

'You just opened a tunnel-sized hole in our security, while we're operational, when we know we've got people looking for us, to get laid!'

'You know, not everyone enjoys your well-developed sense of solitude, partner. I like a little companionship from time to time, yeah.'

'They can use voice mail!'

'All right, I get the point! I made a mistake, I admit it, okay? What more do you want from me?'

I started to say something, then got a grip on myself. He was right, there was no point in playing I-told-you-so. And then I felt bad. He had just saved my ass back there with that chair.

I closed my eyes and exhaled. 'I'm sorry. Shit like what just happened makes me cranky, okay? Usually there's no one around for me to take it out on.'

There was a pause. Then he said, 'I'm sorry, too. It was a dumb mistake. You were right.'

'What happened, anyway? Where did you go? I thought something had happened to you.'

He grinned, obviously coming back to himself. 'Is that your way of telling me you care? 'Cause it gives me a warm feeling, it really does.'

I looked at him. 'I think I liked it better when you were puking.'

He chuckled. 'I just walked across the street to Lumpini to take a leak. I heard you shout, but it still took me a minute to cut off the stream and get Nessie put away.'

Before I could think better of it, I asked, "'Nessie'?"

'You know, the Loch Ness Monster. I had a girlfriend once who named my . . .'

'I get it, I get it.'

'Anyway, I came running as fast as I could. Why'd you follow me out, anyway?'

I told him about the feeling I'd gotten about 'Tiara' being a set-up.

'Damn, son,' he said, 'you are good. I have to admit, that whole thing went right by me. I promise I'll never call you paranoid again.'

The cab pulled up in front of Chong Nonsi station. We got out and watched it pull away. 'You see a sewer?' I asked, looking around. 'We need to dump the knives. And the handkerchief.'

'Dump them?'

'Yeah. We don't want to be carrying anything that would connect us with a recent multiple homicide, do we?'

'Partner, I'll have you know that the knives in question are a Benchmade AFCK and a Fred Perrin La Griffe. These are high-quality instruments of destruction and not so easy to come by. It would be wasteful in the extreme to "dump" them.'

I looked at him. 'It would be "wasteful in the extreme" to have the prosecution use them as evidence of why we should spend the rest of our lives in a Thai prison.'

'All right, I understand where you're coming from. Tell you what, how about if I sterilize them? Alcohol, bleach, whatever. You tell me how and I'll do it. Plus you can have either one you want.'

I paused for a moment. If we cleaned them, I supposed, the risk would be manageable. It would have been safer, more thorough, to get rid of them entirely, but maybe this was one of the many battles with Dox that wasn't worth fighting.

I said, 'I'll take the La Griffe.'

He looked crestfallen. 'Shit, man, I want the La Griffe. It's so cool.'

I rolled my eyes. 'All right, whatever. I'll take the AFCK.'

He brightened. 'Thanks, partner. You're a good man.'

'Since you're feeling so magnanimous,' I said, 'let's keep moving for a while. I want to do a few more things to break the connection between us and what just happened in front of the club.'

He shook his head. 'I don't have a problem with that.'

See? You get a little by giving a little, I thought.

We found a street sewer that worked nicely for the handkerchief and the knife I had used on Perry Mason and friends. As I was dumping them in, Dox said, 'Wait, there's this, too.' He reached into a pocket. 'Here. I think it's some kind of hypodermic.'

I looked at it and nodded. 'That's exactly what it is.'

The device was flesh-colored and looked vaguely like a plastic joy-buzzer. Where the button would be on a joy-buzzer, though, was a short, thick needle, maybe 16-gauge. The needle was covered in some kind of wax that was hard enough to protect the user from an accidental stick, but soft enough to give way under strong pressure. The back of it was sticky, and I realized it had been adhered to Perry Mason's palm as he approached me.

'Slick,' I said, musing. 'I've never seen something like this before. It must be custom. Look.' I stuck it to my palm and turned my hand upward so he could see it. 'I thought what was going on back there was supposed to be a snatch. I was right. The four Thai guys grab me. The white guy moves in and hits me in the leg with an open-hand strike, or just grabs me and squeezes, whatever. Then what's in this thing – I'm betting a veterinary anesthetic, something with fentanyl, droperidol, whatever – gets injected, just like a snakebite. They've probably got a dose in here that could put down a Clydesdale. I'm unconscious in seconds and they drag me into the van. Yeah, that's why they had the atropine and naloxone in the glove compartment – to immediately reverse cardiac and respiratory suppression, make sure they don't accidentally lose the patient. That was the plan, anyway.'

'What about me?'

I thought for a minute. 'I'm not sure. But I would guess I was the main target. First they want to separate us. If they can pick me up, they could always deal with you later. Remember, they were tracking your cell phone.'

'I doubt that you'll let me forget.'

'Or if you'd actually gone off with Tiara, they'd have that. She probably would have suggested her apartment, told you she had a hot roommate and they had this fantasy about a threesome with a big, strong, white man. Not that you would fall for something like that.'

'No, not me, I'm immune to that kind of thing.'

'If you go to the apartment, you get ambushed there. If you take her back to your hotel room instead, she makes a call and lets them know where to go and how to proceed.'

'Who were they all, do you think?'

I considered for a moment. 'I don't know. The Thais were tough, but they weren't professionals. They felt like street muscle. The white guy, though, he was impressive. He was an operator, and I guarantee you this wasn't the first time he'd done a snatch.'

'Company man, you think?'

'Definitely a possibility. But then why the Thais?'

He shrugged. 'Maybe he was working on the fly. Didn't have time to assemble a proper team.'

'Yeah, could be that.'

I looked at the syringe for another moment, then slipped it into my shirt pocket, needle-side out. 'We're keeping the knives,' I said. 'I guess this might come in handy, too.'

We went up the stairs, bought tickets, then headed to the platform. Dox said, 'Where are we going, anyway?'

'To his hotel. The Silom Holiday Inn. He had a room key on him. I took it.'

'What, are we going to try every door in the hotel? I know that place. It used to be the Crowne Plaza. They probably have seven hundred rooms.'

I thought about Perry Mason. About the lack of identifying pocket litter, even in the van. About how smooth his approach had been, and how confident he'd been when we faced off.

He was a careful man, I could see that. A survivor. Yeah, look at his everyday carry, the quality knives, the Casio G-Shock watch. He was a good Boy Scout. He minded the details, looked for small advantages.

The kind of guy who knew to park a van so that the cargo could be loaded from the side it was being carried in from, because doing so would save a few seconds if he had to bug out. That kind of guy.

The kind who would insist on a hotel room on a low floor and next to a stairwell for the same reason.

'How many floors is the hotel?' I asked.

'I don't know exactly. It's got two towers. One is maybe fifteen floors, the other about twenty-five.'

'You want to bet that this guy's room will be on one of the first five floors and adjacent to a stairwell? Figure two stairwells per tower, three rooms either right next to or directly across from each stairwell. Total of sixty doors to check. Fewer if we're lucky.'

He grinned. 'No, I wouldn't take that bet.'

I nodded. 'I wouldn't, either. Let's go.'

15

We rode the sky train two exits to Surasak and got off. As we walked the short distance to the hotel, I said, 'We don't know for sure that the room is empty. So when we get the right door, we need to go in fast and hard, surprise anyone who might be in there, overwhelm them. Okay?'

'Okay. Who goes first?'

'I'll go first. You back me up.'

'Don't I always?'

'When you're not trying to make it with a *katoey*, yeah.'

'Hey, man . . .'

'Hang on a minute, there's a drugstore. You speak a little Thai, right?'

'Yeah, some.'

'We need a few supplies to clean the knives. And our hands, too. Bleach and alcohol.'

'I'll be right back.'

'Get a toothbrush, too. And some rubber gloves. Four pairs.'

'Four pairs of rubber gloves? Shit, man, they're going to think I'm some kind of deviant.'

'Dox, if the shoe fits . . .'

'Yeah, yeah. I'm going.'

Dox went into the drugstore and came out a few minutes later carrying a plastic grocery bag. When we were in sight of the hotel, I said, 'All right. Let me go ahead. You wait one minute and follow me in. It's better if the two of us aren't seen together. Meet me on the first floor – not the lobby, the one above it – by the elevators.'

'Which tower?'

'What are they called?'

'I don't remember.'

I thought for a moment. 'Whichever one is closest to the lobby entrance where we're going in. Worst case, you go to the wrong one, you don't see me, you adjust.'

'All right, sounds like a plan.'

I went in and headed straight for the elevators, just another hotel guest tired from an evening of carousing in nearby Patpong and heading to his room to sleep it off. There was a security guy in front of the elevator bank, but he did nothing more than return my nod of greeting and let me pass. I noted a camera in front of the elevators, and hoped there wouldn't be more of them.

I took the elevator to the seventh floor. I got out and glanced around. No cameras. Excellent. If this had been The Four Seasons or The Oriental or one of the other high-end hotels in town, we would have had a problem. With cameras in the corridors, you can only try two or three doors before security understands what's happening and comes running. But the Holiday Inn didn't have quite that level of service.

I took the stairs down to the first floor and waited. Dox showed up a minute later, emerging directly from the elevator. It would have been smarter if he'd gone to a different floor and walked down as I had, just in case anyone on the lobby level was watching where the elevator was going, but okay, not such a big deal. Certainly not worth mentioning right now.

We started by the stairwell nearest the elevators and

worked our way up. Each floor took less than a minute. No luck going up. On five, we walked over to the second stairwell and started down again. On the third floor we found what we were looking for: to the right of the stairwell, room 316. I slid the card in and the reader lit up in green. I turned the handle, shoved the door open, and burst inside.

It was a simple room, not a suite. The lights were on in the main room, straight ahead; the bathroom, to the right, was dark. If anyone was in here, it was unlikely he'd be sitting in a dark bathroom, and I checked the main room first. It was empty. The fact that the door opened at all – that the interior dead bolt wasn't engaged – was encouraging, of course. If someone security conscious had been in the room, he would have engaged the dead bolt. And the fact that there had been no sounds of someone being startled, no reactive movement anywhere, that was good, too. Still, I had to be sure. I checked the bathroom. Empty. I even checked the closet and under the bed, something that, but for his recent chagrin, would doubtless have elicited some comment from Dox. Nothing. We were in.

We pulled on the gloves and started looking around. Unfortunately, the room was as clean as the van. There was a change of clothes in one of the dresser drawers, an empty suitcase against a wall. Some toiletries in the bathroom. Other than that, nothing.

Dox was checking the closet. 'Safe's locked,' I heard him say.

I walked over. Yeah, there it was, a typical hotel unit. I tried it and it was indeed locked.

'Told you,' he said. 'Well, you had a damn good idea about getting into the room, I'll give you that. But I'm no safecracker, and I doubt you are, either. I think we've reached a dead end.'

'Maybe,' I said, looking at the safe. 'Maybe not.'

I walked over to the desk, picked up the phone, and hit the button for room service. Dox looked at me quizzically, but didn't say anything.

The phone rang once, then someone picked up. 'Yes, Mr Winters, how may I help you?' the voice on the other end said.

'Huh?' I said, looking at Dox. 'You've got me down as Mr Winters?'

'Uh, yes, sir, "Mr Mitchell William Winters" is what we have on the list. Are you not Mr Winters?'

'Winters! I thought you said Vintners. I must be losing my hearing. Sorry about that.'

'No trouble at all, Mr Winters. How may I help you?'

'Well, I was hoping you could tell me what sort of exercise equipment you have down there.'

'Exercise equipment, sir?'

'Yes, you know, stationary bicycles, weights, a sauna, that sort of thing.'

'Ah, you must want the fitness center, sir. This is room service.'

'Room service? Good God, I'm losing my mind along with my hearing. I'm so sorry to have disturbed you.'

'Not at all, sir. But the fitness center is closed now. It will reopen at six o'clock in the morning, and someone will be able to assist you then. In the meantime, if you like, you can access it with your room key.'

'I see. Well, that's very helpful. Thank you very much.'

I hung up and turned to Dox. 'Mitchell William Winters,' I said. 'Or at least that's the name he's checked in under.'

He nodded. 'Okay, but now what? "Open sesame" to the safe?'

213

'No, I thought it would be better if you call down to the front desk and tell them you've forgotten the PIN you used to lock it.'

'Me? You want me to do that?'

I looked at him. 'Do I look like "Mitchell William Winters" to you?'

He shrugged. 'Well no, now that you mention it, you don't. But you don't look like a John Rain, either.'

'That's not the point. My real name could *be* Winters, it still wouldn't matter. We just don't want to provoke any questions, or make anything look out of order.'

'I know, I know, just keeping you on your toes is all. You sure no one on the staff would recognize this guy?'

I shook my head. 'I wouldn't worry about that. I don't think he was the kind of guy who wanted to be noticed, or who would have done anything that would get him noticed.' I might have added, *unlike someone we know,* but that would have been counterproductive.

I glanced at my watch. It was past midnight. I wanted to get this over with and be out of here.

'Look, they won't ask for ID,' I said. 'The fact that you're calling from the room is all the security they'll think they need.'

'Sounds like you've done this before, partner.'

'And even if they ask for ID, you tell them everything is in the safe.'

'Yeah, and after that?'

I struggled not to get exasperated. Working alone definitely had a few advantages.

'You improvise,' I said. 'Weren't you a Marine?'

He looked at me. 'Hell, yes, son.' He started to pick up the phone.

'Wait, wait. Get out of your clothes first. Put on one of

the hotel robes. Turn on the shower as though you're about to get in it, or better yet as though you've got a guest in there – it'll make them want to leave faster.'

He grinned. 'Ordinarily, partner, seeing me half-naked makes people want to stick around.'

'You can call Tiara when we're done.'

His grin turned into a frown.

'You want to make it look like you own the room,' I told him. 'This is *your* room, they're here to help you, but at your invitation, okay?'

'Yeah, yeah, I got it. What, have they got a master PIN or something?'

I nodded. 'It's what they use if a guest forgets his personal PIN, or dies in the room, or whatever. Theoretically, only the manager knows it.'

'Okay, then.'

'And whoever they send up, don't let him look inside the safe. He probably won't, he'll probably be discreet, but be ready and don't give him a chance. Winters might have a gun in there, who knows, and we don't want that kind of attention.'

'Yeah, good point.'

'One more thing. Ask him if he can tell you what PIN you used. Usually the safes are configured so that the person using the master can view the last twelve PINs that have been input.'

'But if we've already got the safe open . . .'

'We'll still want to close it up using the same PIN. If someone checks later, we don't want it to look like someone else was in here and got in the safe.'

'You're a thorough man, Mr Rain. I like that about you.' He started to undress. I walked into the bathroom, turned on the shower, and got him a robe.

Once he was changed, I handed him the phone and pressed the button for the front desk. He explained the problem, said yes twice, thanked them, and hung up.

'Okay,' he said, 'they're on their way up to open Mr Winters's safe.'

'*Your* safe.'

He frowned. 'Look, man, I ain't stupid, all right? I understand.'

'Listen, Dox, I don't tell you how to snipe because you're the best at it and I've got nothing to teach you there. But on these things, I'm telling you, you have to get in the right mindset or little signs will come to the surface and give you away.'

He flushed slightly. 'All right, all right. I don't mean to be sensitive. Just get off that Tiara stuff, all right?'

I shook my head. 'I'm sorry, I can't do that.'

For a second, his frown started to deepen. Then he laughed.

'Yeah, I guess I'm just asking too much there,' he said.

'Give me your gloves,' I said. 'And try to touch as little as possible while they're off.'

He removed the gloves and handed them to me.

I held out my hand. 'You're a good man, Mr Winters.'

He smiled and we shook.

'Oh, and the knives. I'll clean them up in the bathroom while you take care of the safe.'

He pulled the knives out of his pants and handed them to me. I went into the bathroom and locked the door behind me.

It took only a few minutes to take care of the knives. I disassembled them and used the alcohol first. Quick scrub with the toothbrush. Soapy water. Rinse. Repeat with bleach. I did my hands when I was done, then turned off the sink, put on a fresh pair of gloves, wiped everything down, and reassembled the knives.

The door chimed. I heard Dox walk over to open it.

'Thanks for coming up,' I heard him say. 'I was just about to jump in the shower and uh, I wouldn't have been able to relax in there worrying about forgetting the combination to the safe and all.'

I rolled my eyes. Dox was as deadly a sniper as I've ever known, but we'd have to work on smoothing out some of the rough edges.

I heard them move past my position. There was a bit of muffled conversation. Then they were on their way back to the door. Dox said, 'Thank you again, thank you,' and I heard the door close.

A moment later he opened the bathroom door. 'You can come out now,' he said.

'Any problems?'

'Nope. I think the robe helped, like you said. You know, you're pretty good at this stuff, actually. Hey, maybe we should raid the minibar. This is the opportunity of a lifetime.'

'Was he able to give you the PIN Winters used?'

He nodded. 'Eight-eight-seven-one.'

'Good. Nice work. What did you touch?'

'Just three things. The door handle, the bathroom door handle, and the safe.'

'Okay,' I said, handing him a fresh pair of gloves. 'The alcohol and bleach are in the bathroom. Wash your hands with one, rinse, then use the other. You had Winters's blood on you, too. Then put the gloves on. I'll wipe down the places you touched.'

I grabbed a hand towel and took care of the surfaces he had mentioned, then joined him in the bathroom and did the sink when he was finished there. He pulled on the gloves again and I put the supplies, including the hand towel, into the bag in which we'd brought them. I set the bag down in front of the door so it would be impossible to forget.

We walked over to the safe, which was now open. There were three items inside. A wallet. A passport. And a Treo 650 smartphone.

Dox pulled on his clothes while I checked the items. First, the passport. It was US-issued, and indeed for Mitchell William Winters. Then the wallet, which contained credit cards and an Indonesian driver's license with a Jakarta address, also for Mr Winters. In the billfold, there were Indonesian rupiah, US dollars, Thai baht, and Hong Kong dollars.

Back to the passport. Mr Winters was quite the traveler. He had stamps from all over the world, most recently Thailand, of course.

The Treo was what I was most looking forward to. I picked it up and turned it on. The screen lit up, asking for a password.

Dox said, 'Shit.'

I considered for a moment, then keyed in eight-eight-seven-one.

The screen changed to the home menu. We were in.

'Hot damn, nice going, man!' Dox said, clapping me on the back. 'Shame on old Mr Winters, using the same password in different places.'

I looked at him and raised my eyebrows. 'Do you use different passwords for all your different devices?' I asked.

'Well, uh . . .'

'No one does. In the never-ending battle between security and convenience, convenience always wins.'

'I guess that's true.'

I smiled. 'Of course, now you know better. Remember: security is like a chain. It's only as strong as its weakest link.'

We started going through the Treo – contacts, appointments, memos. There was a lot in the device.

'This is taking too long,' I said. 'Let's put the passport and wallet back in the safe. We'll take the Treo with us. It's possible someone will know it's gone, but I think it'll be worth that risk.'

'Works for me.'

'You leave ahead of me. Don't go out the same way you came in – you don't want that security guard to see you leaving shortly after he saw you come in. Meet me in twenty minutes on the Surawong side of Patpong Two.'

He grinned. 'Sure, I know Patpong.'

'I know you do. But we're just going there to find an Internet café. Don't get distracted.'

'I was afraid you might say that. Why an Internet café?'

'Just a feeling. We might want to follow up on some of what we find in the Treo. We could do this from the laptop at the hotel, but I like to do my surfing anonymously.'

He grinned. 'Me, too. You never know when the government is going to crack down on us pornography hounds.'

Dox went ahead. I put the passport and wallet back in the safe and relocked it. I gave the room a last once-over to make sure we hadn't disturbed anything. It all looked good.

I checked through the peephole. All clear. I opened the door with my shirt and took the stairs down. I used a side exit, then walked down the sois paralleling Silom into Patpong.

16

Twenty minutes later, we were sitting in an Internet bar off Surawang, going through the Treo. The date book was interesting. It had an entry for a meeting at 19:00 the following day. The entry read: *TD, JB, VBM @ CC.*

'Code,' I said, musing.

'Gee, you think?' Dox asked.

I ignored him. 'Let's see what else is in here,' I said.

There were a few dozen names in the contact list. I knew only one of them. Jim Hilger.

'Look at this,' I said, pointing to it.

'Hilger,' Dox said. 'The guy from Hong Kong? The CIA NOC?'

'Yeah, Mr Non-Official Cover. The one who skimmed two million dollars from what Belghazi was paying those Transdniester types who we thought were Russians.'

'That was supposed to be our money, partner. I've been hoping to run into this feller so we could have a good honest talk about it.'

I nodded and went to the memos section. There was only one entry: the confirmation number for an open-ended electronic ticket from Bangkok to Hong Kong.

'Looks like our friend Winters was planning on a visit to Hong Kong,' I said, indicating the entry. 'There's this ticket. And he had Hong Kong dollars in his wallet.'

'Hilger's based in Hong Kong, ain't he? Or he was when we took out Belghazi.'

'Yeah, I'm thinking the same thing.' I went back to the

calendar entry, but still couldn't make sense of Winters's code. I looked at it for about a full minute, but nothing came.

'How does it work?' Dox asked. 'If you stare at it long enough, does it suddenly reveal its secrets?'

I sighed. 'No, probably not. But . . . "at CC" . . . and he's going to be in Hong Kong . . .'

I spun around to the keyboard and brought up Google. I keyed in 'Hong Kong CC.'

I got entries for Hong Kong Correspondence Chess. The Hong Kong Computer Center. The Hong Kong Cricket Club. The Hong Kong Cat Club.

'Ah-ha, the old rendezvous at the Hong Kong Cat Club,' Dox said. 'Those devils, we should have known.'

I could tell that, if Dox and I were going to keep working together, ignoring him was a survival skill I would have to develop. 'Hong Kong Cricket Club,' I said. 'Hong Kong Cat Club. Hong Kong . . . China Club.'

'China Club?'

I nodded. 'It's a private club with a five-star restaurant at the top of the old Bank of China building in Central. They've got one in Beijing now, too, and in Singapore.'

'We didn't get a hit for that, though.'

'Yeah.' I keyed in 'China Club Hong Kong' and hit 'enter.' I got about three million hits, none for what I was looking for.

'You sure about this place?' Dox asked.

'It's exclusive. It wouldn't surprise me if they didn't have a website and I doubt they advertise.' I keyed in a number of variations on what I was looking for until I came up with a phone number. I picked up my cell phone, turned it on, and input the number.

The phone on the other end rang once, then again.

A woman's voice answered: 'Good evening, China Club. How may I assist you?'

'Restaurant reservations,' I said.

'My pleasure,' the voice said.

I waited a moment, then a man's voice said, 'China Club Restaurant. How may I assist you?'

'I'd like to confirm a reservation,' I said. 'Jim Hilger. Tomorrow.'

There was a pause, then the voice said, 'Yes, sir, seven o'clock tomorrow evening, private dining room, party of four.'

'Thank you so much,' I said, smiling.

I hung up and looked at Dox. 'Dinner tomorrow night at the China Club, party of four, private dining room. I think they must have forgotten to invite us.'

He grinned. 'Well, maybe we ought to just join them anyway.'

'I'm beginning to think we should.'

'Do we know who else will be there?'

I shook my head. 'I couldn't ask that. They probably wouldn't have known, and anyway the question would have seemed odd.'

'Well, it was a near thing back there in front of Brown Sugar,' he said, 'but now that I think about it, it might have loosened things up for us, given us the break we're looking for. Nothing like a little serendipity to make a man feel all is right in the universe.'

The massive adrenaline surge that had helped me survive Brown Sugar and its aftermath was ebbing, but I could still feel its effects. Getting to sleep tonight was going to be a bitch.

'So it looks like Hilger was behind Winters,' I said. 'For a while there, I was concerned it was the Israelis.'

'You think Delilah would set us up? I don't believe that. Plus she doesn't know my number.'

'Oh, you didn't get around to giving it to her?'

'Stop it. That wouldn't be right.'

I scrubbed a hand over my face and thought. 'Even before we found that Treo entry, I doubted it was the Israelis. Although if some Russians have your number, I suppose there are a lot of other players who might have gotten ahold of it, the Israelis included. But Delilah only just found out about you. I don't see how the Israelis could have gotten your number that quickly. Plus, they're relatively weak in Asia, which is part of the reason they wanted me to do Manny in the first place. I doubt they have the technical means, on the ground, immediately deployable, to track a cell phone in Bangkok.'

He nodded. 'All right, so we can rule out the Israelites, I agree.'

'Now let's assume that Winters was hooked up with Hilger. It sure looks that way – we've got the entry in the Treo, the Hong Kong connection, the dinner reservation. We think that Hilger is CIA. Does that mean that all this is coming from the CIA?'

'Not necessarily. Hilger might be with the CIA, but he's not synonymous with the CIA.'

'Correct. But the Agency has your phone number, don't they?'

'They do, yeah, they've been a client. Never thought that would be a problem before.'

'Does the Agency know about the work you've done for the Russians?'

'I never told them about it. When I'm not leaving my cell phone on and trying to have my way with the lady-boys, I can actually be fairly discreet.'

I chuckled. 'Well, the Agency might know anyway. They're spies, after all. Winters might have told us he got the number from the Russians to hide the CIA's involvement.'

'Or he might really have gotten it from Ivan.'

'Yeah. No way for us to know, not yet. But whoever Winters was with, they had access to some pretty sophisticated equipment. They had to be able to track your cell phone to Bangkok, which would mean access to the carriers, and they had to pinpoint it at Brown Sugar, which required sophisticated equipment and know-how. Also, they moved fast. We arrived in Bangkok from Manila only two days ago, so they were able to get everything in place in' – I glanced at my watch – 'a little over sixty hours. Pretty impressive.'

'Yeah, but on the other hand, you said those Thai guys weren't pros.'

'No, they weren't. They were outsourced – hell, two of them ran off as soon as they started taking fire.'

'Guess the money wasn't worth it.'

'Exactly. Now, if the snatch had been a CIA op, I would have expected an integrated group from the Agency's paramilitary branch. They've got the operators, and they can move fast if they want to.'

He leaned back in his chair. 'Tell me again. How do we know Hilger is CIA?'

'We don't for sure. But two people implied that he was – Kanezaki, and the late Charles Crawley the third.'

Crawley was the Agency staffer who had tried to hire Dox to take me out. Dox warned me. After which I had what the government likes to call a 'full and frank discussion' with Mr Crawley, uninvited, in his suburban Virginia apartment. He had told me about a Hong Kong NOC, but wouldn't give up the NOC's name. The way Hilger had shown up afterward had left me in no doubt.

'Well, if Hilger's CIA,' Dox said, 'and he was behind Brown Sugar, why did he send a bunch of locals instead of the A-team?'

'He didn't send a bunch of locals. He sent Winters. Winters assembled the local team.'

'I see what you're saying. That's the right way to look at it.'

I looked at him. 'So the question . . .'

'Is, "Who is Old Man Winters?"'

'Right. Was Winters Agency, or not? Right now, I'm guessing not. Which would tell us a lot about what Hilger is really up to.'

I turned to the monitor and Googled 'Mitchell William Winters.' We got no hits.

Dox said, 'It seems that Mr Winters has spent some time flying under the radar.'

'It does. Hang on a minute.'

I went to the bulletin board I used with Tatsu. There was a message waiting from him: the two dead men were named Scott Calver and David Gibbons. That tracked with what Kanezaki had told me. They were both ex-military, Third Special Forces. First Gulf War vets, honorable discharges. After that they entered the State Department Foreign Service, with postings to Amman, Karachi, and Riyadh.

Except for proper names, the message was in Japanese. I translated for Dox. He said, 'So they left the Third Special Forces to become diplomats. Now there's a believable career path.'

'Yeah,' I said. 'At one point, they were Agency. But the message says they left in 2003. Looks like Kanezaki was being straight when he described them as "ex-company."'

I glanced back at the screen. Tatsu's post said the two men had left the government to join 'Gird Enterprises.' I read it to Dox.

'What do you make of that?' he asked.

'A company, I'm guessing. My contact says he has no further information on it, but . . .'

I Googled 'Gird Enterprises' and 'Gird Enterprise.' Nada.

I went back to Tatsu's post. At the bottom, there was an additional paragraph.

When you have a chance, there is something of a personal nature I would like to discuss with you. It's not related to the matter at hand. Will you be in Japan soon? Perhaps we could get together for tea and our small talk, which I confess I quite miss. I hope you are well. Please be careful.

I wondered what the personal matter might be, and hoped that Tatsu and his family were all right. I typed in a message:

I need information on Jim Hilger, American resident in Hong Kong, reportedly a CIA NOC. There's a connection with a man named Mitchell William Winters, probably residing in Jakarta, probably with a US military special operations background, probably with experience in Thailand. Possible connection of both to 'Gird Enterprises.'

And I would very much like to see you for tea and to discuss the personal matter you mention. I hope you and your family are well. Thank you for all your help, and please take care.

'What about Kanezaki?' Dox asked.

I went to that bulletin board. There was a message waiting:

I'm still looking into things, but running into a lot of interference and have to be careful. Anything more you can give me could help.

I typed in, *What can you tell me about 'Gird Enterprises'? Apparently the two departed men left the government for something by that name.* I closed the two bulletin boards and reflexively purged the browser.

'Let's see if there's anything in the news,' I said.

I Googled a few variations on 'Shooting in Manila Shopping Mall CIA.' And came up with a very interesting headline, from the *Washington Post*: 'Two Slain Americans Reported to Be CIA Officers.'

'Shit, look at that,' Dox said.

We read the article. Apparently, 'sources' were claiming that the two dead men were CIA. A CIA spokesman, citing Agency policy, refused to either confirm or deny the affiliations of the men.

We were quiet for a moment. Dox said, 'Kanezaki said they were ex-spooks.'

I nodded. 'He did.'

'Well, I'd have to call this a discrepancy.'

'Yeah.'

'Maybe your lady found out something that might shed some light on the situation. Why don't you give her a call?'

I thought for a moment. For all the reasons Dox and I had just discussed, I didn't think Delilah could have been involved in what had happened in front of Brown Sugar. What was bothering me was that I was *hoping* she hadn't been involved. I realized this was dangerous: it used to be that I would just do the math and accept the results. I didn't hope one way or the other or have any other particular feelings about it. Now I was emotionally invested in the outcome. That made me wonder whether I could trust myself not to skew the data.

I'd have to figure that one out as we went along. If I could.

I called her. There were three rings, then she answered. *'Allo?'*

'It's me. Okay to talk?'

'Okay to talk. I was just going to post you something.'

'Where are you?'

'Bangkok.'

'So am I. Can you meet?'

'No. Gil is here. I have to be careful. And so do you.'

'He's here?' I asked.

She must have heard something in my voice. Or else she had just come to know me well enough to know what I was thinking. Either way, she said, 'Don't even think it.'

I didn't answer. I don't like the feeling of being hunted. I tend to take it personally.

'Don't even think it,' she said again. 'If something happens to him, you will make an enemy of me. I promise.'

All right, Gil was on her team. I needed to remember that.

'I understand,' I said. 'I'll just keep a low profile.'

'Good.'

'Any new info?'

'Yes. It sounds like those men really were CIA. Gil knew them in the first Gulf War. They were all part of the same unit, headed by a man named Jim Huxton, now Jim Hilger.'

Hilger again. Okay.

'What else?'

'Hilger was observed in multiple meetings with Lavi. And he uses CIA cryptonyms. Hilger is "Top Dog." Lavi is "Jew-boy."'

'Well, that's not very politically correct, is it?'

She chuckled.

'I'm serious. You think you could use a crypt like that at a US government agency? Christ, the Transportation Security Administration can't even do an extra check on a Saudi chanting verses from the Koran and mumbling "Allahu Akbar" as he boards a plane, you think the CIA can call an asset "Jew-boy"?'

'That's a good point.'

I picked up the Treo and looked at the date book. 'TD' and 'JB' suddenly took on a whole new meaning.

'What about "VBM"?' I asked.

'"VBM"?'

'Yes, probably another crypt.'

'It doesn't mean anything to me. Gil didn't mention it. Just the two I told you. Why?'

'I'm not sure. Anyway, the two you got were helpful. Thanks.'

'Helpful, how?'

I paused and considered. My sense was that she could be useful, maybe even necessary, but I wanted a chance to think about it before I asked.

'You sure you can't meet?' I asked.

'It's not a good idea. I don't want Gil to get more suspicious than he already is.'

'How much time are you spending with him?'

There was a pause. She said, 'Are you jealous?'

'Yeah, I think I am.'

'That's nice. I like that.'

Damn, I really would have liked to see her. Oh, well. The good news was that her demurral made me trust her. If she'd said no, then allowed me to persuade her, I would have smelled a set-up. Delilah wasn't the wishy-washy type.

'My information is that those guys weren't spooks,' I said. 'They were ex-spooks. Most recently with an outfit called "Gird Enterprises." That mean anything to you?'

'It doesn't. Did you try Google?'

For a moment I was easily able to understand why Dox sometimes got annoyed with me for asking questions that to him must have seemed obvious. 'Of course,' I said. 'There's nothing.'

'I'll look into it,' she said. 'You sure about those guys, though?'

'Not sure, no. But I've got two independent sources, one of them in the organization itself, and their information tracks. My guess is that your people have it wrong, although I don't know why.'

'I don't know what more I can do on that one. I've already asked. If I press further, they'll know something's up.'

There was a pause. 'How long will you be in Bangkok?' I asked.

'I don't know. I'm supposed to post something on our bulletin board about how I'm angry and hurt that you took off, that I want to see you again. I can probably wait a couple days or so to see if you'll contact me.'

'Then let me check on a few things, use the information you gave me. I'll be in touch.'

'Don't keep me out of this. I'm in too deeply already.'

She had good antennae. 'I won't keep you out,' I said.

I imagined her thinking, *Like hell.* But what could she say.

'I'll be in touch,' I told her.

There was a pause. She said, 'You better be.' And clicked off.

I briefed Dox on the cryptonyms and everything else.

'Hilger, Manny, the dear departed Mr Winters, and the mysterious Mr VBM,' he said. 'Damn, partner, sounds like Hong Kong is going to be the place to be.'

'Yeah, but if we go there, are we taking on the whole CIA? Or something else?'

'Well, let's consider. We've got the Israelites telling us one thing, and Kanezaki and your Japanese contact telling us something different. Whose information do you trust more?'

I shrugged. 'Kanezaki's in the best position to know.'

'I agree with that, as long as he's playing it straight.'

'Plus we've got the independent confirmation.'

'Agreed again. So what could have led the Israelites astray?'

I thought for a minute. 'One, someone could be lying. Two, and more likely, I think, someone's just made a mistake. Which isn't so hard to imagine. I mean, Delilah said that Gil knew Hilger and the other two guys when they joined the Company. Then, during surveillance, Gil saw Hilger with Manny. He naturally assumes Hilger is still with the Agency and that Manny is an asset. When the two guys get killed while meeting with Manny, it reinforces the existing assumption that they were active-duty CIA. No one thinks to ask, Have these people moved on to something else? And they can't make too many inquiries because the whole thing is so sensitive. Plus, there's this media leak we just saw in the *Washington Post*. They might have seen that, too. More reinforcement of a mistaken assumption.'

He nodded for a long moment, as though thinking. Then he said, 'You know, maybe we're being too limited with this either/or perspective we've adopted.'

I looked at him, intrigued.

'I mean, look at us,' he went on. 'Are we CIA? No, not really, we're contractors. But the CIA uses us from time to time. And it ain't just us. Hell, these days you've got Halliburton and Blackwater and DynCorp and Vinnell and Kroll-Crucible . . . these outfits are springing up all over, and it can be hard to tell where the government ends and the private sector begins.'

'That's true,' I said.

'Plus you've got the government turning everybody into a bounty hunter by offering twenty-five million for Osama's scrawny ass.'

'Capitalism at work,' I said. 'Supply and demand.'

'I know. Hell, when I was watching us shock and awe the Iraqis on CNN when we first went in, I kept expecting the announcer to say, "This sortie brought to you by Kellogg's Rice Krispies," or something like that. It just ain't as clear as it used to be.'

I nodded. 'You know who is the third largest contributor of forces to the coalition there, after the US and the Brits?'

'Private contractors, son, no doubt about it. We're the wave of the future. Ought to form a union.'

I nodded. 'The US doesn't go out of its way to advertise it, but yeah.'

'Well, that's what I'm talking about.'

He rubbed his chin as though considering something.

'But on balance,' he went on, 'I don't think we're dealing with Uncle Sam here. Not with the Thais, not with the Jewboy thing. And like you said, Christians In Action has a fairly dismal record of being able to run really bad guys like Manny. Plus your Japanese contact, plus Kanezaki, both say those guys in Manila were ex-spooks, not current. That's independent confirmation, far as we know.'

'What about that *Washington Post* report?'

He shrugged. 'Some reporter, fishing. Making the same mistake the Israelites made.'

I nodded. 'Can't disagree with any of that.'

'Plus Hilger did abscond with that two million dollars from Kwai Chung.'

'I'm not sure which way that cuts. He could still be government, just dirty.'

'That's kind of what I'm getting at. What I think is, Hilger *is* Agency, but he's wandered a tad off the reservation.'

I considered. 'That would be a very interesting possibility.'

'Damn straight it's interesting. If I'm right, and the news gets out, the Agency would likely disown Hilger like the wayward child he is. I've seen it happen.'

'He would be vulnerable to that, it's true.'

'So you agree with what I'm saying?'

'I do.'

'Think we ought to go to Hong Kong?'

I looked at him. 'I think we ought to leave in the morning. Bangkok's feeling a little hot after Brown Sugar, anyway.'

I checked a few sites and found a Thai Air flight leaving at 8:00 that morning. I looked at my watch – less than seven hours away. Good. I wanted us out of the country before Hilger got news of what had happened to his man Winters, or at least before he had a chance to react to it. I reserved a seat for me, then one on an 8:25 Cathay Pacific flight for Dox. It would be more secure for us to travel separately. To be doubly sure, I used one of the backup false identities we were traveling under just in case Hilger had thought to put a customs hit on our names. I booked rooms for us in a couple of big, anonymous hotels – the InterContinental on Kowloon for Dox and the Shangri-La on Hong Kong Island for me.

'Glad to see we're going deluxe,' Dox said, as I made the reservations.

'The China Club is members only,' I said. 'We need hotels that can get their guests in.'

'Hey, I'm not complaining.'

'We're going to need some clothes, too,' I said. 'The club is formal. There ought to be a tailor right in the Inter-Continental shopping arcade who can get a suit ready for you while you wait. If not, ask the concierge for a recommendation.'

He smiled. 'I love Hong Kong. Fastest place on earth.'

'Just tell the tailor you want something dark and conservative, a suit,' I said. 'Let him do the rest. He'll pick a tie for you, too.'

'Hey, man, don't you trust my sense of style?'

I thought it best not to answer. I finished up on the computer, then purged the browser again.

Dox said, 'One thing occurs to me. If Winters is supposed to show up for dinner at the China Club and he doesn't, Hilger's going to be concerned. Or maybe Winters was supposed to check in beforehand, and when he doesn't, Hilger might change his plans. Wasn't that what you were worried about, why you tried to make it look like the man hadn't died being interrogated?'

I nodded. 'We'll have to take that into account. But the fact that the meeting place was already decided is encouraging. It would have been more secure for Hilger to have just told people the general venue, and waited until the last moment to give the exact location. My guess is that VBM, whoever he is, isn't all that reachable. Or there are some other limitations on their ability to communicate in real time. And you have to figure this meeting is related to what happened in Manila. They've already been disrupted there once. I doubt they'd want to cancel again just because someone didn't show up or failed to check in. I may be wrong, and if I am we're going to find out, but I have a feeling their dinner's on.'

He leaned back in his chair. 'I'll buy that. What's the general plan?'

I started envisioning things, figuring out what more we'd need and how we were going to get it.

'Manny and Hilger,' I said. 'We take them both out. Manny satisfies the Israeli contract. We get paid. As for Hilger, either he's not CIA at all, or he is and he's off the reservation, but either way he gets disowned postmortem. At which point, the Israelis realize that they don't have a problem with the Agency. It gets everyone off our backs.'

'You know, though, even if the government disowns Hilger, someone might be interested in avenging him. That kind of thing has been known to happen.'

I shrugged. 'I'm willing to take that chance. No matter what, Hilger is where the direct pressure is coming from right now, even more than from the Israelis. I don't see a better way of relieving that pressure than eliminating its source.'

'Seems reasonable to me.'

Part of me wondered how I had wandered along to a point where calmly proposing that we kill two men, one of whom might be CIA, would indeed seem reasonable. I would have to ponder that in my leisure time.

'And,' I said, 'since, as far as I can tell, the reason they wanted relatively "natural" causes for Manny in the first place was their mistaken assumption that he was a CIA asset, we no longer have to be overly constrained in our methods.'

Dox nodded. 'That makes me feel better. Where I was brought up, gentlemen just shot each other. It's more comfortable for me.'

I nodded, then for the second time in as many minutes realized that there were people in the world who might find this kind of conversation strange, who might even be put off by it. I wondered where the new perspective was coming from. I really would have to think about that later.

'The thing is,' I said, 'I don't think we're going to have guns.'

His face fell a little. 'No guns?'

I shook my head. 'I don't think even Kanezaki could get

us what we'd need on this short notice. I'm not sure it would be wise to ask just now, regardless. And my Japanese contact could help us if we were in Tokyo. For Hong Kong . . . not with these time constraints.'

'Well, that sucks. I was kind of picturing myself up on a rooftop with the dreaded M-40A3 and matching AN/ PVS-10 nightscope. It would have been so civilized.'

I nodded. 'That, or I could have just burst into their private room with a forty-five while they were enjoying the Peking duck. But maybe . . .'

He looked at me. 'You're thinking something devious there, partner, I can tell.'

I smiled. 'I'm thinking about Hilger. He was armed last year at Kwai Chung.'

'Armed and dangerous,' he said, nodding. 'That boy was a one-man killing machine. Had his primary in a waist holster or belly band, if I'm remembering correctly, and a backup on his ankle.'

'Think that was a one-time thing?'

'Hell, no. A guy like that, carry for him is routine. He'd feel naked without it.'

'And even if it's not routine, we know he carries when he's operational.'

'Like tomorrow night, for example.'

'For example.'

He stroked his chin and grinned. 'Old Manny might be carrying, too. I would be, after what almost happened to him in Manila.'

'Exactly what I was thinking.'

'Nice of them, to bring the guns for us.'

I nodded. 'All I need to do is get to one of them alone, from behind. Say, in a restroom.'

Dox cleared his throat. 'You're not worried about, you

know, that when you see Manny like you did the last time . . .'

I shook my head, and felt something shift inside me like a block of frozen granite. 'No,' I said. 'I'm not worried at all.'

Part Three

17

Because Winters and company might have tracked Dox's cell phone earlier in the day, the Grand Hyatt was no longer secure. We took extreme care in returning, and stayed just long enough to collect our gear. Then we went to Sukhumvit, using appropriate countersurveillance measures along the way, and took rooms at the Westin. Dox, chastened by the way Winters had almost gotten to us, didn't argue with any of this.

I showered and shaved, then took an excruciatingly hot bath, which ordinarily helps me sleep. But I was still wired from that near miss in front of Brown Sugar. I had to leave for the airport at six o'clock, and if I didn't get some rest soon, the next chance I'd get would be on the plane.

I pulled a chair over to the window and sat in the dark, looking down at Sukhumvit Road and the urban mass beyond it. There wasn't much of a view – the Westin isn't tall enough and the city itself is too congested. I wished for a moment, absurdly, that I was back in my apartment in Sengoku, the quiet part of Tokyo where I'd lived until the CIA and Yamaoto had managed to track me there. I'd never realized at the time how safe I felt there, how peaceful. It seemed a long time ago, and so much had happened in between. I realized I'd never even paused to mourn having been forced to leave. Until this moment, anyway. And now I couldn't afford the distraction.

I thought about the plan Dox and I had come up with.

It seemed sound, up to a point. But I wondered why the solutions I reached for always involved violence.

Violence, my ass. You're talking about killing.

I smiled sardonically. When all you've got are hammers, everything starts to look like a nail.

Maybe my default settings were just horrifyingly stunted. Or warped. Maybe there were other, better ways, ways that long and unfortunate habit was preventing me from seeing.

Yeah, maybe. But the feeling of sitting there in the dark, running through the requirements of the next day's operation, was momentarily so familiar to me that it carried with it the oppressive weight of fate.

I've been killing since that first Viet Cong, near the Xe Kong river, when I was seventeen. I'd kept count for a while, but long ago lost track entirely, something that horrified Midori, rightly, I supposed, when she had asked me about it. Could it really have just been circumstances that got me started so early and kept me going so long, or was there something about me, something intrinsic?

So many people seemed to recognize that I was a killer. Tatsu. Dox. The army shrinks. Carlos Hathcock, the legendary sniper I'd once met in Vietnam.

Why fight it? I thought. *Just accept the evidence.*

I remembered something from a childhood visit to church. Matthew, I think, where Jesus said:

Put your sword back in its place, for all who draw the sword will die by the sword.

I chewed on that for a moment. Then:

Bullshit. God doesn't care. Like Dox said, if he did care, he would have done something by now.

If he did do something, would you even know what it was? Would you be paying attention?

I would if he fucking smote me, or whatever. Which is what I would do.

Maybe that was the point, though. All this time, I'd been expecting – hell, demanding – that God smite me down for my transgressions. And prove himself to me thereby. But what if God weren't really in the smiting business? What if smiting were all man-made, and God preferred to communicate in more subtle ways, ways that men like me chose to pretend weren't even there?

I leaned forward, my elbows on my knees, and looked at my hands as though they might offer me some answer. I wished I could get tired. I wanted so much to just sleep.

I thought of Musashi's *Go Rin No Sho,* the Book of Five Rings, which I've read many times. In his recounting of his over sixty sword duels, and of the half-dozen large-scale battles in which he participated, Musashi had never expressed doubt about the morality of his actions. He seemed to take it as a given that men fought, killed, and died, and I doubted he gave much more thought to any of this than he did to the fact that men breathed and ate and slept. The one was as natural, and immutable, as the other. What mattered was one's proficiency.

Somehow, Musashi had found a way to put down his sword as he got older. By the time he was in his late fifties, he spent most of his time teaching, painting, meditating, practising tea, and writing poetry. And writing his profound book, of course. Eventually, he even managed to die in his bed. I didn't find that notion at all unappealing. I just didn't know how I was going to get there if I didn't find a way to get out of this business.

When people take stock of their lives, I wondered, how do they go about it? From where do they derive their satisfaction, their sense of purpose? Sitting there, alone in that dark room, I tried to find some way to sum up my own existence, to justify who I am. And all I could come up with was:

You're a killer.

I rested my head in my hands. I couldn't think of anything else. Killing is all I've ever really been good at. Killing, and, I suppose, surviving.

But maybe . . . maybe I was missing the point. My nature might be immutable, but the causes to which I lent that nature, that was still for me to decide. And then it occurred to me: the dream I'd had, the one about the two *katana.* That's what the dream had been about.

Regardless of the other services in which it might be employed, a sword is fundamentally a killing instrument. Yeah, you might use it as a doorjamb or as a letter opener, but that's not what it's designed for. It's not what the sword, in its soul, longs to do. But its inherent nature isn't what makes the sword good or bad; rather, the sword's morality is determined by the use to which it is put. There is *katsujinken,* the sword that gives life, or weapon of justice; and *setsuninto,* the sword that takes life, or weapon of oppression. In the dream, some nameless thing had almost caught me because of my inability to decide. I couldn't afford to keep making that mistake in my life.

Could I become *katsujinken?* Was that the answer? Killing Belghazi in Hong Kong a year earlier had prevented the transfer of radiologically tipped missiles to groups that wanted to detonate them in metropolitan areas. Didn't my act there save countless lives? And couldn't something like that . . . offset the other things I've done?

The notion was both appealing and frightening: appealing, because it hinted at the possibility of redemption; frightening, because it also acknowledged the certainty that, one way or the other, eventually I would be judged.

I chuckled ruefully. *Katsujinken* and redemption . . . I was going to continue trying to reconcile East and West until the attempt finally killed me.

I thought about Manny. He was like Belghazi, wasn't he? A lot of good would come from his death.

And his little boy will be marooned in grief for years to follow.

I thought of the delicate way Dox had asked me if I was afraid I might freeze again, and of the simple confidence with which he took me at my word when I told him he needn't worry.

And suddenly the feeling of being frozen, stuck in some nameless purgatory between competing worldviews, began to seem like the worst possibility of all. This was the wrong time to be a philosopher, to be afflicted with doubts. I didn't care what the price was. I didn't care whether it was right or wrong. I was going to finish what I started.

I felt the familiar mental bulkheads sliding shut, sealing off my emotions, focusing me only on the essentials of what needed to be done and how I would do it. Some bloodless, disconnected part of myself, turning the knobs and dials and making sure that things happened as they needed to. Whatever it was, this feeling, it has served me well countless times in my life. I don't know if other people have it, but it's part of my core, part of what makes me who and what I am. But this time, as those partitions moved into place, the part of me being closed off behind them wondered whether this wasn't some further transgression, some further sin. To have been so close to what felt like a difficult epiphany, and to deliberately turn away from it . . .

I sat back in the chair and let my gaze unfocus. I started thinking about how we could do it the way it needed to be done.

I'd been to the China Club once, and knew the general

layout. It was on the top three floors of the old Bank of China building in Central. The elevators stopped at thirteen; the next two floors were accessible only by internal staircases.

I'd need to arrive early, use a pretext for getting in. Maybe I'd be doing advance work for some Japanese corporate titan, checking the place out to see if the boss wanted to shell out all those yen for a membership. The ploy was good. I'd used it before, and it usually brought out the host's deepest desires to show his place off and answer all my innocent questions.

The problem was that Manny knew my face now. I could ameliorate some of that with light disguise, which I assumed I'd have to use anyway because of the high likelihood of security cameras at the building's perimeter and possibly inside. I'm also good at just fading into the background when I need to. But Hilger, who I sensed was a significantly harder target than Manny, would also know my face, as well as Dox's. The CIA had photos of us both, as I'd learned during the Belghazi op a year earlier, and Hilger would have studied them closely, the same way I would have. Getting into the building wouldn't be too difficult. But once we were inside, our ability to move might be curtailed.

I sat and thought more. I could get there early, and probably find a place to hide. A bathroom, a closet, whatever. Dox would arrive later. We might be able to use cameras, as we had at the Peninsula in Manila, and Dox could monitor them and signal me with the commo gear when it was time to move. But where could we position him so he wouldn't be noticed? I pictured him, sitting alone at the China Club's renowned Long March Bar. The Long March Bar was for entertaining and impressing clients.

Anyone sitting by himself for more than a few minutes would stick out. It wasn't going to work.

Of course, if he weren't alone, it would be a little more doable. If he were with, say, an attractive European executive.

I pictured Dox in a Hong Kong–tailored, conservative suit, across from Delilah, probably in a chic but tasteful pantsuit. Dox could be a local corporate expat; Delilah would be the smart European advertising executive trying to land an account with him. That's the kind of deal that got done at the China Club every night. They'd look completely at home.

What the hell, I couldn't sleep anyway. I got up, turned on one of the reading lights, and picked up the cell phone. I slipped in a new SIM card and powered it up, then called Delilah. She answered on the first ring.

'Hey,' I said. 'Hope I'm not waking you.'

'You're not. I'm still jet-lagged.'

'Okay time to talk?'

'It's fine. I'm just sitting in my room.'

I thought about asking her again if she wanted to meet. It seemed like such a waste, with both of us in the same city. Hell, for all I knew, she was in the same hotel, maybe in the room right next to me.

I supposed she was right, though. It would have been stupid to meet now, with Gil watching her. If she had to lose him, she might only get one chance, and I wanted that chance to be the China Club. Also, part of me, maybe not the most mature part, didn't like the idea of being rejected a third time, even if the rejections were for sound reasons and not at all personal.

'I think I've got an opportunity to wrap this whole thing up tomorrow,' I said. 'Finish what I started.'

There was a pause. She said, 'Okay.'

'But I could use your help. If that's a problem, I'll understand. This isn't your mess.'

She chuckled softly. 'If only that were true.'

'All right. If you want to help clean things up, can you get to Hong Kong tomorrow?'

There was another pause. 'I already told Gil that I would stick around Bangkok for a few days in case you contacted me. I don't know how I could explain my sudden urge to travel.'

I thought for a moment. 'Tell him I contacted you. That I apologized for bugging out on you and asked if you could join me in Hong Kong.'

'If I tell him that, he's going to go out there, too, just like he came to Bangkok. To be closer to wherever you resurface so he can get to you right away. And he's suspicious of me now. He's going to want to stay close.'

'Can you manage all that?'

I could feel her weighing the pros and cons. She said, 'Probably.'

'Can you get a flight out first thing in the morning?'

'Of course.'

'Okay. Do it. Check the bulletin board when you get there. Or I'll call you again.'

She was quiet for a moment, and I thought, *Meet me tonight. Just ask me.*

But she didn't. She said, 'Okay. I'll be there.'

I thanked her and hung up.

I powered down the cell phone, turned off the light, and sat down in the chair again. I crossed my legs under me and watched the city lights through the window until one by one, almost imperceptibly, they started to go out.

I thought about Delilah, so near and yet so far.

I hoped I could trust her. I supposed I needed to. But none of that was what worried me.

What worried me was how much I wanted to.

18

Hilger finally finished up the day's financial work – certain aspects of which constituted his cover in Hong Kong; others of which had more to do with his real business, his real mission. With everything that had been going on lately, it hadn't been easy to stay on top of it all.

He stood up from his desk and stretched, then checked his watch. Shit, two in the morning. He had to get home and get some sleep. He had a big day tomorrow.

The phone rang. He sat back down. The caller ID read-out indicated a blocked number, which, he hoped, meant it was Winters calling with good news. He'd been wondering what had been taking so long.

Instead, it was Demeere, another man from his network who had gone to Thailand to help Winters interrogate Rain. Before Hilger had a moment to consider why it was Demeere calling rather than Winters, the team leader, Demeere said, 'Bad news.'

'All right,' Hilger said, his voice calm.

'Winters and the Thais tried to take Rain outside a club in Pathumwan. Rain got away. Winters is dead. So are two of the Thais.'

For once, Hilger's calm came slightly unstuck. He said, 'Shit.' He tried to think of something else to say, but there was nothing, so he said it again. 'Shit.'

Winters was a pro, and Hilger had assumed the man would avoid any unnecessary risks. Worst case, he had expected they might not be able to find Rain, or that Rain might get away when they moved in on him. He hadn't expected casualties. Certainly not Winters.

'What about Dox?' he asked, regaining his focus.

'He got away, too. Two of the Thais briefed me.'

'Do the Thais represent a liability at this point?'

'No. They don't know enough to matter.'

Hilger thought for a moment, then said, 'How did it go down?'

'Apparently Rain saw it coming. He reacted before they were properly in position.'

If Rain had seen Winters coming, he must be damn near psychic. That, or the Thais had slipped somehow. You couldn't expect them to own up to something like that. They were just local muscle, after all. Contractors. With Calver and Gibbons dead from that goat-rope in Manila, Hilger hadn't been able to field a full, professional team.

'How did Winters die?' Hilger asked.

'Rain had a knife.'

Hilger frowned. All that *kali* stuff . . . Winters was supposed to be an expert with blades. 'He beat Winters, with a knife?' he asked, thinking that something was wrong with the story.

'Dox threw a chair at him, it seems. It knocked him down.'

Well, that would do it. 'And then?'

'The Thais said Rain and Dox jumped on him and started stabbing him. There was nothing they could do and they ran away.'

Hilger believed they ran away, all right. He just wondered exactly when in the sequence it had actually happened.

'Were you able to confirm any of this?' he asked.

'Yeah. I've got a contact in the embassy who was able to check with the Thai police. Winters had broken ribs and was killed by a knife wound in the chest. He had defensive wounds on his arms.'

Even in the midst of his anger and sorrow over Winters, Hilger felt a sense of relief that the man had died on his feet. Winters knew a lot, and it would have been a problem if Rain and Dox had managed to interrogate him. Not that Winters had been any sort of pushover – it would have taken a lot to separate him from any information he was intent on keeping – but this way, Hilger didn't have to deal with any doubts at all.

'What do the police make of it?' he asked.

'They think it was a bad drug deal. Winters was traveling sterile. No problem there.'

Damn, Winters had been a good man. Thorough. Losing him was a blow.

Hilger realized he was going to have to call Winters's sister, Elizabeth Shannon. Winters hadn't been married; his sister was his next of kin. Hilger had dated her after the war. She was married now, with a family, but they had stayed friendly. Goddamnit, he was dreading that call. He hated Rain for forcing him to make it.

'What's next?' Demeere asked.

Hilger thought for a moment about telling the man to come to Hong Kong for the meeting with VBM, but then decided not to. It would have been useful to have him there to take Winters's place, but he judged it more important to keep someone on Rain and Dox. He wanted them dead.

'Try to reacquire Rain and Dox,' Hilger told him. 'And use your discretion, but I would advise against trying to render them again. We've lost too many people already, and I don't see how we could do it anyway without a full team in place. If you can find them and the opportunity is there, just take them the fuck out.'

'Roger that,' Demeere said. 'I'll keep you posted.'

Hilger hung up. Christ, the op was coming apart. But he had to find a way to fix it. It had taken him two years to set up this meeting with VBM. And it wasn't just the time he'd invested. It was the things he'd been forced to do to make it possible. Those things were going to haunt him forever, and if there was a God out there, Hilger knew one day there was going to be some explaining to do.

He put his elbows on his desk, closed his eyes, and rested his forehead against his fingertips. Yeah, he'd made some hard calls along the way, calls that no one should have to make. Having to take out that guy in Amman, an American, with a family, hadn't been easy. And having to sit on information that he knew would have saved lives in Bali, in Jakarta, and elsewhere . . . well he was going to have to live with all of that, too.

But a lot of good was coming from it, and that was the thing to focus on. You had to look at the big picture. Were the Brits wrong not to evacuate Coventry when they discovered the Nazis were going to bomb it? If the city had been evacuated, the Nazis would have known their Enigma code had been compromised, and the whole Allied war effort would have been jeopardized. The people of Coventry had to be sacrificed so that others might live. It wasn't pretty when you said it out loud, but that's what had happened. The difference was, today the politicians didn't have the balls to make those decisions. So the hard work had devolved to men like himself.

It was funny, he thought, that democracy couldn't survive if it tried to adhere top to bottom to its own ideals. He knew that it was men like himself, working behind the scenes, on their own, doing what no one else could face, who made democracy function, who saved it from the knowledge of its own inherent hypocrisy, who kept it sleeping untroubled at night.

The irony was, Rain was a man who might understand all this. Didn't the Japanese even have a name for it? *Honne* and *tatemae* – real truth, and societal façade? English could use a couple of words like that. Their absence from America's lexicon was revealing: not only couldn't we appreciate the necessity, we couldn't even acknowledge the concept.

Rain. He imagined how good it was going to feel when he received confirmation that the man was dead. He was surprised at the intensity of the feeling. Ordinarily, these things weren't personal for him. But three good men were down, and now he had to make that call to Elizabeth Shannon . . . not to mention the pressure all this was putting on his entire operation.

Yeah, he wanted him dead, all right. And Dox, too. He wondered if maybe he would have a chance to do it himself.

19

The flight to Hong Kong the next morning was uneventful. After the restless night I'd just had, I was glad to sleep through most of it. I arrived at Hong Kong International feeling relaxed and refreshed and caught a cab to the Shangri-La.

I checked in, then called Dox on the prepaid unit he was carrying. He was in a cab, on his way to Kowloon.

'Stop at the bug-out point first, take care of that,' I said. 'No sense in both of us being there at the same time. Then check in and get the clothes you need.'

'Will do.'

The bug-out point was a coffee shop near the Man Mo temple on Hollywood Road. When you go operational, or otherwise commit an act that the authorities are apt to frown upon if you're caught, it's wise to choose a backup meeting place to use if it becomes inconvenient to return to your hotel, and to pre-position certain necessary items there: cash, for one thing; and a spare passport, for another, if you're lucky or connected enough to know how to come by such things. You typically want a place that's accessible at all hours and that offers many appropriate hiding spots: the underside of a counter or a bookshelf, the back of a bathroom cabinet, that sort of thing. Whether the op goes well or poorly, your things need to be in place for only a few hours. If the op goes really poorly, you've got bigger problems than someone stumbling across the stash you've taped to, say, the underside of a toilet in an all-night diner.

'When you're done with that,' I said, 'let's meet on the mezzanine level of the Grand Hyatt at sixteen hundred. It's away from the main lobby so it's private, and you'll look right at home there in your new threads.'

'Sounds good. You've got the gear?'

'And everything else.'

'All right, partner, see you soon.'

I turned off the phone and headed over to the hotel shopping arcade, where I got a haircut and a shave. I had them put a bunch of gel in my hair and slick it back – not my usual look, and not a dramatic alteration to my appearance, but lots of small changes would begin to add up. Next, a visit to an optometrist for a pair of rectangular wire-frame glasses that did a nice job of reworking the angles of my face. At the adjacent Pacific Place shopping mall, one stop at Dunhill got me the rest of what I needed: single-breasted, double-vented navy gabardine suit, fitted with inch-and-a-half cuffs in fifteen minutes flat; white Sea Island cotton shirt and flat gold cuff links; brown split-toe lace-ups and navy socks; brown alligator belt and British-tan attaché case. It wasn't terribly cold in Hong Kong, but perhaps just chilly enough to justify the purchase of a pair of brown deerskin gloves, which went into the attaché. I checked myself in the mirror before heading out of the store and liked what I saw: a well-off Japanese businessman, with international experience and taste, in the discreet employ of powerful industrial interests seeking a foothold in Hong Kong through one of its famous business institutions, the China Club. Hopefully I'd even get to keep the clothes when this was done. Hopefully they wouldn't have any bullet holes in them.

I headed back to the hotel and filled the attaché case with the commo gear and other equipment. From the hotel, I caught a cab to the bug-out point, where I taped an extra passport and some other necessaries to the back of a cabinet in the men's room. Then I walked until I found an Internet café, where I checked the bulletin board. No word from Kanezaki. From Tatsu, there was some interesting news. His post said:

Jim Hilger: Works as a financial adviser in Hong Kong for high net worth clients. Cannot confirm his possible CIA affiliations, although sources believe there was a connection there at some point. More recently, considered dirty. Suspected to be involved in black market arms trading, including Israeli weapons to various separatist groups in the region. Suspected of operating 'Murder, Inc.' type organization, trading on former military and possible intelligence skills and contacts.

Mitchell William Winters: Gulf War I veteran, Third Special Forces. No other information.

Looking forward to seeing you. Take care of yourself.

All right, the more I·learned, the more it seemed that Dox and I were right. Either Hilger was running his own show, or he was so far off the government reservation that he might as well be.

I Googled 'Two Slain Americans Reported to Be CIA Officers' to follow up on the story we'd seen the day before in the *Washington Post*. This time there were dozens of hits – the other services were starting to pick up the story. I went to the *Post*'s site because they seemed to be breaking the news. There was a new story, this one headlined, 'Americans Killed in Manila Connected to Mysterious Company.'

The *Post* had picked up the Gird Enterprises information and was running with it. They'd done some digging, and apparently the address listed in the company's articles of incorporation was an empty suite in a New Jersey office park. The *Post* had contacted the law firm that had drawn up the articles; when told who was calling and why, the lawyer they reached hung up. Interesting.

I caught a cab to the Grand Hyatt and called Delilah from the lobby.

'Hey,' she said. 'I was wondering when you were going to call.'

'Sorry. I had a lot of things to do to get ready. How soon can you be in the lobby of the Grand Hyatt?'

'Fifteen minutes.'

'Good. See you then.' I clicked off.

I walked up the black granite stairs that curved along the wall to the mezzanine level. The mezzanine was open to the opulent lobby below, and would provide a good vantage point for ensuring that Delilah came alone.

Dox wasn't there yet. I stood looking down at the lobby, explaining to the woman who offered to seat me that I preferred to wait and watch for my acquaintances, who ought to be arriving soon.

Delilah got there in fifteen minutes as promised. She looked around the lobby, then up at the mezzanine. I nodded when she saw me, then watched her cross the lobby and start up the long, winding stairs. No one came in after her. If Gil was keeping tabs, it was at a distance. So far.

I offered her my hand as she approached, just a business acquaintance greeting her for a post-meeting drink. We shook, then stood looking down at the lobby. Harry's bug detector lay in my pocket without stirring.

'Dox is on his way,' I said. 'Let's just keep an eye out for him.'

'All right.'

In fact, I wanted to watch the lobby for a little longer to make sure she had come alone. She knew what I was doing, of course, but under the circumstances couldn't really object.

'Where's Gil?' I asked.

'He's here. I told him you contacted me and wanted to meet me in Hong Kong. Right now he's probably just sitting in his hotel room, waiting for me to call.'

I would have liked to take the fight to him. I've never been inclined to simply run and hide. A tactical retreat, sure, but at a minimum you leave booby traps along the way. Or you circle behind the people who are hunting you until you're hunting them. It's just the way I work, the way I've always done things.

But all I said was, 'We'll try to get this over with before he gets too antsy.'

Dox showed ten minutes later. Damn, I'd never seen him like this – a perfectly tailored charcoal suit, white spread-collar shirt, and a monochrome blue tie. The only thing that was out of place was the goatee – I'd forgotten to mention that. It was too memorable and anyway we needed to alter his appearance as much as possible. I thought it ought to go.

Unlike Delilah, Dox looked up before he looked anywhere else. It was reflex for him to check for sniper hides, and he saw us immediately. He crossed the lobby and headed up the stairs.

He walked over to where we were standing and shook Delilah's hand. 'It's nice to see you again,' he said.

I realized that the latent formality Delilah seemed to evoke in him would be perfect for the job at hand. Dox, whose acting skills, in my opinion, still needed polishing, would automatically comport himself like the perfect gentleman, businessman, and solicitous host, which was exactly who he was supposed to be today.

She gave him a warm smile and said, 'Likewise.'

'Sorry I'm a little late. I had some trouble getting fitted in this suit. They're not used to the big guys in these parts.'

'You look great,' she said, nodding her head appreciatively.

He actually blushed. One day I would have to ask Delilah what her secret was. 'Thank you,' he said. 'You do, too.'

She did look great. She was wearing a charcoal pantsuit with a fitted double-breasted jacket, short to the waist with the buttons set low across the chest. Underneath was a crisp white blouse open at the neck. The pants were also fitted, with a slight flare below the knee; farther down, a pair of deep purple flats, a little less dressy than pumps but better for maneuver. The whole thing was set off with a pair of diamond stud earrings and a simple platinum link necklace. She was carrying a leather attaché case and a small clutch. Her blonde hair was down and blown out – the perfect attention-getter in Hong Kong, and something that could be expected to draw attention away from Dox, whom Hilger might recognize.

We sat down and ordered tea. I briefed them on what I had just learned from my 'source in Japan,' and on the latest news from the *Washington Post*. We all agreed that, although Gil's information was to the contrary, the jury was in on Jim Hilger. Now all that remained was to carry out his sentence. And Manny's.

We spent some time mapping things out. Through the hotel, I had already arranged a visit to the China Club for later that afternoon, and Dox and Delilah needed to do the same. Reservations shouldn't be a problem; all they had to do was get there early enough to ensure getting seats at one of the small tables in the bar. We'd communicate via the commo gear. We would use the wireless video transmitters that Dox and I had employed in Manila, but this time we would supplement them with audio, and the combination would let us know when tonight's targets arrived, where they were positioned, and, most important, when one of them excused himself from dinner to attend a call of nature. I was confident I could find an appropriate place to hide on the premises; Dox and Delilah would monitor it all from the bar and keep me apprised of whatever I needed to know. As for Manny and Hilger, I would use my hands on the first one that presented a target of opportunity, then immediately proceed to the other. With any luck, at that point I would be armed. VBM, whoever he was, would go down, too, if he got in the way, but other than that he meant nothing to me.

If this had been a sniping operation, I would have been the sniper; Dox and Delilah, the spotters. The division of labor isn't always necessary, but it's almost always useful. Having a partner spot, assess, and monitor the target enables the sniper to focus on a single task: killing. In this case, it would have been distracting for me to have to try to gauge whether and when Hilger or Manny might be moving toward my position; to adjust, if they went elsewhere; to react, if they did something I hadn't predicted. Dox and Delilah, angled with their backs to the wall and monitoring everything on the laptop like two businesspeople discussing a PowerPoint presentation, would provide some welcome cushioning from all those vagaries. And backup, if something went wrong.

I looked at my watch. It was almost five o'clock. Time for me to go.

'You take the attaché,' I said, setting it on the table and discreetly removing the items I would need. 'Everyone carries a bag in Hong Kong and you have to look the part. The commo gear, the laptop, everything is inside.'

'What about you?'

I eased my hips forward and started slipping the items

I'd removed from the attaché into my front pockets. 'I'll find something on the way. Something the right size for adhesive-backed, wireless audio and video transmitters.'

He grinned. 'What the well-dressed man is carrying these days, I understand.'

I looked at him, trying to decide, then said, 'I think you're going to have to lose the goatee. It's too noticeable.'

He looked at me as though I'd suggested a vasectomy. 'Son, I've been wearing this goatee for over twenty years.'

'That's my point. If Hilger has file photos, and I'm sure he does, the trademark goatee will be front center. The suit and the beautiful lady by your side are helpful, but losing the facial hair would be better.'

'Well, the suit is a new look, it's true, but I've been known to have a beautiful lady by my side from time to time,' he said. 'So that part's not exactly a disguise for me.' He rubbed the beard. 'Damn, I feel like Samson here on the chopping block.' He turned to Delilah. 'Well, your name is Delilah.'

She smiled. 'I think you'll look great without it.'

'Really?'

She nodded. 'You've got good bones. Why hide them?'

Dox smiled and looked at me. 'Someone get me a razor!' he said. Then he turned back to Delilah. 'You know, I've never considered myself the marrying type. But if you ever get tired of my partner here, I believe I'd like to propose to you.'

She laughed.

'Did I say something funny?' Dox asked.

'All right, I've got to go,' I said, standing up. 'You should get there in, say, forty-five minutes, before the bar fills up. And before Hilger and company arrive.'

They stood and we all shook hands again, staying in our roles. I went downstairs, took a cab to the Mandarin

Oriental, then crossed the street and ducked into a luggage store. They were selling a number of high-quality, but essentially boring business bags . . . and one mahogany-colored, lid-over, Tanner Krolle attaché. *Expensive,* I thought, playing with the latches, which clicked open with the quiet assurance of a bank vault or the door on a Rolls-Royce, *but life is short . . .*

Five minutes later, I was circling the old Bank of China building, attaché in hand. At over half a century of age, the Art Deco–influenced building was, by Hong Kong standards, ancient. At fifteen stories, it was also a pygmy, and with the steel-masted HSBC headquarters looming to its right and the fountain-like, fiber optic–controlled light show of the Cheung Kong Center rising up behind it, it had the air of a structure that has been granted some miraculous reprieve from the engines of progress that must have demolished its contemporaries to make room for the behemoths that now surrounded it. A condemned man, still dignified, but now living on borrowed time.

I noted all points of ingress and egress, the direction of traffic, the presence of cameras. There was a single entrance in use, on the western side, along a short, single-lane street that was all that separated the building from its giant neighbors. On the other side of the street, directly across from the building's entrance, was a large industrial dumpster that would make for good cover and concealment if for some reason I needed it. Four elevators, two security cameras, center. One bored-looking guard behind a desk, right. A stairwell and fire door, left. An office worker emerged from the stairwell as I approached, and as the door eased closed behind him, I noted he wasn't holding a swipe card or other key. The stairwell doors were accessible from the interior, then, at least on the ground floor. To be expected, it's true –

you can't very well lock people in if there's a fire — but it's good to have confirmation.

I stepped onto one of the elevators, running a hand along my slicked hair as I did so to obscure my face while I checked for more cameras. There it was, a ceiling-mounted dome model. I pressed the button with a knuckle and kept my head down on the trip up. I reminded myself of who I was and why I was here: Watanabe, an advance man examining the China Club on behalf of certain Japanese industrial interests.

I got off on thirteen and looked around. A winding wooden staircase curved upward to my left, its banister supported by some sort of Chinese-style metal latticework. The walls were white; the floors, dark wood, with that density and slight unevenness that's only acquired with generations of use. A flat panel monitor by the staircase was running stock quotes from the Hang Seng index. There was a hush to the place, a feeling of money, old and new; status, acquired and sought; ambition, barely concealed behind pin-striped suits and cocktail party smiles. The Bank of China might have moved its headquarters to I. M. Pei's triangular black glass tower a few blocks to the southwest, but the ghosts of the drive and wealth to which the new headquarters stood in monument were all still at home right here.

And yet there was an air of whimsy to the place, as well. There was a sitting area crowded with overstuffed chairs and couches covered in slipcovers of bubble-gum pink and lime green and baby blue. The lamp shades hovering above the end tables were of similar glowing hues. And those grave wooden floors gave way to brightly colored kilim rugs. It was as though the proprietor had designed the place both in homage to Hong Kong's titanic ambitions, and also to gently mock them.

A pretty Chinese woman in black pants and a white Mao jacket emerged from a coatroom to my right. 'May I help you?' she asked.

I nodded, and switched on a heavy Japanese accent. 'I am Watanabe.' As though that explained everything.

She picked up a clipboard and glanced at whatever was written on it. 'Ah yes, Mr Watanabe, the Shangri-La called to tell us you'd be visiting. Would you like me to show you around?'

'Yes,' I said, with a half bow. 'Very good.'

The woman, whose name was May, was an excellent guide, and helpfully answered all my questions. Such as: Where are the private dining rooms? Fifteenth floor. Do you have any that would be appropriate for a small party – say, four people? Yes, two such rooms. And how are the upper floors accessible? Only by the winding internal staircases.

May's guided tour took about ten minutes. Given the earliness of the hour, there weren't yet any other patrons on the premises, and the staff was busy laying out silver and crystal and adjusting tablecloths and otherwise preparing for what would no doubt be another capacity-crowd evening for the club.

When we were done, I asked May if it would be all right if I wandered around a bit by myself. She told me that would be fine, and that I if I had any additional questions I should simply ask.

Watanabe-san gave the place a thorough examination, starting with the main dining room on the fourteenth floor and the charming Long March Bar adjacent to it. He observed the positions of the restrooms on the thirteenth and fourteenth floors, and noted that there was no restroom on fifteen, meaning that diners enjoying the private banquet rooms there would have to descend a floor to use the facilities. He wandered around the splendid library, and briefly enjoyed the view of Central from the rooftop observation deck. And of course he made sure to take a peek in all the private dining rooms, paying particular attention to the two that had been set for parties of four. In these, Watanabe stepped inside and paused for an extra moment to admire the furnishings, even running the backs of his fingers along the astonishingly thick interior doorjambs, which in each room was of more than adequate stature for the placement of a miniature audio and video transmitter.

So that we could keep the signal weak and therefore less susceptible to bug detectors, I also placed repeaters in various places outside the private dining rooms and along the stairs down to the fourteenth floor. Before heading down to the elevators on thirteen, I ducked into the fourteenth-floor restroom. As restrooms go, this one was impressive. The floor was white marble, and I noted with satisfaction that my new Dunhill split-toes were utterly noiseless on its polished surface. To my right was a bank of sinks, all solid white ceramic. Folded terrycloth washcloths were laid out neatly on a shelf just above them in lieu of ordinary paper towels, along with an array of special soaps, lotions, and tonics. Straight ahead, a bank of urinals; like the sinks, all heavy white ceramic. To my left were stalls that could more properly be described as closets, separated as they were by marble walls and featuring floor-to-ceiling mahogany doors.

The stalls looked promising, although I was concerned that, after his recent experience in Manila, Manny might have some sort of phobic reaction if he entered a restroom and noticed that one of the stall doors was closed. But then I noticed something that might be even better.

Between the sinks and the urinals was a large mahogany door. On it hung a brass sign with black lettering:

BUILDING ORDINANCE
(CHAPTER 123)
NOTICE DANGER
LIFT MACHINERY
UNAUTHORIZED
ACCESS PROHIBITED
DOOR TO BE KEPT LOCKED

Interesting, I thought. If the passenger elevators went up only to thirteen, this access must be to a freight unit. The door opened out, and there were three sets of heavy brass hinges running up its left side. I tried it, and, per the ordinance, found it was indeed locked. The lock, though, was a cheap single wafer model, what you might find on an old desk or filing cabinet. It wasn't there to protect valuables, just to comply with a local building ordinance. After all, who in his right mind other than a maintenance man would want to access the lift machinery?

I didn't even need a lock pick – I simply forced the mechanism with a turn of the Benchmade folder. Then I slipped the knife into the crack between the door and the jamb and eased the door open. The hinges gave a long squeal and I thought, *Shit, hadn't thought of that. Should have brought some lubricant.*

I glanced inside. There was a small corridor, providing, I supposed, maintenance access to the elevators. It looked good. There were variables – Manny might have a new bodyguard, or might otherwise not show up alone, or he might not come at all – but this could work.

But what about those hinges. I walked back to the sinks and picked up one of the bottles of lotion. *Gardner's Hand Lotion,* the label advised, *Replete with Lavender and Other Essential Oils.* Well, it wasn't WD-40, but let's see. I emptied a healthy amount onto one of the wash towels, then wiped down the hinges. I swung the door open and closed a few times, and the essential oils worked their magic. The squealing stopped.

I wiped down the bottle, put it back on the shelf, and tossed the wash towel into a basket that the China Club had thoughtfully provided for this very purpose. I exited the restroom and began to descend the winding staircase. A waiter on his way up passed me but paid no attention.

Two-thirds of the way down, I had a clear view of the elevators and the coatroom from which May had emerged when I first arrived. The area was empty. May must have been elsewhere for the moment, attending some aspect of preparing the restaurant. She might wonder at not having seen me leave, but I felt I could count on her to assume she had simply failed to notice my departure. Hopefully she would forgive Mr Watanabe his rudeness in not saying thank you and a proper good-bye.

I turned around and went back up the stairs. This time I really did use the bathroom – I didn't know how long I'd be without access. Then I opened the closet door again and stepped inside. I pulled the door shut behind me and waited for my eyes to adjust to the darkness. There was just a little light coming from the elevator shaft behind me. The lack of illumination in here wasn't the problem though – what I really needed to see was the bathroom, and, with the heavy mahogany door closed, that was impossible.

I set down the attaché and popped the hinges. The case opened with a muted double click. I pulled out the Surefire E1E mini-light I was carrying and twisted it on, then slipped into the deerskin gloves. I looked around to see what I might have to work with.

Propped against the wall to my right was a mop in a bucket. On the floor, a plunger and a few rudimentary tools, including a screwdriver. I opened the door, then slid the screwdriver between the door and the jamb on the hinged side at eye level. I pulled the door inward. The steel shaft of the screwdriver created tremendous pressure on the hinged surfaces around it, and something had to give. But it wouldn't be those heavy brass hinges – instead, the wood itself provided the path of least resistance, and the edge of the door and jamb deformed around the screwdriver as I pulled relentlessly toward me. I went back and forth several times until I was easily able to almost close the door with the screwdriver still in the way.

I stepped outside. I closed the door, then opened it without a problem. Just wanted to make sure that nothing was going to stick as a result of my handiwork. It would have been embarrassing to have to call for Dox to come let me out. I looked at the dent I had made at the intersection of the door and jamb. It was virtually unnoticeable. Even if someone put his eye right up to it, all he would see inside was darkness.

I went back inside, closed the door, and put my eye up to the jamb.

Perfect. I had a clear view of the area to my right, which included the urinals and stalls. Every time I heard someone come in, it would be a simple matter to visually confirm who it was.

I repeated the operation on the knob side of the door. When I was done, I had a view of the entrance and sinks. I checked from the outside and confirmed again that the door opened and closed without a problem, and that the second hole, too, was unnoticeable.

I slipped an earpiece and lapel mike into place and checked the illuminated dial of my watch. Almost six o'clock. Dox and Delilah should be arriving anytime now.

269

I wouldn't be able to use the gear to communicate with them until they were in the building – fifteen floors of steel and concrete would block the signal for sure.

At just after six o'clock, I heard Dox's soft twang. 'Hey, partner, it's me. Are you there?'

It felt good to hear him. 'Yeah, I'm here. The men's room on the fourteenth floor.'

'Well, that's a nice coincidence. I was just going to use that very facility. Can you hear me? I'm on my way in.'

A moment later, I heard the restroom door open, then footsteps on the marble. Dox moved past my position. The goatee was gone, and I was pleased at the way its absence changed his appearance.

He stepped up to one of the urinals and started to use it. Looking over at the open stall doors, then to his right, he said, 'Looks like you've got a good spot. Where are you?'

'The closet. To your right.'

'Ah-hah, I should have known. Hey, man, no peeking.'

'Don't worry,' I said, surprising myself with a rare rejoinder, 'from this far, I can only make out large objects.'

He chuckled. 'That's a good one. Say, you don't hang around in men's rooms habitually, do you? You seem awfully good at it.'

All right, I should have known better than to try to one-up him. 'Where's Delilah?' I asked.

'She grabbed us a table in the dreaded Long March Bar.'

'Crowded?'

'Not yet, but it's filling up. No sign of our friends. I sure hope they show. If they don't, I'll start to worry something might have happened to them.'

'Yeah, that would be too bad.'

He zipped up and headed over to the sink, winking at my position en route. 'Ooh, look at these fancy soaps. I like this place. Ordinarily I'm not terribly fastidious about washing my hands after urination, but tonight I believe I'll make an exception.'

I checked through the other hole and watched Dox lathering his hands. 'Damn,' he said, 'I can't get used to the way I look in these clothes and without my trusty goatee. You think Delilah meant it when she said I have good bones?'

'I'm sure she did,' I said, feeling a little impatient. 'Look, you might want to hurry. If our friends show up, you don't want to accidentally pass them in the hallway. Even without the goatee that was hiding your good bones.'

He dried his hands with a towel and tossed it in the basket. 'Okay, partner, that's a fair point. I'll be in the bar, keeping your girlfriend company. Seriously, I'll be right here, talking into your ear the whole time. If you need me, I'll come running.'

Even in the midst of all the annoying palaver, it felt good to hear him say that. 'Thanks,' I said. 'I know you will.'

20

A few minutes later, I heard Delilah. 'Hey, John. Just checking the gear.'

'I hear you.'

'Good. We're in the bar. We've got a nice table in the far corner. You can talk to us anytime. We'll monitor the transmitters and let you know what's going on. Any problems, just let us know.'

'Okay,' I said.

Dox said, 'We'll switch off now so we don't bore you with our pretend conversations about strategic partnership opportunities in Asia and how we're getting traction with our paradigm shifts and inflection points. Unless you want to listen in, just to make sure I'm behaving myself with your girlfriend.'

'Please, shut it down,' I said.

He laughed. 'Okay. Remember, we can still hear you, so if you need anything, just speak up.'

'Okay.'

He cut out.

I waited for nearly an hour in silence. Three times, someone came in to use the restroom. Each time, I checked to see if it was Manny or Hilger. It was possible that one or both of them might stop in on their way to the private dining room, in which case Delilah and Dox wouldn't be able to warn me. But it was always someone else.

The closet was fairly roomy, and I was able to move around a bit, do a few squats and stretches. There was a time when I could go to top speed without a warm-up, but that sort of thing was getting harder lately, and I wanted to stay limber.

I was doing some isometric neck exercises when Dox came back on. 'Okay, partner,' he said, 'our guests have arrived. They're being seated right now.'

'How many?'

'Two, it looks like. Hilger and Manny. Hang on, let me change frequencies and listen in for a minute.'

A moment later, he came back on. 'Yeah, it's just the two of them. Hilger asked the hostess to escort "Mr Eljub" when he arrives. So it looks like it's going to be just the three of them. You were right, Hilger didn't change the plans.'

'Eljub,' Delilah said.

I asked, 'What of it?'

'I'm . . . not sure. Just wondering who the mystery guest might be.'

'I'm more concerned about where he's sitting. And about whether he gets up.'

'Of course.'

I said, 'Dox, can you switch the audio so that I can listen in, too?'

'I can, but then you won't be able to hear Delilah and me.'

'That's okay. You can cut back in anytime you think you need to.'

'Gotcha. Okay, here you go.'

There was a hiss, and then I was listening to Manny and Hilger. Hilger's voice I remembered from listening to him through a parabolic microphone in front of Kwai Chung. He had a memorably slow, confident, reassuring way of speaking. Manny's voice was higher; his tone, higher-strung. It sounded as though he was complaining to Hilger about

273

security, specifically about having to leave his bodyguard outside.

'He can do you more good monitoring the entrance than he could have in here,' Hilger told him.

I wondered if he believed that – there were pros and cons, as I saw it – or if he was just trying to placate Manny, who struck me as a bit of a whiner.

Manny said, 'I don't think so. Anyway, after what happened in Manila, I feel more comfortable with him close by.'

'I've told you, I'm known at this club and I don't have a bodyguard. If we post a man outside the door, it's only going to make the staff curious about who I'm entertaining. Curiosity is the last thing we need tonight.'

'He could have just eaten with us. The staff wouldn't know his role.'

'That's true, but then we wouldn't be able to speak freely. Look, I told you, Rain is in Bangkok. We almost had him there yesterday. He's on the run now, and my men are pursuing him. You don't have anything to worry about.'

For a moment I wondered anew whether Hilger's operation was in fact CIA. He certainly sounded like the government, describing an 'almost had him' as a comforting sign of success. I sensed he would have been right at home spouting off about 'catastrophic successes' and the other such doublespeak of the age.

Manny said, 'I want to know when you get him.'

'Of course.'

Well, Hilger's going to have a little explaining to do to Manny later tonight, I thought. On the other hand, if things went as planned, Hilger wouldn't be any more able to explain than Manny would be to listen.

The audio cut out. There was a hiss, and Dox was back in

my ear. 'Saw Hilger pull some bug-detection gear from an attaché,' he said. 'Glad we're using video. I'm gonna go dark for ten minutes or they might pick up the signal.'

'Good,' I said. The transmitters broadcast on radio frequency, which is present in the background in any urban location, and we were using low signal strength, boosted outside the room by the repeaters I'd put in place. So the concern wasn't the transmitters' ambient presence, only their susceptibility to a deliberate sweep, which might follow the signal they emitted like a trail of electronic bread crumbs. Once the sweep was completed, we could safely come back online.

After ten minutes, I heard Dox again. 'Okay, here we go. I'll switch you over.'

Another hiss, and I was listening to Hilger and Manny again. Manny was saying, 'He knows he's important. It's going to his head.'

Hilger chuckled.

'I mean it, that's why he's late. He's just showing us that he can make us wait for him, and that he knows we'll put up with it. Arabs. This is just like them.'

'Let's remember that we're all friends tonight, all right?' Hilger said. 'No nationalities around this table. No stupid allegiances.'

I thought I heard the sound of glasses clinking.

They were quiet after that. Ten minutes passed, then I heard the sound of a knock on their door, of chairs being pushed back. Hilger said, 'Hello, Mr Eljub. Welcome.'

At last, I thought. *Mr VBM.*

'Ali, hello,' Manny said. 'Glad you could make it.'

'Please, call me Ali,' a new voice said, in accented English that I had trouble placing. Arab, maybe, with something European behind it. Whoever he was, he must have been talking to Hilger, Manny had already presumed. Or else they knew each other.

'Ali, welcome,' Hilger said again. 'Please, have a seat.'

I heard chairs being moved around. Hilger said, 'You had a good flight, I hope?'

'Uneventful. But slow. There's so much airline security these days!'

This provoked a laugh. Hilger said, 'And the hotel?'

'I don't think I can complain about a suite at The Four Seasons. Thank you for taking care of it.'

'My pleasure.'

I heard another knock at their door. Hilger said, 'Yes.'

There was a woman's voice, asking them about drinks.

'Shall we order?' the man called Ali said. 'I'm starving.'

'Yeah, it's gotten pretty late for dinner,' Manny said, and I thought, *Not just a whiner. Passive-aggressive, too.* Not that my growing distaste for him would be a factor one way or the other. I wasn't feeling anything right now other than the usual, slightly heightened focus of being in the middle of an op. And I was going to keep it that way until after it was too late to make a difference.

'All right, let's,' Hilger said. 'Ali, let me suggest the . . .'

There was a hiss. Dox cut in: 'We've got something interesting here, partner. Listen to your lady.'

Delilah said, 'It's not Eljub. It's Al-Jib. Ali Al-Jib.'

'I don't know the name,' I said. 'Should I?'

'What about A. Q. Khan?' she asked.

Khan again. 'Yeah, I know of Khan,' I told her, thinking of my conversation with Boaz and Gil in Nagoya. 'Pakistani scientist, nuclear starter kit, et cetera. It was in the news a little over a year ago, then it died down, right? The outgoing CIA director, George Tenet, was bragging about it.'

'Yeah, how Christians In Action was down Khan's throat

and up his ass and in some other hard-to-reach places, too,' Dox added.

'I think it was more like "inside his residence, inside his facilities, inside his rooms,"' Delilah said. 'But yes, that was the propaganda the US was putting out. They were hailing Khan's arrest as a great victory. But then why is the US still investigating his network? Why is the International Atomic Energy Agency doing the same?'

'Oh, you know,' Dox said. 'In these matters, the government usually continues the investigation just to determine whether what they've achieved is merely a "great victory," or if it could in fact be more accurately described as a "historic triumph." I'm sure they don't think the network's still operational after all that clever spying they did to stop it.'

'It is operational,' Delilah said. 'Despite the arrests. It's like Al Qaeda – the leadership is damaged, but then new, less centralized actors begin to emerge in its place.'

'Al-Jib?' I asked.

'Exactly. Ali Al-Jib is part of this new generation. He was educated in East Germany, the Central Institute of Nuclear Research in Rossendorf. There are more like him, men who were trained behind the Iron Curtain and then lost to the world's intelligence services in the turmoil following the end of the Cold War. A lucky find of some Soviet-era documents pointed us in the right direction.'

'Maybe we should switch the frequency back to Hilger and company,' I said. 'Not that this isn't interesting, but we don't want to get distracted.'

'You don't understand,' Delilah said. 'Al-Jib is a dangerous man, very dangerous. What Lavi does with conventional explosives, Al-Jib is trying to do with nuclear weapons. We've been hunting him for a long time and he is exceedingly difficult to track. We can't let him walk out of here tonight.'

'Look,' I said, 'he sounds like he's another problem child, it's true. But we've got our hands full as it is. Hilger and Manny are the primaries. That's going to be hard enough to do. Let's not complicate it by rearranging our priorities in the middle of the proceedings.'

'You don't understand,' she said again.

'I do understand. These aren't my decisions to make. Your people hired me to do a job, I'm doing it. If they wanted to hire me to do Al-Jib, too, they should have brought it up sooner and I would have priced it in. And they damn well shouldn't have turned on me after one little hitch in Manila.'

'Is that what this is about?' she said. 'You won't do this . . . out of spite?'

'I won't do it because it's not sensible to do it. We've got two targets already. If I put Al-Jib at the head of the line, it reduces the chances that I'll be able to get to the other two. So let's just stick to the plan.

'Jeez, partner,' Dox said. 'I don't know.'

'Goddamnit,' I said, 'what happened to all that "The judge and the executioner, they're different roles" shit you were spouting at me the other day?'

'I think I meant that more as a guideline than a rule, man,' he said. 'And this feels like, you know, an exigency.'

We were all quiet for a moment. I thought, *This is exactly what I'm talking about, we're arguing about this idiot Al-fucking-Jib instead of monitoring what's going on in the room. Getting distracted, jeopardizing the whole operation.*

'If the opening is there,' I said, 'I'll take him out. But Hilger and Manny are still the priority. Okay?'

There was a pause, then Delilah said, 'Okay.'

278

'Good. Now switch the frequency back. Please.'

We went back to Hilger and company. It sounded like Hilger was making a sales pitch. Something about diversified investments, Asian emerging markets equities, average yields of over twenty-five percent.

'What about your commission?' Al-Jib asked.

'The twenty-five percent yields are after my commission, which is twenty percent.'

'Twenty percent. Is that in keeping with American SEC regulations?'

'Not at all. But then, not much of what I can do is likely to be approved by the SEC.'

Al-Jib laughed. 'I have to tell you, your proposal is interesting and I think there is a lot you might be able to do for my people, but I would not have agreed to meet you. Not even with the people who vouched for you. Your former affiliations are too ... suspect. There are people who believe you are still in the employ of the US government.'

'That impression can be useful in my work. I don't go out of my way to dispel it.'

'I understand. Still, it can be hard for men to trust each other even when they are from the same village. When they come from such different villages as ours, the suspicions linger, do they not?'

'They do. But I hope the test you devised was adequate to ease your doubts.'

'More than adequate. Killing a US diplomat in Amman ... there are some things that a US government agent simply cannot do.'

Hilger laughed. 'It was a creative solution. I'm glad it worked.'

'You never told me one thing, though. How did you

manage to have the Jordanians blame Al Qaeda for the man's death?'

'That was a case of someone rounding up the "usual suspects,"' Hilger replied. 'When a senior member of USAID is assassinated, someone has to be blamed. Who better than AQ?'

'Yes,' Al-Jib said. 'I suppose that's true.'

They were quiet for a moment. Then Hilger said, 'One thing that's so useful about my ambiguous status with the United States government is that I'm in touch with many, many people who are in a position to do me favors. They're receiving the same twenty-five percent you will be, and are always looking for an opportunity to invest something more. So tonight, in addition to the logistics of setting up your accounts and transferring funds, I would very much like to talk about what you need that the US government might unwittingly provide. I'd like to help with all that, too.'

'For your usual twenty percent fee?'

'Of course. Everything I do involves personal risk.'

'I don't begrudge you. I only wanted to confirm. If you can provide what I need, I think we'll both be satisfied with the arrangement.'

'Tell me, then,' Hilger said. 'I'm intrigued.'

There was a moment of quiet, then Al-Jib said, 'As you know, Dr Khan's organization was chiefly able to provide know-how and machinery to its customers. The missing link in our product lineup was always material.'

'Uranium? Plutonium?'

'Either one is greatly desired.'

'If it's uranium you need, highly enriched is your best bet. The US National Nuclear Security Administration and the International Atomic Energy Administration are supervising the repatriation of HEU from all over the world right now, and I have extensive contacts in both organizations. You might have heard of the program – the Global Threat Reduction Initiative, a joint operation between the United States and Russia to secure Soviet-era nuclear fuel.'

'Yes, I know of it.'

'Then you probably know that six kilograms of highly enriched uranium was just repatriated from the Czech Republic to Russia. The transfer was secret until it was completed, but I knew about it beforehand. There are others that are being secretly planned even as we speak. HEU is being moved from Bulgaria, Libya, Romania, Serbia, and Uzbekistan. With your background, I don't think I need to tell you how many opportunities there are en route for a diversion.'

'What will it cost?' Al-Jib asked, and I thought, *Nice sales pitch. The guy's ready to whip out his checkbook.*

'A lot,' Hilger said, and they all laughed.

Manny said, 'What did I tell you, Ali?'

Al-Jib said, 'Yes, it seems we can do business together.'

Manny said, 'I've been telling you that for what, three years? I've made a lot of money with this man and he's done me a lot of favors.'

Hilger said, 'Cheers,' and I heard glasses clinking.

Manny said, 'Excuse me for a minute.' I heard a chair sliding back, then their door open and close.

My heart rate started to pick up speed. There was a hiss, then Dox cut in. 'Manny's on his way out,' he said. 'Probably going to take a leak.'

'I heard him,' I said. 'I'm ready.'

'Delilah and I will stay on this frequency so we can hear you if there's a problem,' he said. 'But I'm done talking unless you need me.'

'All right,' I said. I was a little surprised Delilah hadn't

281

mentioned the discussion we just overheard as a way of reintroducing the critical importance of killing Al-Jib. I knew she was stubborn and didn't easily accept the word 'no.' But I supposed the compromise I offered had persuaded her.

I rotated my head left, then right, cracking the joints. I squatted down to make sure that, if my knees needed to pop, they would do so now. I twisted my torso left, then right, swung my arms around, and took two short, sharp breaths. Okay.

I looked through the hole facing the bathroom door, thinking, *Come on, Manny, come on* . . .

But Manny didn't show. A minute went by, then two. If he was just heading down here from the private dining room, he should have arrived by now. Maybe he didn't need the bathroom after all. Or maybe he went down to the one on thirteen. I wouldn't have expected him to bypass the closer facilities, but maybe he didn't know there was one on this floor. Or maybe he stopped to make a phone call, or to try to chat up a waitress. Could be anything. The main thing was, he wasn't coming.

I said into the lapel microphone, 'Manny isn't here yet. He must have gone somewhere else.'

Delilah said, 'Shit.'

'Can you take a look?' I asked. 'Dox should stay put. It's not likely, but also not impossible that Manny would recognize him.'

'No problem,' she said.

I heard the door open. I looked through the hole. It wasn't Manny. But it was still someone interesting. I leaned toward my lapel and whispered to Delilah, 'Wait.'

She said, 'Understood.'

My new visitor had the dark hair and skin of a Filipino.

Inside his cheap suit was a body with the approximate dimensions of a refrigerator. From his size, the way he was dressed, and the way he was scoping the bathroom, I made him as a bodyguard. Manny's bodyguard.

This was the guy Hilger had insisted wait outside. Manny must have used his cell phone to call him after stepping out of the private dining room. The call, and the elevator ride up, explained Manny's delay in reaching my position. He really had turned paranoid about public restrooms.

Not without reason.

The bodyguard was heading right toward me, looking at the closet door. He was going to check it.

I put my left foot against the doorjamb, grasped the handle, and leaned back so that the door was supporting about a hundred and fifty pounds of pressure. A moment later, I felt a mild pull from the other side. If we'd been in a real tug-of-war, the guy might have been able to budge me, but he wasn't trying to force the door, just to confirm that it was locked as the sign advertised. It didn't move a millimeter. I felt him let go, heard him walking back to the entrance. I heard the bathroom door open, heard him say, 'It's clear.'

I kept my position. Manny might try the door, too.

I heard a new set of footsteps in the room. Manny's voice: 'Thank you. Just wait outside, if you don't mind.'

The man said, 'Of course.'

I heard the door close. Manny's footsteps, drawing nearer. Then stopping.

He had seen the closet door. He was wondering whether the bodyguard had checked it. *Of course he's checked it,* he'd be thinking. *He's a bodyguard. Still, no harm confirming . . .*

Sure enough, his footsteps came closer, then stopped again, and I felt another mild tug on the door. Then the pressure eased, and I heard him walking off to my right.

I eased off the pressure I was keeping on the door and looked through the first hole I had made. Manny was using the urinal farthest from me. He was facing the wall, but his peripheral vision would detect motion when I opened the door. I would have to move fast.

I took one quick peek through the other hole to confirm that the bodyguard had indeed walked out. He had. It was just Manny and me, the way it was supposed to be.

It wasn't like the last time. I thought of nothing that wasn't operational. Nothing.

I gave him a little time to finish what he was doing. If I didn't, he'd wind up pissing on the floor, and maybe on me.

He started shaking off. I took two quick, silent breaths. *Go.*

I swung the door open, took a long step past the door, pivoted, and strode directly toward him.

His head snapped in my direction and his mouth dropped open. His eyes popped wide and his arms started to come up.

Adrenaline constricts the throat. This is why a person, suddenly terrified, finds himself squeaking in a high-pitched voice, or whispering, or unable even to make a sound. Manny, his recent restroom anxieties suddenly realized, had just gotten a massive dose. So although his bodyguard was just outside the door, he remained silent.

He started to turn toward me, but it was already too late. I stepped behind him, jammed my left knee in his lower back, and jerked him toward me by the shoulders. His body folded backward around my knee. I put my foot back on the floor and swept my left arm counterclockwise around his neck so that his face was pressed against my lower rib cage and my forearm was braced against the back of his neck.

I took my left wrist in my right hand, shoved his lower body forward against the urinal, and jerked up with my forearm. His spine arched to the limit of its natural give, and for a split second our forward momentum froze. Then his neck broke. The crack was loud, but not quite loud enough for the guard to have heard outside that solid mahogany entrance door. His body went rubbery and I slipped my arms under his to stop him from slumping to the floor.

I dragged him into the closet and closed the door behind us. I patted him down, but he wasn't armed. *Shit.*

I thought for a moment. If the bodyguard were right outside the door, and I expected he was, I couldn't just walk past him. He had checked the bathroom before Manny entered, and it had been empty at the time. Someone new walking out now wouldn't figure. Anyway, the point wasn't to get past him, it was to get his gun. If his back was to me, I might manage it despite his size. But if he saw me coming, things might get messy. If there was a commotion, even if I disarmed him and headed directly upstairs for Hilger and Al-Jib, I might already have lost the element of surprise.

I heard the bathroom door open. I checked through the peephole: a middle-aged Chinese man in a business suit. He looked harmless, and the bodyguard must have decided it was all right for him to pass. He went into one of the stalls and closed the door.

Another minute and the bodyguard was going to check up on Manny. I was running out of time.

I left the closet, strode noiselessly over to the second stall, eased its door closed, and got back in the closet. The floor-to-ceiling mahogany stall door would obscure the question of whether someone was actually in there, and, if the guard poked his head in, he would now likely assume Manny was using one of the stalls. I doubted he'd want to disturb his client at such a delicate moment by calling out, but his reticence would last only so long. I might have bought myself a minute or two, but the clock was still ticking.

And then I had an idea.

21

'Delilah,' I whispered.

She answered instantly. 'I'm here.'

'Manny's done. But there's a bodyguard standing out-side the bathroom. I can't get past him. In another couple of minutes, he's going to come in and check on Manny. There's also someone using one of the stalls and I need to buy another couple minutes so he can finish and get the hell out.'

'Tell me what to do,' she said.

'Dox, do you still have that syringe we took off Winters?'

'Got it right here, partner,' he said.

'Give it to Delilah. Delilah, you won't have any trouble getting close to the guard. Make it look like you're about to head into the wrong restroom. Then flirt with him, distract him until the guy in the stall leaves. When he does, you nail the guard with the syringe.'

'What's in it?' she asked.

'Dox, give her the syringe. I'll explain on the way.'

'Already did, partner. She's getting up now.'

'It's a knockout cocktail. All you have to do is palm it and slap him with it. It works like a snakebite.'

'That's "all" I have to do? Don't I have to hit a vein or an artery?'

'If we want the drug to work fast, you do.'

'Veins and arteries tend to be pretty small moving targets.'

'Look, just flirt with the guy, okay? Get him so his back is facing the bathroom door. I'll hit him in the head with whatever I can find in here. But he's a gorilla, I don't know if a shot to the head will be enough. Although it should stun him for long enough for you to slap the syringe down on his carotid. If you miss, I'll figure something else out.'

'All right.'

'He's probably armed, a shoulder or hip carry. Whatever else happens, we have to disarm him. That's our best chance with the other two.'

'Okay.'

I clicked on the Surefire and looked around the closet. None of the tools I saw would be helpful. No hammer, no wrench. For a second, I thought of the knife, then rejected it because of the mess it would make. All right, I would have to use my hands. I started to put the Surefire back in my pocket, then looked at it. Shit, I had almost overlooked something so obvious. I had been thinking of it only as a flashlight, when in fact, gripped tightly in my fist with the hard edge slightly protruding, it would make a serviceable yarawa stick.

I heard the toilet flush, and a moment later the Chinese man emerged from the stall.

I heard Delilah say, 'Here we go.' Then, in a tipsy, slightly flirtatious tone, 'Excuse me, isn't that the ladies' room?'

Her lapel mike picked up the guard saying, 'No, miss, this is the men's room.' She must have been standing close.

'Oh my God, I would have felt so silly if I'd walked in there! You don't know where the ladies' room is, do you?'

'I think it's just around the corner.'

The Chinese guy walked over to the sinks and started examining the various choices among the soaps and lotions.

Can you just wash your hands and get the fuck out? I thought. *Better yet, don't wash them at all. I promise not to tell anyone.*

Delilah said, 'Are you the doorman or something?'

The man chuckled. Good, she was reeling him in. 'No, I'm just waiting for someone.'

The Chinese guy selected one of the soaps and began thoroughly washing his hands. He was taking so long that I was half-tempted to pop out of the closet, break his neck, and drag him inside.

He turned off the sink, picked up one of the towels, and began leisurely drying his hands.

'Oh, you're here with someone, then,' Delilah said. 'Too bad.'

The guard said, 'Too bad?'

'Well,' she said, 'my date is being a jerk, and . . .' She laughed. 'I'm sorry, I think I've had too much to drink. I'm not usually like this.'

The guard said, 'No, that's all right. I don't mind at all.'

The Chinese guy kept rubbing away with the towel.

Come on, buddy, there can't be a single fucking water molecule left on you. . . .

Finally he tossed the towel into the basket under the sink.

If you comb your hair now, I thought, *or examine your teeth, or adjust your tie, I will kill you.*

But the man decided not to engage in any of these fatal activities. He simply walked out the door.

Delilah said, 'You're so nice. I'm sorry I was so forward just now.'

The guard said, 'I'm used to forward women. I like them.'

'Really?' she asked. 'Where are you from?'

'I need his back to me,' I said, emerging from the closet and heading toward the door. 'Now.'

The guard said, 'I'm Filipino.'

'It is,' Delilah said, without changing her tone at all.

And while the bodyguard was busy trying to process that non sequitur, I stepped out of the bathroom behind him and nailed him in the base of the skull with a hammer-fist, one end of the Surefire leading the way. He grunted and his body shivered, but he didn't go down. Damn, this guy had a hell of a thick skull. I went to hit him again, but Delilah had already moved in, slapping him with the syringe on the side of the neck, over the carotid. He grunted again and started groping for something under his jacket. I caught his arm to stop him. He tried to turn toward me. Delilah reached in and smoothly retrieved what he had been going for – a Kimber Pro CDP II in a hip holster carry.

The guy managed to turn all the way around and face me. He reached out as though to grapple with me, but then his feet went out from under him, from the blow or the injection I wasn't sure. He crashed into me and I caught him under the arms and around the back. I stumbled backward through the bathroom door, grunting with the effort. The guy must have weighed two hundred and fifty pounds. Delilah followed us through, closing the door behind us. I saw her eject the Kimber's magazine, check its load, and pop it back in. She pulled back the slide a half inch, nodded as though she liked what she saw, and let the slide go.

'Brace the door,' I said, straining to support the dead weight in my arms. 'Don't want anyone coming in.'

She pressed her right toes against the door, her heel wedged to the floor, and took a long step back with her other leg. I dragged the guard into the closet and dumped him on top of his erstwhile client. I stepped over them both and closed the door behind me.

Someone tried the bathroom door. When it didn't open, the person knocked. Delilah kept her foot in place and said, 'We're cleaning in here, sorry. Please use the restroom on thirteen.'

Cleaning, I thought. *That's one way to put it.*

The knocking stopped.

I walked over and said, 'Give me the gun.'

She shook her head. 'Just go. I'll take care of the rest.'

'Come on, this isn't what you do.'

'It's what I have to do.'

'Let me finish what I started. With a gun, I can take care of them both.'

I thought that was what she would want to hear, but she shook her head again.

'Look,' I said, 'where are you going to hide that cannon with what you're wearing? It's bigger than your purse.'

She took a deep breath and said, 'You fulfilled your contract with Manny. You'll be paid. Now just go.'

'Will you give me the fucking gun? I don't know how much time we have.'

She looked at me, and for a second I thought I'd convinced her. But then she opened the door and walked out into the corridor to the stairway. I went out after her. She held the gun low along her right leg.

I heard Dox in my ear. 'What's the status there, ladies and gentlemen, your conversation is making me nervous.'

'I'll handle the rest, Dox,' Delilah said, still heading for the stairs. 'You should just go. Now would be a good opportunity.'

'Come on, Delilah,' he said, 'we're not just going to leave you. You can rely on my partner. I've seen his shooting, believe me, he hits things and they don't get back up.'

We stopped on the landing between the stairs up to the fifteenth floor and down to the thirteenth. From here, we could only go up to fifteen, down to thirteen, or back along the corridor to the restrooms. For a moment, I thought of just grabbing her and trying to take the gun. But she was keeping her gun side away from me – keeping it away deliberately. I doubted I could disarm her without either harming her or getting shot myself. Neither was an attractive alternative.

I took her by the arm and started to say, 'Damn it, Delilah . . .'

There was a sound at the top of the stairs above us. We both looked. It was Hilger and Al-Jib, descending toward us. Hilger was holding a gun in a two-handed grip, close to his body and pointing at the floor. He looked at me and I saw hard recognition in his eyes.

Shit. They must have gotten suspicious about Manny taking so long, and emerged to investigate.

'Step out of the way, John,' Hilger said. 'We just want to leave. There's no need for anyone to get killed here.'

Delilah was holding the Kimber, but it was clear to me that Hilger had the advantage. His weapon was more at the ready, for one thing. He had the high ground, for another. Also, presumably the gun he was holding was familiar to him, was presumably the very gun he trained with, whereas Delilah was relying on someone else's weapon, a four-inch-barrel .45 that was probably too big for her. Delilah must have recognized all this, too, or she would already have tried for a shot.

But then why hadn't Hilger already dropped us? I'd seen his combat shooting skills in front of Kwai Chung and knew he was formidable. And then I realized: *He's known here. This is part of his cover. He doesn't want to shoot.*

Al-Jib didn't say anything. He looked scared. This was Hilger's show.

'No problem,' I said, showing my hands. 'Our business wasn't with you. We're finished.'

At a minimum, I had to get us onto level ground. Better yet, let them go down the stairs past us. Then the high ground would be ours. They'd be struggling to keep us covered and descend the stairs backward at the same time.

Hilger frowned. 'Manny?'

'Manny's done. You and I are quits.'

His eyes narrowed. 'We're not quits.'

Well, so much for lulling him.

Delilah said, 'You can go. But not your friend.'

'Sorry, we're both going to leave,' Hilger said. 'Around you or through you, your choice.'

'I don't have a problem with around,' I said, thinking, *Goddamnit, Delilah, follow my lead.*

I heard Dox in my ear. 'I know what's going on, folks, but I can't help you while they're above you on the stairs. You've got to let 'em down past fourteen.'

'Let's just do as he says,' I said to Delilah, referring, of course, to Dox.

There was a long pause. I supposed she just instinctively didn't want to take herself from between Al-Jib and an escape path.

But she was tactical, she must have understood the situation. Our position relative to Hilger and Al-Jib was untenable. It was as though she was just trying to delay things, slow Al-Jib down. But why would she . . .

A stair creaked on one of the risers below. I don't know if it was intuition, or a sixth sense, or what, but I ducked. I heard the *pffft* of a suppressed pistol and a round cracked into the wall behind me.

I sprang to my right, down the corridor toward the bathroom. As I did so I saw Gil, moving toward us from below, his gun out. I heard Delilah scream, 'No!' A second later, gunfire erupted from the stairs above us.

I blasted open the bathroom door and stumbled inside. 'Get out of the bar!' I said to Dox through the lapel mike. I ran for the closet, opened the door, and got inside. 'Gil's here. Delilah must have called him. They're on the stairs. We're blown. There's nothing we can do.'

'Yeah, sounds like a shooting gallery out there,' he said. 'The patrons here are all freaking out, can you hear them?'

I heard shouting and other sounds of panic in the background. Dox, characteristically, sounded almost soporifically calm. I pulled out the Surefire and twisted it on. The attaché was where I'd left it. I grabbed it and headed back to the freight elevator. I pressed the button on the wall and waited.

'If you can get to the closet where I was hiding,' I said, 'there's freight elevator access. Otherwise, your only way down is on thirteen.'

'Already thought of all that. But I can't get to either with the OK Corral in between.'

Goddamn, he was cool under pressure. For a second I loved him for it.

'I know. But you can't just stay in the bar, either. If Gil and Delilah drop Hilger and Al-Jib, they might come for you.'

'I don't think Delilah . . .'

'Delilah called Gil, damn it. What do you think, she said, "Promise not to hurt them," and he said, "Sure, honey, whatever you say"?'

Come on, where the hell was the elevator. Delilah would know I would come this way. If Gil managed to drop Hilger and Al-Jib, this would be his next stop.

Dox said, 'Okay, I hear what you're saying. I'll just find some more hospitable place to wait this out.'

'At some point, you're going to get a crowd from the fifteenth-floor private dining rooms and the restaurant on fourteen stampeding for the exits,' I said. 'Let them carry you with them.'

'Yeah, that's pretty much what I had in mind. What about you?'

'I'm waiting for the freight elevator right now. But once the doors close and it goes down, we'll lose contact. The range of this gear is too short.'

'Well, what the hell are you waiting for? Go on, git. We'll hook up at the bug-out point.'

The elevator arrived. I stepped inside and held the 'door open' button. I glanced up – no dome camera. That was only for the passenger units.

'It's here,' I said. 'I can hold it for you.'

'Don't be stupid, man. Just take it down, then send it back up when you get off. I don't even know if I'm going out that way. I'll probably just drift out with the crowd once Hilger and the rest have finished killing each other.'

I didn't want to leave him, but what he said made sense. 'Good luck,' I said, and pressed the button for the lobby. The doors closed and the elevator started down.

Damn it, I hated to let Hilger go. We'd been so close to having this whole thing wrapped up. I thought for a moment.

The dumpster opposite the entrance. If I hid behind it, and Hilger made it out, an opportunity might present itself. A long shot, true, but there wasn't much downside.

Thirty seconds later, the doors opened on the lobby level. The security guard I had seen earlier was right in front of them. He had a gun drawn, a .38 Special, and was holding it too far in front of his body. He barely glanced at me as he charged inside.

He yelled something at me in Chinese – 'Get out,' probably. Before he even had a chance to think about what was happening, I dropped the attaché, grabbed the outstretched gun in both hands, pivoted, and twisted it away from him. He cried out in shock and fear. Then he backed up against the elevator wall and started yelling in Chinese again. This time I assumed it was something like 'Oh, shit!' or perhaps the time-honored 'Don't shoot!'

I picked up the attaché, stepped out of the elevator, and glanced around. All clear. I reached inside and pressed the button for thirteen. The doors closed, and the bug-eyed guard disappeared behind them, getting him out of my hair and preventing him from seeing what I was going to do next. Hopefully Dox already would be waiting for the guy when he arrived on thirteen. He could just haul him out and ride the elevator straight back down.

I walked across the street to the dumpster and examined my options. Good cover and concealment from both sides. But it was a little far from the elevator bank for my tastes. If Hilger hit the ground running and went immediately left or right from the elevators, I might lose him. If I could find the right spot, better to be waiting right there as he emerged.

I walked back over. The guard's desk. That would do. I started to duck down behind it.

The stairwell door blew open to my left, ricocheting off the wall. Al-Jib dashed out. I brought the gun up and tried to track him, but he had already gone around the corner.

The door blew open again. I spun back toward it. This time it was Delilah. She stuck her head out and checked left and right, the Kimber in a two-handed grip just below her chin. She saw me and said, 'Where did he go? Which way?'

'Where's Hilger?' I said.

'Upstairs! Goddamn you, where is Al-Jib!'

I cocked my head to the left. She took off without another word.

I turned and took two steps toward the guard's desk. I stopped. I took one more step. Then I said, 'Fuck!' I turned and ran after Delilah, heaving the attaché in the direction of the dumpster en route.

I saw her head into Statue Square park and sprinted after her. She raced past one of the fountains inside, the couples sitting around it turning their heads to watch as she blew by them. I sprinted after her, dodging pedestrians. We crossed the square, then weaved through the thick traffic on Chater Road. I could see Al-Jib, about fifteen meters ahead of Delilah. He was running flat out but she was gaining. Damn, she was fast.

He bolted across Connaught without slowing at all. A taxi screeched to a halt in front of him, the driver laying on the horn. Al-Jib knocked down a pedestrian but kept going. Someone yelled something. The cab started to move forward again and then Delilah cut in front of it. The driver laid on the horn again. I flew past him a few paces behind Delilah.

Al-Jib raced up Edinburgh, toward the Star Ferry. If his timing was bad, he was about to meet a dead end, in the form of the southern end of Victoria Harbor. If his timing was good, though, he might just catch a departing ferry. The Star Ferry route between Central and Tsim Sha Tsui has been a major commuting line between Hong Kong and Kowloon for over a century, and the enormous, two-deck, open-air pedestrian ferries, some seemingly as old as the inception of the service, depart every seven minutes, each usually jammed with hundreds of passengers.

Al-Jib ran into the ferry terminal. Delilah followed him. I got inside a few seconds later and looked around. There were crowds of people and for a second I looked around wildly, not seeing her. Then I spotted a disturbance in the crowd on one of the stairwells – there she was, heading up the stairs. A woman was getting up from the floor and was yelling. Delilah must have lost Al-Jib for a moment, then figured out he had knocked over the woman tearing up the stairs. I followed, just a few lengths behind now. A crowd of passengers was heading down the stairs to our left. Shit, a ferry had come in a minute or two earlier – that meant it would already be leaving. We got to the concourse level and I saw Al-Jib, far ahead now. He seemed to recognize his desperate opportunity. He sprinted faster, vaulting over the turnstiles to the departure pier. He knocked a table over as he leaped and coins spilled to the concrete floor. The attendant bellowed something in Chinese.

We went over the turnstiles after him. The pier was empty – the passengers had already boarded the ferry. A worker stood along the gunwale on the lower deck, using a pole to push the lumbering craft from the pier. Al-Jib sprinted straight toward the boat, leaped, and fell across the guardrail, nearly knocking the worker over in the process. Delilah followed two meters behind him. I saw her leap onto the guardrail and pull herself over. The worker shouted something but didn't try to stop the boat. It kept moving forward. Its stern was about to pull clear of the end of the pier.

I shoved the .38 into the back of my pants and kept running. *Come on, come on . . .*

Even as I launched myself through the air, I saw that I wasn't going to make it. I slammed into one of the old tires strung up just below the deck to cushion the boat while it was docking. The tire might have been adequate for watercraft, but seemed to offer considerably less padding for a human torso, and I had the wind partially knocked out of me. But I was able to haul myself up to the guardrail.

I scrambled over it onto the deck and rolled to my feet.

Delilah and Al-Jib had disappeared into the mass of passengers, but there was a path of sorts, slightly less packed with people than the areas around it, that told me where to look. I pulled the pistol and set off into the crowd. I was glad there were no security people on board to complicate things. The Star Ferry is about as secure as a sidewalk.

But after just a few meters, the path I'd been following closed up. There were scores of people down here, maybe hundreds, and I couldn't pick up any vibe in the crowd that might have indicated where Delilah and Al-Jib had headed. In less than seven minutes, we'd be landing in Kowloon. It would be hard to stop him from leaping onto the pier there as we were docking and taking off into the crowd. We had to contain him here.

I moved toward the stern, beyond the rows of wooden seats, but couldn't see through the mass of people who hadn't gotten seats and were standing. 'Delilah?' I called out. 'Delilah!'

'Here,' I heard her say, from somewhere in front of me. 'I . . .'

Something cut her off. I heard the report of a big gun. There were screams. Suddenly the crowd was shoving back toward me. The people ahead were trying to get away from the shooting.

I pushed forward. All at once, the crowd was behind me like a receding tide. And then I saw.

Somehow Al-Jib had gotten behind Delilah and managed to wrest the Kimber from her. He was standing behind her, one arm around her neck, the other holding the barrel of the gun to her temple.

I stopped, pulled the .38, and pointed it at him with a

two-handed grip. They were eight meters away. I was still winded from the chase, and the deck of the ferry was rolling with the harbor's currents. And Al-Jib was holding her like a shield, with only part of his head exposed. I was too far to risk the shot.

'Drop the gun!' he screamed. 'Drop it or by Allah I will put her brains on the floor!'

'Don't,' I said, as calmly as I could. 'Because then I'll have to put your brains on the floor, too.'

'Drop it! Drop it!' he screamed again.

'Listen,' I said over the wind that was blowing across the deck. 'I don't know who you are. I don't care. My business was with Manny, and that business is done. As far as I'm concerned, you're free to leave. But not if you harm the lady. Then I have to kill you, understand?'

He looked at me, his eyes desperate, but I could tell he was thinking. He couldn't shoot Delilah. If he did, in the time it took him to bring the gun around to me I would turn him into hamburger.

'Let's think this through,' I said. 'Let's find a way to all walk away from here. Why don't you lower your gun a little. And then I'll lower mine a little. And then we'll go from there.'

He started to relax, just slightly. I thought, *Okay.*

'No!' Delilah shouted. 'Shoot him!'

Goddamnit, I would if you would just work with me. . . .

Al-Jib's grip around her neck tightened. 'Drop the gun!' he screamed again.

Delilah was staring at me, her eyes full of rage. 'Shoot him!' she rasped. 'Goddamn you, shoot him!'

He was choking her, intentionally or unintentionally, I didn't know. I realized I was losing control of the situation. He was so strung out he might pull the trigger without even meaning to. Or he might shoot just to shut her up. Or he might otherwise miscalculate.

'Drop the fucking gun!' he screamed again. 'Or I swear . . .'

In one smooth motion, Delilah shrugged her head downward and slapped the gun up with her right hand. It discharged into the ceiling. I was so juiced with adrenaline it sounded like not more than a firecracker.

Al-Jib started to bring the gun back down. Delilah caught it in both hands. It discharged again.

I moved in. Delilah was between us, in front of his torso, and they were moving. I was still too far to risk the shot.

He let go of her neck and used both hands to try to wrestle the gun away from her. It didn't work. He looked up, saw me heading toward him, and realized he had lost.

He let go of the gun and started to turn to run. But the muzzle velocity of a bullet from a .38 is eight hundred and fifty feet per second. Since I was now less than twenty feet from him, the round I fired reached him in about one-fortieth of a second, give or take. Which turned out to be slightly faster than he could move out of the way. The bullet caught him in the face. He spun around from the impact and stumbled back toward the railing. I followed him, focusing on his torso, ready to finish him off.

I heard two more shots from alongside me. They caught Al-Jib in the side. In my peripheral vision I saw Delilah walk past me, holding the Kimber in a two-handed grip, as implacable as the angel of death.

Al-Jib tried to straighten. Delilah kept moving in. She shot him twice in the head. His hands flew up and he went over the railing, into the dark water below.

For a long second, I looked at her. I was still holding the gun in a combat grip.

She stood panting for a moment, returning my look, but not in a focused way. She lowered the Kimber.

I hesitated for a moment, grappling with the knowledge that she had called Gil. Then something in her eyes, her posture, made the decision for me. I lowered the .38 and stuck it in my waistband.

I looked toward the bow. The lights of Tsim Sha Tsui were less than a minute away.

A few wordless seconds passed. Then Delilah handed me the Kimber. 'Here,' she said. 'I've got no place to conceal this, like you said. And we might need it.'

I stuck the second gun in my waistband and looked at her, trying to find words.

She said, 'I had to. For you, too.'

'What do you mean, for me?'

'One day, Al-Jib and his type will detonate a nuclear weapon inside a city. A half-million people are going to die. Innocent people – families, children, babies. When that happens, it won't be because I could have stopped it but didn't. And you couldn't bear that burden any more than I could. I won't let you.'

I realized there was a lot of shouting and commotion around the side of the boat where the passengers would be exiting any minute. While we were engaging Al-Jib, I'd been too focused to notice.

Delilah and I walked forward, into the crowd. The people closest to us recognized that we had been involved in what just happened, and gave us wide berth. The farther forward we moved into the crowd, though, the less we encountered that kind of courtesy. The people closer to the front hadn't seen what happened. They didn't know who we were and they didn't care. They had heard shooting and a commotion, and just wanted to get the hell off the ferry as soon as it docked. We reached a point where the crowd was so dense that we were lost in it, just two more scared passengers. We couldn't move farther forward. We simply had to wait, along with everyone else.

A few seconds later, we were docking. The moment the boat was in position, people started surging off it. There was a lot of shouting in Chinese and I wasn't sure what was being said. I did know that we wanted to get out of there before anyone started pointing at us.

We headed out of the pier building, past the clock tower and the crowds shopping in the area. We cut through the underpass below Salisbury Road, then headed east to the impossibly dense and crowded shopping districts around Nathan. An Asian man and a gorgeous blonde – we would be easy to pick up from a description of what had happened on the ferry, and at the China Club just before that. But I didn't want us to split up yet. I wanted to finish this.

We reached the southeast corner of Kowloon Park and went inside. The park, set on a sprawling knoll above the streets below, was dark and, at this hour, reasonably deserted. We walked past the skeletal aviary and the silhouetted Chinese-style gardens to the Sculpture Walk, where we sat on the steps of a small amphitheater beside one of the Walk's silent statues. I took out the prepaid cell phone, turned it on, and called Dox on the throwaway he was carrying.

He picked up immediately. 'Hey, partner, I hope that's you.'

I couldn't help smiling at the sound of his voice. 'It's me. Are you okay?'

'I'm fine. I'm here at the bug-out point. Where are you?'

'Kowloon.'

'Pardon me for asking, but isn't that the wrong direction?'

'Unfortunately. Delilah and I chased Al-Jib onto the Star Ferry.'

'How'd that turn out?'

'With Al-Jib dead.'

'Well, that's a happy outcome. Another victory for the good guys, and a blow to the forces of evil. What about Delilah?'

'She's fine. She's right here with me.'

'Ah-ha, so that's why you hightailed it to Kowloon. You sure we have time for that sort of thing right now?'

'I'm sure we don't. What happened with Hilger and Gil?'

'If you're talking about the guy who was shooting at Hilger, he's dead.'

'How do you know?'

'Hilger shot him, and when Delilah went to help, old Ali just about fucking flew over them and headed down the stairs. After that, Gil was doing a damn fine job of returning Hilger's fire upside down and on his back from the stairs, but eventually Hilger put another round in him and then imitated Ali's levitation trick. He paused just long enough to turn and shoot the sumbitch point-blank in the head.'

'Goddamn, I wish we'd managed to get you a gun.'

'Yeah, I would have liked to shoot him, and the opportunity was there. I did manage to sling a chair at him from the landing as he made his getaway, at least. It knocked him down, but he kept going after that.'

'You and the chairs,' I said. 'You ought to market it. *"Chair-fung-do."*'

He laughed. 'Yeah, the odd piece of furniture can come in handy from time to time, I've discovered. Anyway, I couldn't get to Hilger in time after he was down, seeing as he was armed and dangerous and I was only dangerous.

These jobs can be awkward without a proper rifle at hand. I don't know how you do it.'

'It doesn't matter,' I said. 'Hilger's known in the club. Hell, he had reservations there tonight. The police are going to pick him up for sure. And then we'll see if we were right about him running his own operation.'

'Think the powers that be will disown him?'

I paused and considered. 'I'm getting the feeling he has . . . enemies. People who might like to see that happen, yeah.'

'What gives you that feeling?'

'I'm not sure. I want to check something out, and then I'll let you know.'

'All right. Finish your quickie, and let's meet at the airport. The old City of Life just doesn't feel as welcoming now as it did this morning.'

'Give me an hour.'

'Sure, take as much time as you need. I don't see any reason to hurry. It's not like half the Hong Kong police force would be looking for someone of your description or anything like that.'

'All right,' I said, 'I see your point.' I told him where he could retrieve the bug-out kit I'd put in place. He said he would grab it and be on the way.

I clicked off and looked at Delilah.

'Gil's dead,' I said. 'Dox saw Hilger shoot him in the head, point-blank.'

She nodded, her jaw set, then said, 'What else?'

I briefed her on the rest of what Dox had told me.

'I'm going to meet him at the airport now,' I said. 'You coming?'

She shook her head. 'Not yet. I don't have my passport.'

I didn't say anything. I was still pissed that she had called Gil. I was trying to let it go.

'Anyway,' she said, 'I need to brief my people on what just happened here. There are going to be a lot of questions.'

'You going to be able to weather it?'

'I'm not sure. Al-Jib dead will certainly help. That is a major victory, major. If he'd gotten away, I don't know what would have happened.'

She was talking unusually fast. I noticed that her hands were trembling.

'You okay?' I asked, looking at her.

She nodded. I saw her eyes were filling up.

'You never . . .' I started to say. I paused, then went on. 'That was your first time, wasn't it.'

She nodded again and her tears spilled over. She started to shake.

My anger dissipated. I put my arm around her and pulled her close. 'You did the right thing,' I said. 'Just like they trained you. You'll be okay.'

She shook her head. 'I don't know what's wrong with me. I should be happy, I should be exulting that he's dead. I mean, I was exulting, right after. But now . . .'

I kissed the top of her head. 'Your mind knows what's what. It'll just take a little while for your gut to catch up. You'll see.'

She wiped her face and looked at me. 'I was so afraid he was going to get away. I wanted you to shoot him. When he had that gun to my head, I thought I was going to die and all I cared about was that you shoot him first, so I would know.'

I nodded. 'When you're certain you're going to die, and you don't, it stays with you for a long time after. Sometime

I'll have to tell you about what happened to me outside of Kwai Chung last year.'

'You never did tell me that whole story.'

'Well, are you going to give me the chance?'

She laughed a little and touched my cheek. 'Let's meet somewhere. I don't want it to end like this. I want . . . I want that to look forward to.'

I shrugged. 'I've got your number. And we've got the bulletin board.'

She smiled. 'We'll always have the bulletin board.'

I laughed. 'Well, it's not Paris, but we'll figure something out.'

Her hand slipped around to the back of my neck and caressed me there, absently, gently. It felt good.

'Thank you for trusting me,' she said. 'I wanted to say that to you in Phuket, but I didn't. I wanted to tell you . . . how much it means to me.'

How someone could smell so good after chasing a terrorist a quarter mile, almost dying in his grasp, and then killing him, was a mystery I knew I would always savor.

'Sounds like trusting you in Phuket wasn't the brightest move I've ever made,' I said.

She looked at me, her eyes fierce. 'Yes, it was. And as for calling Gil tonight . . .'

I shook my head. 'I understand why you did it.'

'I had to. I told him it was Al-Jib, not you, that you were helping us. But he didn't believe me about you. And when I saw him take a shot at you . . .'

I realized I was touching her leg. I started to say, 'I know, I heard you,' but she pulled me in and kissed me.

I stopped talking. The kiss went from zero to sixty in about two nanoseconds. Where we were sitting, it was very dark.

What the hell, it wasn't like Dox had never kept me waiting.

I took the Airport Express train from Kowloon station and called Dox when I arrived. He was already there. We met on the departures level, in front of United Airlines. He was still in his suit, an attaché in each hand.

He grinned as I walked up to him. 'I think this one's yours,' he said, handing it to me. 'Saw it next to a dumpster in front of the Bank of China building as I exited the premises. Unless you meant to throw it away . . .'

'No, I was just blowing the ballast to chase after Al-Jib. I'm glad to have it back. Traveling without luggage can be conspicuous.'

'And we all know how much you hate to be conspicuous,' he said, staring at my neck.

I said, 'What?'

His grin achieved galactic proportions. 'Partner, I believe that's lipstick on your collar. You've been a bad boy. And here we are, in the middle of an operation and everything. Next thing I know, you'll be leaving your cell phone on and trying to hump a *katoey* into submission and committing similar such indiscretions. If you keep this up, people are going to start suspecting you're human, and the unpleasant burden of explaining otherwise will fall entirely to me.'

My hand wandered up to my collar. 'I . . . I just . . .'

'You don't have to explain. Combat will do that to a man, I know. Bet you didn't even need the Viagra this time, either.'

'No, I just thought of Tiara.'

He laughed. 'That's good, you got me there, man! Damn, you're always going to have that over me. Hey, you think the Israelites will pay us, after all this?'

'I'd say they'd better. And then some.'

'I'm sure Delilah will strenuously advocate our cause. She's a nice lady.'

'I don't know what her position is going to be now. They're going to ask her a lot of questions.'

'Well, if things don't work out for her with her people, as far as I'm concerned she's always welcome to join our happy band of freelancers. Like I said, we're the wave of the future. The nation-states of the world are just going to outsource all their defense needs so they can watch more television, you'll see.'

I shook my head. 'I don't think Delilah would be comfortable as a freelancer. It's not who she is.'

'Well, hopefully she won't ever have to face that decision. It ain't a happy moment in a soldier's life, as you know.'

'No, it's not,' I said.

'Well? Where to, from here?'

'I've got some business in Tokyo. On the way over here, I made a reservation on an Asiana flight that goes through Seoul. It leaves at . . .' I looked at my watch. 'Oh-dark-thirty. Two hours.'

'What about Rio? You still hanging your hat there?'

'Mostly. I'll probably head back after Tokyo.'

'Maybe I'll come visit you there. Them Brazilian girls . . . man, don't even get me started.'

'I try not to.'

He laughed.

'Yeah, come on down,' I said. 'It would be good to see you. We can go to another adult bar.'

He laughed again. 'I'd like that. I really would.'

We were quiet for a moment. I said, 'What about you? Where are you heading?'

'Gonna go visit my folks in the States, I think. It's been a while and I miss them.'

I nodded, trying to imagine it. I lost my parents so many years earlier that the simple concept of visiting the folks, of visiting anyone, is almost alien. But maybe I could find a way.

I said, 'They've got a good son.'

He beamed. 'They do. And I'm lucky to have them, too.' He glanced at his watch. 'Got a Cathay Pacific flight that leaves for L.A. at twenty-three thirty-five. So I'd better beat feet.'

I held out my hand.

He looked at me and said, 'Son, just because I was recently nearly inducted as a new member of the Accidental Katoey Love Association doesn't mean you're not allowed to show your feelings for me.'

Oh God, I thought. But then there I was, hugging the big bastard in the middle of the airport.

22

I slept like a dead man on the trip to Seoul. There was a five-hour layover, then a short flight to Tokyo.

I wondered where I should stay. When I was living in the city, I maintained a relationship with several hotels that held a suitcase for me while I was 'out of town,' just in case. But those arrangements were out of date now, and I couldn't be sure the hotels in question would still have my gear. And even if they did, it was possible the relationship had been exposed in the interim. I decided it would be safer to do something new.

I arrived at Narita airport at a little after noon. I took the JR Express train to Tokyo station, then walked unburdened by anything other than my attaché to the Four Seasons in Marunouchi. I asked if they had any rooms available. Only a suite, they told me. I told them a suite would be fine.

For an excessive price in the lobby concession store, I bought a pair of khaki pants and a navy merino wool sweater. In the room, I showered and shaved with the razor and other amenities the hotel had thought to provide. I called housekeeping and told them I would like to avail myself of their one-hour pressing services. My suit looked like I'd been living in it.

I walked into Ginza to buy clean underwear, a fresh shirt, and a few other such necessities for the fugitive on the move. The weather was cold and crisp – my favorite in Tokyo – and the wind had a clean winter bite to it. Being back felt good. It even felt oddly right.

I looked around as I walked, more in appreciation of my surroundings than to check my back. The topography had changed a bit since my last visit. Some of the stores were different, and a number of new buildings had gone up, and Starbucks had continued its kudzu-like infiltration of lobbies and storefronts. But the feel of the city was all the same: the way you could transition from the Stygian gloom of a Hibiya train underpass to the glittering shops of Ginza in just a few dozen paces; the air of money to be made and spent, of dreams realized and broken; the beautiful people in the shops and the sharp-elbowed old women in the train stations; the sense that everyone you pass in the pricey restaurant windows and on the smart sidewalks and in the solemn silences of the city's small shrines wants to be here, here in Tokyo, here and nowhere else.

I thought of Yamaoto, and wondered when, if ever, it might be safe for me to move back here. Fond as I was of Rio, it didn't really feel like home, and as I walked through Tokyo I suspected it never would.

I bought what I needed and went back to the hotel. My suit, pressed to perfection, was already hanging in the suite's ample closet. I changed, left the hotel, and made my way to a cell phone shop, where I bought a prepaid unit. I used it to call Kanezaki.

'*Hai,*' he answered.

I gave him my usual 'hey' in response.

There was a pause. He said, 'You're in Tokyo.'

Ah, the relentless march of caller ID and other such complicating technologies. 'Yes,' I told him. 'I wanted to update you on what I've found out about Manila. And I think you owe me a bit of an update, too.'

'I haven't been able to learn that much . . .'

'Don't bullshit me. You know that makes me angry.'

312

There was another pause. 'Where are you?'

'I'm watching you right now.'

'You're watching . . . what do you mean?'

I smiled, imagining him looking suddenly over his shoulder or through his office window. 'Just kidding. I'm at Tokyo station. Marunouchi South exit.'

'I'm near the embassy. I can meet you in ten minutes, how's that?'

'That's fine. Call me when you get here.'

I clicked off.

I didn't think he'd have any inclination to bring company. And I certainly hadn't given him time. Still, I crossed the street and watched the entrance from afar. Old habits die hard.

He showed up by taxi ten minutes later, alone. He got out and waited, knowing I would want to see him before I showed myself.

I circled around, using taxis and pedestrians for cover, then moved in from his blind spot. But he turned before I could get close enough to say *ta-da*. Good for him.

'Hey,' he said, and smiled. He held out his hand and we shook.

'Let's get out of here,' I said. 'I doubt the Japanese government wastes a lot of time trying to shadow you CIA types, but just in case.'

We spent a half hour making sure we were alone, then ducked into Tsuta, a coffee shop I used to frequent in Minami Aoyama. I was glad to find Tsuta weathering the Starbucks storm. The last time I'd been here, I had been with Midori. That had been a good afternoon, strange under the circumstances but full of weird and foolish promise. And it was so long ago.

We sat down across from each other at one of the two

tables and ordered espressos. I looked him over. It had been a year since I'd last seen him, and he seemed older now, more mature. There was a confidence that he'd lacked before, a new substance, a kind of weight. Kanezaki, I realized, wasn't a kid anymore. He was managing some serious matters, and those matters were in turn molding him. As Dox's favorite philosopher said, when you look into the abyss, the abyss also looks into you.

We made small talk for a while. The table next to us was occupied by two elderly Japanese women. I doubted they could speak English, which Kanezaki and I were using – hell, I doubted they could hear much at all – but we kept our voices low all the same.

After the espressos arrived, I said, 'I think it's time for you to level with me.'

He took a sip from his demitasse, nodded appreciatively, and said, 'I don't know what you mean.'

I knew he would tell me eventually. I also knew he would make me struggle for it, so that I would feel I had won something, that the information I extracted had worth. I wished we could skip the intermediate dance steps, but this was the way Kanezaki always played it.

Well, maybe there was a way we could accelerate things. 'It's probably just a coincidence,' I said, 'but every time we talked or otherwise corresponded over the last few days, things I told you wound up in the *Washington Post* right afterward.'

He didn't say anything, but I detected the trace of a satisfied smile.

'So,' I said, 'if you want me to tell you what happened in Manila, and what just happened in Hong Kong, you're going to have to go first.'

I picked up my demitasse and leaned back in my chair. I

let the aroma play around my face for a moment, then took a small sip. Ah, it was good. Strong but not overwhelming; bitter, but not over-extracted; light, but with density in the play of flavors. I've drunk coffee in Paris, Rome, and Rio. Hell, I've even drunk it in Seattle, where the bean is a local religion. But in my mind nothing beats Tsuta.

Kanezaki waited a long time, the better to convince me that he was talking only under duress. I was halfway through my espresso when he said, 'How do you know about Hong Kong?'

I knew he would crack, and I couldn't help smiling a little. I said, 'Because I just came from there.'

He looked at me and said, 'Holy shit.'

'So? This time you go first.'

He sighed. 'All right. Hilger was running a private op.'

'What do you mean, "private"?'

'Let me amend that. I should have said "semiprivate." Like the post office: private, but government-subsidized.'

He took a sip from his demitasse. 'What is intelligence, to the policymakers? It's just a product. Hell, in the community we even call it a product. We call the policymakers "consumers." And what do all consumers want?'

'Low prices?' I offered.

He chuckled. 'If the consumer is rich enough so that price doesn't matter.'

'Then choice,' I said.

He nodded. 'Exactly. And if you don't like what one store is trying to sell you, you'll spend your money somewhere else. Look at what the White House did in the run-up to Iraq. They didn't like what the CIA was telling them, so they set up a Pentagon unit and did their shopping there, instead.'

'So Hilger . . .'

'Look, think of it this way: the basis exists for a competitive, free market for intelligence. Regardless of the structure that exists by law, policymakers will always look to different factions to satisfy policymaking requirements, and develop those factions if they don't already exist.'

I took a sip of espresso. 'Hilger's one of the factions?'

He nodded. 'For almost a decade, he's been building his own network. In a sense, he's created a privatized intelligence service, and his product is good. A lot of policymakers have come to rely on it.'

'What happened, did the CIA get jealous?'

'That's not the point. Sure, he was able to do things that the Agency can't – he's got no oversight, for one thing. But that's exactly the problem. He's his own extra-governmental institution.'

'And what are you doing here with me?'

He was quiet for a moment. Then he said, 'Hilger was corrupt. And I'm not just talking about the two million dollars he made off with from Kwai Chung last year. I'm talking about much worse than that. Remember the US diplomat who was assassinated in Amman a few years ago?'

I nodded.

'That was Hilger, making his bones.'

That tracked with the conversation I had overheard in the China Club. I nodded.

'Look,' he said, 'why do you think it's so hard for us to penetrate terrorist cells? Because there's a simple admission test: kill a high-profile American, or carry out some other atrocity. If you can do that, you're in. Well, the CIA can't do that.'

'But apparently, Hilger can.'

'Can and did. Hilger created access to terrorists by being a terrorist. The thing in Jordan, deals with that guy Belghazi you took out last year, black market arms, money launder-ing . . . I've got evidence that he knew about the Bali bombing before the fact. Two hundred people died there. The two bombings in Jakarta, too. After all that, you think he even remembered who he was or what he was trying to do?'

'I don't know.'

'It's like Nixon's "madman" theory. You want people to think you're a madman, you have to start doing mad things. In which case, you might as well be mad. What's the difference?'

'Tell me why you were leaking to the *Post*.'

He shrugged. 'I had to put pressure on Hilger's network. Publicity equals pressure.'

'The first story said the men in Manila were spooks, not ex-spooks.'

'They were ex-spooks, like I told you. But if the story was that they were current, Langley would face more questions, and Hilger would feel more heat.'

'So those "well-placed sources" the stories mentioned . . .'

'Yeah, you're talking to him.'

I nodded in appreciation. 'What about "Gird Enter-prises"?'

'One of Hilger's front companies, I think. We'll know soon enough. The media is all over it now.'

'Now that you leaked it.'

'Of course,' he said, sounding and for a moment even looking very much like Tatsu.

'Are you sure that taking down Hilger was the right thing to do?' I asked. 'He'd gotten pretty close to this guy Al-Jib . . .'

'Ali Al-Jib?' he asked, his eyes wide.

'You know any others?'

317

'How do you know this?'

'Because they were meeting at the China Club in Hong Kong last night.'

'They were meeting . . . holy shit, where is Al-Jib now?'

'I expect he's being fished out of Victoria Harbor. Unless he was able to swim for shore with five bullets in him.'

He shook his head as though incredulous. 'That was you, at the China Club?'

I shrugged.

He shook his head again. 'Someone ought to give you a medal.'

'I'd settle for just getting paid. Anyway, how do you know Hilger wasn't trying to develop Al-Jib, run him somehow? Maybe Al-Jib would have led to other sources.'

He took a breath and let it out. 'Who knows what Hilger was up to with Al-Jib? The man was dirty.'

I took a sip from the demitasse. 'So what happens to him now?'

He shrugged. 'I don't think he has much of a chance, but I don't have all the information yet. What happened at the China Club?'

I told him, leaving out Dox's and Delilah's involvement.

He sat silently while I briefed him, shaking his head as though incredulous. When I was done, he said, 'You did Manny, too. Unbelievable. You really should get a medal.'

'I wish I'd thought to come to you a week ago and ask what it would be worth to you for me to take these guys out. I probably could have retired on it.'

'That would be a tragic loss. Guess I can't ask you who you were working for this time?'

'Guess you're right.'

'It's okay. I can imagine.'

'You can imagine all you want.'

318

'Well, from what you've told me, I don't think Hilger can survive this. His supporters are all going to be running for cover.'

'I don't know,' I said. 'I get the feeling this guy is a survivor. Look at the way he turned things around at Kwai Chung last year, and made off with two million US in the process. I wouldn't underestimate him.'

'I'm not,' he said.

I finished my espresso and set down the demitasse. 'Are you still in touch with Tatsu?' I asked.

'A bit,' he said, his tone guarded, and I knew they were in touch a lot.

I nodded. 'Spend time with him. He's walked the narrow path you seem to be on for a long time, and somehow he hasn't managed to fall off. That's rare. You should try to learn his secret.'

'What path are you talking about?'

'The one where the end justifies the means.'

He nodded.

'Well,' I said, getting up, 'seeing as I've just eliminated two of the entries on Uncle Sam's nonexistent terrorism hit list, I guess I can count on you to pay for the coffee?'

He stood and smiled. 'My pleasure.'

I looked at him. 'Is this on you, though? Or the government?'

'It's on me.'

I nodded. 'That's what I thought.'

I held out my hand and we shook. *'Ki o tsukero yo,'* I said. Be careful.

'So shimasu,' he told me. I will.

23

Hilger sat in the Dragonair departures area at Hong Kong International, waiting for his flight to Shanghai. The sun was up and he was exhausted.

It had been a long night. Deleting the files hadn't required much time. They were all electronic, after all. And collecting his essential gear hadn't been a problem, either, as much of it was kept in a bag that served as the civilian equivalent of the bug-out kits they had been taught to use in the military. It had been the phone calls that had taken a while. There were the people in his network, who needed to be warned. There were the family members, who needed to be prepared. And there were the politicians, who needed to be importuned. Each set of calls had been more difficult than the one that preceded it.

He wasn't worried about himself. He'd been ready for a day like this, and his backup systems had worked well. Even if they hadn't, and he'd been forced to take a fall or even worse, he could have handled it. What was hard to come to grips with was the total unraveling of his op. He'd been so close to achieving so much. America was in mortal danger, and wasn't doing enough to safeguard against it. With his operation crippled, he thought the worst was now inevitable.

He'd read an article once, about the wildfires they have every few years in Southern California. Some expert was explaining that, because of the encroachment of suburban development on woodlands, the small fires nature employed to clear out the underbrush were no longer permissible. As a result, year after year, the underbrush got thicker and drier and more ready to combust. Sooner or later, the expert said, something will always set that underbrush off. It's almost mathematically certain.

He looked at a WMD attack on America in much the same terms. There was so much post-Soviet matériel out there, and so many fanatics who wanted to use it, that it was just a matter of time. But no one wanted to accept this fact, any more than the Los Angeles suburban homeowners wanted to accept that a little annual soot on their wood siding might be a small price to pay to avoid a fucking holocaust. It was just how people's minds worked. There wasn't much you could do about it.

He shook his head, disgusted. It all made him think of the way municipalities install traffic lights. After a certain number of auto fatalities at a given intersection, the politicians say, 'Hmm, we ought to put in a light there.' They were going to do the same thing when New York had disappeared under a mushroom cloud.

Or maybe he was giving the idiots too much credit. Hell, losing New York . . . maybe they would just pause for a minute, then go back to renaming French fries and prohibiting gay marriage and the other priorities of the day.

Yeah, the politicians were in thrall to Big Oil, or brain-dead, or both. If anyone was going to prevent a cataclysm, it would be Hilger, and the team he had built.

He sighed. Al-Jib was one of his linchpins. If Hilger just could have learned a little more about the man's contacts, where his knowledge had been disseminated, they might actually have been able to stuff some of the fucking genie back in the bottle. But not now. Al-Jib probably wouldn't touch Hilger after this. That is, assuming the man was still alive. The blonde in the China Club, whoever she was, had taken off after him like a hungry lioness hot on a gazelle.

Well, there were little silver linings in the cloud. When his pissant National Security Council contact had started back-pedaling about whether the White House could support Hilger in the face of another mess, Hilger had just told the man what a shame it would be when Hilger's client list came to light, with the contact's name and those of several other prominent political personages on it. The helpless silence that had followed that warning was one of the most satisfying sounds Hilger had ever heard. The contact's plan of simply saying 'I have no recollection of that event, Senator,' and 'I don't recall that meeting, Senator,' and 'I can't imagine I would have done that, Senator, because that would be wrong,' suddenly just wasn't going to be adequate, and the piece of shit knew it.

Hilger had gone on to explain that he was no Edwin Wilson. If he went down, lots of people would be coming with him, first among them Mr NSC contact. Do I need to explain further? Hilger had asked. No, the contact had told him in a tight, emasculated voice. He had made himself perfectly clear.

Wilson had been an operative the Agency allegedly fired back in 1971, but who had gone on acting like a spook afterward, carrying out assassinations, laundering money, and selling plastic explosives to countries like Libya, until he was jailed in 1983. Wilson claimed that he'd never left the Agency and that the whole thing had been a sanctioned op; the government, predictably, claimed he was fabricating. Hilger didn't know the truth – that information would be very closely held, just as it was for him – but he suspected the whole thing had been an op. After all, how do you get close to a man like Kaddafi? By selling him what he wants. There were people who understood this principle then, just as there were people, like Hilger, who understood it today.

Wilson's error, though, had been his failure to collect evidence implicating his paymasters. Hilger had been much better prepared. The people who had been greedy enough to invest their money with him had been stupid, too. NSC staffers just couldn't explain being on the same client list as unsavorables like Manny. They would have to back Hilger, or go down with him.

As for the Agency, he knew the last thing they would want would be another Wilson scandal. Even if they denied Hilger, the press would go into a frenzy over a repeat. All those resultant congressional committees, and questions under oath, examination of finances, new layers of over-sight . . . no one wanted any of that, there was so much more important work to be done. Plus, Hilger's contacts were putting out the word that Hilger had been behind Manny's death. And if Al-Jib turned up not breathing, that would be attributed to Hilger, too. All, of course, with the understanding that the new director could take whatever credit for the op he wanted. Politicians tended to be as resistant to that kind of opportunity as junkies were to a fix. The Hong Kong police and Hong Kong liaison could be bought off the same way. With the right mix of sense and incentives, the whole thing could be put to sleep pretty quietly.

Of course, the Jim Hilger cover was permanently blown, and at a minimum Hong Kong's Chinese overlords would declare him persona non grata and boot him out. Hilger had decided to save them the trouble. He already had an established identity, and a presence he had been careful to cultivate, in Shanghai. When the authorities showed up at his Hong Kong apartment, or at his office, as perhaps they already had, he wasn't going to be there to greet them.

He was going to miss that view from Two IFC, though. Well, it wasn't like there were no skyscrapers in Shanghai. The city was growing so fast, and had so many foreigners, that he'd have no trouble fitting in there and gearing up again.

He thought of Rain for a moment, and could actually feel his face contorting with rage as he did so. He was surprised at his own reaction. After all, Rain hadn't acted with knowledge. He'd been hired for a job and he'd done it. Hilger used people like him all the time; it wasn't personal. So why was Hilger taking it so personally now? It was stupid. Yes, the man had screwed up everything. And in the process, cost Hilger years of effort and unknowingly endangered millions of innocents. But he hadn't meant it, he hadn't known. Hilger should just let it go.

Or he should just find the bastard and shoot him in the head. It wasn't justified, it wasn't even mature, but it would probably help him sleep better.

And that fucking Dox, too. Someone had nailed him with a chair as he'd hauled ass down the China Club stairs, and he had a pretty good idea of who it was. He had a welt on his back the size and color of an eggplant.

One thing at a time, though. First, Shanghai. Then, probably, more damage control. Then salvaging what he could of his operation.

Then it would be time for Rain and Dox. And God help them then.

24

After leaving Kanezaki at Tsuta, I called Tatsu. I asked him if he felt like an early dinner. He told me that would be fine. I told him I would meet him at Tsukumo Ramen, one of the best noodle shops in the city. Rio's cuisine is wonderful, but ramen is comfort food for me, and Tsukumo is one of the best. I'd missed it and was glad for the chance to return.

I stopped at an Internet café in Aoyama on the way. There was a message waiting from Delilah. It said:

Dox was right, Gil is dead. I never liked him, and yet I feel so sad. Without men like him, I don't know what would happen to the world. My government won't acknowledge his affiliations, of course. Only his citizenship. But at least his family will be able to bury him and properly mourn. One day, I hope to tell them what happened. They should know he was a hero.

My people have transferred your payment in accordance with the instructions you gave them. You've been paid in full for Lavi. You have also been paid the same amount for Al-Jib. And there is a bonus.

I don't know what's next. There are a lot of meetings going on right now, with me as the subject. For the most part, I don't care.

I would like to see you again. I hope it will be soon.

– D

I checked the bulletin board I had established with Boaz and Gil. There was a message waiting. It read like an invoice, and matched what Delilah had told me. Next to the amount she had described as a 'bonus,' it said:

No hard feelings. With a little smiley face.

I almost laughed. It had to be Boaz.

I checked the account I had given them. The money was all there. I transferred Dox half of everything, then went to meet Tatsu. I would respond to Delilah later.

I took a cab to Hiro and walked. Tatsu was already sitting at the counter when I came in. He got up, shuffled over, and shook my hand. He was wearing a broad smile and it felt good to be with someone who was so happy to see me. Then I realized he was getting the same smile from me.

It was early enough so that we were able to get a table. We ordered *marukyu* ramen, prepared with fresh noodles and homemade Hokkaido mozzarella over a miso base, and a couple of Yebisu beers. We made small talk throughout the meal, just as we had discussed, and I was almost alarmed at how much I enjoyed his conversation. Dining with company was becoming addictive.

When we were done with the ramen and lingering over a second beer, I asked, 'Is everything all right?'

'"All right"?'

'You said you wanted to talk about something personal. Which, as everyone knows, isn't like you.'

He smiled. 'Everything is fine, thank you.'

'Your family? Your daughters?'

'Everyone is fine, fine. I'm a grandfather now, you know. My eldest daughter.'

'Yes, you mentioned she was pregnant last time we talked. A boy, right?'

He nodded, and for a moment there was no trace of the sadness that I could usually see in his eyes. 'A beautiful little boy,' he said, beaming.

I bowed my head. 'Congratulations, my friend. I'm happy for you.'

He nodded again. 'Anyway. The personal matter isn't mine. It's yours.'

I shook my head, not following him.

He reached into a battered briefcase, pulled out a manila envelope, and handed it to me. I reached inside and withdrew a short stack of black-and-white photos. Even before my mind grasped the content, I noted the circumstances: from the slightly blurred background, compressed perspective, and shallow depth of field, I knew the photos were taken from a distance through a telephoto lens.

In them, Midori sat at an outdoor restaurant table in what looked like America, maybe New York. A baby stroller was parked next to her. A Japanese child, not much more than an infant, sat on her lap, facing her. Midori was making a face – pursing her lips and puffing out her cheeks – and the child was reaching for her nose, laughing.

My heart started thudding. It always does, when I pause to really imagine her, to indulge the razor-clear memories of the time we spent together. But seeing a photograph, literally a snapshot of the life she was living a world away, heightened the reaction. I tried not to show it.

'She's . . . married?' I asked, warring emotions roiling inside me.

'No. Not married.'

'Then . . .'

I looked at him. He nodded and smiled, a profound and strangely gentle sympathy in his eyes.

My instincts, so keenly honed for combat, can be almost laughably useless in matters of the heart. The pounding in my chest intensified, my body understanding fully even as my mind struggled to catch up. I looked away, not wanting him to see my face.

I remembered our last night together, in a room at the

Park Hyatt in Tokyo nearly two years earlier. We had made love furiously, despite Midori's new knowledge of who I was and what I had done to her father; despite our understanding that it would be the last time; despite knowing the cost.

I didn't know what the hell to say. 'Oh, my God,' I think is what came out.

I tried to pull myself together, but couldn't really manage it. Eventually, though, I was able to revert to some sort of operational default. I found myself asking, 'Who took the photo? You?'

There was a pause, then he said, 'No. It was taken by Yamaoto's people.'

I looked at him. My expression was neutral again. Thinking of Yamaoto helped me focus. It put me back on familiar ground.

'Why?'

'She is your only known civilian nexus. Yamaoto has people watch her from a distance, from time to time, in case you reappear in her life.'

'Bastard needs a course in anger management.'

'You defeated him twice. First, in intercepting the disk. Second, in dispatching his lieutenant, Murakami. He is a vain man with a long memory.'

'Is she . . . are they, in danger?'

'I don't believe so. He is interested in her only as a means to get to you.'

'How did you acquire the photo?'

'A search of one of his affiliate's belongings.'

'Sanctioned search?'

He shook his head. 'Not exactly.'

'Then there's a chance the affiliate doesn't know the photos are missing.'

'I can assure you he doesn't. My men downloaded the contents of his digital camera, but otherwise didn't molest it. He has no way of knowing his belongings were examined. Yamaoto has no way of knowing you have discovered the existence of . . . your son.'

There was a strange corporeality to those last words. They seemed to linger in the air.

A son, I thought. It made no sense. My father had a son. But not I.

'It's . . . he's a boy?' I asked.

He nodded. 'I made some discreet inquiries. She calls him Koichiro. Ko-chan.'

'How do you even know . . . how can you be sure he's mine?'

He shrugged. 'He looks like you, don't you think?'

I couldn't even go there. I felt confused, and realized I was in some kind of mild shock.

'Why did you show me this?' I asked, feeling like I was groping, flailing. I was thinking, *Because I had made my adjustment. It was over, she might as well have been dead and gone, I was consoling myself with memories.*

Tormenting yourself, you mean.

'Would you have preferred that I hadn't?' he asked.

'What's the difference? Even if I wanted to, even if she wanted me to, I couldn't contact her while Yamaoto is watching.'

I paused and felt a flush of anger. I looked at him and said, 'That's why you told me.'

He shrugged. 'Certainly some of my motives were selfish. Some weren't. You know as well as I do that you need a connection, you need something to pull you off the nihilistic path you've been treading. It seems that fate has taken a hand.'

329

'Right. To get out of the killing business, all I need to do is kill a few more people.'

'It does seem paradoxical when you put it that way. But yes, I believe you have accurately described the heart of the matter.'

I shook my head, trying to understand. 'I can't see them unless I take out Yamaoto first.'

'Yes.'

'And Yamaoto is smart. He understands this dynamic. Which means he's probably tightened his security as a result.'

'He most certainly has.'

I looked at him. 'For Christ's sake, why don't you just arrest this fucking guy? What do they pay you for?'

'Yamaoto is a prominent politician, with many protectors, as you know. If I tried to arrest him, I would simply lose my job. He is inaccessible by ordinary means.'

'I don't even know if she would see me. Why hasn't she contacted me?'

'Does she have your address?'

'No. But she could have contacted you.'

He shrugged. 'Perhaps she is ambivalent. Who wouldn't be? True, she didn't contact you. On the other hand, she had your baby. She is the mother of your son.'

'Oh, my God,' I said again. I felt dizzy.

'It's a strange thing, having a child,' he said. 'It completely alters your most fundamental priorities. When my eldest daughter was born, I realized that I would do anything – anything – to protect her. If I had to set myself on fire to save her from something, I would do it with the utmost relief and gratitude. It's quite a thing, quite a privilege, to care about someone so much that the measure of the worth of your own life is changed by it.'

'I don't know if I'm ready for all that,' I said. I felt like I was outside my body, that someone else was talking.

'Of course you're not. No one ever is. Because there's a responsibility that comes with the privilege.' He licked his lips. 'When my little son died, there was nothing I could do to save him. All the things I would have done, would have been overjoyed to do, were meaningless. You can't imagine the impact of knowing that the most precious thing over which you have full control – your own life – is useless as barter or bribe to save the life of your child.'

He took a swallow from his beer mug. 'You see? For your whole life, you've believed the sun revolved around the earth. You are about to discover otherwise. With everything that implies.'

I didn't know what to say. My head was spinning but I ordered us another round.

We drank in silence for a while after that. At one point Tatsu asked if I wanted to be alone. I told him no, I wanted him there, wanted his company. I just needed to think.

Three rounds later, I said to him, 'I can't figure this out. Not in one night. But there's one thing I am going to do. And I need your help to do it.'

25

It took Tatsu a few days to manage it, but eventually he was able to discover where I could find Manny's Filipina wife. I had a feeling that, after what had almost happened to him in Manila, Manny might have sent her to stay with her family outside the city, and it turned out I had been right.

While I waited for the information, I stayed at my suite at the Four Seasons. It was a beautiful hotel and a good base from which to revisit the many areas in the city I had missed during my recent exile. I avoided those areas I had once frequented often enough to be recognized if I were to return, not wanting to do anything that might put me on Yamaoto's radar screen. But there were plenty of places I had patronized anonymously before, and which I could therefore safely visit again: bars like Teize and Bo Sono Ni in Nishi Azabu; shrines like Tomioka Hachimangu, where the wisteria would be blooming soon; bright boulevards like Chuo-dori in Ginza and dim alleyways and backstreets too obscure to name.

Tatsu had been right, I realized, about the earth and the sun. Everything I saw measured correctly against the template in my memory, and yet the contours were subtly and indescribably different. The thought that I had become a father was overwhelming. I'd never even seen my child outside of a few surveillance photos, never even suspected his existence until just a few days before, and yet suddenly I felt connected to a possible future in a way I had never imagined. And it wasn't just that I had a son; my parents, a posthumous grandchild. It was the connection the child gave me with Midori, something I intuitively sensed could never be denied, not even after what I had done to her father. I didn't know if a life to come could trump a death dealt previously, but I wondered at the possibility. It filled me with frightful hope.

I responded to Delilah's post, telling her that I needed a vacation like I've never needed one before. I had some things to take care of over the next few days, but after that I could meet her anywhere. She asked me if I'd ever been to Barcelona. I told her I hadn't, but that I'd always wanted to go. We agreed to be in touch over the next few days, while her situation sorted itself out and while I tied off a few loose ends of my own.

Every day I checked various news sites, chief among them the *Washington Post*. I was hoping to see Hilger's name in the papers. Publicity, as Kanezaki knew, would put Hilger out of business, might even make his protectors turn on him. But so far there was nothing, and I had a feeling there never would be. Hilger was too smart.

The shooting at the China Club and on the Star Ferry got a lot of press in the *South China Morning Post* and other local English language papers. Witnesses had provided descriptions of various people involved, but so far the only 'arrest' had been of a Caucasian man – Gil – who had died of gunshot wounds before he could be questioned. Manny's body had been identified. His bodyguard had been revived with nothing worse than a horse tranquilizer hangover and a huge lump on the back of his head, and the man had identified his late client for the police. And a body had been fished out of the turbid waters of Victoria Harbor. Police were checking dental records and DNA, but weren't yet able to say who the dead man was.

I was in an Internet café in Minami Azabu, one of my favorite parts of the city, early in the evening, when Tatsu's message came. It was brief: an address in Batangas, about a two-hour drive south of Manila. Characteristically, he asked no questions about why I might want this information, but a brief note, at the bottom of his post, indicated that he might already know:

It was very good to see you the other night. I think we should try to meet more often. Neither of us is getting younger.

Let me know how you would like to proceed in the matter we discussed. Obviously you would have the benefit of all my resources to assist you.

Good luck with what you have to do first.

The benefit of all my resources. Well, that was saying a lot. It wasn't just his position with the Keisatsucho, the Japanese FBI. That would be the least of it. Tatsu had his own loyal cadre of men, along with other assets that would make a grizzled spymaster sit up and beg. I'd have to think about it. But first things first.

I made the appropriate travel arrangements on the Internet, moved money from one offshore account into another, then stopped at a Citibank to make a large cash withdrawal – the full amount I had been paid for Manny. I took the entire amount in ten-thousand-yen notes, which amounted to four bricks, each five hundred notes high, and put it all in the attaché.

I walked out and did a bit of shopping in the area: traditional Japanese sweets like *daifuku* and *sakura-mochi* and *kashiwa-mochi*; a kimono and *geta* slippers; several packages of high-end calligraphy paper. Each store wrapped the items exquisitely – after all, they were obviously gifts – and placed them in a elegant bag.

My shopping completed, I stopped in a Kinko's, where I cut down the contents of one of the calligraphy paper packages so it would accommodate the bricks of cash. I resealed the package and placed it back in the appropriate bag.

I checked out of the hotel early the next morning and caught a flight to Manila. I arrived at nine-thirty and had no trouble passing through customs along with the dozens of other visiting businessmen from Tokyo, all of us bearing traditional gifts from exotic Japan. I took a cab to the Mandarin Oriental in Makati. I explained to them that, although I wasn't a guest, I had business in town and would like to rent a car and driver for half the day. I would of course pay cash. They told me that would be fine, and I was immediately provided with a Mercedes E230 and driver. I gave him the address and we set off.

The weather was hot and sticky, as it usually is in the region, and the sky was full of the kind of pollution that almost begs to be washed away in some violent thunderstorm to come. While we drove, I replaced the innocuous contents of the attaché with the four bricks of cash.

The urban knot of Metro Manila unraveled as we drove, and soon we were moving past rice paddies and coconut groves. I had seen the same countryside just a few days earlier, but today it felt different. Unwelcoming, maybe. Maybe unforgiving.

I looked out the window at the fields and farm animals and wondered whether the woman would have learned of Manny's demise. It had been only a few days, and I supposed it wasn't impossible that somehow the news wouldn't yet have reached her.

The roads we drove on became narrower, with more frequent and deeper potholes. Twice the driver had to stop and ask for directions. But eventually we pulled up in front of a low-slung, ramshackle dwelling at the end of a dirt road with paddies all around. A few gaunt cows swished their tails near the house, and chickens and small dogs ran freely. There were a dozen people sitting out front in plastic chairs. An extended family, I sensed, but more than could be living in this small dwelling. Something had happened, some tragedy, you might have guessed, and the visitors were here to offer support, to help the survivors make it through.

I saw Manny's wife, seated across from two other young women who might have been her sisters. The boy sat listlessly on the lap of an older woman, perhaps his grandmother. I knew the scene well, and for a moment my resolve faltered. And then, ironically, the same icy blinders that had moved in to allow me to finish Manny started to close again, and enabled me to move forward this time, as well.

I got out of the car. Conversation, I noticed, had come to a halt. The assembled people eyed me curiously. I took the attaché and walked confidently over to Manny's wife. I bowed my head before speaking.

'I am an attorney, representing the estate of Manheim Lavi,' I said to her. In the suit, carrying the attaché, I felt I looked the part. And if the average lawyer carries himself stiffly at moments like this one, then that part of the act was spot-on, too, because I was having a hard time even looking at her.

She came to her feet. She was petite and very pretty, and, like many Filipinas, looked younger than she probably was.

'Yes?' she asked, in lightly accented English.

'Mr Lavi left clear instructions with my firm, to be carried out in the event of his death. That certain funds were to be transferred to you, for the benefit of . . . your son.'

I knew Manny might already have provided for them.

Although, with a primary family back in Johannesburg, he might not have. I didn't care. That wasn't the point.

The little boy ran over from his grandmother. He must have gotten spooked seeing his mother talking to a stranger. His arms were outstretched and he was saying, 'Mama, Mama.'

The woman picked him up with some effort and he clutched her tightly. He had regressed, I noted, from the trauma of the news he must have just received. *That's normal,* I told myself. *That's normal.*

She shook her head. 'Funds?'

I cleared my throat. 'Yes. From Mr Lavi's estate. Here.'

I went to hand her the attaché, but she couldn't take it with the boy in her arms.

I felt oddly light-headed. Maybe it was the heat, the humidity.

'This is yours,' I said, setting the case down in front of her. I cleared my throat again. 'I hope . . . my firm hopes it will be helpful. And I am very sorry for your loss.'

The boy started to cry weakly. The woman stroked his back. I swallowed, bowed my head again, and turned to walk back to the car.

Christ, I almost felt sick. Yeah, it must have been the heat. I got in the car. As we drove away I looked back. They were all watching me.

We drove past the paddies, the indifferent farm animals. I sat slumped in the seat. In my head, the boy cried out, *Mama, Mama,* again and again, and I thought I might never stop hearing his voice.

We drove. The potholes in the road felt like craters.

'Stop,' I said to the driver. 'Stop the car.'

He pulled over to the side of the dirt road. I opened the door and stumbled out, barely making it in time. I clutched the side of the door and leaned forward and everything inside me came up, everything. Tears were streaming down my face and snot was running out of my nose and I felt like my stomach itself might tear loose from its moorings and make its way onto the potholed road I stood on.

Finally it subsided. I stood for a moment, sucking air, then wiped my face, spat, and got back in the car. The driver asked me if I was all right. I nodded. It was the climate, I said. You'd think I'd be used to it, but I'm not.

I had him take me to the airport. I didn't know where I would go from there. Wherever it was, I knew that everything I've done, it would all be coming with me.

Acknowledgments

John Rain's fans seem to think he keeps getting better (I, of course, prefer the phrase 'even better') as he goes along. To the extent this is so, I owe much to the advice and other support I continue to receive from a number of good people. My thanks to:

My agents, Nat Sobel and Judith Weber of Sobel Weber Associates, and my editor, David Highfill at Putnam, for helping me find the true notes and eliminate the false ones.

Michael Barson (master of Yubiwaza), Dan Harvey, and Megan Millenky at Putnam, for doing such an amazing job of getting out the word on John Rain.

Dexter Domingo, for giving me multiple insider's tours of Manila; Yannette Edwards, for her suggestion that Rain should visit the Philippines, which jump-started the entire book; and Doug and Susan Patteson, for getting Rain better acquainted with Manila and other Southeast Asian environs, for otherwise drawing on their extensive experience in the region to help me refine not just the locales, but the entire story, and for their insights into all things Rain.

Jim Dunn, who came to know and love Bangkok during his service in the Vietnam War, for sharing his historical perspective on the city and refreshing Rain's recollections thereby; David Gibbons, for sharing his extensive knowledge of Thailand and for being the best guide an author could ever ask for through Bangkok and Phuket; novelist Christopher G. Moore, for sharing his insights about life in Bangkok and Thai culture; novelist Marcus Wynne, for sharing his experiences with Bangkok, knives, and the Special Ops community; and Bangkokbob – whoever you are, www.bangkokbob.net is a wonderful resource.

Massad Ayoob of the Lethal Force Institute, for sharing his awe-inspiring knowledge of and experience with firearms tools and tactics, and for helpful comments on the manuscript.

Tony Blauer, for again sharing with Rain his profound knowledge of the psychology, physiology, and tactics of violence.

The dreaded Carl, who thank God is still out there, for teaching me so much, for being the inspiration behind Dox, and for sharing his thoughts about 'catch and release' programs.

Again and always, sensei Koichiro Fukasawa of Wasabi Communications, a singular window on everything Japan and Japanese, for years of insight, humor, and friendship, and for helpful comments on the manuscript.

Matt Furey, for providing the Combat Conditioning bodyweight exercises that Rain uses in this book to stay in top shape (and that his author uses, too).

Lori Kupfer, for years of friendship, for continued insights into what sophisticated, sexy women like Delilah wear and how they think, and for helpful comments on the manuscript.

Janelle McCuen, Miss Creative Force, for making sure that Rain knows his telephoto lenses.

Matt Powers, for once again ensuring that Rain knows his wines, for leading the good fight against 'like' and 'you know,' and for helpful comments on the manuscript.

Evan Rosen, M.D. Ph.D., and Peter Zimetbaum, M.D., for once again offering (reluctant) expert advice on some of the killing techniques in this book, and for helpful comments on the manuscript. Actually, I don't think the advice is so reluctant anymore. I think they're starting to enjoy it.

Ernie Tibaldi, a thirty-one-year veteran agent of the FBI, for continuing to generously share his encyclopedic knowledge of law enforcement and personal safety issues, and for helpful comments on the manuscript.

William Scott Wilson, for *The Lone Samurai: The Life of Miyamoto Musashi*, a book that represents a significant part of John Rain's emerging philosophy.

The extraordinarily eclectic group of philosophers, bad-asses (mostly retired), and deviants who hang out at Marc MacYoung's and Dianna Gordon's www.nononsenseself-defense.com. The amount I've learned from you all is hard to put in words, and you're all great company during those long lonely nights of approaching deadlines, too. In particular, thanks to Dave Bean, for sharing his knowledge of firearms and for steering me to backstory sources for various aspects of this book; Jack 'Spook' Finch, Mr Lawsey, Lawsey himself, veteran of the Vietnam War's Easter Offensive, Operation Just Cause, Operation Desert Storm, and Silver Star awardee, for sharing his experiences with 'the cost of it,' for making Rain a Kimber man, and for helpful comments on the manuscript; Frank 'Pancho' Garza, ex-Marine, for showing by his example what it's like to be one of the toughest hombres out there and yet with a heart as soft as beaver fur; Dianna 'Mrs Velociraptor' Gordon, for 'defending my readers' by helping me hone everything from punctuation to backstory to character, and for teaching Dox to be a gentleman around Delilah; Montie Guthrie, for sharing his knowledge of and experience with firearm tools and tactics, for teaching Rain that 'nothing good can come of this,' and that, for the bad guy, 'it is never your turn,' and for helpful comments on the manuscript; Drew Anderson, Wim 'Chimpy' Demeere, Ed Fanning, Michael 'Mama Duck' Johnson, and David Organ, for sharing their thoughts on invisibility in crowds; Marc 'Animal' MacYoung, the Tiresius of civilization and the street, for deepening my understanding of urban survival tactics, how crowds react to violence, how operators carry themselves, how Klingons decloak and Predators conceal themselves, and for helpful comments on the manuscript; Slugg, for sharing his insights on what permits men to do bad things for good purposes and how they live with it after, on how high-pressure interrogations are conducted and resisted, for demonstrating by his presence how a big man can disappear, and for helpful comments on the manuscript; Tristan Sutrisno, former Army Special Forces, Vietnam veteran, and keeper of the dreaded Nessie, for sharing his experience with combat and killing and on living with it after. A special thank you to Terry Trahan, a man who has seen the darkness and now lives in the light, for sharing the experiences that inspired this story, for getting me up to speed on knives and related matters, and for helpful comments on the manuscript.

My friends at Café Borrone in Menlo Park, California, for serving the best breakfasts – and especially coffee – that any writer could ask for.

Naomi Andrews and Dan Levin, Eve Bridberg, Vivian Brown, Alan Eisler, Judy Eisler, Shari Gersten and David Rosenblatt, Tom Hayes, novelist Joe Konrath, Owen and Sandy Rennert, Ted Schlein, Hank Shiffman, and Caryn Wiseman, for helpful comments on the manuscript and many valuable suggestions and insights along the way.

Most of all, to my wife, Laura, for more than I can put in words. And the research on the 'love scenes' was great, too.

Author's Note

The Manila, Bangkok, Phuket, Hong Kong, Kowloon, Tokyo, and Batangas locales that appear in this book are described, as always, as I have found them. The backstory on A. Q. Khan and the CIA is real.

The **Rough Guide** to

Manila and Lake Taal

T here's no denying that Manila is intimidating: a massive, clamorous, unkempt megaopolis with appalling traffic. It's also a city with no focal point, no proper centre. To some Manileños, the ritzy central business district of Makati is the city centre, to others it might be the sprawl of Quezon City to the north, the largely residential area of Greenhills, or atmospheric Manila Bay, with its seafront boulevard and bohemian bars and clubs. Each is a city in its own right. Roads run everywhere like capillaries, and suburbs and shanty towns act as connecting tissue between new centres of population. It is this apparent lack of order, though, that gives Manila its character. The anarchic charm sweeps you along.

The key tourist district is the area fronting **Manila Bay** along **Roxas Boulevard**, taking in the neighbourhoods of **Ermita** and **Malate**, and stretching north to the old walled city of **Intramuros** and over the Pasig River to **Chinatown**, also known as **Binondo**. On Manila Bay are landmarks such as **Rizal Park** and the *Manila Hotel*. **Makati** is the business district, built around the main thoroughfare of Ayala Avenue, and home to five-star hotels such as the *Peninsula Manila*.

Manila's main artery is Epifaño de los Santos Avenue, or **EDSA** – stretching from Caloocan in the north to Pasay in the south.

City transport

Like all the roads in the capital, **EDSA** is in a perpetual state of chaos. There are so many vehicles that at peak times it can be a sweaty battle of nerves just to move a few hundred metres. **Buses** and **jeepneys** - utilitarian passenger vehicles modelled on American World War II jeeps – belch smoke with impunity, turning the air into a toxic miasma. Fortunately, Manila's **taxis** are not expensive – many visitors use them all the time.

Accommodation

Most of Manila's budget accommodation is in the Manila Bay enclaves of **Ermita** and **Malate**. In **Makati**, there is mid-range accommodation in and around the red light district of **Burgos** Street at the northern end of Makati Avenue, a 15-minute walk north of the *Peninsula*.

Ermita

Mabini Pension 1337 A. Mabini St ☏ 02/523 3930. Convenient, friendly and well established. Rooms are large and some have a/c, but all could do with a lick of paint.

Manila Hotel One Rizal Park ☏ 02/527 0011, ⓦ www.manila-hotel.com.ph. Estimable establishment that is past its best but nevertheless reeks of history, at least in the old wing where General Douglas MacArthur stayed during World War II; if you've got $2000 to spare you can stay a night in his suite.

Malate

Adriatico Arms 561 J Nakpil St ☎ 02/521 0736. A pleasant refuge of a hotel in an unbeatable location. The 28 a/c rooms are smallish, but well-kept and functional. Right next door is *Café Adriatico*, where you can sit and watch the beautiful people stroll by.
Bianca's Garden 2139 Adriatico St ☎ 02/526 0351. This idyllic provincial-style retreat on the southern edge of the tourist area bustle is popular with backpackers and divers stopping off in Manila for a few nights on their way to the beach. Eleven quaint rooms - some in the main house, some set around a garden courtyard - with stone floors and iron four-poster beds. The terrace and swimming pool are a big selling point.

Makati

Mandarin Oriental Manila Makati Ave ☎ 02/750 8888, Ⓦ www.mandarin-oriental.com. Five-star establishment that serves as a good landmark in Makati, opposite Citibank and a short walk from the shops. The hotel's *Captain's Bar* is a popular venue for live music.

The Peninsula Manila Ayala Ave corner Makati Ave ☎ 02/887 2888, Ⓦ www. manila.peninsula.com. Ostentatious five-star that takes up a city block and has a cheesily opulent lobby where people go to see and be seen. There are seven restaurants and rooms are as you'd expect at this price, with fancy furnishings and mod cons.

Around Burgos Street

City Garden Hotel Makati 7870 Makati Ave corner Kalayaan Ave ☎ 02/899 1111, Ⓦ www.citygarden-hotels.com. A comfortable boutique hotel with well-maintained rooms, small rooftop swimming pool and giddy views from the rooftop cafe.

Oxford Suites P. Burgos St corner Durban St ☎ 02/899 7988. One of the best hotels on the Burgos strip, with 223 rooms and suites, gymnasium, 24hr coffee shop and fourth-floor restaurant.

The City

To see Manila's major sights you will have to sweat it out in traffic and be prepared for delays, but at least the main attractions such as the old walled city of **Intramuros** and the nightlife of **Malate** are close to one another, grouped along the crescent sweep of Manila Bay and Roxas Boulevard, with the green oasis of **Rizal Park** close at hand too. **Intramuros**, the old Spanish capital, is the one part of the metropolis where you get a real sense of history. It was begun in the 1570s and remains a monumental, if partially ruined, relic of the Spanish occupation, a city within a city, separated from the rest of Manila by its crumbling walls. The Romanesque **Manila Cathedral**, originally built in 1571, has been destroyed six times down the centuries by a combination of fire, typhoon, earthquake and war. A few hundreds metres to the south of the cathedral stands **San Agustin Church**, with a magnificent Baroque interior, *trompe l'oeil* murals and a vaulted ceiling and dome. Dating back to 1587, it's the oldest stone church in the Philippines, and contains the tomb of Miguel Lopez de Legazpi, the founder of Manila. Next to the church, the former **Augustinian monastery** houses a museum of icons and artefacts, along with an eighteenth-century Spanish pipe organ that was recently restored. The monastery was the centre of Augustinian power in the Philippines, and played host to illustrious guests such as the governor general and religious dignitaries from Europe. The splendid **Casa Manila**, a restored colonial-era house, lies opposite San Agustin on General Luna Street in the Plaza San Luis Complex. The upstairs family latrine is a two-seater, which allowed husband and wife to gossip out of earshot of the servants while simultaneously going about their business. The ruins of **Fort Santiago** stand at the northwestern end of Intramuros, a five-minute walk from the cathedral. The seat of the colonial powers of both Spain and the US, Fort Santiago was also a prison and torture chamber under the Spanish regime and the scene of countless military-police atrocities during the Japanese occupation. In the **Rizal Shrine Museum** inside the grounds, you can see the room where the writer and revolutionary José Rizal spent the hours before his execution in Bagumbayan, the open space that has now become **Rizal Park**. On the other side of the Pasig River, much of the presidential home, **Malacañang Palace**, is off-limits to the public, although you can visit the wing that houses the **Malacañang Museum**. Further north, the **Chinese Cemetery** was established by affluent Chinese merchants in the 1850s because the Spanish would not allow foreigners to be buried in Spanish cemeteries. Many of the tombs resemble houses, with fountains, balconies and, in at least one case, a small swimming pool. It has become a sobering joke in the Philippines that this "accommodation" is among the best in the city.

Makati

Makati was an expanse of swampland until the Ayala family, one of the country's most influential business dynasties, started developing it at the end of the nineteenth century. It is now Manila's business district and chock-full of plush hotels, international restaurant chains and air-conditioned malls.

Eating

Filipinos are fond of Western franchise **restaurants** of the kind you can see in every capital city – all of Manila's malls and business districts are full of familiar names such as *Starbucks* and *T.G.I. Friday's*.

Ermita and Malate

Almost everyone who dines out in **Ermita** and **Malate** does so in the trendy area around J. Nakpil Street.

Bistro Remedios 1911 M. Adriatico St, Remedios Circle. Informal and homey little restaurant with pretty Filipiniana interiors and charming staff. The food is exclusively Filipino, with cholesterol-filled fried pig's knuckles, beefy stews and hefty chunks of roast pork.
Café Nakpil 644 J Nakpil St. One of the great survivors of Nakpil Street, this unpretentious but still fashionable little bistro pulls in an eclectic crowd for its pizzas, tasty curries and Thai dishes. The wine list is only average,

so stick with cold San Miguel or one of the fresh juices.
Kamayan 532 Padre Faura corner A. Mabini St, Ermita. The word *kamayan* means "with your hands", which is how you eat here, without knife and fork. A traditional selection of unpretentious native dishes are dished up, including grilled fish, spicy crab, roast chicken and some good vegetables. The staff are dressed in elegant Filipino costumes and strolling minstrels work the tables doing requests.

Makati

Many restaurants in Makati are either in **Ayala Center** or the newer Greenbelt mall.

Carpaccio 7431 Yakal St. Popular but never uncomfortably busy, this casual little restaurant tucked

away down a side street behind Makati Fire Station serves excellent regional Italian food and has a good, affordable wine list. The speciality is carpaccio – the beef carpaccio is delicious – but almost everything is good, including the home-made ice creams and sorbets. Expats love this place, and it's also got a loyal following among the Filipino office crowd.

Oody's Level 2, Greenbelt 3. Excellent choice for a quick, affordable light meal. The speciality here is noodles in all forms, including Thai, Japanese, Italian and Filipino. The rice meals are good value at less than P200; the bagooong rice is very fishy, but goes down well with a glass or two of fresh fruit juice.

Sentro 1771 Level 2, Greenbelt 3. Well-run, straightforward Filipino restaurant that's packed with office workers at lunchtime and the pre-cinema crowd in the evenings. The affordable menu includes modern variations of classics such as *adobo*, *pancit* and *Bicol express*.

Around P. Burgos Street

Handlebar 31 Polaris St Hospitable biker bar owned by a group of Harley fanatics. It's primarily for drinkers (with lots of sport on the TVs) but the food also makes it worth a visit. The menu is nothing exotic, just solid, satisfying pizzas, burgers and pasta, or pies serves with peas and mash.

Hossein's Persian Kebab 7857 LKV Building, Makati Ave. The unpretentious old *Hossein's* was closed to make way for this glitzy new version with froufrou decor and prices to match. If you're not in the mood for a brain sandwich, there are dozens of curry and kebab dishes. The food is very good, but it's become a little expensive in recent years.

Drinking and nightlife

Few visitors to Manila are disappointed by the buoyant, gregarious nature of its **bars and clubs.** This is a city that rarely sleeps and one that offers a full range of fun, from the offbeat watering holes and gay bars of Malate to the chic wine bars of arriviste areas such as Nicanor Garcia Street in Makati.

Ermita and Malate

Ermita and Malate went through a transformation in the early 1990s, when most of the girlie bars were closed down and independent nightspots opened.

Bedrock Bar & Grill Restaurant 1782 M. Adriatico St, Malate. Two live pop or mellow-rock bands play three sets every night until 4am and there's no entrance fee, which makes it popular with students. Stone-grilled food includes a hunk of premium Kobe beef for P850.

Bed J Nakpil corner Maria Orosa St. This new and brash - some say outrageous - addition to the Malate night scene is a gay club that also welcomes straights. Whatever you are, you'll need to be a hardcore partier to last the pace; bed doesn't warm up until midnight and is still buzzing at dawn. The music is loud and the crowd is an entertaining mix of starlets, wannabees, expats and curious sightseers.

Hobbit House 1801 A. Mabini St, Ermita. In the 1980s a young Manila entrepreneur decided to open a bar that would pay homage to his favourite book, *The Lord of the Rings*. He staffed it with twenty midgets and a legend was born. *Hobbit House* has somehow endured, still employing short people, with nightly appearances at 9pm by a variety of local bands, some good, some miserably bad. It has also become a notorious tourist trap, with busloads of visitors brought in every night to have their photographs taken alongside the diminutive staff.

Makati

Makati has a reputation as a yuppie ghetto frequented by office workers spilling out of the nearby banks and corporate skyscrapers.

Conway's *Shangri-La Makati Hotel*, Makati Ave. The most popular happy hour in Makati, with all-you-can-drink San Miguel for P180 (6–9pm) and some good live music (6pm–1am). The crowd is a happy and hard-drinking mix of young Filipino *corpies* (corporate types), expats and travelling executives staying at the hotel.

Club Government 7840 Makati Ave. Makati's biggest gay club has pumped-up acid jazz, disco and tribal music, plus guest DJs on most nights. P200

entrance (Mon-Sat) and two-for-one beers every Wednesday.

Around P. Burgos Street

Heckle & Jeckle Villa Building, Jupiter St corner Makati Ave. *Heckle & Jeckle* scooped everyone when it became the first bar in the Philippines to show live English Premier League football on Saturday and Sunday nights from 10pm. Live bands on Fridays.
Jools 5043-5045 P. Burgos St. A camp, flamboyant

Burgos Street institution with cheesy but fun cabaret shows every night from 7pm until 4am. There are also excellent live bands every evening and downstairs there's an English pub, the Woodman's Head, with traditional ale and football on the TV.

Lake Taal and around

The compact but busy city of **Tagaytay**, 70km south of Manila, sits on a 600-metre-high ridge overlooking **Lake Taal** and **Taal Volcano**, and because of the cool climate — on some days it even gets foggy — the area around is a popular weekend retreat from the heat of the nearby capital. Taal Volcano, which stands right in the middle of the lake, is said to be the smallest active volcano in the world, and there are occasional rumblings that force the authorities to issue evacuation warnings to local inhabitants. It's worth spending the night down by the lakeshore, where there's affordable accommodation, and taking the opportunity to climb the volcano. The departure point for trips across **Lake Taal** to the **volcano** is the small town of **Talisay** on the lake's northern shore; here you arrange to hire a boat and a guide.

Accommodation

It's best to stay down by the lake, which is quieter and more convenient if you intend to climb the volcano.

Mountain Side Just beyond the barrio of Leynes on the lake's north shore, 8km west of Talisay ☎ 043/773 0138. Comfortable, cheap rooms with fans and bath. A boat to the volcano costs P800 including a guide.

San Roque Beach Resort Less than 1km west of Talisay and close to the lakeshore ☎ 0918/290 8384. Accommodation here is mainly in nipa huts with room for two or more.

Eating and drinking

The ridge above the volcano has dozens of **restaurants**, though it has also been rather overrun by big chains and fast-food joints. Two hundred metres east of the *Taal Vista Lodge Hotel* is *Josephine's*, an institution among Filipinos, serving good home-style Filipino dishes such as sour *sinigang* soup with mounds of steamed rice. Look out also for street vendors selling the local speciality, delicious **buko** (coconut) **pie**.

Written by David Dalton

The Story in the Novel
and for the Screen

I get a lot of questions about whether the Rain books will be made into movies. It hasn't happened yet, although Jet Li had a film rights option at one point and Barrie Osborne, Oscar-winning producer of the *Lord of the Rings* trilogy, has one now. To help the option holders get a movie made, I've adapted the first book, *Rain Fall*, into a screenplay, and thought I'd offer an excerpt here to illustrate how a story must change when it moves from novel to screen.

Novels and movies are not stories themselves; they're ways of storytelling. The trick in adapting a novel for the screen, therefore, is to identify not the essence of the novel, but rather of the story, and then to retain that essence in moving the story to a medium with its own tendencies, limitations, and possibilities.

Novels are made of words; movies are made primarily of images and sound (yes, movies contain dialogue, and might include a voiceover, both of which are composed of words, but we're talking about the tendencies of these forms of storytelling, not the outer limits of their possibilities). Because movies are about sight and sound, things that can't be seen or heard on the screen have no place in the screenplay. It follows, then, that elements of a novel that can't be seen or heard have to be transformed into images and sounds if their essence is to be expressed on the screen. This difference makes it particularly difficult to adapt a first-person narrative like *Rain Fall*, where much of what you learn – indeed, much of what drives the story – comes from the protagonist's own thoughts and voice, neither of which can drive a movie.

What follows is the first chapter of *Rain Fall*, then the same parts of the story as they appear in the screenplay. If you're curious, read both, and keep in mind the following questions:

1. Who's the protagonist? How is he introduced?
2. What do you know about the protagonist and what kind of person he is? How do you know it?
3. What's happening in the story? How do you know it's happening?
4. Where does the story take place? How can you tell?

If you think about these questions as you read the excerpts below, you'll come away with a deeper appreciation of the possibilities and limitations of each medium, and of the craft of storytelling generally. And if you haven't read the other Rain books yet, the chapter below will provide a good introduction. Enjoy.

I

Harry cut through the morning rush-hour crowd like a shark fin through water. I was following from twenty meters back on the opposite side of the street, sweating with everyone else in the unseasonable October Tokyo heat, and I couldn't help admiring how well the kid had learned what I'd taught him. He was like liquid the way he slipped through a space just before it closed, or drifted to the left to avoid an emerging bottleneck. The changes in Harry's cadence were accomplished so smoothly that no one would recognize he had altered his pace to narrow the gap on our target, who was now moving almost conspicuously quickly down Dogenzaka toward Shibuya Station.

The target's name was Yasuhiro Kawamura. He was a career bureaucrat connected with the Liberal Democratic Party, or LDP, the political coalition that has been running Japan almost without a break since the war. His current position was vice minister of land and infrastructure at the Kokudokotsusho, the successor to the old Construction Ministry and Transport Ministry, where he had obviously done something to seriously offend someone because serious offense is the only reason I ever get a call from a client.

I heard Harry's voice in my ear: 'He's going into the Higashimura fruit store. I'll set up ahead.' We were each sporting a Danish-made, microprocessor-controlled receiver small enough to nestle in the ear canal, where you'd need a flashlight to find it. A voice transmitter about the same size goes under the jacket lapel. The transmissions are burst UHF, which makes them very hard to pick up if you don't know exactly what you're looking for, and they're scrambled in case you do. The equipment freed us from having to maintain constant visual contact, and allowed us to keep moving for a while if the target stopped or changed direction. So even though I was too far back to see it, I knew where Kawamura had exited, and I could continue walking for some time before having to stop to keep my position behind him. Solo surveillance is difficult, and I was glad I had Harry with me.

About twenty meters from the Higashimura, I turned off into a drugstore, one of the dozens of open-façade structures that line Dogenzaka, catering to the Japanese obsession with health nostrums and germ fighting. Shibuya is home to many different *buzoku*, or tribes, and members of several were represented here this morning, united by a common need for one of the popular bottled energy tonics in which the drugstores specialize, tonics claiming to be bolstered with ginseng and other exotic ingredients but delivering instead with a more prosaic jolt of ordinary caffeine. Waiting in front of the register were several gray-suited *sarariman* – 'salary man,' corporate rank and file – their faces set, cheap briefcases dangling from tired hands, fortifying themselves for another interchangeable day in the maw of the corporate machine. Behind them, two empty-faced teenage girls, their hair reduced to steel-wool brittleness by the dyes they used to turn it orange, noses pierced with oversized rings, their costumes meant to proclaim rejection of the traditional route chosen by the *sarariman* in front of them but offering no understanding of what they had chosen instead. And a gray-haired retiree, his skin sagging but his face oddly bright, probably in Shibuya to avail himself of one of the area's well-known sexual services, which he would pay for out of a pension account that he kept hidden from his wife, not realizing that she knew what he was up to and simply didn't care.

I wanted to give Kawamura about three minutes to get his fruit before I came out, so I examined a selection of bandages that gave me a view of the street. The way he had ducked into the store looked like a move calculated to flush surveillance, and I didn't like it. If we hadn't been hooked up the way we were, Harry would have had to stop abruptly to maintain his position behind the target. He might have had to do something ridiculous, like tie his shoe or stop to read a street sign, and Kawamura, probably peering out of the entranceway of the store, could have made him. Instead, I knew Harry would continue past the fruit store; he would stop about twenty meters ahead, give me his location, and fall in behind when I told him the parade was moving again.

The fruit store was a good spot to turn off, all right – too good for someone who knew the route to have chosen it by accident. But Harry and I weren't going to be flushed out by amateur moves out of some government antiterrorist primer. I've had that training, so I know how useful it is.

I left the drugstore and continued down Dogenzaka, more slowly than before because I had to give Kawamura time to come out of the store. Shorthand thoughts shot through my mind: Are there enough people between us to obscure his vision if he turns when he comes out? What shops am I passing if I need to duck off suddenly? Is anyone looking up the street at the people heading toward the station, maybe helping Kawamura spot surveillance? If I had already drawn any countersurveillance attention, they might notice me now, because before I was hurrying to keep up with the target and now I was taking my time, and people on their way to work don't change their pace that way. But Harry had been the one walking point, the more conspicuous position, and I hadn't done anything to arouse attention before stopping in the drugstore.

I heard Harry again: 'I'm at one-oh-nine.' Meaning he had turned into the landmark 109 Department Store, famous for its collection of 109 restaurants and trendy boutiques.

'No good,' I told him. 'The first floor is lingerie. You

354

going to blend in with fifty teenage girls in blue sailor school uniforms picking out padded bras?'

'I was planning to wait outside,' he replied, and I could imagine him blushing.

The front of 109 is a popular meeting place, typically crowded with a polyglot collection of pedestrians. 'Sorry, I thought you were going for the lingerie,' I said, suppressing the urge to smile. 'Just hang back and wait for my signal as we go past.'

'Right.'

The fruit store was only ten meters ahead, and still no sign of Kawamura. I was going to have to slow down. I was on the opposite side of the street, outside Kawamura's probable range of concern, so I could take a chance on just stopping, maybe to fiddle with a cell phone. Still, if he looked, he would spot me standing there, even though, with my father's Japanese features, I don't have a problem blending into the crowds. Harry, a pet name for Haruyoshi, being born of two Japanese parents, has never had to worry about sticking out.

When I returned to Tokyo in the early eighties, my brown hair, a legacy from my mother, worked for me the way a fluorescent vest does for a hunter, and I had to dye it black to develop the anonymity that protects me now. But in the last few years the country has gone mad for *chappatsu,* or tea-color dyed hair, and I don't have to be so vigilant about the dye anymore. I like to tell Harry he's going to have to go *chappatsu* if he wants to fit in, but Harry's too much of an *otaku,* a geek, to give much thought to issues like personal appearance. I guess he doesn't have that much to work with, anyway: an awkward smile that always looks like it's offered in anticipation of a blow, a tendency to blink rapidly when he's excited, a face that's never lost its baby fat, its pudginess accentuated by a shock of thick black hair that on bad days seems almost to float above it. But the same qualities that keep him off magazine covers confer the unobtrusiveness that makes for effective surveillance.

I had reached the point where I was sure I was going to have to stop when Kawamura popped out of the fruit store and reentered the flow. I hung back as much as possible to increase the space between us, watching his head bobbing as he moved down the street. He was tall for a Japanese and that helped, but he was wearing a dark suit like ninety percent of the other people in this crowd – including Harry and me, naturally, so I couldn't drop back too far.

Just as I'd redeveloped the right distance, he stopped and turned to light a cigarette. I continued moving slowly behind and to the right of the group of people that separated us, knowing he wouldn't be able to make me moving with the crowd. I kept my attention focused on the backs of the suits in front of me, just a bored morning commuter. After a moment he turned and started moving again.

I allowed myself the trace of a satisfied smile. Japanese don't stop to light cigarettes; if they did, they'd lose weeks over the course of their adult lives. Nor was there any reason, such as a strong headwind threatening to blow out a match, for him to turn and face the crowd behind him. Kawamura's obvious attempt at countersurveillance simply confirmed his guilt.

Guilt of what I don't know, and in fact I never ask. I insist on only a few questions. Is the target a man? I don't work against women or children. Have you retained anyone else to solve this problem? I don't want my operation getting tripped up by someone's idea of a B-team, and if you retain me, it's an exclusive. Is the target a principal? I solve problems directly, like the soldier I once was, not by sending messages through uninvolved third parties like a terrorist. The concerns behind the last question are why I like to see independent evidence of guilt: It confirms that the target is indeed the principal and not a clueless innocent.

Twice in eighteen years the absence of that evidence has stayed my hand. Once I was sent against the brother of a newspaper editor who was publishing stories on corruption in a certain politician's home district. The other time it was against the father of a bank reformer who showed excessive zeal in investigating the size and nature of his institution's bad debts. I would have been willing to act directly against the editor and the reformer, had I been retained to do so, but apparently the clients in question had reason to pursue a more circuitous route that involved misleading me. They are no longer clients, of course. Not at all.

I'm not a mercenary, although I was nothing more than that once upon a time. And although I do in a sense live a life of service, I am no longer samurai, either. The essence of samurai is not just service, but loyalty to his master, to a cause greater than himself. There was a time when I burned with loyalty, a time when, suffused with the samurai ethic I had absorbed from escapist novels and comics as a boy in Japan, I was prepared to die in the service of my adopted liege lord, the United States. But loves as uncritical and unrequited as that one can never last, and usually come to a dramatic end, as mine did. I am a realist now.

As I came to the 109 building I said, 'Passing.' Not into my lapel or anything stupid like that; the transmitters are sensitive enough so that you don't need to make any subtle movements that are like billboards for a trained counter-surveillance team. Not that one was out there, but you always assume the worst. Harry would know I was passing his position and would fall in after a moment.

Actually, the popularity of cell phones with earpieces makes this kind of work easier than it once was. It used to be that someone walking alone and talking under his breath was either demented or an intelligence or security agent. Today you see this sort of behavior all the time among Japan's *keitai,* or cell phone, generation.

The light at the bottom of Dogenzaka was red, and the crowd congealed as we approached the five-street intersection in front of the train station. Garish neon signs and massive video monitors flashed frantically on the buildings around us. A diesel-powered truck ground its gears as it slogged through the intersection, laborious as a barge in a muddy river, its bullhorns blaring distorted right-wing patriotic songs that momentarily drowned out the bells commuters on bicycles were ringing to warn pedestrians out of the way. A street hawker angled a pushcart through the crowds, sweat running down the sides of his face, the smell of steamed fish and rice following in his zigzagging wake. An ageless homeless man, probably a former *sarariman* who had lost his job and his moorings when the bubble burst in the late eighties, slept propped against the base of a streetlight, inured by alcohol or despair to the tempest around him.

The Dogenzaka intersection is like this night and day, and at rush hour, when the light turns green, over three hundred people step off the curb at the same instant, with another twenty-five thousand waiting in the crush. From here on, it was going to be shoulder to shoulder, chest to back. I would keep close to Kawamura now, no more than five meters, which would put about two hundred people between us. I knew he had a commuter pass and wouldn't need to go to the ticket machine. Harry and I had purchased our tickets in advance so we would be able to follow him right through the wickets. Not that the attendant would notice one way or the other. At rush hour, they're practically numbed by the hordes; you could flash anything, a baseball card, probably, and in you'd go.

The light changed, and the crowds swept into one another like a battle scene from some medieval epic. An invisible radar I'm convinced is possessed only by Tokyoites prevented a mass of collisions in the middle of the street. I watched Kawamura as he cut diagonally across to the station, and maneuvered in behind him as he passed. There were five people between us as we surged past the attendant's booth. I had to stay close now. It would be chaos when the train pulled in: five thousand people pouring out, five thousand people stacked fifteen deep waiting to get on, everyone jockeying for position. Foreigners who think of Japan as a polite society have never ridden the Yamanote at rush hour.

The river of people flowed up the stairs and onto the platform, and the sounds and smells of the station seemed to arouse an extra sense of urgency in the crowd. We were swimming upstream against the people who had just gotten off the train, and as we reached the platform the doors were already closing on handbags and the odd protruding elbow. By the time we had passed the kiosk midway down the platform, the last car had passed us and a moment later it was gone. The next train would arrive in two minutes.

Kawamura shuffled down the middle of the platform. I stayed behind him but hung back from the tracks, avoiding his wake. He was looking up and down the platform, but even if he had spotted Harry or me earlier, seeing us waiting for the train wasn't going to unnerve him. Half the people waiting had just walked down Dogenzaka.

I felt the rumble of the next train as Harry walked past me like a fighter jet buzzing a carrier control tower, the slightest nod of his head indicating that the rest was with me. I had told him I only needed his help until Kawamura was on the train, which is where he had always gone during our previous surveillance. Harry had done his usual good work in helping me get close to the target, and, per our script, he was now exiting the scene. I would contact him later, when I was done with the solo aspects of the job.

Harry thinks I'm a private investigator and that all I do is follow these people around collecting information. To avoid the suspicious appearance of a too-high mortality rate for the subjects we track, I often have him follow people in whom I have no interest, who of course then provide some measure of cover by continuing to live their happy and oblivious lives. Also, where possible, I avoid sharing the subject's name with Harry to minimize the chances that he'll come across too many coincidental obituaries. Still, some of our subjects do have a habit of dying at the end of surveillance, and I know Harry has a curious mind. So far he hasn't asked, which is good. I like Harry as an asset and wouldn't want him to become a liability.

I moved up close behind Kawamura, just another commuter trying to get a good position for boarding the train. This was the most delicate part of the operation. If I flubbed it, he would make me and it would be difficult to get sufficiently close to him for a second try.

My right hand dipped into my pants pocket and touched a microprocessor-controlled magnet, about the size and weight of a quarter. On one side the magnet was covered with blue worsted cloth, like that of the suit Kawamura was wearing. Had it been necessary, I could have stripped away the blue to expose a layer of gray, which was the other color

Kawamura favored. On the opposite side of the magnet was an adhesive backing.

I withdrew the magnet from my pocket and protected it from view by cupping it in my hands. I would have to wait for the right moment, when Kawamura's attention was distracted. Mildly distracted would be enough. Maybe as we were boarding the train. I peeled off the wax paper covering the adhesive and crumbled it into my left pants pocket.

The train emerged at the end of the platform and hurtled toward us. Kawamura pulled a cell phone out of his breast pocket. Started to input a number.

Okay, do it now. I brushed past him, placing the magnet on his suit jacket just below the left shoulder blade, and moved several paces down the platform.

Kawamura spoke into the phone for only a few seconds, too softly for me to hear over the screeching brakes of the train slowing to a halt in front of us, and then slipped the phone back in his left breast pocket. I wondered whom he had called. It didn't matter. Two stations ahead, three at the most, and it would be done.

The train stopped and its doors opened, releasing a gush of human effluent. When the outflow slowed to a trickle, the lines waiting on either side of the doors collapsed inward and poured inside, as though someone had hit the reverse switch on a giant vacuum. People kept jamming themselves in despite the warnings that 'The doors are closing,' and the mass of commuters grew more swollen until we were all held firmly in place, with no need to grip the overhead handles because there was nowhere to fall. The doors shut, the car lurched forward, and we moved off.

I exhaled slowly and rotated my head from side to side, hearing the bones crack in my neck, feeling the last remnants of nervousness drain away as we reached the final moments. It has always been this way for me. When I was a teenager, I lived for a while near a town that had a network of gorges cutting through it, and at some of them you could jump from the cliffs into deep swimming holes. You could see the older kids doing it all the time – it didn't look so far up. The first time I climbed to the top and looked down, though, I couldn't believe how high I was, and I froze. But the other kids were watching. And right then, I knew that no matter how afraid I was, no matter what might happen, I was going to jump, and some instinctive part of me shut down my awareness of everything except the simple, muscular action of running forward. I had no other perceptions, no awareness of any future beyond the taking of those brisk steps. I remember thinking that it didn't even matter if I died.

Kawamura was standing in front of the door at one end of the car, about a meter from where I was positioned, his right hand holding one of the overhead bars. I needed to stay close now.

The word I had gotten was that this had to look natural: my specialty, and the reason my services are always in demand. Harry had obtained Kawamura's medical records from Jikei University Hospital, which showed that he had a condition called complete heart block and owed his continuing existence to a pacemaker installed five years earlier.

I twisted so that my back was to the doors – a slight breach of Tokyo's minimal train etiquette, but I didn't want anyone who might speak English to see the kinds of prompts that were going to appear on the screen of the PDA computer I was carrying. I had downloaded a cardiac interrogation program into it, the kind a doctor uses to adjust a patient's pacemaker. And I had rigged it so that the PDA fed infrared commands to the control magnet.

The only difference between my setup and a cardiologist's was that mine was miniaturized and wireless. That, and I hadn't taken the Hippocratic oath.

The PDA was already turned on and in sleep mode, so it powered up instantly. I glanced down at the screen. It was flashing 'pacing parameters.' I hit the Enter key and the screen changed, giving me an option of 'threshold testing' and 'sensing testing.' I selected the former and was offered a range of parameters: rate, pulse width, amplitude. I chose rate and quickly set the pacemaker at its lowest rate limit of forty beats per minute, then returned to the previous screen and selected pulse width. The screen indicated that the pacemaker was set to deliver current at durations of .48 milliseconds. I decreased the pulse width as far as it would go, then changed to amplitude. The unit was preset at 8.5 volts, and I started dropping it a half volt at a time. When I had taken it down two full volts, the screen flashed, 'You have now decreased unit amplitude by two volts. Are you sure you want to continue to decrease unit amplitude?' I entered, 'Yes' and went on, repeating the sequence every time I took it down two volts.

When the train pulled into Yoyogi Station, Kawamura stepped off. Was he getting off here? That would be a problem: the unit's infrared had limited range, and it would be a challenge to operate it and follow him closely at the same time. *Damn, just a few more seconds,* I thought, bracing to follow him out. But he was only allowing the people behind him to leave the train, and stopped outside the doors. When the Yoyogi passengers had exited he got back on, followed closely by several people who had been waiting on the platform. The doors closed, and we moved off again.

At two volts, the screen warned me that I was nearing minimum output values and it would be dangerous to further decrease output. I overrode the warning and took the unit down another half volt, glancing up at Kawamura as I did so. He hadn't changed his position.

When I reached a single volt and tried to go farther, the screen flashed, 'Your command will set the unit at minimum output values. Are you certain that you wish to enter this command?' I entered 'Yes.' It prompted me one more time anyway: 'You have programmed the unit to minimum output values. Please confirm.' Again I entered, 'Yes.' There was a one-second delay, then the screen started flashing bold-faced letters: **Unacceptable output values. Unacceptable output values.**

I closed the cover, but left the PDA on. It would reset automatically. There was always the chance that the sequence hadn't worked the first time around, and I wanted to be able to try again if I had to.

There wasn't any need. As the train pulled into Shinjuku Station and jerked to a stop, Kawamura stumbled against the woman next to him. The doors opened and the other passengers flowed out, but Kawamura remained, gripping one of the upright bars next to the door with his right hand and clutching his package of fruit with his left, commuters shoving past him. I watched him rotate counterclockwise until his back hit the wall next to the door. His mouth was open; he looked slightly surprised. Then slowly, almost gently, he slid to the floor. I saw one of the passengers who had gotten on at Yoyogi stoop down to assist him. The man, a mid-forties Westerner, tall and thin enough to make me think of a javelin, somehow aristocratic in his wireless glasses, shook Kawamura's shoulders, but Kawamura was past noticing the stranger's efforts at succor.

'*Daijoubu desu ka?*' I asked, my left hand moving to support Kawamura's back, feeling for the magnet. Is he all right? I used Japanese because it was likely that the Westerner wouldn't understand it and our interaction would be kept to a minimum.

'*Wakaranai,*' the stranger muttered. I don't know. He patted Kawamura's increasingly bluish cheeks and shook him again – a bit roughly, I thought. So he did speak some Japanese. It didn't matter. I pinched the edge of the magnet and pulled it free. Kawamura was done.

I stepped past them onto the platform and the in-flow immediately began surging onto the train behind me. Glancing through the window nearest the door as I walked past, I was stunned to see the stranger going through Kawamura's pockets. My first thought was that Kawamura was being robbed. I moved closer to the window for a better look, but the growing crush of passengers obscured my view.

I had an urge to get back on, but that would have been stupid. Anyway, it was too late. The doors were already sliding shut. I saw them close and catch on something, maybe a handbag or a foot. They opened slightly and closed again. It was an apple, falling to the tracks as the train pulled away.

Now let's see how the same sequence is written for the screen:

AERIAL SHOT - TOKYO - MORNING

High-rises. Signs in Japanese. Neon giving way
to daylight. The first commuters beginning to hit
the streets.

INT. JOHN RAIN'S APARTMENT - MORNING

A one-bedroom apartment, small and neat. A
couch, a wooden Wing Chun training dummy, a huge
collection of jazz CDs, a high-end stereo
system, a bookshelf with volumes in English and
Japanese. A desk and computer. The apartment is
unadorned except for several posters of jazz
musicians.

JOHN RAIN, mixed Asian/Caucasian, about forty,
lies on his back on a futon, already awake. A
digital CD alarm clock on the floor next to him
reads 5:59. At 6:00, the clock goes off: a jazz
standard. Rain listens for a moment, then gets
up. He's wearing boxers; he's in serious shape.

Rain pulls open the bedroom curtains, cracks his
neck, and looks out on the city below him. In
quick cuts he showers, shaves, and selects a
suit from a neatly arranged closet. Next to the
hanging suits are several martial arts 'gis'
(white uniforms) and worn black belts. He makes
a cappuccino in a high-end machine.

Dressed now, Rain slips on a watch. He picks up
a handheld computer and presses a button. The

screen flashes PACEMAKER INTERROGATION PROGRAM.
Rain pockets the computer, then checks through
the peephole of the door before going out.

EXT. JAPANESE MINISTRY OF CONSTRUCTION - MORNING

YASUHIRO KAWAMURA, a ranking bureaucrat in his
sixties, approaches the bland façade of the
ministry, briefcase in hand. He's pale and looks
unwell. He pauses to take a last drag on a
cigarette, then grinds it out decisively on the
sidewalk. He coughs violently. When it passes,
he takes a deep breath and starts up the steps.

INT. JAPANESE MINISTRY OF CONSTRUCTION -
SECURITY DESK

Two uniformed GUARDS sit behind a table. To
their right is a walk-through metal detector.
Kawamura enters.

                    GUARD #1
          Good morning, Kawamura-san. You're
          early today.

                    KAWAMURA
          Yes, a busy day. Good morning.

Kawamura starts to walk around the metal
detector.

                    GUARD #2
        Sir, if you could just step through
        the metal detector...

Kawamura looks at him, irritated.

                    GUARD #1
                  (to Guard #2)
        Kawamura-san has a pacemaker. He
        doesn't need to go through the metal
        detector.
                  (to Kawamura)
        I'm sorry, sir. We're still changing
        over from the night shift. He didn't
        know.
                    GUARD #2
        But...

Guard #1 silences him with a stare.

                    GUARD #2
                  (bowing his head)
        I apologize, sir.

Kawamura nods and continues inside. He pauses
and pats his pocket.

                    KAWAMURA
        Damn it, I forgot my key.

                    GUARD #1
        I'm sorry, sir?

                    KAWAMURA
My office key. I went home late last
night and must have left it in my
office. Can you let me in?

                    GUARD #1
I would, sir, but I have to stay
here. My shift doesn't end for
another half hour.

                    KAWAMURA
I see. Well then, why don't you lend
me your key for a few minutes.

                    GUARD #1
My key?

                    KAWAMURA
I'll just let myself into my office,
get my own key, and come right back.

                    GUARD #1
Sir, I'm really not supposed to give
out the security key —

                    KAWAMURA
I have a lot to do and I'm in a
hurry. I'll be back in five minutes.

                    GUARD #1
Yes, sir.
          (pulling out a key)
Please, sir, five minutes.

                        KAWAMURA
                    (takes the key)
        Yes, yes.

INT. JAPANESE MINISTRY OF CONSTRUCTION -
ELEVATOR

Kawamura rides the elevator to the top floor. As
the doors open, he takes three quick breaths and
steps out into the:

CORRIDOR

Empty. Kawamura looks left and right, but sees
no one. He strides down to one of the offices. He
double checks the nameplate next to the door,
which says 'Minister of Construction,' and uses
the guard's key to open the door.

OFFICE

The office is well decorated and there are many
wall photos of the minister together with
domestic and foreign dignitaries. Kawamura takes
a CD from one of his suit pockets and inserts it
into the bay on a desktop computer. He works the
keyboard, looking up nervously as he does so.
After a moment, a message appears on the screen:
COPYING.

INT. JAPANESE MINISTRY OF CONSTRUCTION -
SECURITY DESK

Kawamura returns the guard's key with a nod. He keeps moving and continues outside.

EXT. JAPANESE MINISTRY OF CONSTRUCTION

The moment Kawamura leaves the building, he opens his cell phone and punches in a number. He holds the phone to his ear and keeps walking.

EXT. TOKYO STREET - MORNING

Rain cruises along a heavily trafficked street on a motorcycle. Something in his pocket RINGS loudly. He reaches in and pulls out the handheld computer. On the screen, a message blinks: CELL PHONE ACQUIRED: TRIANGULATING. The screen switches over to a street map with a moving, blinking light: Kawamura's cell phone signal. Rain takes the motorcycle into a smooth U-turn.

EXT. TOKYO SIDEWALK - SHIBUYA - MORNING

It's high rush hour and there's a lot of car and pedestrian traffic. Kawamura walks briskly, glancing behind periodically. As he passes a glass phone booth, a man inside turns his head to watch him: it's Rain.

Rain checks Kawamura's wake, then leaves the phone booth and falls in behind him.

As Kawamura walks, he becomes more agitated. He increases his pace and his backward glances

become more frequent. Rain maintains his
distance and keeps people between himself and
Kawamura for cover.

Kawamura ducks into a fruit store, forcing Rain
to move past his position. Rain stops at a news
stand and pulls out the handheld computer. The
blinking light — Kawamura's cell phone — is
stationary. But after a moment, it begins moving
again.

Rain watches for a long beat, his back to the
sidewalk, then turns and falls in behind
Kawamura.

EXT. TOKYO SIDEWALK - SHIBUYA

Rain reenters the flow behind Kawamura and
follows him. Kawamura is now carrying a gift-
wrapped box of fruit. They approach a large
structure. A sign says SHIBUYA STATION.

INT. SHIBUYA TRAIN STATION

The platform, one of dozens in this station, is
packed with commuters. It's noisy: ANNOUNCEMENTS
IN JAPANESE BLARE from loudspeakers; various
MUSICAL CHIMES announce the arrival and
departure of RUMBLING TRAINS; people SHOUT into
their cell phones. Amidst the thick, shifting
crowds, Rain moves close to Kawamura,
undetected.

The train arrives. Kawamura, Rain, and hundreds
of other people surge onto it. The doors close.

INT. SUBWAY CAR

As the passengers jostle for position, Rain
stumbles against Kawamura. Kawamura looks
frightened and suspicious, but seems relieved
when Rain mumbles an apology and moves away.

CLOSE ON KAWAMURA'S BACK

Rain has placed some sort of cloth-covered disk,
presumably adhesive-backed, over Kawamura's left
shoulder blade.

BACK TO SCENE

Rain takes out the handheld and begins to work
the keypad.

The screen flashes INFRARED PACEMAKER
INTERROGATION SEQUENCE. Rain hits the enter key.
The screen changes to RATE, PULSE WIDTH,
AMPLITUDE.

Rain chooses RATE and sets Kawamura's pacemaker
at its lowest rate limit of 40 BEATS PER MINUTE.

Kawamura blinks several times as though
confused. His hand rises slowly and he rubs his
chest.

The screen now reads PULSE WIDTH: .48 MILLI-
SECONDS. Rain decreases the pulse width as far
as it will go, then changes to AMPLITUDE.

Kawamura is now pale and perspiring. Rain
glances at him, then returns his attention to
the computer.

The screen reads 8.5 VOLTS. Rain takes it down
two volts, and the screen flashes YOU HAVE NOW
DECREASED UNIT AMPLITUDE BY TWO VOLTS. ARE YOU
SURE YOU WANT TO CONTINUE TO DECREASE UNIT
AMPLITUDE? Rain enters YES.

The train stops at the next station and the
doors open. Kawamura and a number of other
passengers get off. Rain tenses to follow, but
then sees that Kawamura was only making way for
the people behind him. Rain waits. After a
moment Kawamura gets back on. The doors close
and the train leaves.

The screen now reads 3.0 VOLTS.

Kawamura is quite pale now. He looks confused.
He rubs his chest as though intuiting that
something has gone wrong within it.

Rain drops the amplitude to ONE VOLT. The
screen flashes YOUR COMMAND WILL SET THE UNIT AT
MINIMUM OUTPUT VALUES. ARE YOU CERTAIN YOU WISH
TO ENTER THIS COMMAND? Rain enters YES. There is
a one-second delay, then the screen begins

flashing bold-faced letters: UNACCEPTABLE OUTPUT
VALUES.

The train pulls to a stop at the next station.
Kawamura has gone gray. His eyes are fluttering.
As the doors open, he slumps with his back
against the wall.

Passengers flow off the train, but Kawamura
remains. His mouth is open; he looks slightly
surprised. Then he slides slowly to the floor.

Rain closes the handheld and drops it into his
jacket pocket.

Passengers begin to get on the train. One of
them, a mid-forties Caucasian STRANGER, sees
Kawamura and stoops to help him. The stranger
shakes Kawamura's shoulders, but Kawamura's eyes
have rolled up and he seems not to notice.

Rain bends as though to assist, supporting
Kawamura's back.

                    RAIN
        Is he all right?

                    STRANGER
              (looking at Kawamura)
        I don't know.

                    RAIN
        I'll get help.

Rain stands and squeezes past oncoming
passengers to get off the train.

INT. TRAIN STATION

Rain moves away from the train. He's holding
something in his hand: the cloth-covered
pacemaker interrogation device.

Rain drops the device into his pocket and
glances back at the train. Through the open
doors, he sees the stranger going through
Kawamura's pockets. Rain pauses, surprised. The
stranger rips open Kawamura's fruit box and
empties it. Apples and oranges roll out and fall
to the tracks below.

Rain takes a step forward as though to get back
on. But the doors close and the train pulls
away.

I hope you enjoyed this introduction to adapting a novel
for the screen. You can learn more about Rain on my
website, www.barryeisler.com, and if you're particularly
interested in storytelling, check out the For Writers link,
which contains additional articles and suggestions for
further reading.

Cheers,
Barry Eisler
October 30, 2006

Read an exclusive extract from
the next John Rain thriller

Last Assassin

by Barry Eisler

Published March 2007

I

I've never liked doing a job in a new place. You don't know how to get in and out undetected, you don't know what tools you'll need to access the target, you don't know where you'll stick out and where you'll be able to fade into the background or disappear in a crowd.

To compensate, I start by studying the area from afar, move in only when I've learned as much as possible, and always arrive early enough to become familiar with the local terrain before it's time to act. Tactics like these have kept me alive, and even reasonably prosperous, during more than a quarter century of doing the thing I've always been best at.

But this time the preparation was reflex, not necessity. I wasn't on a job, for one thing; I was done with the life. Or almost done. There was one last thing, a big one, but I didn't want to face that just yet. Barcelona was supposed to be an interlude: pleasure, not business, and it was disturbing that some part of my mind seemed not to understand the difference.

Still, in alien circumstances, we tend to cling to habit, and so I found myself defaulting to my usual approach. I should have known better. Barcelona was unfamiliar, but the real territory I was trying to navigate isn't marked on any map.

I flew JAL from Tokyo via Amsterdam and arrived at Barcelona El Prat on a mild winter evening with nothing more than the plain carry-on bag in my hand and the cheap business suit on my back. On my feet were a pair of plain brown leather loafers, purchased in a mass market Aoyama men's store; on my nose, nonprescription steel-framed eyeglasses, calculated to obscure my features; in my pocket, a guidebook in Japanese. For my first days in the city, I would be an anonymous salaryman, recently divorced, his children grown and out of the house, seeking distraction through travel slightly more intrepid than last year's jaunt to Hawaii or Saipan. When Delilah arrived I would morph into something else.

The staff at Le Meridien hotel on Las Ramblas spoke their delightfully Catalan-accented English slowly, as my own halting, heavily Japanese-accented attempts indicated I would need. I certainly looked the part. My face is courtesy mostly of my Japanese father, and what vestiges my American mother contributed to the mix were diminished by surgery many years ago. The act came easily, too. I've had a lifetime to practice playing roles: no drama school training, true, but if you've lasted as long as I have in a business as literally cutthroat as mine, you learn a thing or two.

I was tired. Jet lag had been a nonissue in my thirties, a nuisance in my forties, and now it was more noticeable than ever. I went straight to my room, ate a room service meal, took a hot bath, and slept fitfully through the night.

I got up at dawn. I'd never been to Barcelona before, and wanted to see the city at first light, not yet on its feet, not yet wearing its makeup. I showered quickly and went out just as the sun was cresting the horizon. I scanned the street as I moved past the lobby window, then checked ambush positions from in front of the hotel. Everything looked fine.

I walked out to Las Ramblas, my breath fogging just slightly in the morning-chilled sea air, and paused. Ten meters down, three men in sanitation overalls and rubber boots were rolling up a dripping hose; the cobblestones were still slick from their work. I stood silently and didn't let them notice me. They finished with the hose, got in a truck, and drove off. When the sound of the engine had faded, it was followed only by silence, and I smiled, pleased to have the city to myself for a while.

I strolled east into the Barri Gòtic, the gothic quarter. I sensed I had arrived during a tenuous interlude between the departure of the night's last revelers and the morning's first arrivals, and I paused, enjoying the feeling that I was privy to some secret transition. I wandered for a long time, listening to my footfalls on the narrow stone streets, enjoying the aroma of fresh bread and ground coffee, watching as the area's residents gradually emerged from behind the centuries-old façades of scarred but stalwart dwellings to start another day.

After a breakfast of croissants and coffee *cortado*, I paid a visit to Ganivetería Roca, a famous cutlery store I'd read about while preparing for the trip. There, among the pewter razors and steel scissors and related items, I selected a Benchmade folder with a three-inch blade. I'd gotten used to carrying a knife in the last year or so, and no longer felt comfortable without something sharp close at hand.

Now properly outfitted, I started my customary systematic exploration of the city. I wouldn't feel at ease here until I had learned how best to blend, or how to escape, should my attempts at blending fail. So I went everywhere, that day and for the five days and nights after, at all times, by all means of transit. I absorbed the layout of the streets and alleys; the location of police stations and security cameras; the rhythms and rituals of pedestrians and tourists and shopkeepers.

But there were so many distractions: the mingled smell

of tapas and shawarma among the winding alleyways of El Raval; the sounds of music and laughter echoing in the public squares of Gràcia; the feel of the sea breeze on my face and in my hair on the peaks of Montjuic and Tibidabo. I liked that the locals took for granted morning mass in six-hundred-year-old cathedrals. I liked the contrasts: gothic and *modernista*; mountains and sea; historical weight and exuberant esprit.

And the distractions weren't limited to the city itself. I was also suddenly aware of parents with infants. They were everywhere: walking their babies in strollers, holding them in their arms, gazing at their small faces with crippling devotion. Tatsu, my sometime nemesis and current friend in the Keisatsucho, the Japanese FBI, had warned me this would be the case, and, as in so many other matters, he had been right.

What Tatsu hadn't prepared me for, what he couldn't, were the thousand other ways his news about Midori had left me ambivalent, confused, almost in shock. I had nearly canceled with Delilah, but then decided not to. I owed her an explanation, for one thing. I still wanted to see her, wanted it a lot, for another.

I never could have predicted the affection I'd developed for Delilah, or that she seemed to have developed for me. Certainly our initial encounters were inauspicious. First there was Macau, where we learned we were working the same target. Then Bangkok and Hong Kong, where she was supposed to be working me. And yet the inherent mistrust born of working for competing intelligence organizations – Delilah, for the Mossad, and I, freelance at the time for the CIA – had paradoxically provided a stable foundation. Each of us recognized in the other a professional, an operator with an agenda, someone for whom business imperatives would always trump personal desire. All of that became the basis for respect, even mutual understanding, and ultimately provided the context for the indulgence of undeniable personal chemistry. The sex couldn't lead anywhere, we both knew it. So why not enjoy what we had, whatever it was, for as long as it lasted?

But it did last, and it deepened. We spent a month together in Rio, after which Delilah had defied her paymasters when they ordered her to set me up. Defy, hell, she had very nearly betrayed them. She had warned me what was coming, and then worked with me to straighten things out. There must have been something between us, something worthwhile, if we had managed to avoid so many potentially lethal obstacles, and Barcelona was going to be the time and place to figure out what.

On the day Delilah was due to arrive, I checked out of Le Meridien and did some shopping in preparation for my transition from anonymous salaryman to the more cosmopolitan persona I think of as the real me. I bought pants, shirts, and a navy cashmere blazer at Aramis in Eixample; underwear, socks, and a few accessories at Furest on the Plaça de Catalunya; shoes at Casas in La Ribera; and a leather carrying bag to put it all in at Loewe, on the ground floor of the magnificent Casa Lleó Morera building on the Passeig de Gràcia. I paid cash for everything. When I was done, I found a restroom and changed into some of the new clothes, then caught a cab to the Hotel La Florida, where Delilah had made a reservation.

The ride from the city center took about twenty minutes, much of it up the winding road to the top of Mount Tibidabo. I had already reconnoitered the hotel and environs, of course, during my exploration of the city, but the approach was every bit as impressive the second time around. In the late afternoon sunlight, as the cab zigged and zagged its way up the steep mountain road, the city and all its possibilities appeared below me, then disappeared, then came tantalizingly back. And then vanished once again.

When the cab reached the entrance to the hotel, seven stories of taupe-painted plaster and balconied windows overlooking Barcelona and the Mediterranean beyond, a bellhop opened the door and welcomed me. I paid the driver, looked around, and got out. I had no particular reason to think Delilah or her people wanted me dead – if I had, I never would have agreed to meet her here – but still, I stood for a moment as the cab drove away, checking likely ambush positions. There weren't many. Exclusive properties like La Florida aren't welcoming to people who seem to be waiting around without a good reason. The hotels assume the lurker is a paparazzo waiting to shoot a celebrity with a camera, not a killer possessed of rather more lethal means and intent, but the result is the same: inhospitable terrain, which today would work in my favor.

The bellhop stood by, holding my bag with quiet professionalism. The grounds were impressive, and he must have been accustomed to guests pausing to enjoy the moment of their arrival. When I was satisfied, I nodded and followed him inside.

The lobby was bright yet intimate, all limestone and walnut and glass. There was only one small sitting area, currently unoccupied. It seemed I had no company. My alertness stayed high, but the tension I felt dropped a notch.

A pretty woman in a chic business suit came over with a glass of sparkling water and inquired after my journey. I told her it had been fine.

'And your name, sir?' she asked, in lightly Catalan-accented English.

'Ken,' I replied, giving her the name I had told Delilah I would be traveling under. 'John Ken.'

'Of course, Mr Ken, we've been expecting you. Your other party has already checked in.' She nodded to a young man behind the counter, who came around and handed her a key. 'We have you in room three-oh-nine – my favorite in the hotel, if I may say so, because of the views. I think you'll enjoy it.'

'I'm sure I will.'

'May I have someone assist with your bag?'

'That's all right. I'd like to wander around a little before going to the room. See a bit of the hotel. It's beautiful.'

'Thank you, sir. Please let us know if there's anything else you need.'

I nodded my thanks and moved off. For a little while, I 'wandered' around the first floor, checking everything – eclectic gift shop, low-key bar, comfortable lounge, spacious stairwells, abundant elevators – and found nothing out of place.

I took the stairs to the third floor, paused outside 309, and listened for a moment. The room within was quiet. I placed my bag and empty glass on the ground, took off my jacket, crouched, and loudly slipped the key into the lock. Nothing. I held the jacket in front of the door and opened it a crack. Still nothing. If there was a shooter in there, he was disciplined. I shot my head over and back. I saw only a short hallway and part of a room beyond. I detected no movement.

I stood up, eased the Benchmade from my front pocket, and silently thumbed it open. 'Hello?' I called out, stepping inside.

No answer. No sound. I let the door close. It clicked audibly behind me.

'Hello?' I called out again.

Nothing.

'That's weird . . . must be the wrong room,' I muttered, loudly enough to be heard. I opened the door and let it close. To anyone hiding inside, it would sound as though I had left.

Still nothing.

I padded down the hallway, toe-heel, pausing after each step to listen. My newly purchased soft-soled Camper shoes were silent on the polished wood floor.

At the end of the hallway, I could see the entire room but for the bathroom. The closet door was open. Probably that was Delilah, knowing I would approach tactically and wanting to make it easier for me, but I wasn't sure yet.

There was a note on the bed, conspicuous in the middle of the flawless white quilt. I ignored it. If this had been my setup, I would have put the note on the bed and then nailed the target from the balcony or bathroom while he went to read it.

The glass doors to the balcony were closed, the curtains open, and I could see no one was out there. Probably Delilah again, lowering my blood pressure.

All that remained was the bathroom, and I started to relax a little. The worst part about clearing a room, especially if you have only a knife and the other guy might have a gun, is traversing the 'fatal funnel,' where the enemy has the dominant position and a clear field of fire. In this case, narrowing down the ambush points to just the bathroom reduced my vulnerability considerably.

I walked to the side of the open bathroom door. I paused and listened. All quiet. I waved the jacket in front of the door to see if it would draw fire – nothing – then burst inside. The bathroom was empty.

I let out a long breath and walked past the glass-enclosed shower to the window. The views, as promised, were stunning: the city and the sea to one side; the snowcapped peaks of the Pyrenees to the other. I looked out for a few minutes, unwinding.

I went back to the door and looked through the peephole. All clear. I retrieved my bag and the glass, brought them into the room, and picked up the note from the bed. It said: *I'm at the indoor pool. Come join me. – D.*

Hard to argue with that. I checked the room for weapons first, then paused for a moment, just breathing, until I felt calmer. I pocketed the note, threw my jacket over a chair, and headed out. A minute later, I entered an expansive glass-and-stone solarium with vaulted ceilings and a sparkling, stainless-steel-bottomed swimming pool.

Delilah was on her back on one of the red upholstered lounge chairs surrounding the pool. She wore a one-piece cobalt-blue bathing suit that showed off her curves perfectly. Her blond hair was tied back, and oversized sunglasses concealed her features. She looked every inch the movie star.

I glanced around. No one set off my radar. It troubled me for a moment that even now, with all we had been through, all we had shared, I still felt I had to be careful. I wondered whether I'd ever be able to completely relax with her, or with anyone. Maybe I could hope for something like that with Midori. After all, isn't that why medieval kings married off their sons and daughters, to seal blood alliances and make murder unthinkable? Wasn't it the idea that children trump everything, even the most deep-seated resentments and rivalries, that they trump even hate?

I walked closer and paused, just a few feet behind her.

I wanted to see whether she might sense my presence. Delilah's antennae were as sensitive as any I've known, but on the other hand there aren't many people who can move as quietly as I can.

I waited a few seconds. She didn't notice me.

'Hey,' I said softly.

She sat up and turned toward me, then pulled off the sunglasses and broke into a gorgeous smile.

'Hey,' she said.

'I've been standing here awhile. I thought you'd notice.'

Her smile lingered. 'Maybe I was just indulging you. I know you like to feel stealthy.'

She stood up and gave me a long, tight hug. I caught a hint of the perfume she wore, a scent I've encountered nowhere else and that I will always equate with her.

There were people around, but we were suddenly kissing passionately. It was always like this when we'd been apart for a while, and sometimes even when we hadn't been. There was just something about the two of us that wouldn't let us keep our hands off each other. I don't know what it was, but sometimes it was overpowering.

I had to sit down on the lounge chair before the condition she had caused attracted further attention. She laughed, knowing exactly why I had broken the embrace, and sat down next to me, her hand on my leg.

'How long have you been here?' she asked.

'I just arrived a few minutes ago.'

'Not the hotel. The city. Barcelona.'

I paused, then admitted, 'A few days.'

She shook her head. 'What a waste. I could have gotten here earlier, you know. But I knew you'd want to have a look around alone first.'

'Guess I'm getting predictable.'

'I understand. I'm just worried I'll have nothing new to show you.'

I looked into her blue eyes. 'I want you to show me everything.'

Her hand moved on my leg, playful, insistent. 'All right. Shall we start with the room?'

We hurried, but getting back to the room seemed to take a lot longer than my trip to the pool a few minutes earlier. We made it, though, and I had her out of that bathing suit before the door had closed behind us.

I kicked off my shoes and we moved into the room, kissing again, Delilah pulling off my shirt and pants. I paused at the foot of the bed to get out of my boxers. Delilah scrambled up and reached suddenly under one of the pillows. Even though I'd checked there already, I tensed, but then saw it was only a condom. It was a measure of her own abandon that she hadn't reached more slowly – she knew my habits, and what could set me off – but also of mine, that I hadn't spotted the move in time to have done anything about it.

She lay back and I moved up on top of her, advancing between her open legs. She kissed me again and was rolling the condom onto me even as I moved inside her. For a second I thought of Midori and was glad we were being smart this time. We hadn't been, in Phuket.

We made love hard and fast. We didn't talk, talk was beside the point, it was just moans and breathing and finally a pair of sharp groans that were probably heard in the adjacent room.

As we lay side by side after, catching our breath, I realized that, for a few minutes, my nearly constant security aware-ness had been temporarily eclipsed by blind lust, and then by its afterglow. On the one hand, it was liberating, hell, it was life affirming to realize I could have a moment like that. But at the same time, it was worrisome. I hadn't told Delilah yet what I'd learned about Midori. I didn't know how to tell her, or when. What I did know was that I had never needed my skills as much as I would need them for what I planned to do next.

BARRY EISLER

THE LAST ASSASSIN

> 'I've never liked doing a job in a new place. You don't know
> how to get in and out undetected, you don't know what tools
> you'll need to access the target, you don't know where
> you'll stick out and where you'll be able to fade into the
> background or disappear into a crowd.'

When John Rain learns that his former lover, Midori, has been raising
their child in New York, he senses a chance for reconciliation – perhaps
even redemption – and a chance to get out of the killing game. But
Midori is being watched by Rain's enemies, and his sudden appearance
put mother and child in extreme danger.

To save them, Rain is forced to use the same deadly talents he had been
hoping to leave behind. With the help of Tatsu, his friendly nemesis in
the Japanese FBI, and Dox, the ex-marine sniper whose laid-back style
masks a killer as deadly as Rain himself, Rain races against time to
bring his enemies into the open and eliminate them once and for all.
But to finish the job, he'll need one more ally: Israeli intelligence agent
Delilah, a woman who represents an altogether different kind of threat.

Meet JOHN RAIN at www.barryeisler.com